EVERYMAN, I will go with thee,

and be thy guide,

In thy most need to go by thy side

WALTER HORATIO PATER

Born at Shadwell, London, in 1839. Educated at Oxford, and elected a Fellow of Brasenose in 1864. Resigned tutorship in 1880 to devote himself to writing, and continued to live chiefly at Oxford until his death in 1894.

WALTER PATER

Marius the Epicurean

INTRODUCTION BY
OSBERT BURDETT

DENT: LONDON
EVERYMAN'S LIBRARY
DUTTON: NEW YORK

NO. 903

SBN: 460 00903 6

INTRODUCTION

In the year 1885, when *Marius the Epicurean* was first published, Walter Horatio Pater, then in his forty-sixth year, ceased to make his home entirely at Oxford, and began to reside during the vacations at Earl's Terrace, Kensington. In a life outwardly so uneventful this was a considerable change, for the Oxford don, who had found the duties of tutor at Brasenose, where he had been elected a Fellow soon after taking his degree, an encroachment on a leisure devoted wholly to literary composition, had hitherto shown no inclination for society, but preferred to confine himself to a few intimates, though among these were now numbered some admirers from the outside world. Of these admirers, the most fervent and the most enduring was George Moore, and it is George Moore, who, until the end of his life, continued to call *Marius* 'the golden book of English prose', that has left us the most vivid glimpse of Pater at this moment of singular emergence in an otherwise secluded life.

All who have been attracted by Pater's writings are familiar with their author's mask, for mask, rather than face, seems the appropriate term for the bald head, the heavy, dark moustache, the no less heavy jaw, that confront us in the likenesses. Nothing less like the connoisseur in criticism, the advocate of exquisite sensibility, could be imagined; and the contrast between the extreme formality of appearance, with the grave frock coat, the dogskin gloves, the invariable tall hat, the uniform (as we may call it) of social convention carried to its last detail, and the Epicurean philosopher, whose pursuit of beauty had given him a place apart among his contemporaries, surprised every one. At first glance, the figure of Pater appeared to Moore to be 'almost uncouth', until, on closer acquaintance, he decided it to be a screen carefully prepared to protect its deviser from the world. His manner, at first, was equally formal, and it never wholly thawed, not because Pater was cold or frigid, but because there was in him something that shrank from direct experience, and could cope only with the mirror of emotion, in art, in architecture, or in books.

In the tenth and eleventh chapters of *Avowals* the reader will find how George Moore, who prided himself, a little rashly, on his genius for intimacy, tried, and had to abandon, his attempt to become intimate with one who had a genius for reserve.

From the point of vantage conferred by the reputation that had come to him after the publication of *The Renaissance* in 1873, Pater now ventured into London society, and in his calm, polite, but mainly observant way, enjoyed savouring at a certain remove the sweets of fame. These were really valuable to him by encouraging his easily discouraged productivity. Beyond question, the substance of all he had to say was condensed in the conclusion to *The Renaissance*, and this stands apart from his other writings, so far as any of them define or recommend an attitude of life to others, not only by the impassioned flame that burns, for once audibly, among the embers of a style that is best when it smoulders, and like real embers sinks, here and there, into dead ashes, but because for once it lingers clearly in the memory; the thought as clearly as the words. The other essays, for all the memorable passages that continue to be the chosen quarry of anthologists have a curious quality of elusiveness. While we read them, we seem to pursue a careful and subtle process of reasoning, but once the book has been laid aside, and we ask ourselves what Pater has said about Botticelli, or Giorgione, or Pico of Mirandola, our memory falters. The impression that fell lightly, flake by flake of snow, and so transformed the subject for us, has the other quality of snow: it vanishes; and thus a good criticism will warn the reader, especially of *Marius*, the longest and most ambitious of Pater's works, not to be disappointed if incidents, passages, or chapters alone linger with him, but to remark that certain effects, like that of snow or of a group of glowing embers, are none the less real because they seem to be contradictory—the beauty residing in a certain condition that is not abiding in the things themselves, but comes like a fleeting miracle in the winter's night, or is only possible in the last and most friendly stages of a dying fire.

Marius, then, though called a narrative, is not strictly a narrative, but a series of essays in 'sensation and ideas', strung upon a single, and intentionally not very individual, character. The hero, as we may call him, is one of Pater's typical spectators, thoughtful humanity rather than a man, and the background chosen for him is one of those debatable periods in which Pater delighted; for he loved to consider alternatives, and even in thought he shrank from the intellectual equivalent of action: the moment of decision, of making up one's mind. Marius, 'a boy living in an old country house, half farm, half villa', is born in the second century, when Christianity was being tolerated, and when it was possible for him to compare it with the old religion of Numa that still survived in the country where he lived, and with the fashionable Stoic philosophy practised so carefully by the Emperor Marcus Aurelius, whose secretary Marius in time becomes. Thus, to set these alternatives before us, rather than to decide between them, is the purpose of the book. It leaves Marius on the threshold of Christianity, but this it would be more than rash to call the goal of his pilgrimage. Suspension of judgment was Pater's characteristic, and it is, therefore, an idle criticism to assert, as some have done, that it is a fault of the book to be equally partial to both sides. We may not sympathize with such indefiniteness, or with the temperament that cherished it, but such a temperament was Pater's, and such a temperament is delineated here.

The threshold, the border, was his province, and the careful reader, noticing, possibly with a trace of impatience, that the externals of Christianity seem to absorb him exclusively, will remember a sentence on the second page, a sentence in which the religion of Numa is lingered over lovingly, precisely because it was 'a religion of usages and sentiment rather than of facts and belief'. Beyond 'usages' and 'sentiment' Pater could not commit himself, and it was well said of him that he saw religion, 'not as a drama but as a tableau'. That is why his characters, with few exceptions, are static not dynamic, why his style is monotonous, why his backgrounds suggest tapestry, why his argument, though moving, does not seem itself to move. You must be precisely aware of that which he has to give, or you will be in danger of overlooking virtues not to be found in work more emphatic than his own. A tableau is not a drama; a tapestry is not a picture, but tableau and tapestry have decorative qualities, passages of colour, mysteries of repose, that we would not exchange, or even compare with other forms of beauty.

So approached, *Marius* offers a much wider choice than would seem possible for any one anticipating the different pleasures of narrative. The most human, and one of the most satisfying chapters, is the second, 'White Nights', with its loving glimpses of things dear to mankind in every age, homely incidents within and without the house, domestic and religious, with the little touches of description in which Pater, at his best, excelled. Then the story of Cupid and Psyche, translated from the pages of Apuleius, becomes an exquisite interlude, and not an interruption of the theme. The passion that underlay Pater's habitual reserve, and rarely broke through his writings, except in the conclusion to *The Renaissance* already mentioned, is severely restrained in *Marius the Epicurean*, but there is one chapter in it, the chapter called 'Manly Exercises', which bears a definite relation to the most individual of his *Imaginary Portraits*.

Among these, the one that stands out most vividly in the memory is that called 'Denys l'Auxerrois', the extraordinary, fantastic, and even horrible story in which a stranger comes, like a Pagan god, to trouble a medieval community, and to convulse it at last with blood and carnage. A similar theme is the subject of 'Apollo in Picardy', to be found in *Miscellaneous Studies*, because a second volume of *Imaginary Portraits* was never completed. These are interesting, not only because they are the most vivid and unforgettable of Pater's studies, the nearest to exciting narrative of all he wrote, but because they give a glimpse of the forces that lay behind his reserve, and show how the imagination of this austere and restrained man would seek, sometimes, an outlet at the opposite pole from his customary correctitude. His imagination would play with the idea of violence, would rejoice in an outbreak of riot, and, in reaction from his habitual passivity, would linger with an odd delight on bloodshed. In the chapter of *Marius* just mentioned, there is a description of the circus, and there again the crimson pleasure peeps out, while the recoil of Marius himself from the brutal spectacle reveals the author curiously identifying 'action' with crude and horrible manifestations.

One feels from this curious identity of action with brute force, that there was in Pater a need for the control which he sought so carefully, that the mask which he wore before the world was partly self-protective, partly necessary to his own peace, and that the choice for him lay between an almost rigid restraint and the uncurbing of energies that might have proved more than he could master. In the recesses of his nature a fanatic of some kind was lurking, and thus a book like *Marius*, that may seem to cooler natures to recommend an impossible aloofness from experience, may, in truth, have been the wisdom that was the only solution of a temper really difficult for him so to have tamed.

In 1893 he returned permanently to Oxford, having tasted all he cared to taste of society in London. Oxford seemed the proper place for him, and it is characteristic that he should have been always indulgent to the escapades of undergraduates, for his sincere and necessary respect for authority was accompanied by an indulgence for individual cases, and he probably took a vicarious pleasure in the bonfires and periodic rowdiness of the young men who, according to one story, reminded him of 'playful tigers' in high spirits after feeding-time! In spite of his friendships he remained an isolated man, a born bachelor, ending his days with his sisters in a little house in St. Giles, where he indulged his fondness for cats, and dying after a short illness from a heart-attack following pleurisy on July 30th 1894, in the fifty-fifth year of his age.

The influence that he exerted is so striking when compared with the placidity of his uneventful life, that the latter can be described within the limits of an epitaph, for it is no more than the centre of fact from which his influence radiated. To see his work in its due place in the story of English literature is, much more than his own private history, the right introduction to the present volume.

According to family tradition, the Paters derived from Holland, and when Pater was asked whether he was descended from the painter, Jean-Baptiste Pater, he is said to have replied: 'I hope so; I think so; I always say so'. His father, Richard Glode Pater, was a medical man, born in New York, who made his home first at Olney, and then at Shadwell, where Walter Pater was born on August 4th 1839. He was educated at King's School, Canterbury, from which, in 1858, he gained an exhibition at Queen's College, Oxford. A slow developer, with no signs of literary precocity, he took a second class in *Lit. Hum.*, and after reading with private pupils for two years, was elected to a fellowship at Brasenose, when he settled down, happily and naturally, to a quiet scholarly existence. His first essay, a study of Coleridge, less of the poet than of the metaphysician, appeared in 1866, and Pater did not discover himself until the following year, when the characteristic essay on Winckelmann was printed in the *Westminster Review*, to be followed in 1868 by a crucial example of his ornate style, the paper on 'Aesthetic Poetry'. This appeared, to be afterwards withdrawn, in the later volume,

Appreciations. But for the interlude in London already
touched upon, his writings were the only outer events in his
life, the sole active recreation in which was travelling during
his holidays in France and Italy. Though his setting was
Oxford, his profession that of a don, he was not a typical don,
but a man of letters. All his interests were literary and
artistic. The only academic pursuits that he found congenial were the preparation of his lectures, and to criticize
the essays of his pupils. He needed seclusion and stability,
and these Oxford provided as they could be provided
nowhere else.

Meantime the beauty of Gothic, first at Canterbury and
then at Oxford, had laid its spell upon him, and for a while
he had fallen under the influence of Ruskin's writings, though
it was not until he had read a life of Winckelmann and visited
Italy in person that philosophy yielded to art as the decisive
preoccupation of his mind. The 'usages' and 'sentiment' of
Christianity never entirely lost their hold on him, but the
scepticism of his time destroyed his intellectual assent while
leaving his imagination and emotions starved of nearly all
they craved for. Thus he turned to art, and sought to create
a kind of religion out of the pursuit of beauty, which was being
passionately followed by many in protest against the ugliness of industrialism on every hand. Pater, then, has a
definite place in the growth of the Romantic Movement,
which gradually developed first into the Pre-Raphaelite phase
and then into the aesthetic. This second phase his writings
crystallized—before it degenerated into extravagance and
became, in some circles, a fashionable artistic pose. With
religion thought to have been undermined by the crude
materialism which was then the prevalent scientific fashion,
and with an increasingly ugly civilization in the world without,
there seemed to be nothing left for sensitive people but an
epicurean philosophy. Beauty and truth seemed to have
parted company, or to be found together only in works of art,
or at moments in nature, or in transient experience. That
creed was defined with burning conviction in the conclusion
to *The Renaissance*. In *Marius the Epicurean* its application
to life was portrayed in the 'sensations and ideas' of its hero,
set deliberately in an epoch of transition in the past.

But while this creed had stood like a beacon for many in
the earlier book, its successor, *Marius*, was valued less for its
content than for its form. It was welcomed by many as a

great piece of modern prose, and convinced them that prose could be a beautiful art while eschewing, unlike Ruskin's Biblical cadences, any infusion of rhetoric. With the exception of De Quincey, the earlier Romantics had tended to overlook the art of prose, and Pater's grave, intricate sentences appeared like a revelation. Moreover, unlike those who were caught by Flaubert's theory of the unique word and the only epithet, he sought the sentence, and the sentence in relation to the paragraph, and the paragraph as a movement in the chapter. It was a continuous melody that he devised, seeking to draw the reader along with the movement of a sluggish river. The numerous parentheses, for which he prepared by writing his first drafts on alternate lines of ruled paper, deliberately exchanged a quick flow of rhythm for pauses, for charming little eddies by the way. Now that the Romantic Movement has come to be questioned, that the aesthetic attitude has long passed out of fashion, *Marius* remains what it was first found to be: the achievement of one of the most individual styles in English prose-literature.

Returning to it after thirty years, W. B. Yeats called it 'the only great prose in modern English'.[1] But it was right that the final definition, which should do justice both to its statuesqueness and to its dignity, should have been found by George Moore. Always writing about the book and always praising it, only within a few weeks of his death did he find its final definition. 'In the pages of Pater, the English language lies in state.' That expresses exactly and unforgettably, on the one hand, the beauty, and on the other the folds, as of a mortcloth, in this style. Because of that achievement, whatever our personal response to its peculiarity may be, *Marius the Epicurean* remains a landmark in the prose of its century, with a niche of its own, wherein it can remain secure whatever departures or returns of thought may sway the attention of discriminating readers.

OSBERT BURDETT.

---

[1] *Autobiographies.* By W. B. Yeats, page 373. Macmillan, 1926.

SELECT BIBLIOGRAPHY

WORKS. *Studies in the History of the Renaissance*, 1873; later editions appeared as *The Renaissance: Studies in Art and Poetry* (2nd edition, 1877; 3rd, 1888). *Marius the Epicurean*, 1885. *Imaginary Portraits*, 1887. *Appreciations*, 1889; new edition, 1890. *Plato and Platonism*, 1893 (part had already appeared in periodical form in 1892). *Greek Studies*, 1895. *Miscellaneous Studies*, 1895. *Gaston de Latour*, 1896 (an unfinished romance, most of which had appeared in periodical form in 1888). Essays from *The Guardian*, 1901 (privately printed in 1897). *The Chant of the Celestial Sailors*, 1829 (a short poem, privately printed).

The periodicals to which Pater chiefly contributed—other than *The Guardian* (see above)—were: *Westminster Review*, 1866–7; *Fortnightly Review*, 1869, 1870, 1871, 1874, 1876–7–8, 1880, 1888–9, 1890, 1892; *Macmillan's Magazine*, 1876, 1878, 1885–6–7–8–9, 1892; *New Review*, 1890, 1892; *Contemporary Review*, 1892, 1894; *Harper's Magazine*, 1893; *Nineteenth Century*, 1894. These articles went to make up most of his books, only *Marius the Epicurean* first appearing in book form. Pater also wrote an Introduction to C. L. Shadwell's translation of Dante's *Purgatorio*, 1892. Complete editions of his works appeared in 1901 and 1910 and were reprinted in 1967.

BIOGRAPHY AND CRITICISM. A. C. Benson, *Walter Pater*, 1906; A. Symons *A Study of Walter Pater*, 1932; G. Tillotson, *Criticism and the 19th Century*, 1951; R. V. Johnson, *Walter Pater*, 1961; A. Ward, *Walter Pater: The Idea in Nature*, 1966.

TO
HESTER AND CLARA

CONTENTS

PART THE FOURTH

PART THE FIRST

CHAPTER I

'THE RELIGION OF NUMA'

As, in the triumph of Christianity, the old religion lingered latest in the country, and died out at last as but paganism— the religion of the villagers, before the advance of the Christian Church; so, in an earlier century, it was in places remote from town-life that the older and purer forms of paganism itself had survived the longest. While, in Rome, new religions had arisen with bewildering complexity around the dying old one, the earlier and simpler patriarchal religion, 'the religion of Numa', as people loved to fancy, lingered on with little change amid the pastoral life, out of the habits and sentiment of which so much of it had grown. Glimpses of such a survival we may catch below the merely artificial attitudes of Latin pastoral poetry; in Tibullus especially, who has preserved for us many poetic details of old Roman religious usage.

> At mihi contingat patrios celebrare Penates,
> Reddereque antiquo menstrua thura Lari:

—he prays, with unaffected seriousness. Something liturgical, with repetitions of a consecrated form of words, is traceable in one of his elegies, as part of the order of a birthday sacrifice. The hearth, from a spark of which, as one form of old legend related, the child Romulus had been miraculously born, was still indeed an altar; and the worthiest sacrifice to the gods the perfect physical sanity of the young men and women, which the scrupulous ways of that religion of the hearth had tended to maintain. A religion of usages and sentiment rather than of facts and belief, and attached to very definite things and places—the oak of immemorial age, the rock on the heath fashioned by weather, as if by some dim human art, the shadowy grove of ilex, passing into which one exclaimed involuntarily, in consecrated phrase, Deity is in this Place! *Numen Inest!* —it was in natural harmony with the temper of a quiet people amid the spectacle of rural life, like that simpler faith between

3

man and man, which Tibullus expressly connects with the period when, with an inexpensive worship, the old wooden gods had been still pressed for room in their homely little shrines.

And about the time when the dying Antoninus Pius ordered his golden image of Fortune to be carried into the chamber of his successor (now about to test the truth of the old Platonic contention, that the world would at last find itself happy, could it detach some reluctant philosophic student from the more desirable life of celestial contemplation, and compel him to rule it), there was a boy living in an old country-house, half farm, half villa, who, for himself, recruited that body of antique traditions by a spontaneous force of religious veneration such as had originally called them into being.   More than a century and a half had passed since Tibullus had written; but the restoration of religious usages, and their retention where they still survived, was meantime come to be the fashion through the influence of imperial example; and what had been in the main a matter of family pride with his father, was sustained by a native instinct of devotion in the young Marius.   A sense of conscious powers external to ourselves, pleased or displeased by the right or wrong conduct of every circumstance of daily life —that *conscience*, of which the old Roman religion was a formal, habitual recognition, was become in him a powerful current of feeling and observance.   The old-fashioned, partly puritanic awe, the power of which Wordsworth noted and valued so highly in a northern peasantry, had its counterpart in the feeling of the Roman lad, as he passed the spot, 'touched of heaven', where the lightning had struck dead an aged labourer in the field: an upright stone, still with mouldering garlands about it, marked the place.   He brought to that system of symbolic usages, and they in turn developed in him further, a great seriousness—an impressibility to the sacredness of time, of life and its events, and the circumstances of family fellowship; of such gifts to men as fire, water, the earth, from labour on which they live, really understood by him as gifts—a sense of religious responsibility in the reception of them.   It was a religion for the most part of fear, of multitudinous scruples, of a year-long burden of forms; yet rarely (on clear summer mornings, for instance) the thought of those heavenly powers afforded a welcome channel for the almost stifling sense of health and delight in him, and relieved it as gratitude to the gods.

The day of the 'little' or private *Ambarvalia* was come, to be celebrated by a single family for the welfare of all belonging to it, as the great college of the Arval Brothers officiated at Rome in the interest of the whole state. At the appointed time all work ceases; the instruments of labour lie untouched, hung with wreaths of flowers, while masters and servants together go in solemn procession along the dry paths of vineyard and cornfield, conducting the victims whose blood is presently to be shed for the purification from all natural or supernatural taint of the lands they have 'gone about'. The old Latin words of the liturgy, to be said as the procession moved on its way, though their precise meaning was long since become unintelligible, were recited from an ancient illuminated roll, kept in the painted chest in the hall, together with the family records. Early on that day the girls of the farm had been busy in the great portico, filling large baskets with flowers plucked short from branches of apple and cherry, then in spacious bloom, to strew before the quaint images of the gods—Ceres and Bacchus and the yet more mysterious Dea Dia—as they passed through the fields, carried in their little houses on the shoulders of white-clad youths, who were understood to proceed to this office in perfect temperance, as pure in soul and body as the air they breathed in the firm weather of that early summer-time. The clean lustral water and the full incense-box were carried after them. The altars were gay with garlands of wool and the more sumptuous sort of blossom and green herbs to be thrown into the sacrificial fire, fresh gathered this morning from a particular plot in the old garden, set apart for the purpose. Just then the young leaves were almost as fragrant as flowers, and the scent of the bean-fields mingled pleasantly with the cloud of incense. But for the monotonous intonation of the liturgy by the priests, clad in their strange, stiff, antique vestments, and bearing ears of green corn upon their heads, secured by flowing bands of white, the procession moved in absolute stillness, all persons, even the children, abstaining from speech after the utterance of the pontifical formula, *Favete linguis !*—Silence! Propitious Silence!—lest any words save those proper to the occasion should hinder the religious efficacy of the rite.

With the lad Marius, who, as the head of his house, took a leading part in the ceremonies of the day, there was a devout effort to complete this impressive outward silence by that inward tacitness of mind, esteemed so important by religious Romans in the performance of these sacred functions. To him the sustained stillness without seemed really but to be waiting upon that interior, mental condition of preparation or expectancy,

for which he was just then so intently striving. The persons
about him, certainly, had never been challenged by those
prayers and ceremonies to any ponderings on the divine nature:
they conceived them rather to be the appointed means of setting
such troublesome movements at rest. By them, 'the religion
of Numa', so staid, ideal, and comely, the object of so much
jealous conservatism, though of direct service as lending sanction
to a sort of high scrupulosity, especially in the chief points of
domestic conduct, was mainly prized as being, through its
hereditary character, something like a personal distinction—
as contributing, among the other accessories of an ancient
house, to the production of that aristocratic atmosphere which
separated them from newly-made people. But in the young
Marius, the very absence from those venerable usages of all
definite history and dogmatic interpretation had already
awakened much speculative activity; and to-day, starting from
the actual details of the divine service, some very lively surmises, though scarcely distinct enough to be thoughts, were
moving backwards and forwards in his mind, as the stirring
wind had done all day among the trees, and were like the passing
of some mysterious influence over all the elements of his nature
and experience. One thing only distracted him—a certain pity
at the bottom of his heart, and almost on his lips, for the sacrificial victims and their looks of terror, rising almost to disgust
at the central act of the sacrifice itself, a piece of everyday
butcher's work, such as we decorously hide out of sight; though
some then present certainly displayed a frank curiosity in the
spectacle thus permitted them on a religious pretext. The old
sculptors of the great procession on the frieze of the *Parthenon*
at Athens have delineated the placid heads of the victims led
in it to sacrifice, with a perfect feeling for animals in forcible
contrast with any indifference as to their sufferings. It was
this contrast that distracted Marius now in the blessing of his
fields, and qualified his devout absorption upon the scrupulous
fulfilment of all the details of the ceremonial, as the procession
approached the altars.

The names of that great populace of 'little gods', dear to the
Roman home, which the pontiffs had placed on the sacred list
of the *Indigitamenta*, to be invoked, because they can help, on
special occasions, were not forgotten in the long litany—Vatican
who causes the infant to utter his first cry, Fabulinus who
prompts his first word, Cuba who keeps him quiet in his cot,
Domiduca especially, for whom Marius had through life a

particular memory and devotion, the goddess who watches over one's safe coming home. The urns of the dead in the family chapel received their due service. They also were now become something divine, a goodly company of friendly and protecting spirits, encamped about the place of their former abode—above all others, the father, dead ten years before, of whom, remembering but a tall, grave figure above him in early childhood, Marius habitually thought as a genius a little cold and severe.

Candidus insuetum miratur limen Olympi,
Sub pedibusque videt nubes et sidera.—

Perhaps!—but certainly needs his altar here below, and garlands to-day upon his urn. But the dead genii were satisfied with little—a few violets, a cake dipped in wine, or a morsel of honeycomb. Daily, from the time when his childish footsteps were still uncertain, had Marius taken them their portion of the family meal, at the second course, amidst the silence of the company. They loved those who brought them their sustenance; but, deprived of these services, would be heard wandering through the house, crying sorrowfully in the stillness of the night.

And those simple gifts, like other objects as trivial—bread, oil, wine, milk—had regained for him, by their use in such religious service, that poetic and as it were moral significance, which surely belongs to all the means of daily life, could we but break through the veil of our familiarity with things by no means vulgar in themselves. A hymn followed, while the whole assembly stood with veiled faces. The fire rose up readily from the altars, in clean, bright flame—a favourable omen, making it a duty to render the mirth of the evening complete. Old wine was poured out freely for the servants at supper in the great kitchen, where they had worked in the imperfect light through the long evenings of winter. The young Marius himself took but a very sober part in the noisy feasting. A devout, regretful after-taste of what had been really beautiful in the ritual he had accomplished took him early away, that he might the better recall in reverie all the circumstances of the celebration of the day. As he sank into a sleep, pleasant with all the influences of long hours in the open air, he seemed still to be moving in procession through the fields, with a kind of pleasurable awe. That feeling was still upon him as he awoke amid the beating of violent rain on the shutters, in the first storm of the season. The thunder which startled him from sleep seemed to make the solitude of his chamber almost painfully complete, as if the nearness of those angry clouds shut him up in a close place alone in the world. Then he thought of the sort of protection which that day's ceremonies assured. To procure an agreement with the gods—*Pacem deorum exposcere*: that was the meaning of what they had all day been busy upon. In a faith, sincere but half-suspicious, he would fain have those Powers at least not against him. His own nearer household gods were all around his bed. The spell of his religion as a part of the very essence of home, its intimacy, its dignity and security, was forcible at that moment; only, it seemed to involve certain heavy demands upon him.

CHAPTER II

WHITE-NIGHTS

To an instinctive seriousness, the material abode in which the childhood of Marius was passed had largely added. Nothing, you felt, as you first caught sight of that coy, retired place,—surely nothing could happen there, without its full accompaniment of thought or reverie. *White-nights!* so you might interpret its old Latin name.[1] 'The red rose came first,' says a quaint German mystic, speaking of 'the mystery of so-called *white* things', as being 'ever an afterthought—the doubles, or seconds, of real things, and themselves but half-real, half-material—the white queen, the white witch, the white mass, which, as the black mass is a travesty of the true mass turned to evil by horrible old witches, is celebrated by young candidates for the priesthood with an unconsecrated host, by way of rehearsal'. So, white-nights, I suppose, after something like the same analogy, should be nights not of quite blank forgetfulness, but passed in continuous dreaming, only half veiled by sleep. Certainly the place was, in such case, true to its fanciful name in this, that you might very well conceive, in face of it, that dreaming even in the daytime might come to much there.

The young Marius represented an ancient family whose estate had come down to him much curtailed through the extravagance of a certain Marcellus two generations before, a favourite in his day of the fashionable world at Rome, where he had at least spent his substance with a correctness of taste Marius might seem to have inherited from him; as he was believed also to resemble him in a singularly pleasant smile, consistent however, in the younger face, with some degree of sombre expression when the mind within was but slightly moved.

As the means of life decreased, the farm had crept nearer and nearer to the dwelling-house, about which there was therefore a trace of workday negligence or homeliness, not without its picturesque charm for some, for the young master himself

[1] *Ad Vigilias Albas.*

among them. The more observant passer-by would note, curious as to the inmates, a certain amount of dainty care amid that neglect, as if it came in part, perhaps, from a reluctance to disturb old associations. It was significant of the national character, that a sort of elegant *gentleman* farming, as we say, had been much affected by some of the most cultivated Romans. But it became something more than an elegant diversion, something of a serious business, with the household of Marius; and his actual interest in the cultivation of the earth and the care of flocks had brought him, at least, intimately near to those elementary conditions of life, a reverence for which, the great Roman poet, as he has shown by his own half-mystic preoccupation with them, held to be the ground of primitive Roman religion, as of primitive morals. But then, farm-life in Italy, including the culture of the olive and the vine, has a grace of its own, and might well contribute to the production of an ideal dignity of character, like that of nature itself in this gifted region. Vulgarity seemed impossible. The place, though impoverished, was still deservedly dear, full of venerable memories, and with a living sweetness of its own for to-day.

To hold by such ceremonial traditions had been a part of the struggling family pride of the lad's father, to which the example of the head of the state, old Antoninus Pius—an example to be still further enforced by his successor—had given a fresh though perhaps somewhat artificial popularity. It had been consistent with many another homely and old-fashioned trait in him, not to undervalue the charm of exclusiveness and immemorial authority, which membership in a local priestly college, hereditary in his house, conferred upon him. To set a real value on these things was but one element in that pious concern for his home and all that belonged to it, which, as Marius afterwards discovered, had been a strong motive with his father. The ancient hymn—*Jana Novella !*—was still sung by his people, as the new moon grew bright in the west, and even their wild custom of leaping through heaps of blazing straw on a certain night in summer was not discouraged. The privilege of augury itself, according to tradition, had at one time belonged to his race; and if you can imagine how, once in a way, an impressible boy might have an *inkling*, an inward mystic intimation, of the meaning and consequences of all that, what was implied in it becoming explicit for him, you conceive aright the mind of Marius, in whose house the auspices were still carefully consulted before every undertaking of moment.

The devotion of the father then had handed on loyally—and that is all many not unimportant persons ever find to do—a certain tradition of life, which came to mean much for the young Marius. The feeling with which he thought of his dead father was almost exclusively that of awe; though crossed at times by a not unpleasant sense of liberty, as he could but confess to himself, pondering, in the actual absence of so weighty and continual a restraint, upon the arbitrary power which Roman religion and Roman law gave to the parent over the son. On the part of his mother, on the other hand, entertaining the husband's memory, there was a sustained freshness of regret, together with the recognition, as Marius fancied, of some costly self-sacrifice to be credited to the dead. The life of the widow, languid and shadowy enough but for the poignancy of that regret, was like one long service to the departed soul; its many annual observances centring about the funeral urn—a tiny, delicately carved marble house, still white and fair, in the family chapel, wreathed always with the richest flowers from the garden. To the dead, in fact, was conceded in such places a somewhat closer neighbourhood to the old homes they were thought still to protect, than is usual with us, or was usual in Rome itself—a closeness which the living welcomed, so diverse are the ways of our human sentiment, and in which the more wealthy, at least in the country, might indulge themselves. All this Marius followed with a devout interest, sincerely touched and awed by his mother's sorrow. After the deification of the emperors, we are told, it was considered impious so much as to use any coarse expression in the presence of their images. To Marius the whole of life seemed full of sacred presences, demanding of him a similar collectedness. The severe and archaic religion of the villa, as he conceived it, begot in him a sort of devout circumspection lest he should fall short at any point of the demand upon him of anything in which deity was concerned. He must satisfy with a kind of sacred equity, he must be very cautious lest he be found wanting to, the claims of others, in their joys and calamities—the happiness which deity sanctioned, or the blows in which it made itself felt. And from habit, this feeling of a responsibility towards the world of men and things, towards a claim for due sentiment concerning them on his side, came to be a part of his nature not to be put off. It kept him serious and dignified amid the Epicurean speculations which in after years much engrossed him, and when he had learned to think of all religions as indifferent, serious amid many fopperies and through many languid days, and made him anticipate all his life long as a thing towards which he must carefully train himself, some great occasion of self-devotion, such as really came, that should consecrate his life, and, it might be, its memory with others, as the early Christian looked forward to martyrdom at the end of his course, as a seal of worth upon it.

The traveller, descending from the slopes of Luna, even as he got his first view of the *Port-of-Venus*, would pause by the way, to read the face, as it were, of so beautiful a dwelling-place, lying away from the white road, at the point where it began to decline somewhat steeply to the marsh-land below. The building of pale red and yellow marble, mellowed by age, which he saw beyond the gates, was indeed but the exquisite fragment of a once large and sumptuous villa. Two centuries of the play of the sea-wind were in the velvet of the mosses which lay along its inaccessible ledges and angles. Here and there the marble plates had slipped from their places, where the delicate weeds had forced their way. The graceful wildness which prevailed in garden and farm gave place to a singular nicety about the actual habitation, and a still more scrupulous sweetness and order reigned within. The old Roman architects seem to have well understood the decorative value of the floor—the real economy there was, in the production of rich interior effect, of a somewhat lavish expenditure upon the surface they trod on. The pavement of the hall had lost something of its evenness; but, though a little rough to the foot, polished and cared for like a piece of silver, looked, as mosaic-work is apt to do, its best in old age. Most noticeable among the ancestral masks, each in its little cedarn chest below the cornice, was that of the wasteful but elegant Marcellus, with the quaint resemblance in its yellow waxen features to Marius, just then so full of animation and country colour. A chamber, curved ingeniously into oval form, which he had added to the mansion, still contained his collection of works of art; above all, that head of Medusa, for which the villa was famous. The spoilers of one of the old Greek towns on the coast had flung away or lost the thing, as it seemed, in some rapid flight across the river below, from the sands of which it was drawn up in a fisherman's net, with the fine golden laminae still clinging here and there to the bronze. It was Marcellus also who had con-trived the prospect-tower of two stories with the white pigeon-house above, so characteristic of the place. The little glazed windows in the uppermost chamber framed each its dainty landscape—the pallid crags of Carrara, like wildly twisted snowdrifts above the purple heath; the distant harbour with its freight of white marble going to sea; the lighthouse temple of *Venus Speciosa* on its dark headland, amid the long-drawn curves of white breakers. Even on summer nights the air there had always a motion in it, and drove the scent of the new-mown hay along all the passages of the house.

Something pensive, spellbound, and but half real, something cloistral or monastic, as we should say, united to this exquisite order, made the whole place seem to Marius, as it were, *sacellum*, the peculiar sanctuary, of his mother, who, still in real widow-hood, provided the deceased Marius the elder with that secondary sort of life which we can give to the dead, in our intensely realized memory of them—the 'subjective immortality', to use a modern phrase, for which many a Roman epitaph cries out plaintively to widow or sister or daughter, still in the land of the living. Certainly, if any such considerations regarding them do reach the shadowy people, he enjoyed that secondary existence, that warm place still left, in thought at least, beside the living, the desire for which is actually, in various forms, so great a motive with most of us. And Marius the younger, even thus early, came to think of women's tears, of women's hands to lay one to rest, in death as in the sleep of childhood, as a sort of natural want. The soft lines of the white hands and face, set among the many folds of the veil and stole of the Roman widow, busy upon her needlework, or with music sometimes, defined themselves for him as the typical expression of maternity. Helping her with her white and purple wools, and caring for her musical instruments, he won, as if from the handling of such things, an urbane and feminine refinement, qualifying duly his country-grown habits—the sense of a certain delicate blandness, which he relished, above all, on returning to the 'chapel' of his mother, after long days of open-air exercise, in winter or stormy summer. For poetic souls in old Italy felt, hardly less strongly than the English, the pleasures of winter, of the hearth, with the very dead warm in its generous heat, keeping the young myrtles in flower, though the hail is beating hard without. One important principle, of fruit afterwards in his Roman life, that relish for the country fixed deeply in him; in the winters especially, when the sufferings of the animal world become so palpable even to the least observant. It fixed in him a sympathy for all creatures, for the almost human troubles and sicknesses of the flocks, for instance. It was a feeling which had in it something of religious veneration for life as such—for that mysterious essence which man is powerless to create in even the feeblest degree. One by one, at the desire of his mother, the lad broke down his cherished traps and springes for the hungry wild birds on the salt marsh. A white bird, she told him once, looking at him gravely, a bird which he must carry in his bosom across a crowded public place—his own soul was like that! Would it reach the hands of his good genius on the opposite side, unruffled and unsoiled? And as his mother became to him the very type of maternity in things, its unfailing pity and protectiveness, and maternity itself the central type of all love;—so, that beautiful dwelling-place lent the reality of concrete outline to a peculiar ideal of home, which throughout the rest of his life he seemed, amid many distractions of spirit, to be ever seeking to regain.

And a certain vague fear of evil, constitutional in him, enhanced still further this sentiment of home as a place of tried security. His religion, that old Italian religion, in contrast with the really light-hearted religion of Greece, had its deep undercurrent of gloom, its sad, haunting imageries, not exclusively confined to the walls of Etruscan tombs. The function of the conscience, not always as the prompter of gratitude for benefits received, but oftenest as his accuser before those angry heavenly masters, had a large part in it; and the sense of some unexplored evil, ever dogging his footsteps, made him oddly suspicious of particular places and persons. Though his liking for animals was so strong, yet one fierce day in early summer, as he walked along a narrow road, he had seen the snakes breeding, and ever afterwards avoided that place and its ugly associations, for there was something in the incident which made food distasteful and his sleep uneasy for many days afterwards. The memory of it, however, had almost passed away, when at the corner of a street in Pisa he came upon an African showman exhibiting a great serpent: once more, as the reptile writhed, the former painful impression revived: it was like a peep into the lower side of the real world, and again for many days took all sweetness from food and sleep. He wondered at himself indeed, trying to puzzle out the secret of that repugnance, having no particular dread of a snake's bite, like one of his companions, who had put his hand into the mouth of an old garden-god and roused there a sluggish viper. A kind of pity even mingled with his aversion, and he could hardly have killed or injured the animals, which seemed already to suffer by the very circumstance of their life, being what they were. It was something like a fear of the supernatural, or perhaps rather a moral feeling, for the face of a great serpent, with no grace of fur or feathers, so different from quadruped or bird, has a sort of humanity of aspect in its spotted and clouded nakedness. There was a humanity, dusty and sordid and as if far gone in corruption, in the sluggish coil, as it awoke suddenly into one metallic spring of pure enmity against him. Long afterwards, when it happened that at Rome he saw, a second time, a showman with his serpents, he remembered the night which had then followed, thinking, in Saint Augustine's vein, on the real greatness of those little troubles of children, of which older people make light; but with a sudden gratitude also, as he reflected how richly possessed his life had actually been by beautiful aspects and imageries, seeing how greatly what was repugnant to the eye disturbed his peace.

Thus the boyhood of Marius passed; on the whole, more given to contemplation than to action. Less prosperous in fortune than at an earlier day there had been reason to expect, and animating his solitude, as he read eagerly and intelligently, with the traditions of the past, already he lived much in the realm of the imagination, and became betimes, as he was to continue all through life, something of an idealist, constructing the world for himself in great measure from within, by the exercise of meditative power. A vein of subjective philosophy, with the individual for its standard of all things, there would be always in his intellectual scheme of the world and of conduct, with a certain incapacity wholly to accept other men's valuations. And the generation of this peculiar element in his temper he could trace up to the days when his life had been so like the reading of a romance to him. Had the Romans a word for *unworldly*? The beautiful word *umbratilis* perhaps comes nearest to it; and, with that precise sense, might describe the spirit in which he prepared himself for the sacerdotal function hereditary in his family—the sort of mystic enjoyment he had in the abstinence, the strenuous self-control and *ascêsis*, which such preparation involved. Like the young Ion in the beautiful opening of the play of Euripides, who every morning sweeps the temple floor with such a fund of cheerfulness in his service, he was apt to be happy in sacred places, with a susceptibility to their peculiar influences which he never outgrew; so that often in after-times, quite unexpectedly, this feeling would revive in him with undiminished freshness. That first, early boyish ideal of priesthood, the sense of dedication, survived through all the distractions of the world, and when all thought of such vocation had finally passed from him, as a ministry, in spirit at least, towards a sort of hieratic beauty and order in the conduct of life.

And now what relieved in part this over-tension of soul was the lad's pleasure in the country and the open air; above all, the ramble to the coast, over the marsh with its dwarf roses and wild lavender, and delightful signs, one after another—the abandoned boat, the ruined flood-gates, the flock of wild birds —that one was approaching the sea; the long summer-day of idleness among its vague scents and sounds. And it was characteristic of him that he relished especially the grave, subdued, northern notes in all that—the charm of the French or English notes, as we might term them—in the luxuriant Italian landscape.

CHAPTER III

Dilexi decorem domus tuae.

THAT almost morbid religious idealism, and his healthful love of the country, were both alike developed by the circumstances of a journey, which happened about this time, when Marius was taken to a certain temple of Aesculapius, among the hills of Etruria, as was then usual in such cases, for the cure of some boyish sickness. The religion of Aesculapius, though borrowed from Greece, had been naturalized in Rome in the old republican times; but had reached under the Antonines the height of its popularity throughout the Roman world. That was an age of valetudinarians, in many instances of imaginary ones; but below its various crazes concerning health and disease, largely multiplied a few years after the time of which I am speaking by the miseries of a great pestilence, lay a valuable, because partly practicable, belief that all the maladies of the soul might be reached through the subtle gateways of the body.

Salus, salvation, for the Romans, had come to mean bodily sanity. The religion of the god of bodily health, *Salvator*, as they called him absolutely, had a chance just then of becoming the one religion; that mild and philanthropic son of Apollo surviving, or absorbing, all other pagan godhead. The apparatus of the medical art, the salutary mineral or herb, diet or abstinence, and all the varieties of the bath, came to have a kind of sacramental character, so deep was the feeling, in more serious minds, of a moral or spiritual profit in physical health, beyond the obvious bodily advantages one had of it; the body becoming truly, in that case, but a quiet handmaid of the soul. The priesthood or 'family' of Aesculapius, a vast college, believed to be in possession of certain precious medical secrets, came nearest perhaps, of all the institutions of the pagan world, to the Christian priesthood; the temples of the god, rich in some instances with the accumulated thank-offerings of centuries of a tasteful devotion, being really also a kind of hospitals for the

17

sick, administered in a full conviction of the religiousness, the
refined and sacred happiness, of a life spent in the relieving
of pain.

Elements of a really experimental and progressive knowledge
there were doubtless amid this devout enthusiasm, bent so
faithfully on the reception of health as a direct gift from God;
but for the most part his care was held to take effect through a
machinery easily capable of misuse for purposes of religious
fraud. Through dreams, above all, inspired by Aesculapius
himself, information as to the cause and cure of a malady was
supposed to come to the sufferer, in a belief based on the truth
that dreams do sometimes, for those who watch them carefully,
give many hints concerning the conditions of the body—those
latent weak points at which disease or death may most easily
break into it. In the time of Marcus Aurelius these medical
dreams had become more than ever a fashionable caprice.
Aristeides, the 'Orator', a man of undoubted intellectual power,
has devoted six discourses to their interpretation; the really
scientific Galen has recorded how beneficently they had inter-
vened in his own case, at certain turning-points of life; and a
belief in them was one of the frailties of the wise emperor himself.
Partly for the sake of these dreams, living ministers of the god,
more likely to come to one in his actual dwelling-place than
elsewhere, it was almost a necessity that the patient should
sleep one or more nights within the precincts of a temple consecrated to his service, during which time he must observe
certain rules prescribed by the priests.

For this purpose, after devoutly saluting the *Lares*, as was
customary before starting on a journey, Marius set forth one
summer morning on his way to the famous temple which lay
among the hills beyond the valley of the Arnus. It was his
greatest adventure hitherto; and he had much pleasure in all
its details, in spite of his feverishness. Starting early, under
the guidance of an old serving-man who drove the mules, with
his wife who took all that was needful for their refreshment on
the way and for the offering at the shrine, they went, under the
genial heat, halting now and then to pluck certain flowers seen
for the first time on these high places, upwards, through a long
day of sunshine, while cliffs and woods sank gradually below
their path. The evening came as they passed along a steep
white road with many windings among the pines, and it was
night when they reached the temple, the lights of which shone
out upon them pausing before the gates of the sacred enclosure,

while Marius became alive to a singular purity in the air. A rippling of water about the place was the only thing audible, as they waited till two priestly figures, speaking Greek to one another, admitted them into a large, white-walled, and clearly lighted guest-chamber, in which, while he partook of a simple but wholesomely prepared supper, Marius still seemed to feel pleasantly the height they had attained to among the hills.

The agreeable sense of all this was spoiled by one thing only, his old fear of serpents; for it was under the form of a serpent that Aesculapius had come to Rome, and the last definite thought of his weary head before he fell asleep had been a dread either that the god might appear, as he was said sometimes to do, under this hideous aspect, or perhaps one of those great sallow-hued snakes themselves, kept in the sacred place, as he had also heard was usual.

And after an hour's feverish dreaming he awoke—with a cry, it would seem, for someone had entered the room bearing a light. The footsteps of the youthful figure which approached and sat by his bedside were certainly real. Ever afterwards, when the thought arose in his mind of some unhoped-for but entire relief from distress, like blue sky in a storm at sea, would come back the memory of that gracious countenance which, amid all the kindness of its gaze, had yet a certain air of pre-dominance over him, so that he seemed now for the first time to have found the master of his spirit. It would have been sweet to be the servant of him who now sat beside him speaking.

He caught a lesson from what was then said, still somewhat beyond his years, a lesson in the skilled cultivation of life, of experience, of opportunity, which seemed to be the aim of the young priest's recommendations. The sum of them, through various forgotten intervals of argument, as might really have happened in a dream, was the precept, repeated many times under slightly varied aspects, of a diligent promotion of the capacity of the eye, inasmuch as in the eye would lie for him the determining influence of life: he was of the number of those who, in the words of a poet who came long after, must be 'made perfect by the love of visible beauty'. The discourse was conceived from the point of view of a theory Marius found afterwards in Plato's *Phaedrus*, which supposes men's spirits susceptible to certain influences, diffused, after the manner of streams or currents, by fair things or persons visibly present— green fields, for instance, or children's faces—into the air around them, acting, in the case of some peculiar natures, like

potent material essences, and conforming the seer to themselves
as with some cunning physical necessity.   This theory,[1] in itself
so fantastic, had, however, determined in a range of methodical
suggestions, altogether quaint here and there from their cir-
cumstantial minuteness.   And throughout, the possibility of
some vision, as of a new city coming down 'like a bride out of
heaven', a vision still indeed, it might seem, a long way off,
but to be granted perhaps one day to the eyes thus trained, was
presented as the motive of this laboriously practical direction.

'If thou wouldst have all about thee like the colours of some
fresh picture, in a clear light,' so the discourse recommenced
after a pause, 'be temperate in thy religious motions, in love, in
wine, in all things, and of a peaceful heart with thy fellows.'
To keep the eye clear by a sort of exquisite personal alacrity
and cleanliness, extending even to his dwelling-place; to dis-
criminate, ever more and more fastidiously, select form and
colour in things from what was less select; to meditate much on
beautiful visible objects, on objects, more especially, connected
with the period of youth—on children at play in the morning,
the trees in early spring, on young animals, on the fashions and
amusements of young men; to keep ever by him if it were but
a single choice flower, a graceful animal or sea-shell, as a token
and representative of the whole kingdom of such things; to
avoid jealously, in his way through the world, everything
repugnant to sight; and, should any circumstance tempt him
to a general converse in the range of such objects, to disentangle
himself from that circumstance at any cost of place, money, or
opportunity; such were in brief outline the duties recognized,
the rights demanded, in this new formula of life.   And it was
delivered with conviction; as if the speaker verily saw into the
recesses of the mental and physical being of the listener, while
his own expression of perfect temperance had in it a fascinating
power—the merely negative element of purity, the mere freedom
from taint or flaw, in exercise as a positive influence.   Long
afterwards, when Marius read the *Charmides*—that other
dialogue of Plato, into which he seems to have expressed the
very genius of old Greek temperance—the image of this speaker
came back vividly before him, to take the chief part in the
conversation.

It was as a weighty sanction of such temperance, in almost
visible symbolism (an outward imagery identifying itself with

[1] Ἡ ἀπορρόη τοῦ καλλοῦς.

unseen moralities), that the memory of that night's double experience, the dream of the great sallow snake and the utterance of the young priest, always returned to him, and the contrast therein involved made him revolt with unfaltering instinct from the bare thought of any excess in sleep, or diet, or even in matters of taste, still more from any excess of a coarser kind.

When he awoke again, still in the exceeding freshness he had felt on his arrival, and now in full sunlight, it was as if his sickness had really departed with the terror of the night: a confusion had passed from the brain, a painful dryness from his hands. Simply to be alive and there was a delight; and as he bathed in the fresh water set ready for his use, the air of the room about him seemed like pure gold, the very shadows rich with colour. Summoned at length by one of the white-robed brethren, he went out to walk in the temple garden.   At a distance, on either side, his guide pointed out to him the *Houses of Birth and Death*, erected for the reception respectively of women about to become mothers, and of persons about to die; neither of those incidents being allowed to defile, as was thought, the actual precincts of the shrine.   His visitor of the previous night he saw nowhere again.   But among the official ministers of the place there was one, already marked as of great celebrity, whom Marius saw often in later days at Rome, the physician Galen, now about thirty years old.   He was standing, the hood partly drawn over his face, beside the holy well, as Marius and his guide approached it.

This famous well or conduit, primary cause of the temple and its surrounding institutions, was supplied by the water of a spring flowing directly out of the rocky foundations of the shrine.   From the rim of its basin rose a circle of trim columns to support a cupola of singular lightness and grace, itself full of reflected light from the rippling surface, through which might be traced the wavy figurework of the marble lining below as the stream of water rushed in.   Legend told of a visit of Aesculapius to this place, earlier and happier than his first coming to Rome: an inscription around the cupola recorded it in letters of gold. 'Being come unto this place the son of God loved it exceedingly' —*Huc profectus filius Dei maxime amavit hunc locum*—and it was then that that most intimately human of the gods had given men the well, with all its salutary properties.   The element itself when received into the mouth, in consequence of its entire freedom from adhering organic matter, was more like a draught of wonderfully pure air than water; and after tasting, Marius was told many mysterious circumstances concerning it, by one and another of the bystanders: he who drank often thereof might well think he had tasted of the Homeric *lotus,* so great became his desire to remain always on that spot: carried to other places, it was almost indefinitely conservative of its fine qualities: nay! a few drops of it would amend other water; and it flowed not only with unvarying abundance but with a volume so oddly rhythmical that the well stood always full to the brim, whatever quantity might be drawn from it, seeming to answer with strange alacrity of service to human needs, like a true creature and pupil of the philanthropic god. Certainly the little crowd around seemed to find singular refreshment in gazing on it. The whole place appeared sensibly influenced by the amiable and healthful spirit of the thing. All the objects of the country were there at their freshest. In the great park-like enclosure for the maintenance of the sacred animals offered by the convalescent, grass and trees were allowed to grow with a kind of graceful wildness; otherwise, all was wonderfully nice. And that freshness seemed to have something moral in its influence, as if it acted upon the body and the merely bodily powers of apprehension, through the intelligence; and to the end of his visit Marius saw no more serpents.

A lad was just then drawing water for ritual uses, and Marius followed him as he returned from the well, more and more impressed by the religiousness of all he saw, on his way through a long cloister or corridor, the walls wellnigh hidden under votive inscriptions recording favours from the son of Apollo, and with a distant fragrance of incense in the air, explained when he turned aside through an open doorway into the temple itself. His heart bounded as the refined and dainty magnificence of the place came upon him suddenly, in the flood of early sunshine, with the ceremonial lights burning here and there, and withal a singular expression of sacred order, a surprising cleanliness and simplicity. Certain priests, men whose countenances bore a deep impression of cultivated mind, each with his little group of assistants, were gliding round silently to perform their morning salutation to the god, raising the closed thumb and finger of the right hand with a kiss in the air, as they came and went on their sacred business, bearing their frankincense and lustral water. Around the walls, at such a level that the worshippers might read, as in a book, the story of the god and his sons, the brotherhood of the *Asclepiadae,* ran a series of imageries, in low relief, their delicate light and shade being heightened, here and there, with gold. Fullest of inspired and sacred expression, as if in this place the chisel of the artist had indeed dealt not with marble but with the very breath of feeling and thought, was the scene in which the earliest generation of the sons of Aesculapius were transformed into healing dreams; for 'grown now too glorious to abide longer among men, by the aid of their sire they put away their mortal bodies, and came into another country, yet not indeed into Elysium nor into the Islands of the Blest. But being made like to the immortal gods, they began to pass about through the world, changed thus far from their first form that they appear eternally young, as many persons have seen them in many places—ministers and heralds of their father, passing to and fro over the earth, like gliding stars! Which thing is, indeed, the most wonderful concerning them!' And in this scene, as throughout the series, with all its crowded personages, Marius noted on the carved faces the same peculiar union of unction, almost of hilarity, with a certain self-possession and reserve, which was conspicuous in the living ministrants around him.

In the central space, upon a pillar or pedestal, hung, *ex voto*, with the richest personal ornaments, stood the image of Aesculapius himself, surrounded by choice flowering plants. It presented the type, still with something of the severity of the earlier art of Greece about it, not of an aged and crafty physician, but of a youth, earnest and strong of aspect, carrying an *ampulla* or bottle in one hand, and in the other a traveller's staff, a pilgrim among his pilgrim worshippers; and one of the ministers explained to Marius this pilgrim guise.—One chief source of the master's knowledge of healing had been observation of the remedies resorted to by animals labouring under disease or pain—what leaf or berry the lizard or dormouse lay upon its wounded fellow; to which purpose for long years he had led the life of a wanderer, in wild places. The boy took his place as the last comer, a little way behind the group of worshippers who stood in front of the image. There, with uplifted face, the palms of his two hands raised and open before him, and taught by the priest, he said his collect of thanksgiving and prayer (Aristeides has recorded it at the end of his *Asclepiadae*) to the Inspired Dreams:

'O ye children of Apollo! who in time past have stilled the waves of sorrow for many people, lighting up a lamp of safety before those who travel by sea and land, be pleased, in your great condescension, though ye be equal in glory with your elder brethren the Dioscuri, and your lot in immortal youth be as theirs, to accept this prayer, which in sleep and vision ye have inspired. Order it aright, I pray you, according to your loving-kindness to men. Preserve me from sickness; and endue my body with such a measure of health as may suffice it for the obeying of the spirit, that I may pass my days unhindered and in quietness.'

On the last morning of his visit Marius entered the shrine again, and just before his departure the priest, who had been his special director during his stay at the place, lifting a cunningly contrived panel, which formed the back of one of the carved seats, bade him look through. What he saw was like the vision of a new world, by the opening of some unsuspected window in a familiar dwelling-place. He looked out upon a long-drawn valley of singularly cheerful aspect, hidden, by the peculiar conformation of the locality, from all points of observation but this. In a green meadow at the foot of the steep olive-clad rocks below, the novices were taking their exercise. The softly sloping sides of the vale lay alike in full sunlight; and its distant opening was closed by a beautifully formed mountain, from which the last wreaths of morning mist were rising under the heat. It might have seemed the very presentment of a land of hope, its hollows brimful of a shadow of blue flowers; and lo! on the one level space of the horizon, in a long dark line, were towers and a dome: and that was Pisa.—Or Rome, was it? asked Marius, ready to believe the utmost, in his excitement.

All this served, as he understood afterwards in retrospect, at once to strengthen and to purify a certain vein of character in him. Developing the ideal, pre-existent there, of a religious beauty, associated for the future with the exquisite splendour of the temple of Aesculapius, as it dawned upon him on that morning of his first visit—it developed that ideal in connexion with a vivid sense of the value of mental and bodily sanity. And this recognition of the beauty, even for the aesthetic sense, of mere bodily health, now acquired, operated afterwards as an influence morally salutary, counteracting the less desirable or hazardous tendencies of some phases of thought, through which he was to pass.

He came home brown with health to find the health of his mother failing; and about her death, which occurred not long afterwards, there was a circumstance which rested with him as the cruellest touch of all, in an event which for a time seemed to have taken the light out of the sunshine. She died away from home, but sent for him at the last, with a painful effort on her part, but to his great gratitude, pondering, as he always believed, that he might chance otherwise to look back all his life long upon a single fault with something like remorse, and find the burden a great one. For it happened that, through some sudden, incomprehensible petulance, there had been an angry childish gesture, and a slighting word, at the very moment of her departure, actually for the last time. Remembering this he would ever afterwards pray to be saved from offences against his own affections; the thought of that marred parting having peculiar bitterness for one who set so much store, both by principle and habit, on the sentiment of home.

CHAPTER IV

THE TREE OF KNOWLEDGE

O mare! O littus! verum secretumque Μουσεῖον,
quam multa invenitis, quam multa dictatis!

Pliny's Letters.

IT would hardly have been possible to feel more seriously than
did Marius in those grave years of his early life. But the death
of his mother turned seriousness of feeling into a matter of the
intelligence: it made him a questioner; and, by bringing into
full evidence to him the force of his affections and the probable
importance of their place in his future, developed in him
generally the more human and earthly elements of character.
A singularly virile consciousness of the realities of life pronounced itself in him; still however as in the main a poetic
apprehension, though united already with something of personal
ambition and the instinct of self-assertion. There were days
when he could suspect, though it was a suspicion he was careful
at first to put from him, that that early, much cherished religion
of the villa might come to count with him as but one form of
poetic beauty, or of the ideal, in things; as but one voice, in a
world where there were many voices it would be a moral weakness not to listen to. And yet this voice, through its forcible
preoccupation of his childish conscience, still seemed to make
a claim of a quite exclusive character, defining itself as essentially
one of but two possible leaders of his spirit, the other proposing
to him unlimited self-expansion in a world of various sunshine.
The contrast was so pronounced as to make the easy, light-
hearted, unsuspecting exercise of himself, among the temptations
of the new phase of life which had now begun, seem nothing less
than a rival *religion*, a rival *religious* service. The temptations,
the various sunshine, were those of the old town of Pisa, where
Marius was now a tall schoolboy. Pisa was a place lying just
far enough from home to make his rare visits to it in childhood
seem like adventures, such as had never failed to supply new
and refreshing impulses to the imagination. The partly decayed
pensive town, which still had its commerce by sea, and its

fashion at the bathing-season, had lent, at one time the vivid memory of its fair streets of marble, at another the solemn outline of the dark hills of Luna on its background, at another the living glances of its men and women, to the thickly gathering crowd of impressions, out of which his notion of the world was then forming. And while he learned that the object, the experience, as it will be known to memory, is really from first to last the chief point for consideration in the conduct of life, these things were feeding also the idealism constitutional with him—his innate and habitual longing for a world altogether fairer than that he saw. The child could find his way in thought along those streets of the old town, expecting duly the shrines at their corners, and their recurrent intervals of garden-courts, or side-views of distant sea. The great temple of the place, as he could remember it, on turning back once for a last look from an angle of his homeward road, counting its tall grey columns between the blue of the bay and the blue fields of blossoming flax beyond; the harbour and its lights; the foreign ships lying there; the sailors' chapel of Venus, and her gilded image, hung with votive gifts; the seamen themselves, their women and children, who had a whole peculiar colour-world of their own—the boy's superficial delight in the broad light and shadow of all that was mingled with the sense of power, of unknown distance, of the danger of storm and possible death.

To this place, then, Marius came down now from *White-nights*, to live in the house of his guardian or tutor, that he might attend the school of a famous rhetorician, and learn, among other things, Greek. The school, one of many imitations of Plato's Academy in the old Athenian garden, lay in a quiet suburb of Pisa, and had its grove of cypresses, its porticoes, a house for the master, its chapel and images. For the memory of Marius in after-days, a clear morning sunlight seemed to lie perpetually on that severe picture in old grey and green. The lad went to this school daily betimes, in state at first, with a young slave to carry the books, and certainly with no reluctance, for the sight of his fellow-scholars, and their petulant activity, coming upon the sadder sentimental moods of his childhood, awoke at once that instinct of emulation which is but the other side of sympathy; and he was not aware, of course, how completely the difference of his previous training had made him, even in his most enthusiastic participation in the ways of that little world, still essentially but a spectator. While all their heart was in their limited boyish race, and its transitory prizes,

he was already entertaining himself, very pleasurably meditative, with the tiny drama in action before him, as but the mimic,
preliminary exercise for a larger contest, and already with an
implicit epicureanism. Watching all the gallant effects of their
small rivalries—a scene in the main of fresh delightful sunshine
—he entered at once into the sensations of a rivalry beyond
them, into the passion of men, and had already recognized a
certain appetite for fame, for distinction among his fellows, as
his dominant motive to be.

The fame he conceived for himself at this time was, as the
reader will have anticipated, of the intellectual order, that of
a poet perhaps. And as, in that grey monastic tranquillity of
the villa, inward voices from the reality of unseen things had
come abundantly; so here, with the sounds and aspects of the
shore, and amid the urbanities, the graceful follies, of a bathing-
place, it was the reality, the tyrannous reality, of things visible
that was borne in upon him. The real world around—a present
humanity not less comely, it might seem, than that of the old
heroic days—endowing everything it touched upon, however
remotely, down to its little passing tricks of fashion even, with
a kind of fleeting beauty, exercised over him just then a great
fascination.

That sense had come upon him in all its power one exceptionally fine summer, the summer when, at a somewhat earlier age
than was usual, he had formally assumed the dress of manhood,
going into the Forum for that purpose, accompanied by his
friends in festal array. At night, after the full measure of those
cloudless days, he would feel wellnigh wearied out, as if with
a long succession of pictures and music. As he wandered
through the gay streets or on the seashore, the real world
seemed indeed boundless, and himself almost absolutely free
in it, with a boundless appetite for experience, for adventure,
whether physical or of the spirit. His entire rearing hitherto
had lent itself to an imaginative exaltation of the past; but
now the spectacle actually afforded to his untired and freely
open senses, suggested the reflection that the present had, it
might be, really advanced beyond the past, and he was ready to
boast in the very fact that it was modern. If, in a voluntary
archaism, the polite world of that day went back to a choicer
generation, as it fancied, for the purpose of a fastidious self-
correction, in matters of art, of literature, and even, as we have
seen, of religion, at least it improved, by a shade or two of
more scrupulous finish, on the old pattern; and the new era,

like the *Neu-zeit* of the German enthusiasts at the beginning of our own century, might perhaps be discerned, awaiting one just a single step onward—the perfected new manner, in the consummation of time, alike as regards the things of the imagination and the actual conduct of life. Only, while the pursuit of an ideal like this demanded entire liberty of heart and brain, that old, staid, conservative religion of his childhood certainly had its being in a world of somewhat narrow restrictions. But then, the one was absolutely real, with nothing less than the reality of seeing and hearing—the other, how vague, shadowy, problematical! Could its so limited probabilities be worth taking into account in any practical question as to the rejecting or receiving of what was indeed so real, and, on the face of it, so desirable?

And, dating from the time of his first coming to school, a great friendship had grown up for him, in that life of so few attachments—the pure and disinterested friendship of schoolmates. He had seen Flavian for the first time the day on which he had come to Pisa, at the moment when his mind was full of wistful thoughts regarding the new life to begin for him to-morrow, and he gazed curiously at the crowd of bustling scholars as they came from their classes. There was something in Flavian a shade disdainful, as he stood isolated from the others for a moment, explained in part by his stature and the distinction of the low, broad forehead; though there was pleasantness also for the new-comer in the roving blue eyes which seemed somehow to take a fuller hold upon things around than is usual with boys. Marius knew that those proud glances made kindly note of him for a moment, and felt something like friendship at first sight. There was a tone of reserve or gravity there, amid perfectly disciplined health, which, to his fancy, seemed to carry forward the expression of the austere sky and the clear song of the blackbird on that grey March evening. Flavian indeed was a creature who changed much with the changes of the passing light and shade about him, and was brilliant enough under the early sunshine in school next morning. Of all that little world of more or less gifted youth, surely the centre was this lad of servile birth. Prince of the school, he had gained an easy dominion over the old Greek master by the fascination of his parts, and over his fellow-scholars by the figure he bore. He wore already the manly dress; and standing there in class, as he displayed his wonderful quickness in reckoning, or his taste in declaiming Homer, he was like a carved figure in motion, thought Marius, but with that indescribable gleam upon it which the words of Homer actually suggested, as perceptible on the visible forms of the gods—

οἷα θεοὺς ἐπενήνοθεν αἰὲν ἐόντας.

A story hung by him, a story which his comrades acutely connected with his habitual air of somewhat peevish pride. Two points were held to be clear amid its general vagueness—a rich stranger paid his schooling, and he was himself very poor, though there was an attractive piquancy in the poverty of Flavian which in a scholar of another figure might have been despised. Over Marius too his dominion was entire. Three years older than he, Flavian was appointed to help the younger boy in his studies, and Marius thus became virtually his servant in many things, taking his humours with a sort of grateful pride in being noticed at all, and, thinking over all this afterwards, found that the fascination experienced by him had been a sentimental one, dependent on the concession to himself of an intimacy, a certain tolerance of his company, granted to none beside.

That was in the earliest days; and then, as their intimacy grew, the genius, the intellectual power of Flavian began its sway over him. The brilliant youth who loved dress, and dainty food, and flowers, and seemed to have a natural alliance with, and claim upon, everything else which was physically select and bright, cultivated also that foppery of words, of choice diction, which was common among the *élite* spirits of that day; and Marius, early an expert and elegant penman, transcribed his verses (the euphuism of which, amid a genuine original power, was then so delightful to him) in beautiful ink, receiving in return the profit of Flavian's really great intellectual capacities, developed and accomplished under the ambitious desire to make his way effectively in life. Among other things he introduced him to the writings of a sprightly wit, then very busy with the pen, one Lucian—writings seeming to overflow with that intellectual light turned upon dim places, which, at least in seasons of mental fair weather, can make people laugh where they have been wont, perhaps, to pray. And, surely, the sunlight which filled those well-remembered early mornings in school, had had more than the usual measure of gold in it! Marius, at least, would lie awake before the time, thinking with delight of the long coming hours of hard work in the presence of Flavian, as other boys dream of a holiday.

It was almost by accident at last, so wayward and capricious was he, that reserve gave way, and Flavian told the story of his father—a freedman, presented late in life, and almost against his will, with the liberty so fondly desired in youth, but on condition of the sacrifice of part of his *peculium*—the slave's diminutive hoard—amassed by many a self-denial, in an existence necessarily hard. The rich man, interested in the promise of the fair child born on his estate, had sent him to school. The meanness and dejection, nevertheless, of that unoccupied old age defined the leading memory of Flavian, revived sometimes, after this first confidence, with a burst of angry tears amid the sunshine. But nature had had her economy in nursing the strength of that one natural affection; for, save his half-selfish care for Marius, it was the single, really generous part, the one piety, in the lad's character. In him Marius saw the spirit of unbelief, achieved as if at one step. The much admired freedman's son, as with the privilege of a natural aristocracy, believed only in himself, in the brilliant, and mainly sensuous gifts, he had, or meant to acquire.

And then, he had certainly yielded himself, though still with untouched health, in a world where manhood comes early, to the seductions of that luxurious town, and Marius wondered sometimes, in the freer revelation of himself by conversation, at the extent of his early corruption. How often, afterwards, did evil things present themselves in malign association with the memory of that beautiful head, and with a kind of borrowed sanction and charm in its natural grace! To Marius, at a later time, he counted for as it were an epitome of the whole pagan world, the depth of its corruption, and its perfection of form. And still, in his mobility, his animation, in his eager capacity for various life, he was so real an object, after that visionary idealism of the villa. His voice, his glance, were like the breaking in of the solid world upon one, amid the flimsy fictions of a dream. A shadow, handling all things as shadows, had felt a sudden real and poignant heat in them.

Meantime, under his guidance, Marius was learning quickly and abundantly, because with a good will. There was that in the actual effectiveness of his figure which stimulated the younger lad to make the most of opportunity; and he had experience already that education largely increased one's capacity for enjoyment. He was acquiring what it is the chief function of all higher education to impart, the art, namely, of so relieving the ideal or poetic traits, the elements of distinction, in our everyday life—of so exclusively living in them—that the unadorned remainder of it, the mere drift or debris of our days, comes to be as though it were not. And the consciousness of this aim came with the reading of one particular book, then fresh in the world, with which he fell in about this time—a book which awakened the poetic or romantic capacity as perhaps some other book might have done, but was peculiar in giving it a direction emphatically sensuous. It made him, in that visionary reception of everyday life, the seer, more especially, of a revelation in colour and form. If our modern education, in its better efforts, really conveys to any of us that kind of idealizing power, it does so (though dealing mainly, as its professed instruments, with the most select and ideal remains of ancient literature) oftenest by truant reading; and thus it happened also, long ago, with Marius and his friend.

CHAPTER V

THE GOLDEN BOOK

THE two lads were lounging together over a book, half-buried in a heap of dry corn, in an old granary—the quiet corner to which they had climbed out of the way of their noisier companions on one of their blandest holiday afternoons. They looked round: the western sun smote through the broad chinks of the shutters. How like a picture! and it was precisely the scene described in what they were reading, with just that added poetic touch in the book which made it delightful and select, and, in the actual place, the ray of sunlight transforming the rough grain among the cool brown shadows into heaps of gold. What they were intent on was, indeed, the book of books, the 'golden' book of that day, a gift to Flavian, as was shown by the purple writing on the handsome yellow wrapper, following the title. *Flaviane !*—it said,

Flaviane !	*Flaviane !*	*Flaviane !*
lege	*Vivas !*	*Vivas !*
Feliciter !	*Floreas !*	*Gaudeas !*

It was perfumed with oil of sandal-wood, and decorated with carved and gilt ivory bosses at the ends of the roller.

And the inside was something not less dainty and fine, full of the archaisms and curious felicities in which that generation delighted, quaint terms and images picked fresh from the early dramatists, the lifelike phrases of some lost poet preserved by an old grammarian, racy morsels of the vernacular, and studied prettinesses:—all alike, mere playthings for the genuine power and natural eloquence of the erudite artist, unsuppressed by his erudition, which, however, made some people angry, chiefly less well 'got-up' people, and especially those who were untidy from indolence.

No! it was certainly not that old-fashioned, unconscious ease of the early literature, which could never come again; which, after all, had had more in common with the 'infinite patience' of Apuleius than with the hack-work readiness of his detractors, who might so well have been 'self-conscious' of going slipshod. And at least his success was unmistakable as to the precise literary effect he had intended, including a certain tincture of 'neology' in expression—*nonnihil interdum elocutione novella parum signatum*—in the language of Cornelius Fronto, the contemporary prince of rhetoricians. What words he had found for conveying, with a single touch, the sense of textures, colours, incidents! 'Like jewellers' work! Like a myrrhine vase!'— admirers said of his writing. 'The golden fibre in the hair, the gold threadwork in the gown marked her as the mistress'— *aurum in comis et in tunicis, ibi inflexum hic intextum, matronam profecto confitebatur*—he writes, with his 'curious felicity', of one of his heroines. *Aurum intextum :* gold fibre:—well! there was something of that kind in his own work. And then, in an age when people, from the emperor Aurelius downwards, prided themselves unwisely on writing in Greek, he had written for Latin people in their own tongue; though still, in truth, with all the care of a learned language. Not less happily inventive were the incidents recorded—story within story— stories with the sudden, unlooked-for changes of dreams. He had his humorous touches also. And what went to the ordinary boyish taste, in those somewhat peculiar readers, what would have charmed boys more purely boyish, was the adventure: the bear loose in the house at night, the wolves storming the farms in winter, the exploits of the robbers, their charming caves, the delightful thrill one had at the question: 'Don't you know that these roads are infested by robbers?'

The scene of the romance was laid in Thessaly, the original land of witchcraft, and took one up and down its mountains, and into its old weird towns, haunts of magic and incantation, where all the more genuine appliances of the black art, left behind her by Medea when she fled through that country, were still in use. In the city of Hypata, indeed, nothing seemed to be its true self.—'You might think that through the murmuring of some cadaverous spell, all things had been changed into forms not their own; that there was humanity in the hardness of the stones you stumbled on; that the birds you heard singing were feathered men; that the trees around the walls drew their leaves from a like source. The statues seemed about to move, the walls to speak, the dumb cattle to break out in prophecy; nay! the very sky and the sunbeams, as if they might suddenly cry out.' Witches are there who can draw down the moon, or at least the lunar *virus*—that white fluid she sheds, to be found, so rarely, 'on high, heathy places: which is a poison. A touch of it will drive men mad'.

And in one very remote village lives the sorceress Pamphile, who turns her neighbours into various animals. What true humour in the scene where, after mounting the rickety stairs, Lucius, peeping curiously through a chink in the door, is a spectator of the transformation of the old witch herself into a bird, that she may take flight to the object of her affections—into an owl! 'First she stripped off every rag she had. Then opening a certain chest she took from it many small boxes, and removing the lid of one of them, rubbed herself over for a long time, from head to foot, with an ointment it contained, and after much low muttering to her lamp, began to jerk at last and shake her limbs. And as her limbs moved to and fro, out burst the soft feathers: stout wings come forth to view: the nose grew hard and hooked: her nails were crooked into claws; and Pamphile was an owl. She uttered a queasy screech; and, leaping little by little from the ground, making trial of herself, fled presently, on full wing, out of doors.'

By clumsy imitation of this process, Lucius, the hero of the romance, transforms himself, not as he had intended into a showy winged creature, but into the animal which has given name to the book; for throughout it there runs a vein of racy, homely satire on the love of magic then prevalent, curiosity concerning which had led Lucius to meddle with the old woman's appliances. 'Be you my Venus,' he says to the pretty maid-servant who has introduced him to the view of Pamphile, 'and let me stand by you a winged Cupid!' and, freely applying the magic ointment, sees himself transformed, 'not into a bird, but into an ass!'

Well! the proper remedy for his distress is a supper of roses, could such be found, and many are his quaintly picturesque attempts to come by them at that adverse season; as he contrives to do at last, when, the grotesque procession of Isis passing by with a bear and other strange animals in its train, the ass following along with the rest suddenly crunches the chaplet of roses carried in the high priest's hand.

Meantime, however, he must wait for the spring, with more than the outside of an ass; 'though I was not so much a fool, nor so truly an ass,' he tells us, when he happens to be left alone with a daintily spread table, 'as to neglect this most delicious fare, and feed upon coarse hay'. For, in truth, all through the book, there is an unmistakably real feeling for asses, with bold touches like Swift's, and a genuine animal breadth. Lucius was the original ass, who peeping slyly from the window of his hiding-place forgot all about the big shade he cast just above him, and gave occasion to the joke or proverb about 'the peeping ass and his shadow'.

But the marvellous, delight in which is one of the really serious elements in most boys, passed at times, those young readers still feeling its fascination, into what French writers call the *macabre*—that species of almost insane preoccupation with the materialities of our mouldering flesh, that luxury of disgust in gazing on corruption, which was connected, in this writer at least, with not a little obvious coarseness. It was a strange notion of the gross lust of the actual world, that Marius took from some of these episodes. 'I am told,' they read, 'that when foreigners are interred, the old witches are in the habit of out-racing the funeral procession, to ravage the corpse'—in order to obtain certain cuttings and remnants from it, with which to injure the living—'especially if the witch has happened to cast her eye upon some goodly young man.' And the scene of the night-watching of a dead body lest the witches should come to tear off the flesh with their teeth, is worthy of Théophile Gautier.

But set as one of the episodes in the main narrative, a true gem amid its mockeries, its coarse though genuine humanity, its burlesque horrors, came the tale of Cupid and Psyche, full of brilliant, life-like situations, *speciosa locis*, and abounding in lovely visible imagery (one seemed to see and handle the golden hair, the fresh flowers, the precious works of art in it!), yet full also of a gentle idealism, so that you might take it, if you chose, for an allegory. With a concentration of all his finer literary gifts, Apuleius had gathered into it the floating star-matter of many a delightful old story.

THE STORY OF CUPID AND PSYCHE

In a certain city lived a king and queen who had three daughters exceeding fair. But the beauty of the elder sisters, though pleasant to behold, yet passed not the measure of human praise, while such was the loveliness of the youngest that men's speech was too poor to commend it worthily and could express it not at all. Many of the citizens and of strangers, whom the fame of this excellent vision had gathered thither, confounded by that matchless beauty, could but kiss the finger-tips of their right hands at sight of her, as in adoration to the goddess Venus herself. And soon a rumour passed through the country that she whom the blue deep had borne, forbearing her divine dignity, was even then moving among men, or that by some fresh germination from the stars, not the sea now, but the earth, had put forth a new Venus, endued with the flower of virginity.

This belief, with the fame of the maiden's loveliness, went daily farther into distant lands, so that many people were drawn together to behold that glorious model of the age. Men sailed no longer to Paphos, to Cnidus or Cythera, to the presence of the goddess Venus: her sacred rites were neglected, her images stood uncrowned, the cold ashes were left to disfigure her forsaken altars. It was to a maiden that men's prayers were offered, to a human countenance they looked, in propitiating so great a godhead: when the girl went forth in the morning they strewed flowers on her way, and the victims proper to that unseen goddess were presented as she passed along. This conveyance of divine worship to a mortal kindled meantime the anger of the true Venus. 'Lo! now, the ancient parent of nature,' she cried, 'the fountain of all elements! Behold me, Venus, benign mother of the world, sharing my honours with a mortal maiden, while my name, built up in heaven, is profaned by the mean things of earth! Shall a perishable woman bear my image about with her? In vain did the shepherd of Ida prefer me! Yet shall she have little joy, whosoever she be, of her usurped and unlawful loveliness!' Thereupon she called to her that winged, bold boy, of evil ways, who wanders armed by night through men's houses, spoiling their marriages; and stirring yet more by her speech his inborn wantonness, she led him to the city, and showed him Psyche as she walked.

'I pray thee,' she said, 'give thy mother a full revenge. Let this maid become the slave of an unworthy love.' Then, embracing him closely, she departed to the shore and took her throne upon the crest of the wave. And lo! at her unuttered will, her ocean-servants are in waiting: the daughters of Nereus are there singing their song, and Portunus, and Salacia, and the tiny charioteer of the dolphin, with a host of Tritons leaping through the billows. And one blows softly through his sounding sea-shell, another spreads a silken web against the sun, a third presents the mirror to the eyes of his mistress, while the others swim side by side below, drawing her chariot. Such was the escort of Venus as she went upon the sea.

Psyche meantime, aware of her loveliness, had no fruit thereof. All people regarded and admired, but none sought her in marriage. It was but as on the finished work of the craftsman that they gazed upon that divine likeness. Her sisters, less fair than she, were happily wedded. She, even as a widow, sitting at home, wept over her desolation, hating in her heart the beauty in which all men were pleased.

And the king, supposing the gods were angry, inquired of the oracle of Apollo, and Apollo answered him thus: 'Let the damsel be placed on the top of a certain mountain, adorned as for the bed of marriage and of death. Look not for a son-in-law of mortal birth; but for that evil serpent-thing, by reason of whom even the gods tremble and the shadows of Styx are afraid'.

So the king returned home and made known the oracle to his wife. For many days she lamented, but at last the fulfilment of the divine precept is urgent upon her, and the company make ready to conduct the maiden to her deadly bridal. And now the nuptial torch gathers dark smoke and ashes: the pleasant sound of the pipe is changed into a cry: the marriage hymn concludes in a sorrowful wailing: below her yellow wedding-veil the bride shook away her tears; insomuch that the whole city was afflicted together at the ill-luck of the stricken house.

But the mandate of the god impelled the hapless Psyche to her fate, and, these solemnities being ended, the funeral of the living soul goes forth, all the people following. Psyche, bitterly weeping, assists not at her marriage but at her own obsequies, and while the parents hesitate to accomplish a thing so unholy the daughter cries to them: 'Wherefore torment your luckless age by long weeping? This was the prize of my extraordinary beauty! When all people celebrated us with divine honours, and in one voice named the New Venus, it was then ye should have wept for me as one dead. Now at last I understand that that one name of Venus has been my ruin. Lead me and set me upon the appointed place. I am in haste to submit to that well-omened marriage, to behold that goodly spouse. Why delay the coming of him who was born for the destruction of the whole world?'

She was silent, and with firm step went on the way. And they proceeded to the appointed place on a steep mountain, and left there the maiden alone, and took their way homewards dejectedly. The wretched parents, in their close-shut house, yielded themselves to perpetual night; while to Psyche, fearful and trembling and weeping sore upon the mountain-top, comes the gentle Zephyrus. He lifts her mildly, and, with vesture afloat on either side, bears her by his own soft breathing over the windings of the hills, and sets her lightly among the flowers in the bosom of a valley below.

Psyche, in those delicate grassy places, lying sweetly on her dewy bed, rested from the agitation of her soul and arose in peace. And lo! a grove of mighty trees, with a fount of water, clear as glass, in the midst; and hard by the water, a dwelling-place, built not by human hands but by some divine cunning. One recognized, even at the entering, the delightful hostelry of a god. Golden pillars sustained the roof, arched most curiously in cedar-wood and ivory. The walls were hidden under wrought silver:—all tame and woodland creatures leaping forward to the visitor's gaze. Wonderful indeed was the craftsman, divine or half-divine, who by the subtlety of his art had breathed so wild a soul into the silver! The very pavement was distinct with pictures in goodly stones. In the glow of its precious metal the house is its own daylight, having no need of the sun. Well might it seem a place fashioned for the conversation of gods with men!

Psyche, drawn forward by the delight of it, came near, and, her courage growing, stood within the doorway. One by one, she admired the beautiful things she saw; and, most wonderful of all! no lock, no chain, nor living guardian protected that great treasure house. But as she gazed there came a voice—a voice, as it were unclothed of bodily vesture—'Mistress!' it said, 'all these things are thine. Lie down, and relieve thy weariness, and rise again for the bath when thou wilt. We thy servants, whose voice thou hearest, will be beforehand with our service, and a royal feast shall be ready'.

And Psyche understood that some divine care was providing, and, refreshed with sleep and the bath, sat down to the feast. Still she saw no one: only she heard words falling here and there, and had voices alone to serve her. And the feast being ended, one entered the chamber and sang to her unseen, while another struck the chords of a harp, invisible with him who played on it. Afterwards the sound of a company singing together came to her, but still so that none was present to sight; yet it appeared that a great multitude of singers was there.

And the hour of evening inviting her, she climbed into the bed; and as the night was far advanced, behold a sound of a certain clemency approaches her. Then, fearing for her maiden-hood in so great solitude, she trembled, and more than any evil she knew dreaded that she knew not. And now the husband, that unknown husband, drew near, and ascended the couch, and made her his wife; and lo! before the rise of dawn he had departed hastily. And the attendant voices ministered to the needs of the newly married. And so it happened with her for a long season. And as nature has willed, this new thing, by continual use, became a delight to her: the sound of the voice grew to be her solace in that condition of loneliness and uncertainty.

One night the bridegroom spoke thus to his beloved: 'O Psyche, most pleasant bride! Fortune is grown stern with us, and threatens thee with mortal peril. Thy sisters, troubled at the report of thy death and seeking some trace of thee, will come to the mountain's top. But if by chance their cries reach thee, answer not, neither look forth at all, lest thou bring sorrow upon me and destruction upon thyself'. Then Psyche promised that she would do according to his will. But the bridegroom was fled away again with the night. And all that day she spent in tears, repeating that she was now dead indeed, shut up in that golden prison, powerless to console her sisters sorrowing after her, or to see their faces; and so went to rest weeping.

And after a while came the bridegroom again, and lay down beside her, and embracing her as she wept, complained: 'Was this thy promise, my Psyche? What have I to hope from thee? Even in the arms of thy husband thou ceasest not from pain. Do now as thou wilt. Indulge thine own desire, though it seeks what will ruin thee. Yet wilt thou remember my warning, repentant too late'. Then, protesting that she is like to die, she obtains from him that he suffer her to see her sisters, and present to them moreover what gifts she would of golden ornaments; but therewith he ofttimes advised her never at any time, yielding to pernicious counsel, to inquire concerning his bodily form, lest she fall, through unholy curiosity, from so great a height of fortune, nor feel ever his embrace again. 'I would die a hundred times,' she said, cheerful at last, 'rather than be deprived of thy most sweet usage. I love thee as my own soul, beyond comparison even with Love himself. Only bid thy servant Zephyrus bring hither my sisters, as he brought me. My honeycomb! My husband! Thy Psyche's breath of life!' So he promised; and after the embraces of the night, ere the light appeared, vanished from the hands of his bride.

And the sisters, coming to the place where Psyche was

abandoned, wept loudly among the rocks, and called upon her by name, so that the sound came down to her, and running out of the palace distraught, she cried: 'Wherefore afflict your souls with lamentation? I whom you mourn am here'. Then, summoning Zephyrus, she reminded him of her husband's bidding; and he bare them down with a gentle blast. 'Enter now,' she said, 'into my house, and relieve your sorrow in the company of Psyche your sister.'

And Psyche displayed to them all the treasures of the golden house, and its great family of ministering voices, nursing in them the malice which was already at their hearts. And at last one of them asks curiously who the lord of that celestial array may be, and what manner of man her husband? And Psyche answered dissemblingly: 'A young man, handsome and mannerly, with a goodly beard. For the most part he hunts upon the mountains'. And lest the secret should slip from her in the way of further speech, loading her sisters with gold and gems, she commanded Zephyrus to bear them away.

And they returned home, on fire with envy. 'See now the injustice of fortune!' cried one. 'We, the elder children, are given like servants to be the wives of strangers, while the youngest is possessed of so great riches, who scarcely knows how to use them. You saw, sister! what a hoard of wealth lies in the house; what glittering gowns; what splendour of precious gems, besides all that gold trodden under foot. If she indeed hath, as she said, a bridegroom so goodly, then no one in all the world is happier. And it may be that this husband, being of divine nature, will make her too a goddess. Nay! so in truth it is. It was even thus she bore herself. Already she looks aloft and breathes divinity, who, though but a woman, has voices for her handmaidens, and can command the winds.' 'Think,' answered the other, 'how arrogantly she dealt with us, grudging us these trifling gifts out of all that store, and when our company became a burden, causing us to be hissed and driven away from her through the air! But I am no woman if she keep her hold on this great fortune; and if the insult done us has touched thee too, take we counsel together. Meanwhile let us hold our peace, and know naught of her, alive or dead. For they are not truly happy of whose happiness other folk are unaware.'

And the bridegroom, whom still she knows not, warns her thus a second time, as he talks with her by night: 'Seest thou what peril besets thee? Those cunning wolves have made ready for thee their snares, of which the sum is that they persuade thee to search into the fashion of my countenance, the seeing of which, as I have told thee often, will be the seeing of it no more for ever. But do thou neither listen nor make answer to aught regarding thy husband. Besides, we have sown also the seed of our race. Even now this bosom grows with a child to be born to us, a child, if thou but keep our secret, of divine quality; if thou profane it, subject to death'. And Psyche was glad at the tidings, rejoicing in that solace of a divine seed, and in the glory of that pledge of love to be, and the dignity of the name of mother. Anxiously she notes the increase of the days, the waning months. And again, as he tarries briefly beside her, the bridegroom repeats his warning: 'Even now the sword is drawn with which thy sisters seek thy life. Have pity on thyself, sweet wife, and upon our child, and see not those evil women again'. But the sisters make their way into the palace once more, crying to her in wily tones: 'O Psyche! and thou too wilt be a mother! How great will be the joy at home! Happy indeed shall we be to have the nursing of the golden child. Truly if he be answerable to the beauty of his parents, it will be a birth of Cupid himself'.

So, little by little, they stole upon the heart of their sister. She, meanwhile, bids the lyre to sound for their delight, and the playing is heard: she bids the pipes to move, the quire to sing, and the music and the singing come invisibly, soothing the mind of the listener with sweetest modulation. Yet not even thereby was their malice put to sleep: once more they seek to know what manner of husband she has, and whence that seed. And Psyche, simple over-much, forgetful of her first story, answers: 'My husband comes from a far country, trading for great sums. He is already of middle age, with whitening locks'. And therewith she dismisses them again.

And returning home upon the soft breath of Zephyrus one cried to the other: 'What shall be said of so ugly a lie? He who was a young man with goodly beard is now in middle life. It must be that she told a false tale: else is she in very truth ignorant what manner of man he is. Howsoever it be, let us destroy her quickly. For if she indeed knows not, be sure that her bridegroom is one of the gods: it is a god she bears in her womb. And let that be far from us! If she be called mother of a god, then will life be more than I can bear'.

So, full of rage against her, they returned to Psyche, and said to her craftily: 'Thou livest in an ignorant bliss, all incurious of thy real danger. It is a deadly serpent, as we certainly know, that comes to sleep at thy side. Remember the words of the oracle, which declared thee destined to a cruel beast. There are those who have seen it at nightfall, coming back from its feeding. In no long time, they say, it will end its blandishments. It but waits for the babe to be formed in thee, that it may devour thee by so much the richer. If indeed the solitude of this musical place, or it may be the loathsome commerce of a hidden love, delight thee, we at least in sisterly piety have done our part'. And at last the unhappy Psyche, simple and frail of soul, carried away by the terror of their words, losing memory of her husband's precepts and her own promise, brought upon herself a great calamity. Trembling and turning pale, she answers them: 'And they who tell those things, it may be, speak the truth. For in very deed never have I seen the face of my husband, nor know I at all what manner of man he is. Always he frights me diligently from the sight of him, threatening some great evil should I too curiously look upon his face. Do ye, if ye can help your sister in her great peril, stand by her now'.

Her sisters answered her: 'The way of safety we have well considered, and will teach thee. Take a sharp knife, and hide it in that part of the couch where thou art wont to lie: take also a lamp filled with oil, and set it privily behind the curtain. And when he shall have drawn up his coils into the accustomed place, and thou hearest him breathe in sleep, slip then from his side and discover the lamp, and, knife in hand, put forth thy strength, and strike off the serpent's head'. And so they departed in haste.

And Psyche left alone (alone but for the furies which beset her) is tossed up and down in her distress, like a wave of the sea; and though her will is firm, yet, in the moment of putting hand to the deed, she falters, and is torn asunder by various apprehension of the great calamity upon her. She hastens and anon delays, now full of distrust, and now of angry courage: under one bodily form she loathes the monster and loves the bridegroom. But twilight ushers in the night; and at length in haste she makes ready for the terrible deed. Darkness came, and the bridegroom; and he first, after some faint essay of love, falls into a deep sleep.

And she, erewhile of no strength, the hard purpose of destiny assisting her, is confirmed in force. With lamp plucked forth, knife in hand, she put by her sex; and lo! as the secrets of the bed became manifest, the sweetest and most gentle of all creatures, Love himself, reclined there, in his own proper loveliness! At sight of him the very flame of the lamp kindled more gladly! But Psyche was afraid at the vision, and, faint of soul, trembled back upon her knees, and would have hidden the steel in her own bosom. But the knife slipped from her hand; and now, undone, yet ofttimes looking upon the beauty of that divine countenance, she lives again. She sees the locks of that golden head, pleasant with the unction of the gods, shed down in graceful entanglement behind and before, about the ruddy cheeks and white throat. The pinions of the winged god, yet fresh with the dew, are spotless upon his shoulders, the delicate plumage wavering over them as they lie at rest. Smooth he was, and, touched with light, worthy of Venus his mother. At the foot of the couch lay his bow and arrows, the instruments of his power, propitious to men.

And Psyche, gazing hungrily thereon, draws an arrow from the quiver, and trying the point upon her thumb, tremulous still, drave in the barb, so that a drop of blood came forth. Thus fell she, by her own act, and unaware, into the love of Love. Falling upon the bridegroom, with indrawn breath, in a hurry of kisses from eager and open lips, she shuddered as she thought how brief that sleep might be. And it chanced that a drop of burning oil fell from the lamp upon the god's shoulder. Ah! maladroit minister of love, thus to wound him from whom all fire comes; though 'twas a lover, I trow, first devised thee, to have the fruit of his desire even in the darkness! At the touch of the fire the god started up, and beholding the overthrow of her faith, quietly took flight from her embraces.

And Psyche, as he rose upon the wing, laid hold on him with her two hands, hanging upon him in his passage through the air, till she sinks to the earth through weariness. And as she lay there, the divine lover, tarrying still, lighted upon a cypress tree which grew near, and, from the top of it, spake thus to her, in great emotion: 'Foolish one! unmindful of the command of Venus, my mother, who had devoted thee to one of base degree, I fled to thee in his stead. Now know I that this was vainly done. Into mine own flesh pierced mine arrow, and I made thee my wife, only that I might seem a monster beside thee—that thou shouldst seek to wound the head wherein lay the eyes so full of love to thee! Again and again, I thought to put thee on thy guard concerning these things, and warned thee in lovingkindness. Now I would but punish thee by my flight hence'. And therewith he winged his way into the deep sky.

Psyche, prostrate upon the earth, and following far as sight might reach the flight of the bridegroom, wept and lamented; and when the breadth of space had parted him wholly from her, cast herself down from the bank of a river which was nigh. But the stream, turning gentle in honour of the god, put her forth again unhurt upon its margin. And as it happened, Pan, the rustic god, was sitting just then by the waterside, embracing, in the body of a reed, the goddess Canna; teaching her to respond to him in all varieties of slender sound. Hard by, his flock of goats browsed at will. And the shaggy god called her, wounded and outworn, kindly to him and said: 'I am but a rustic herdsman, pretty maiden, yet wise, by favour of my great age and long experience; and if I guess truly by those faltering steps, by thy sorrowful eyes and continual sighing, thou labourest with excess of love. Listen then to me, and seek not death again, in the stream or otherwise. Put aside thy woe, and turn thy prayers to Cupid. He is in truth a delicate youth: win him by the delicacy of thy service'.

So the shepherd-god spoke, and Psyche, answering nothing, but with a reverence to his serviceable deity, went on her way. And while she, in her search after Cupid, wandered through many lands, he was lying in the chamber of his mother, heartsick. And the white bird which floats over the waves plunged in haste into the sea, and approaching Venus, as she bathed, made known to her that her son lies afflicted with some grievous hurt, doubtful of life. And Venus cried angrily: 'My son, then, has a mistress! And it is Psyche, who witched away my beauty and was the rival of my godhead, whom he loves!'

Therewith she issued from the sea, and returning to her golden chamber, found there the lad, sick, as she had heard, and cried from the doorway: 'Well done, truly! to trample thy mother's precepts under foot, to spare my enemy that cross of an unworthy love; nay, unite her to thyself, child as thou art, that I might have a daughter-in-law who hates me! I will make thee repent of thy sport, and the savour of thy marriage bitter. There is one who shall chasten this body of thine, put out thy torch, and unstring thy bow. Not till she has plucked forth that hair, into which so oft these hands have smoothed the golden light, and sheared away thy wings, shall I feel the injury done me avenged'. And with this she hastened in anger from the doors.

And Ceres and Juno met her, and sought to know the meaning of her troubled countenance. 'Ye come in season,' she cried;

'I pray you, find for me Psyche. It must needs be that ye have heard the disgrace of my house.' And they, ignorant of what was done, would have soothed her anger, saying: 'What fault, Mistress, hath thy son committed, that thou wouldst destroy the girl he loves? Knowest thou not that he is now of age? Because he wears his years so lightly must he seem to thee ever but a child? Wilt thou for ever thus pry into the pastimes of thy son, always accusing his wantonness, and blaming in him those delicate wiles which are all thine own?' Thus, in secret fear of the boy's bow, did they seek to please him with their gracious patronage. But Venus, angry at their light taking of her wrongs, turned her back upon them, and with hasty steps made her way once more to the sea.

Meanwhile Psyche, tost in soul, wandering hither and thither, rested not night or day in the pursuit of her husband, desiring, if she might not soothe his anger by the endearments of a wife, at the least to propitiate him with the prayers of a handmaid. And seeing a certain temple on the top of a high mountain, she said: 'Who knows whether yonder place be not the abode of my lord?' Thither, therefore, she turned her steps, hastening now the more because desire and hope pressed her on, weary as she was with the labours of the way, and so, painfully measuring out the highest ridges of the mountain, drew near to the sacred couches. She sees ears of wheat, in heaps or twisted into chaplets; ears of barley also, with sickles and all the instruments of harvest, lying there in disorder, thrown at random from the hands of the labourers in the great heat. These she curiously sets apart, one by one, duly ordering them; for she said within herself: 'I may not neglect the shrines, nor the holy service, of any god there be, but must rather win by supplication the kindly mercy of them all'.

And Ceres found her bending sadly upon her task, and cried aloud: 'Alas, Psyche! Venus, in the furiousness of her anger, tracks thy footsteps through the world, seeking for thee to pay her the utmost penalty; and thou, thinking of anything rather than thine own safety, hast taken on thee the care of what belongs to me!' Then Psyche fell down at her feet, and sweeping the floor with her hair, washing the footsteps of the goddess in her tears, besought her mercy, with many prayers: 'By the gladdening rites of harvest, by the lighted lamps and mystic marches of the Marriage and mysterious Invention of thy daughter Proserpine, and by all beside that the holy place of Attica veils in silence, minister, I pray thee, to the sorrowful heart of Psyche! Suffer me to hide myself but for a few days among the heaps of corn, till time have softened the anger of the goddess, and my strength, outworn in my long travail, be recovered by a little rest'.

But Ceres answered her: 'Truly thy tears move me, and I would fain help thee; only I dare not incur the ill-will of my kinswoman. Depart hence as quickly as may be'. And Psyche, repelled against hope, afflicted now with twofold sorrow, making her way back again, beheld among the half-lighted woods of the valley below a sanctuary builded with cunning art. And that she might lose no way of hope, howsoever doubtful, she drew near to the sacred doors. She sees there gifts of price, and garments fixed upon the door-posts and to the branches of the trees, wrought with letters of gold which told the name of the goddess to whom they were dedicated, with thanksgiving for that she had done. So, with bent knee and hands laid about the glowing altar, she prayed, saying: 'Sister and spouse of Jupiter! be thou to these my desperate fortunes, Juno the Auspicious! I know that thou dost willingly help those in travail with child; deliver me from the peril that is upon me'. And as she prayed thus, Juno in the majesty of her godhead was straightway present, and answered: 'Would that I might incline favourably to thee; but against the will of Venus, whom I have ever loved as a daughter, I may not, for very shame, grant thy prayer'.

And Psyche, dismayed by this new shipwreck of her hope, communed thus with herself: 'Whither, from the midst of the snares that beset me, shall I take my way once more? In what dark solitude shall I hide me from the all-seeing eye of Venus? What if I put on at length a man's courage, and yielding myself unto her as my mistress, soften by a humility not yet too late the fierceness of her purpose? Who knows but that I may find him also whom my soul seeketh after, in the abode of his mother?'

And Venus, renouncing all earthly aid in her search, prepared to return to heaven. She ordered the chariot to be made ready, wrought for her by Vulcan as a marriage-gift, with a cunning of hand which had left his work so much the richer by the weight of gold it lost under his tool. From the multitude which housed about the bedchamber of their mistress, white doves came forth, and with joyful motions bent their painted necks beneath the yoke. Behind it, with playful riot, the sparrows sped onward, and other birds sweet of song, making known by their soft notes the approach of the goddess. Eagle and cruel hawk alarmed not the quireful family of Venus. And the clouds broke away, as the uttermost ether opened to receive her, daughter and goddess, with great joy.

And Venus passed straightway to the house of Jupiter to beg from him the service of Mercury, the god of speech. And Jupiter refused not her prayer. And Venus and Mercury descended from heaven together; and as they went, the former said to the latter: 'Thou knowest, my brother of Arcady, that never at any time have I done anything without thy help; for how long time, moreover, I have sought a certain maiden in vain. And now naught remains but that, by thy heraldry, I proclaim a reward for whomsoever shall find her. Do thou my bidding quickly'. And therewith she conveyed to him a little scrip, in the which was written the name of Psyche, with other things; and so returned home.

And Mercury failed not in his office; but departing into all lands, proclaimed that whosoever delivered up to Venus the fugitive girl, should receive from herself seven kisses—one thereof full of the inmost honey of her throat. With that the doubt of Psyche was ended. And now, as she came near to the doors of Venus, one of the household, whose name was Use-and-Wont, ran out to her, crying: 'Hast thou learned, Wicked Maid! now at last! that thou hast a mistress?' and seizing her roughly by the hair, drew her into the presence of Venus. And when Venus saw her, she cried out, saying: 'Thou hast deigned then to make thy salutations to thy mother-in-law. Now will I in turn treat thee as becometh a dutiful daughter-in-law!'

And she took barley and millet and poppy-seed, every kind of grain and seed, and mixed them together, and laughed, and said to her: 'Methinks so plain a maiden can earn lovers only by industrious ministry: now will I also make trial of thy service. Sort me this heap of seed, the one kind from the others, grain by grain; and get thy task done before the evening'. And Psyche, stunned by the cruelty of her bidding, was silent, and moved not her hand to the inextricable heap. And there came forth a little ant, which had understanding of the difficulty of her task, and took pity upon the consort of the god of Love; and he ran deftly hither and thither, and called together the whole army of his fellows. 'Have pity,' he cried, 'nimble scholars of the Earth, Mother of all things!—have pity upon the wife of Love, and hasten to help her in her perilous effort.' Then, one upon the other, the hosts of the insect people hurried together; and they sorted asunder the whole heap of seed, separating every grain after its kind, and so departed quickly out of sight.

And at nightfall Venus returned, and seeing that task finished with so wonderful diligence, she cried: 'The work is not thine, thou naughty maid, but his in whose eyes thou hast found favour'. And calling her again in the morning: 'See now the grove,' she said, 'beyond yonder torrent. Certain sheep feed there, whose fleeces shine with gold. Fetch me straightway a lock of that precious stuff, having gotten it as thou mayst'.

And Psyche went forth willingly, not to obey the command of Venus, but even to seek a rest from her labour in the depths of the river. But from the river, the green reed, lowly mother of music, spake to her: 'O Psyche! pollute not these waters by self-destruction, nor approach that terrible flock; for, as the heat groweth, they wax fierce. Lie down under yon plane-tree, till the quiet of the river's breath have soothed them. Thereafter thou mayst shake down the fleecy gold from the trees of the grove, for it holdeth by the leaves'.

And Psyche, instructed thus by the simple reed, in the humanity of its heart, filled her bosom with the soft golden stuff, and returned to Venus. But the goddess smiled bitterly, and said to her: 'Well know I who was the author of this thing also. I will make further trial of thy discretion, and the boldness of thy heart. Seest thou the utmost peak of yonder steep mountain? The dark stream which flows down thence waters the Stygian fields, and swells the flood of Cocytus. Bring me now, in this little urn, a draught from its innermost source'. And therewith she put into her hands a vessel of wrought crystal.

And Psyche set forth in haste on her way to the mountain, looking there at last to find the end of her hapless life. But when she came to the region which borders on the cliff that was showed to her, she understood the deadly nature of her task. From a great rock, steep and slippery, a horrible river of water poured forth, falling straightway by a channel exceeding narrow into the unseen gulf below. And lo! creeping from the rocks on either hand, angry serpents, with their long necks and sleepless eyes. The very waters found a voice and bade her depart, in smothered cries of, *Depart hence!* and *What doest thou here? Look around thee!* and *Destruction is upon thee!* And then sense left her, in the immensity of her peril, as one changed to stone.

Yet not even then did the distress of this innocent soul escape the steady eye of a gentle providence. For the bird of Jupiter spread his wings and took flight to her, and asked her: 'Didst thou think, simple one, even thou! that thou couldst steal one drop of that relentless stream, the holy river of Styx, terrible even to the gods? But give me thine urn'. And the bird took the urn, and filled it at the source, and returned to her quickly from among the teeth of the serpents, bringing with him of the waters, all unwilling—nay! warning him to depart away and not molest them.

And she, receiving the urn with great joy, ran back quickly that she might deliver it to Venus, and yet again satisfied not the angry goddess. 'My child!' she said, 'in this one thing further must thou serve me. Take now this tiny casket, and get thee down even unto hell, and deliver it to Proserpine. Tell her that Venus would have of her beauty so much at least as may suffice for but one day's use, that beauty she possessed erewhile being foreworn and spoiled, through her tendance upon the sick-bed of her son; and be not slow in returning.'

And Psyche perceived there the last ebbing of her fortune—that she was now thrust openly upon death, who must go down, of her own motion, to Hades and the Shades. And straightway she climbed to the top of an exceeding high tower, thinking within herself: 'I will cast myself down thence: so shall I descend most quickly into the kingdom of the dead'. And the tower, again, broke forth into speech: 'Wretched Maid! Wretched Maid! Wilt thou destroy thyself? If the breath quit thy body, then wilt thou indeed go down into Hades, but by no means return hither. Listen to me. Among the pathless wilds not far from this place lies a certain mountain, and therein one of hell's vent-holes. Through the breach a rough way lies open, following which thou wilt come, by straight course, to the castle of Orcus. And thou must not go empty-handed. Take in each hand a morsel of barley-bread, soaked in hydromel; and in thy mouth two pieces of money. And when thou shalt be now well onward in the way of death, then wilt thou overtake a lame ass laden with wood, and a lame driver, who will pray thee reach him certain cords to fasten the burden which is falling from the ass: but be thou cautious to pass on in silence. And soon as thou comest to the river of the dead, Charon, in that crazy bark he hath, will put thee over upon the farther side. There is greed even among the dead: and thou shalt deliver to him, for the ferrying, one of those two pieces of money, in such wise that he take it with his hand from between thy lips. And as thou passest over the stream, a dead old man, rising on the water, will put up to thee his mouldering hands, and pray thee draw him into the ferry-boat. But beware thou yield not to unlawful pity.

'When thou shalt be come over, and art upon the causeway, certain aged women, spinning, will cry to thee to lend thy hand to their work; and beware again that thou take no part therein; for this also is the snare of Venus, whereby she would cause thee to cast away one at least of those cakes thou bearest in thy hands. And think not that a slight matter; for the loss of either one of them will be to thee the losing of the light of day. For a watch-dog exceeding fierce lies ever before the threshold of that lonely house of Proserpine. Close his mouth with one of thy cakes; so shalt thou pass by him, and enter straightway into the presence of Proserpine herself. Then do thou deliver thy message, and taking what she shall give thee, return back again; offering to the watch-dog the other cake, and to the ferryman that other piece of money thou hast in thy mouth. After this manner mayst thou return again beneath the stars. But withal, I charge thee, think not to look into, nor open, the casket thou bearest, with that treasure of the beauty of the divine countenance hidden therein.'

So spake the stones of the tower; and Psyche delayed not, but proceeding diligently after the manner enjoined, entered into the house of Proserpine, at whose feet she sat down humbly, and would neither the delicate couch nor that divine food the goddess offered her, but did straightway the business of Venus. And Proserpine filled the casket secretly, and shut the lid, and delivered it to Psyche, who fled therewith from Hades with new strength. But coming back into the light of day, even as she hasted now to the ending of her service, she was seized by a rash curiosity. 'Lo! now,' she said within herself, 'my simpleness! who bearing in my hands the divine loveliness, heed not to touch myself with a particle at least therefrom, that I may please the more, by the favour of it, my fair one, my beloved.' Even as she spoke, she lifted the lid; and behold! within, neither beauty, nor anything beside, save sleep only, the sleep of the dead, which took hold upon her, filling all her members with its drowsy vapour, so that she lay down in the way and moved not, as in the slumber of death.

And Cupid being healed of his wound, because he would endure no longer the absence of her he loved, gliding through the narrow window of the chamber wherein he was holden, his pinions being now repaired by a little rest fled forth swiftly upon them, and coming to the place where Psyche was, shook that sleep away from her, and set him in his prison again, awaking her with the innocent point of his arrow. 'Lo! thine old error again,' he said, 'which had like once more to have destroyed thee! But do thou now what is lacking of the command of my mother: the rest shall be my care.' With these words, the lover rose upon the air; and being consumed inwardly with the greatness of his love, penetrated with vehement wing into the highest place of heaven, to lay his cause before the father of the gods. And the father of gods took his hand in his, and kissed his face, and said to him: 'At no time, my son, hast thou regarded me with due honour. Often hast thou vexed my bosom, wherein lies the disposition of the stars, with those busy darts of thine. Nevertheless, because thou hast grown up between these mine hands, I will accomplish thy desire'. And straightway he bade Mercury call the gods together; and, the council chamber being filled, sitting upon a high throne, 'Ye gods,' he said, 'all ye whose names are in the white book of the Muses, ye know yonder lad. It seems good to me that his youthful heats should by some means be restrained. And that all occasion may be taken from him, I would even confine him in the bonds of marriage. He has chosen and embraced a mortal maiden. Let him have fruit of his love, and possess her for ever'.

Thereupon he bade Mercury produce Psyche in heaven; and holding out to her his ambrosial cup, 'Take it,' he said, 'and live for ever; nor shall Cupid ever depart from thee'. And the gods sat down together to the marriage-feast. On the first couch lay the bridegroom, and Psyche in his bosom. His rustic serving-boy bare the wine to Jupiter; and Bacchus to the rest. The Seasons crimsoned all things with their roses. Apollo sang to the lyre, while a little Pan prattled on his reeds, and Venus danced very sweetly to the soft music. Thus, with due rites, did Psyche pass into the power of Cupid; and from them was born the daughter whom men call Voluptas.

CHAPTER VI

EUPHUISM

So the famous story composed itself in the memory of Marius, with an expression changed in some ways from the original and on the whole graver. The petulant, boyish Cupid of Apuleius was become more like that 'Lord, of terrible aspect', who stood at Dante's bedside and wept, or had at least grown to the manly earnestness of the *Erôs* of Praxiteles. Set in relief amid the coarser matter of the book, this episode of Cupid and Psyche served to combine many lines of meditation, already familiar to Marius, into the ideal of a perfect imaginative love, centred upon a type of beauty entirely flawless and clean—an ideal which never wholly faded from his thoughts, though he valued it at various times in different degrees. The human body in its beauty, as the highest potency of all the beauty of material objects, seemed to him just then to be matter no longer, but, having taken celestial fire, to assert itself as indeed the true, though visible, soul or spirit in things. In contrast with that ideal, in all the pure brilliancy, and as it were in the happy light, of youth and morning and the springtide, men's actual loves, with which at many points the book brings one into close contact, might appear to him, like the general tenor of their lives, to be somewhat mean and sordid. The *hiddenness* of perfect things: a shrinking mysticism, a sentiment of diffidence like that expressed in Psyche's so tremulous hope concerning the child to be born of the husband she has never yet seen—'in the face of this little child, at the least, shall I apprehend thine' —*in hoc saltem parvulo cognoscam faciem tuam*: the fatality which seems to haunt any signal beauty, whether moral or physical, as if it were in itself something illicit and isolating: the suspicion and hatred it so often excites in the vulgar:—these were some of the impressions, forming, as they do, a constant tradition of somewhat cynical pagan experience, from Medusa and Helen downwards, which the old story enforced on him. A book, like a person, has its fortunes with one; is lucky or

53

unlucky in the precise moment of its falling in our way, and often by some happy accident counts with us for something more than its independent value. The *Metamorphoses* of Apuleius, coming to Marius just then, figured for him as indeed *The Golden Book*: he felt a sort of personal gratitude to its writer, and saw in it doubtless far more than was really there for any other reader. It occupied always a peculiar place in his remembrance, never quite losing its power in frequent return to it for the revival of that first glowing impression.

Its effect upon the elder youth was a more practical one: it stimulated the literary ambition, already so strong a motive with him, by a signal example of success, and made him more than ever an ardent, indefatigable student of words, of the means or instrument of the literary art. The secrets of utterance, of expression itself, of that through which alone any intellectual or spiritual power within one can actually take effect upon others, to overawe or charm them to one's side, presented themselves to this ambitious lad in immediate connexion with that desire for predominance, for the satisfaction of which another might have relied on the acquisition and display of brilliant military qualities. In him, a fine instinctive sentiment of the exact value and power of words was connate with the eager longing for sway over his fellows. He saw himself already a gallant and effective leader, innovating or conservative as occasion might require, in the rehabilitation of the mother-tongue, then fallen so tarnished and languid; yet the sole object, as he mused within himself, of the only sort of patriotic feeling proper, or possible, for one born of slaves. The popular speech was gradually departing from the form and rule of literary language, a language always and increasingly artificial. While the learned dialect was yearly becoming more and more barbarously pedantic, the colloquial idiom, on the other hand, offered a thousand chance-tost gems of racy or picturesque expression, rejected or at least ungathered by what claimed to be classical Latin. The time was coming when neither the pedants nor the people would really understand Cicero; though there were some indeed, like this new writer, Apuleius, who, departing from the custom of writing in Greek, which had been a fashionable affectation among the sprightlier wits since the days of Hadrian, had written in the vernacular.

The literary programme which Flavian had already designed for himself would be a work, then, partly conservative or reactionary, in its dealing with the instrument of the literary

art; partly popular and revolutionary, asserting, so to term
them, the rights of the *proletariat* of speech. More than fifty
years before, the younger Pliny, himself an effective witness
for the delicate power of the Latin tongue, had said: 'I am one
of those who admire the ancients, yet I do not, like some others,
underrate certain instances of genius which our own times
afford. For it is not true that nature, as if weary and effete,
no longer produces what is admirable'. And he, Flavian, would
prove himself the true master of the opportunity thus indicated.
In his eagerness for a not too distant fame, he dreamed over all
that, as the young Caesar may have dreamed of campaigns.
Others might brutalize or neglect the native speech, that true
'open field' for charm and sway over men. He would make
of it a serious study, weighing the precise power of every phrase
and word, as though it were precious metal, disentangling the
later associations and going back to the original and native
sense of each,—restoring to full significance all its wealth of
latent figurative expression, reviving or replacing its outworn
or tarnished images. Latin literature and the Latin tongue
were dying of routine and languor; and what was necessary,
first of all, was to re-establish the natural and direct relationship
between thought and expression, between the sensation and the
term, and restore to words their primitive power.

For words, after all, words manipulated with all his delicate
force, were to be the apparatus of a war for himself. To be
forcibly impressed, in the first place; and in the next, to find the
means of making visible to others that which was vividly
apparent, delightful, of lively interest to himself, to the exclusion of all that was but middling, tame, or only half-true even
to him—this scrupulousness of literary art actually awoke in
Flavian, for the first time, a sort of chivalrous conscience. What
care for style! what patience of execution! what research for
the significant tones of ancient idiom—*sonantia verba et antiqua* !
What stately and regular word-building—*gravis et decora con-
structio* ! He felt the whole meaning of the sceptical Pliny's
somewhat melancholy advice to one of his friends, that he should
seek in literature deliverance from mortality—*ut studiis se
literarum a mortalitate vindicet*. And there was everything in
the nature and the training of Marius to make him a full par-
ticipator in the hopes of such a new literary school, with Flavian
for its leader. In the refinements of that curious spirit, in its
horror of profanities, its fastidious sense of a correctness in
external form, there was something which ministered to the

*C 903

old ritual interest, still surviving in him; as if here indeed were involved a kind of sacred service to the mother-tongue.

Here, then, was the theory of Euphuism, as manifested in every age in which the literary conscience has been awakened to forgotten duties towards language, towards the instrument of expression: in fact it does but modify a little the principles of all effective expression at all times. 'Tis art's function to conceal itself: *ars est celare artem*:—is a saying, which, exaggerated by inexact quotation, has perhaps been oftenest and most confidently quoted by those who have had little literary or other art to conceal; and from the very beginning of professional literature, the 'labour of the file'—a labour in the case of Plato, for instance, or Virgil, like that of the oldest of goldsmiths as described by Apuleius, enriching the work by far more than the weight of precious metal it removed—has always had its function. Sometimes, doubtless, as in later examples of it, this Roman Euphuism, determined at any cost to attain beauty in writing— ἐς κάλλος γράφειν—might lapse into its characteristic fopperies or mannerisms, into the 'defects of its qualities', in truth, not wholly unpleasing perhaps, or at least excusable, when looked at as but the toys (so Cicero calls them), the strictly congenial and appropriate toys, of an assiduously cultivated age, which could not help being polite, critical, self-conscious. The mere love of novelty also had, of course, its part there: as with the Euphuism of the Elizabethan age, and of the modern French romanticists, its *neologies* were the ground of one of the favourite charges against it; though indeed, as regards these tricks of taste also, there is nothing new, but a quaint family likeness rather, between the Euphuists of successive ages. Here, as elsewhere, the power of 'fashion', as it is called, is but one minor form, slight enough, it may be, yet distinctly symptomatic, of that deeper yearning of human nature towards ideal perfection, which is a continuous force in it; and since in this direction too human nature is limited, such fashions must necessarily reproduce themselves. Among other resemblances to later growths of Euphuism, its archaisms on the one hand, and its neologies on the other, the Euphuism of the days of Marcus Aurelius had, in the composition of verse, its fancy for the *refrain*. It was a snatch from a popular chorus, something he had heard sounding all over the town of Pisa one April night, one of the first bland and summer-like nights of the year, that Flavian had chosen for the refrain of a poem he was then pondering—the *Pervigilium Veneris*—the vigil, or 'nocturn', of Venus.

Certain elderly counsellors, filling what may be thought a constant part in the little tragi-comedy which literature and its votaries are playing in all ages, would ask, suspecting some affectation or unreality in that minute culture of *form*: Cannot those who have a thing to say, say it directly? Why not be simple and broad, like the old writers of Greece? And this challenge had at least the effect of setting his thoughts at work on the intellectual situation as it lay between the children of the present and those earliest masters. Certainly, the most wonderful, the unique, point, about the Greek genius, in literature as in everything else, was the entire absence of imitation in its productions. How had the burden of precedent, laid upon every artist, increased since then! It was all around one: —that smoothly built world of old classical taste, an accomplished fact, with overwhelming authority on every detail of the conduct of one's work. With no fardel on its own back, yet so imperious towards those who came labouring after it, *Hellas*, in its early freshness, looked as distant from him even then as it does from ourselves. There might seem to be no place left for novelty or originality,—place only for a patient, an infinite, faultlessness. On this question too Flavian passed through a world of curious art-casuistries, of self-tormenting, at the threshold of his work. Was poetic beauty a thing ever one and the same, a type absolute; or, changing always with the soul of time itself, did it depend upon the taste, the peculiar trick of apprehension, the fashion, as we say, of each successive age? Might one recover that old, earlier sense of it, that earlier manner, in a masterly effort to recall all the complexities of the life, moral and intellectual, of the earlier age to which it had belonged? Had there been really bad ages in art or literature? Were all ages, even those earliest, adventurous, matutinal days, in themselves equally poetical or unpoetical; and poetry, the literary beauty, the poetic ideal, always but a borrowed light upon men's actual life?

Homer had said:

> Οἱ δ' ὅτε δὴ λιμένος πολυβενθέος ἐντὸς ἵκοντο,
> Ἱστία μὲν στείλαντο, θέσαν δ' ἐν νηΐ μελαίνῃ . . .
> Ἐκ δὲ καὶ αὐτοὶ βαῖνον ἐπὶ ῥηγμῖνι θαλάσσης.

And how poetic the simple incident seemed, told just thus! Homer was always telling things after this manner. And one might think there had been no effort in it: that here was but the almost mechanical transcript of a time, naturally, intrinsically, poetic, a time in which one could hardly have spoken at all without ideal effect, or the sailors pulled down their boat without making a picture in 'the great style', against a sky charged with marvels. Must not the mere prose of an age, itself thus ideal, have counted for more than half of Homer's poetry? Or might the closer student discover even here, even in Homer, the really mediatorial function of the poet, as between the reader and the actual matter of his experience; the poet waiting, so to speak, in an age which had felt itself trite and commonplace enough, on his opportunity for the touch of 'golden alchemy', or at least for the pleasantly lighted side of things themselves? Might not another, in one's own prosaic and used-up time, so uneventful as it had been through the long reign of these quiet Antonines, in like manner, discover his ideal, by a due waiting upon it? Would not a future generation, looking back upon this, under the power of the enchanted-distance fallacy, find it ideal to view, in contrast with its own languor—the languor that for some reason (concerning which Augustine will one day have his view) seemed to haunt men always? Had Homer, even, appeared unreal and affected in his poetic flight, to some of the people of his own age, as seemed to happen with every new literature in turn? In any case, the intellectual conditions of early Greece had been—how different from these! And a true literary tact would accept that difference in forming the primary conception of the literary function at a later time. Perhaps the utmost one could get by conscious effort, in the way of a reaction or return to the conditions of an earlier and fresher age, would be but *novitas*, artificial artlessness, *naïveté*; and this quality too might have its measure of euphuistic charm, direct and sensible enough, though it must count, in comparison with that genuine early Greek newness at the beginning, not as the freshness of the open fields, but only of a bunch of field-flowers in a heated room.

There was, meantime, all this:—on one side, the old pagan culture, for us but a fragment, for him an accomplished yet present fact, still a living, united, organic whole, in the entirety of its art, its thought, its religions, its sagacious forms of polity, that so weighty authority it exercised on every point, being in reality only the measure of its charm for every one: on the other side, the actual world in all its eager self-assertion, with Flavian himself, in his boundless animation, there, at the centre of the situation. From the natural defects, from the pettiness, of his euphuism, his assiduous cultivation of manner, he was saved by the consciousness that he had a matter to present, very real, at least to him. That preoccupation of the *dilettante* with what might seem mere details of form, after all, did but serve the purpose of bringing to the surface, sincerely and in their integrity, certain strong personal intuitions, a certain vision or apprehension of things as really being, with important results, thus, rather than thus,—intuitions which the artistic or literary faculty was called upon to follow, with the exactness of wax or clay, clothing the model within. Flavian too, with his fine clear mastery of the practically effective, had early laid hold of the principle, as axiomatic in literature: that to know when oneself is interested, is the first condition of interesting other people. It was a principle, the forcible apprehension of which made him jealous and fastidious in the selection of his intellectual food; often listless while others read or gazed diligently; never pretending to be moved out of mere complaisance to other people's emotions: it served to foster in him a very scrupulous literary sincerity with himself. And it was this uncompromising demand for a matter, in all art, derived immediately from lively personal intuition, this constant appeal to individual judgment, which saved his euphuism, even at its weakest, from lapsing into mere artifice.

Was the magnificent *exordium* of Lucretius, addressed to the goddess Venus, the work of his earlier manhood, and designed originally to open an argument less persistently sombre than that protest against the whole pagan heaven which actually follows it? It is certainly the most typical expression of a mood, still incident to the young poet, as a thing peculiar to his youth, when he feels the sentimental current setting forcibly along his veins, and so much as a matter of purely physical excitement, that he can hardly distinguish it from the animation of external nature, the upswelling of the seed in the earth, and of the sap through the trees. Flavian, to whom, again, as to his later euphuistic kinsmen, old mythology seemed as full of untried, unexpressed motives and interest as human life itself, had long been occupied with a kind of mystic hymn to the vernal principle of life in things; a composition shaping itself, little by little, out of a thousand dim perceptions, into singularly definite form (definite and firm as fine-art in metal, thought Marius), for which, as I said, he had caught his 'refrain', from the lips of the young men, singing because they could not help it, in the streets of Pisa. And as oftenest happens also, with natures of genuinely poetic quality, those piecemeal beginnings came suddenly to harmonious completeness among the fortunate incidents, the physical heat and light, of one singularly happy day.

It was one of the first hot days of March—'the sacred day' —on which, from Pisa, as from many another harbour on the Mediterranean, the *Ship of Isis* went to sea, and every one walked down to the shore-side to witness the freighting of the vessel, its launching and final abandonment among the waves, as an object really devoted to the Great Goddess, that new rival, or 'double', of ancient Venus, and like her a favourite patroness of sailors. On the evening next before, all the world had been abroad to view the illumination of the river; the stately lines of building being wreathed with hundreds of many-coloured lamps. The young men had poured forth their chorus—

> Cras amet qui nunquam amavit,
> Quique amavit cras amet—

as they bore their torches through the yielding crowd, or rowed their lanterned boats up and down the stream, till far into the night, when heavy raindrops had driven the last lingerers home. Morning broke, however, smiling and serene; and the long procession started betimes. The river, curving slightly, with the smoothly paved streets on either side, between its low marble parapet and the fair dwelling-houses, formed the main highway of the city; and the pageant, accompanied throughout by innumerable lanterns and wax tapers, took its course up one of these streets, crossing the water by a bridge up-stream, and down the other, to the haven, every possible standing-place, out of doors and within, being crowded with sightseers, of whom Marius was one of the most eager, deeply interested in finding the spectacle much as Apuleius had described it in his famous book.

At the head of the procession, the master of ceremonies, quietly waving back the assistants, made way for a number of women, scattering perfumes. They were succeeded by a company of musicians, piping and twanging, on instruments the strangest Marius had ever beheld, the notes of a hymn, narrating the first origin of this votive rite to a choir of youths, who marched behind them singing it. The tire-women and other personal attendants of the great goddess came next, bearing the instruments of their ministry, and various articles from the sacred wardrobe, wrought of the most precious material; some of them with long ivory combs, plying their hands in wild yet graceful concert of movement as they went, in devout mimicry of the toilet. Placed in their rear were the mirror-bearers of the goddess, carrying large mirrors of beaten brass or silver, turned in such a way as to reflect to the great body of worshippers who followed, the face of the mysterious image, as it moved on its way, and their faces to it, as though they were in fact advancing to meet the heavenly visitor. They comprehended a multitude of both sexes and of all ages, already initiated into the divine secret, clad in fair linen, the females veiled, the males with shining tonsures, and every one carrying a *sistrum*—the richer sort of silver, a few very dainty persons of fine gold—rattling the reeds, with a noise like the jargon of innumerable birds and insects awakened from torpor and abroad in the spring sun. Then, borne upon a kind of platform, came the goddess herself, undulating above the heads of the multitude as the bearers walked, in mystic robe embroidered with the moon and stars, bordered gracefully with a fringe of real fruit and flowers, and with a glittering crown upon the head. The train of the procession consisted of the priests in long white vestments, close from head to foot, distributed into various groups, each bearing, exposed aloft, one of the sacred symbols of Isis—the corn-fan, the golden asp, the ivory hand of equity, and among them the votive ship itself, carved and gilt, and adorned bravely with flags flying. Last of all walked the high priest; the people kneeling as he passed to kiss his hand, in which were those well-remembered roses.

Marius followed with the rest to the harbour, where the mystic ship, lowered from the shoulders of the priests, was loaded with as much as it could carry of the rich spices and other costly gifts, offered in great profusion by the worshippers, and thus, launched at last upon the water, left the shore, crossing the harbour bar in the wake of a much stouter vessel than itself with a crew of white-robed mariners, whose function it was, at the appointed moment, finally to desert it on the open sea.

The remainder of the day was spent by most in parties on the water. Flavian and Marius sailed further than they had ever done before to a wild spot on the bay, the traditional site of a little Greek colony, which, having had its eager, stirring life at the time when Etruria was still a power in Italy, had perished in the age of the civil wars. In the absolute transparency of the air on this gracious day, an infinitude of detail from sea and shore reached the eye with sparkling clearness, as the two lads sped rapidly over the waves—Flavian at work suddenly, from time to time, with his tablets. They reached land at last. The coral-fishers had spread their nets on the sands, with a tumble-down of quaint, many-hued treasures, below a little shrine of Venus, fluttering and gay with the scarves and napkins and gilded shells which these people had offered to the image. Flavian and Marius sat down under the shadow of a mass of grey rock or ruin, where the sea-gate of the Greek town had been, and talked of life in those old Greek colonies. Of this place, all that remained, besides those rude stones, was—a handful of silver coins, each with a head of pure and archaic beauty, though a little cruel perhaps, supposed to represent the siren Ligeia, whose tomb was formerly shown here—only these, and an ancient song, the very strain which Flavian had recovered in those last months. They were records which spoke, certainly, of the charm of life within those walls. How strong must have been the tide of men's existence in that little republican town, so small that this circle of grey stones, of service now only by the moisture they gathered for the blue-flowering gentians among them, had been the line of its rampart! An epitome of all that was liveliest, most animated and adventurous, in the old Greek people of which it was an offshoot, it had enhanced the effect of these gifts by concentration within narrow limits. The band of 'devoted youth', ἱερὰ νεότης—of the younger brothers, devoted to the gods and whatever luck the gods might afford, because there was no room for them at home—went forth, bearing the sacred flame from the mother-hearth; itself a flame, of power to consume the whole material of existence in clear light and heat, with no smouldering residue. The life of those vanished townsmen, so brilliant and revolutionary, applying so abundantly the personal qualities which alone just then Marius seemed to value, associated itself with the actual figure of his companion, standing there before him, his face enthusiastic with the sudden thought of all that; and struck him vividly as precisely the fitting opportunity for a nature like his, so hungry for control, for ascendency over men.

Marius noticed also, however, as high spirits flagged at last, on the way home through the heavy dew of the evening, more than physical fatigue in Flavian, who seemed to find no refreshment in the coolness. There had been something feverish, perhaps, and like the beginning of sickness, about his almost forced gaiety, in this sudden spasm of spring; and by the evening of the next day he was lying with a burning spot on his forehead, stricken, as was thought from the first, by the terrible new disease.

CHAPTER VII

A PAGAN END

For the fantastical colleague of the philosophic emperor Marcus Aurelius, returning in triumph from the East, had brought in his train, among the enemies of Rome, one by no means a captive. People actually sickened at a sudden touch of the unsuspected foe, as they watched in dense crowds the pathetic or grotesque imagery of failure or success in the triumphal procession. And, as usual, the plague brought with it a power to develop all pre-existent germs of superstition. It was by dishonour done to Apollo himself, said popular rumour—to Apollo, the old titular divinity of pestilence, that the poisonous thing had come abroad. Pent up in a golden coffer consecrated to the god, it had escaped in the sacrilegious plundering of his temple at Seleucia by the soldiers of Lucius Verus, after a traitorous surprise of that town and a cruel massacre. Certainly there was something which baffled all imaginable precautions and all medical science, in the suddenness with which the disease broke out simultaneously, here and there, among both soldiers and citizens, even in places far remote from the main line of its march in the rear of the victorious army. It seemed to have invaded the whole empire, and some have even thought that, in a mitigated form, it permanently remained there. In Rome itself many thousands perished; and old authorities tell of farmsteads, whole towns, and even entire neighbourhoods, which from that time continued without inhabitants and lapsed into wildness or ruin.

Flavian lay at the open window of his lodging, with a fiery pang in the brain, fancying no covering thin or light enough to be applied to his body. His head being relieved after a while, there was distress at the chest. It was but the fatal course of the strange new sickness, under many disguises; travelling from the brain to the feet, like a material resident, weakening one after another of the organic centres; often, when it did not kill, depositing various degrees of lifelong infirmity in this member or that; and after such descent, returning upwards

63

again, now as a mortal coldness, leaving the entrenchments of the fortress of life overturned, one by one, behind it.

Flavian lay there, with the enemy at his breast now in a painful cough, but relieved from that burning fever in the head, amid the rich-scented flowers—rare Paestum roses, and the like—procured by Marius for his solace, in a fancied convalescence; and would, at intervals, return to labour at his verses, with a great eagerness to complete and transcribe the work, while Marius sat and wrote at his dictation one of the latest but not the poorest specimens of genuine Latin poetry.

It was in fact a kind of nuptial hymn, which, taking its start from the thought of nature as the universal mother, celebrated the preliminary pairing and mating together of all fresh things, in the hot and genial springtime—the immemorial nuptials of the soul of spring itself and the brown earth; and was full of a delighted, mystic sense of what passed between them in that fantastic marriage. That mystic burden was relieved, at intervals, by the familiar playfulness of the Latin verse-writer in dealing with mythology, which, though coming at so late a day, had still a wonderful freshness in its old age.—'*Amor* has put his weapons by and will keep holiday. He was bidden go without apparel, that none might be wounded by his bow and arrows. But take care! In truth he is none the less armed than usual, though he be all unclad.'

In the expression of all this Flavian seemed, while making it his chief aim to retain the opulent, many-syllabled vocabulary of the Latin genius, at some points even to have advanced beyond it, in anticipation of wholly new laws of taste as regards sound, a new range of sound itself. The peculiar resultant note, associating itself with certain other experiences of his, was to Marius like the foretaste of an entirely novel world of poetic beauty to come. Flavian had caught, indeed, something of the rhyming cadence, the sonorous organ-music of the medieval Latin, and therewithal something of its unction and mysticity of spirit. There was in his work, along with the last splendour of the classical language, a touch, almost prophetic, of that transformed life it was to have in the rhyming middle age, just about to dawn. The impression thus forced upon Marius connected itself with a feeling, the exact inverse of that, known to every one, which seems to say, *You have been just here, just thus, before!*—a feeling, in his case, not reminiscent but prescient of the future, which passed over him afterwards many times, as he came across certain places and people. It

was as if he detected there the process of actual change to a
wholly undreamed-of and renewed condition of human body and
soul: as if he saw the heavy yet decrepit old Roman architecture
about him, rebuilding on an intrinsically better pattern.—
Could it have been actually on a new musical instrument that
Flavian had first heard the novel accents of his verse? And
still Marius noticed there, amid all its richness of expression
and imagery, that firmness of outline he had always relished
so much in the composition of Flavian. Yes! a firmness like
that of some master of noble metal-work, manipulating tenacious
bronze or gold. Even now that haunting refrain, with its
impromptu variations, from the throats of those strong young
men, came floating through the window.

> Cras amet qui nunquam amavit,
> Quique amavit cras amet!

—repeated Flavian, tremulously, dictating yet one stanza more.

What he was losing, his freehold of a soul and body so fortunately endowed, the mere liberty of life above-ground, 'those
sunny mornings in the cornfields by the sea', as he recollected
them one day, when the window was thrown open upon the early
freshness—his sense of all this, was from the first singularly
near and distinct, yet rather as of something he was but debarred
the use of for a time than finally bidding farewell to. That was
while he was still with no very grave misgivings as to the issue
of his sickness, and felt the sources of life still springing essentially unadulterate within him. From time to time, indeed,
Marius, labouring eagerly at the poem from his dictation, was
haunted by a feeling of the triviality of such work just then.
The recurrent sense of some obscure danger beyond the mere
danger of death, vaguer than that and by so much the more
terrible, like the menace of some shadowy adversary in the
dark with whose mode of attack they had no acquaintance,
disturbed him now and again through those hours of excited
attention to his manuscript, and to the purely physical wants
of Flavian. Still, during these three days there was much hope
and cheerfulness, and even jesting. Half-consciously Marius
tried to prolong one or another relieving circumstance of the
day, the preparations for rest and morning refreshment, for
instance; sadly making the most of the little luxury of this or
that, with something of the feigned cheer of the mother who
sets her last morsels before her famished child as for a feast,
but really that he 'may eat it and die'.

On the afternoon of the seventh day he allowed Marius finally to put aside the unfinished manuscript. For the enemy, leaving the chest quiet at length though much exhausted, had made itself felt with full power again in a painful vomiting, which seemed to shake his body asunder, with great consequent prostration. From that time the distress increased rapidly downwards. *Omnia tum vero vitai claustra lababant ;* and soon the cold was mounting with sure pace from the dead feet to the head.

And now Marius began more than to suspect what the issue must be, and henceforward could but watch with a sort of agonized fascination the rapid but systematic work of the destroyer, faintly relieving a little the mere accidents of the sharper forms of suffering. Flavian himself appeared, in full consciousness at last—in clear-sighted, deliberate estimate of the actual crisis—to be doing battle with his adversary. His mind surveyed, with great distinctness, the various suggested modes of relief. He must without fail get better, he would fancy, might he be removed to a certain place on the hills where as a child he had once recovered from sickness, but found that he could scarcely raise his head from the pillow without giddiness. As if now surely foreseeing the end, he would set himself, with an eager effort, and with that eager and angry look, which is noted as one of the premonitions of death in this disease, to fashion out, without formal dictation, still a few more broken verses of his unfinished work, in hard-set determination, defiant of pain, to arrest this or that little drop at least from the river of sensuous imagery rushing so quickly past him.

But at length *delirium*—symptom that the work of the plague was done, and the last resort of life yielding to the enemy— broke the coherent order of words and thoughts; and Marius, intent on the coming agony, found his best hope in the increasing dimness of the patient's mind. In intervals of clearer consciousness the visible signs of cold, of sorrow and desolation, were very painful. No longer battling with the disease, he seemed as it were to place himself at the disposal of the victorious foe, dying passively, like some dumb creature, in hopeless acquiescence at last. That old, half-pleading petulance, unamiable, yet, as it might seem, only needing conditions of life a little happier than they had actually been, to become refinement of affection, a delicate grace in its demand on the sympathy of others, had changed in those moments of full intelligence to a clinging and tremulous gentleness, as he lay—'on the very threshold of death'—with a sharply contracted hand in the hand of Marius, to his almost surprised joy, winning him now to an absolutely self-forgetful devotion. There was a new sort of pleading in the misty eyes, just because they took such unsteady note of him, which made Marius feel as if *guilty*; anticipating thus a form of self-reproach with which even the tenderest ministrant may be sometimes surprised, when, at death, affectionate labour suddenly ceasing leaves room for the suspicion of some failure of love perhaps, at one or another minute point in it. Marius almost longed to take his share in the suffering, that he might understand so the better how to relieve it.

It seemed that the light of the lamp distressed the patient, and Marius extinguished it. The thunder which had sounded all day among the hills, with a heat not unwelcome to Flavian, had given way at nightfall to steady rain; and in the darkness Marius lay down beside him, faintly shivering now in the sudden cold, to lend him his own warmth, undeterred by the fear of contagion which had kept other people from passing near the house. At length about daybreak he perceived that the last effort had come with a revival of mental clearness, as Marius understood by the contact, light as it was, in recognition of him there. 'Is it a comfort,' he whispered then, 'that I shall often come and weep over you?'—'Not unless I be aware, and hear you weeping!'

The sun shone out on the people going to work for a long hot day, and Marius was standing by the dead, watching, with deliberate purpose to fix in his memory every detail, that he might have this picture in reserve, should any hour of forgetfulness hereafter come to him with the temptation to feel completely happy again. A feeling of outrage, of resentment against nature itself, mingled with an agony of pity, as he noted on the now placid features a certain look of humility, almost abject, like the expression of a smitten child or animal, as of one, fallen at last, after bewildering struggle, wholly under the power of a merciless adversary. From mere tenderness of soul he would not forget one circumstance in all that; as a man might piously stamp on his memory the death-scene of a brother wrongfully condemned to die, against a time that may come.

The fear of the corpse, which surprised him in his effort to watch by it through the darkness, was a hint of his own failing strength, just in time. The first night after the washing of the body, he bore stoutly enough the tax which affection seemed to demand, throwing the incense from time to time on the little altar placed beside the bier. It was the recurrence of the thing—that unchanged outline below the coverlet, amid a silence in which the faintest rustle seemed to speak—that finally overcame his determination. Surely, here, in this alienation, this sense of distance between them, which had come over him before though in minor degree when the mind of Flavian had wandered in his sickness, was another of the pains of death. Yet he was able to make all due preparations, and go through the ceremonies, shortened a little because of the infection, when, on a cloudless evening, the funeral procession went forth; himself, the flames of the pyre having done their work, carrying away the urn of the deceased, in the folds of his toga, to its last resting-place in the cemetery beside the highway, and so turning home to sleep in his own desolate lodging.

> Quis desiderio sit pudor aut modus
> Tam cari capitis?—

What thought of others' thoughts about one could there be with the regret for 'so dear a head' fresh at one's heart?

PART THE SECOND

CHAPTER VIII

ANIMULA VAGULA

Animula, vagula, blandula
Hospes comesque corporis,
Quae nunc abibis in loca?
Pallidula, rigida, nudula.

The Emperor Hadrian to his Soul.

FLAVIAN was no more. The little marble chest with its dust and tears lay cold among the faded flowers. For most people the actual spectacle of death brings out into greater reality, at least for the imagination, whatever confidence they may entertain of the soul's survival in another life. To Marius, greatly agitated by that event, the earthly end of Flavian came like a final revelation of nothing less than the soul's extinction. Flavian had gone out as utterly as the fire among those still beloved ashes. Even that wistful suspense of judgment expressed by the dying Hadrian, regarding further stages of being still possible for the soul in some dim journey hence, seemed wholly untenable, and, with it, almost all that remained of the religion of his childhood. Future extinction seemed just then to be what the unforced witness of his own nature pointed to. On the other hand, there came a novel curiosity as to what the various schools of ancient philosophy had had to say concerning that strange, fluttering creature; and that curiosity impelled him to certain severe studies, in which his earlier religious conscience seemed still to survive, as a principle of hieratic scrupulousness or integrity of thought, regarding this new service to intellectual light.

At this time, by his poetic and inward temper, he might have fallen a prey to the enervating mysticism, then in wait for ardent souls in many a melodramatic revival of old religion or theosophy. From all this, fascinating as it might actually be to one side of his character, he was kept by a genuine virility there, effective in him, among other results, as a hatred of what was theatrical, and the instinctive recognition that in vigorous intelligence, after all, divinity was most likely to be found a resident. With this was connected the feeling, increasing with his advance to manhood, of a poetic beauty in mere clearness of thought, the actually aesthetic charm of a cold austerity of mind; as if the kinship of that to the clearness of physical light were something more than a figure of speech. Of all those various religious fantasies, as so many forms of enthusiasm, he could well appreciate the picturesque: that was made easy by his natural Epicureanism, already prompting him to conceive of himself as but the passive spectator of the world around him. But it was to the severer reasoning, of which such matters as Epicurean theory are born, that, in effect, he now betook himself. Instinctively suspicious of those mechanical *arcana*, those pretended 'secrets unveiled' of the professional mystic, which really bring great and little souls to one level, for Marius the only possible dilemma lay between that old, ancestral Roman religion, now become so incredible to him, and the honest action of his own untroubled, unassisted intelligence. Even the *Arcana Celestia* of Platonism—what the sons of Plato had had to say regarding the essential indifference of pure soul to its bodily house and merely occasional dwelling-place—seemed to him, while his heart was there in the urn with the material ashes of Flavian, or still lingering in memory over his last agony, wholly inhuman or morose, as tending to alleviate his resentment at nature's wrong. It was to the sentiment of the body, and the affections it defined—the flesh, of whose force and colour that wandering Platonic soul was but so frail a residue or abstract—he must cling. The various pathetic traits of the beloved, suffering, perished body of Flavian, so deeply pondered, had made him a materialist, but with something of the temper of a devotee.

As a consequence it might have seemed at first that his care for poetry had passed away, to be replaced by the literature of thought. His much pondered manuscript verses were laid aside; and what happened now to one, who was certainly to be something of a poet from first to last, looked at the moment like a change from poetry to prose. He came of age about this time, his own master though with beardless face; and at eighteen, an age at which, then as now, many youths of capacity, who fancied themselves poets, secluded themselves from others chiefly in affectation and vague dreaming, he secluded himself indeed from others, but in a severe intellectual meditation, that salt of poetry, without which all the more serious charm is lacking to the imaginative world. Still with something of

the old religious earnestness of his childhood, he set himself—
Sich im Denken zu orientiren—to determine his bearings, as by
compass, in the world of thought—to get that precise acquaintance with the creative intelligence itself, its structure and
capacities, its relation to other parts of himself and to other
things, without which, certainly, no poetry can be masterly.
Like a young man rich in this world's goods coming of age, he
must go into affairs, and ascertain his outlook. There must be
no disguises. An exact estimate of realities, as towards himself,
he must have—a delicately measured gradation of certainty in
things—from the distant, haunted horizon of mere surmise or
imagination, to the actual feeling of sorrow in his heart, as he
reclined one morning, alone instead of in pleasant company, to
ponder the hard sayings of an imperfect old Greek manuscript,
unrolled beside him. His former gay companions, meeting him
in the streets of the old Italian town, and noting the graver
lines coming into the face of the sombre but enthusiastic student
of intellectual structure, who could hold his own so well in the
society of accomplished older men, were half afraid of him,
though proud to have him of their company. Why this reserve?
—they asked, concerning the orderly, self-possessed youth, whose
speech and carriage seemed so carefully measured, who was
surely no poet like the rapt, dishevelled Lupus. Was he secretly
in love, perhaps, whose toga was so daintily folded, and who
was always as fresh as the flowers he wore; or bent on his own
line of ambition; or even on riches?

Marius, meantime, was reading freely, in early morning for
the most part, those writers chiefly who had made it their
business to know what might be thought concerning that strange,
enigmatic, personal essence, which had seemed to go out altogether, along with the funeral fires. And the old Greek who
more than any other was now giving form to his thoughts was
a very hard master. From Epicurus, from the thunder and
lightning of Lucretius—like thunder and lightning some distance
off, one might recline to enjoy, in a garden of roses—he had
gone back to the writer who was in a certain sense the teacher
of both, Heraclitus of Ionia. His difficult book *Concerning
Nature* was even then rare, for people had long since satisfied
themselves by the quotation of certain brilliant, isolated,
oracles only, out of what was at best a taxing kind of lore.
But the difficulty of the early Greek prose did but spur the
curiosity of Marius; the writer, the superior clearness of whose
intellectual view had so sequestered him from other men, who

had had so little joy of that superiority, being avowedly exacting as to the amount of devout attention he required from the student. 'The many', he said, always thus emphasizing the difference between the many and the few, are 'like people heavy with wine', 'led by children', 'knowing not whither they go'; and yet, 'much learning doth not make wise'; and again, 'the ass, after all, would have his thistles rather than fine gold'.

Heraclitus, indeed, had not under-rated the difficulty for 'the many' of the paradox with which his doctrine begins, and the due reception of which must involve a denial of habitual impressions, as the necessary first step in the way of truth. His philosophy had been developed in conscious, outspoken opposition to the current mode of thought, as a matter requiring some exceptional loyalty to pure reason and its 'dry light'. Men are subject to an illusion, he protests, regarding matters apparent to sense. What the uncorrected sense gives was a false impression of permanence or fixity in things, which have really changed their nature in the very moment in which we see and touch them. And the radical flaw in the current mode of thinking would lie herein: that, reflecting this false or un-corrected sensation, it attributes to the phenomena of experience a durability which does not really belong to them. Imaging forth from those fluid impressions a world of firmly outlined objects, it leads one to regard as a thing stark and dead what is in reality full of animation, of vigour, of the fire of life—that eternal process of nature, of which at a later time Goethe spoke as the 'Living Garment', whereby God is seen of us, ever in weaving at the 'Loom of Time'.

And the appeal which the old Greek thinker made was, in the first instance, from confused to unconfused sensation; with a sort of prophetic seriousness, a great claim and assumption, such as we may understand, if we anticipate in this preliminary scepticism the ulterior scope of his speculation, according to which the universal movement of all natural things is but one particular stage, or measure, of that ceaseless activity wherein the divine reason consists. The one true being—that constant subject of all early thought—it was his merit to have conceived, not as sterile and stagnant inaction, but as a perpetual energy, from the restless stream of which, at certain points, some ele-ments detach themselves, and harden into non-entity and death, corresponding, as outward objects, to man's inward condition of ignorance: that is, to the slowness of his faculties. It is with this paradox of a subtle, perpetual change in all visible things that the high speculation of Heraclitus begins. Hence the scorn he expresses for anything like a careless, half-conscious, 'use-and-wont' reception of our experience, which took so strong a hold on men's memories! Hence those many precepts towards a strenuous self-consciousness in all we think and do, that loyalty to cool and candid reason, which makes strict attentiveness of mind a kind of religious duty and service.

The negative doctrine, then, that the objects of our ordinary experience, fixed as they seem, are really in perpetual change, had been, as originally conceived, but the preliminary step towards a large positive system of almost religious philosophy. Then as now, the illuminated philosophic mind might apprehend, in what seemed a mass of lifeless matter, the movement of that universal life, in which things, and men's impressions of them, were ever 'coming to be', alternately consumed and renewed. That continual change, to be discovered by the attentive understanding where common opinion found fixed objects, was but the indicator of a subtler but all-pervading motion—the sleepless, ever-sustained, inexhaustible energy of the divine reason itself, proceeding always by its own rhythmical logic, and lending to all mind and matter, in turn, what life they had. In this 'perpetual flux' of things and of souls, there was, as Heraclitus conceived, a continuance, if not of their material or spiritual elements, yet of orderly intelligible relationships, like the harmony of musical notes, wrought out in and through the series of their mutations—ordinances of the divine reason, maintained throughout the changes of the phenomenal world; and this harmony in their mutation and opposition was, after all, a principle of sanity, of reality, there. But it happened, that, of all this, the first, merely sceptical or negative step, that easiest step on the threshold, had alone remained in general memory; and the 'doctrine of motion' seemed to those who had felt its seduction to make all fixed knowledge impossible. The swift passage of things, the still swifter passage of those modes of our conscious being which seemed to reflect them, might indeed be the burning of the divine fire: but what was ascertained was that they did pass away like a devouring flame, or like the race of water in the mid-stream—too swiftly for any real knowledge of them to be attainable. Heracliteanism had grown to be almost identical with the famous doctrine of the sophist Protagoras, that the momentary, sensible apprehension of the individual was the only standard of what is or is not, and each one the measure of all things to himself. The impressive name of Heraclitus had become but an authority for a philosophy of the despair of knowledge.

And as it had been with his original followers in Greece, so it happened now with the later Roman disciple. He, too, paused at the apprehension of that constant motion of things— the drift of flowers, of little or great souls, of ambitious systems, in the stream around him, the first source, the ultimate issue, of which, in regions out of sight, must count with him as but a dim problem. The bold mental flight of the old Greek master from the fleeting, competing objects of experience to that one universal life, in which the whole sphere of physical change might be reckoned as but a single pulsation, remained by him as hypothesis only—the hypothesis he actually preferred, as in itself most credible, however scantily realizable even by the imagination—yet still as but one unverified hypothesis, among many others, concerning the first principle of things. He might reserve it as a fine, high, visionary consideration, very remote upon the intellectual ladder, just at the point, indeed, where that ladder seemed to pass into the clouds, but for which there was certainly no time left just now by his eager interest in the real objects so close to him, on the lowlier earthy steps nearest the ground. And those childish days of reverie, when he played at priests, played in many another day-dream, working his way from the actual present, as far as he might, with a delightful sense of escape in replacing the outer world of other people by an inward world as himself really cared to have it, had made him a kind of 'idealist'. He was become aware of the possibility of a large dissidence between an inward and somewhat exclusive world of vivid personal apprehension, and the unimproved, unheightened reality of the life of those about him. As a consequence, he was ready now to concede, somewhat more easily than others, the first point of his new lesson, that the individual is to himself the measure of all things, and to rely on the exclusive certainty to himself of his own impressions. To move afterwards in that outer world of other people, as though taking it at their estimate, would be possible henceforth only as a kind of irony. And as with the *Vicaire Savoyard*, after reflecting on the variations of philosophy, 'the first fruit he drew from that reflection was the lesson of a limitation of his researches to what immediately interested him; to rest peacefully in a profound ignorance as to all beside; to disquiet himself only concerning those things which it was of import for him to know'. At least he would entertain no theory of conduct which did not allow its due weight to this primary element of incertitude or negation, in the conditions of man's life.

Just here he joined company, retracing in his individual mental pilgrimage the historic order of human thought, with another wayfarer on the journey, another ancient Greek master, the founder of the Cyrenaic philosophy, whose weighty traditional utterances (for he had left no writing) served in turn to give effective outline to the contemplations of Marius. There was something in the doctrine itself congruous with the place wherein it had its birth; and for a time Marius lived much, mentally, in the brilliant Greek colony which had given a dubious name to the philosophy of pleasure. It hung, for his fancy, between the mountains and the sea, among richer than Italian gardens, on a certain breezy table-land projecting from the African coast, some hundreds of miles southward from Greece. There, in a delightful climate, with something of transalpine temperance amid its luxury, and withal in an inward atmosphere of temperance which did but further enhance the brilliancy of human life, the school of Cyrene had maintained itself as almost one with the family of its founder; certainly as nothing coarse or unclean, and under the influence of accomplished women.

Aristippus of Cyrene too had left off in suspense of judgment as to what might really lie behind—*flammantia moenia mundi*: the flaming ramparts of the world. Those strange, bold, sceptical surmises, which had haunted the minds of the first Greek inquirers as merely abstract doubt, which had been present to the mind of Heraclitus as one element only in a system of abstract philosophy, became with Aristippus a very subtly practical worldly-wisdom. The difference between him and those obscure earlier thinkers is almost like that between an ancient thinker generally, and a modern man of the world: it was the difference between the mystic in his cell, or the prophet in the desert, and the expert, cosmopolitan, administrator of his dark sayings, translating the abstract thoughts of the master into terms, first of all, of *sentiment*. It has been sometimes seen, in the history of the human mind, that when thus translated into terms of sentiment—of sentiment, as lying already half-way towards practice—the abstract ideas of metaphysics for the first time reveal their true significance. The metaphysical principle, in itself, as it were, without hands or feet, becomes impressive, fascinating, of effect, when translated into a precept as to how it were best to feel and act; in other words, under its sentimental or ethical equivalent. The leading idea of the great master of Cyrene, his theory that things are but shadows, and that we, even as they, never continue in one stay, might indeed have taken effect as a languid, enervating, consumptive nihilism, as a precept of 'renunciation', which would touch and handle and busy itself with nothing. But in the reception of metaphysical *formulae*, all depends, as regards their actual and ulterior result, on the pre-existent qualities of that soil of human nature into which they fall—the company they find already present there, on their admission into the house of thought; there being at least so much truth as this involves in the theological maxim, that the reception of this or that speculative conclusion is really a matter of will. The persuasion that all is vanity, with this happily constituted Greek, who had been a genuine disciple of Socrates and reflected, presumably, something of his blitheness in the face of the world, his happy way of taking all chances, generated neither frivolity nor sourness, but induced, rather, an impression, just serious enough, of the call upon men's attention of the crisis in which they find themselves. It became the stimulus towards every kind of activity, and prompted a perpetual, inextinguishable thirst after experience.

With Marius, then, the influence of the philosopher of pleasure depended on this, that in him an abstract doctrine, originally somewhat acrid, had fallen upon a rich and genial nature, well fitted to transform it into a theory of practice, of considerable stimulative power towards a fair life. What Marius saw in him was the spectacle of one of the happiest temperaments coming, so to speak, to an understanding with the most depressing of theories; accepting the results of a metaphysical system which seemed to concentrate into itself all the weakening trains of thought in earlier Greek speculation, and making the best of it; turning its hard, bare truths, with wonderful tact, into precepts of grace, and delicate wisdom, and a delicate sense of honour. Given the hardest terms, supposing our days are indeed but a shadow, even so, we may well adorn and beautify, in scrupulous self-respect, our souls, and whatever our souls touch upon—these wonderful bodies, these material dwelling-places through which the shadows pass together for a while, the very raiment we wear, our very pastimes and the intercourse of society. The most discerning judges saw in him something like the graceful 'humanities' of the later Roman, and our modern 'culture', as it is termed; while Horace recalled his sayings as expressing best his own consummate amenity in the reception of life.

In this way, for Marius, under the guidance of that old master of decorous living, those eternal doubts as to the *criteria* of truth reduced themselves to a scepticism almost dryly practical, a scepticism which developed the opposition between things as they are and our impressions and thoughts concerning them— the possibility, if an outward world does really exist, of some faultiness in our apprehension of it—the doctrine, in short, of what is termed 'the subjectivity of knowledge'. That is a consideration, indeed, which lies as an element of weakness, like some admitted fault or flaw, at the very foundation of every philosophical account of the universe; which confronts all philosophies at their starting, but with which none have really dealt conclusively, some perhaps not quite sincerely; which those who are not philosophers dissipate by 'common', but unphilosophical, sense, or by religious faith. The peculiar strength of Marius was, to have apprehended this weakness on the threshold of human knowledge, in the whole range of its consequences. Our knowledge is limited to what we feel, he reflected: we need no proof that we feel. But can we be sure that things are at all like our feelings? Mere peculiarities in the instruments of our cognition, like the little knots and waves on the surface of a mirror, may distort the matter they seem but to represent. Of other people we cannot truly know even the feelings, nor how far they would indicate the same modifica- tions, each one of a personality really unique, in using the same terms as ourselves; that 'common experience', which is some- times proposed as a satisfactory basis of certainty, being after all only a fixity of language. But our own impressions!—The light and heat of that blue veil over our heads, the heavens spread out, perhaps *not* like a curtain over anything!—How reassuring, after so long a debate about the rival *criteria* of truth, to fall back upon direct sensation, to limit one's aspirations after knowledge to that! In an age still materially so brilliant, so expert in the artistic handling of material things, with sensible capacities still in undiminished vigour, with the whole world of classic art and poetry outspread before it, and where there was more than eye or ear could well take in—how natural the determination to rely exclusively upon the phenomena of the senses, which certainly never deceive us about themselves, about which alone we can never deceive ourselves!

And so the abstract apprehension that the little point of this present moment alone really is, between a past which has just ceased to be and a future which may never come, became practical with Marius, under the form of a resolve, as far as possible, to exclude regret and desire, and yield himself to the improvement of the present with an absolutely disengaged mind. *America is here and now—here, or nowhere :* as Wilhelm Meister finds out one day, just not too late, after so long looking vaguely across the ocean for the opportunity of the development of his capacities. It was as if, recognizing in perpetual motion the law of nature, Marius identified his own way of life cordially with it, 'throwing himself into the stream', so to speak. He too must maintain a harmony with that soul of motion in things, by constantly renewed mobility of character.

Omnis Aristippum decuit color et status et res.—

Thus Horace had summed up that perfect manner in the reception of life attained by his old Cyrenaic master; and the first practical consequence of the metaphysic which lay behind that perfect manner, had been a strict limitation, almost the renunciation, of metaphysical inquiry itself. Metaphysic—that art, as it has so often proved, in the words of Michelet, *de s'égarer avec méthode,* of bewildering one's self methodically:—one must spend little time upon that! In the school of Cyrene, great as was its mental incisiveness, logical and physical speculation, theoretic interests generally, had been valued only so far as they served to give a groundwork, an intellectual justification, to that exclusive concern with practical ethics which was a note of the Cyrenaic philosophy. How earnest and enthusiastic, how true to itself, under how many varieties of character, had been the effort of the Greeks after Theory—*Theôria*—that vision of a wholly reasonable world, which, according to the greatest of them, literally makes man like God: how loyally they had still persisted in the quest after that, in spite of how many disappointments! In the Gospel of Saint John, perhaps, some of them might have found the kind of vision they were seeking for; but not in 'doubtful disputations' concerning 'being' and 'not-being', knowledge and appearance. Men's minds, even young men's minds, at that late day, might well seem oppressed by the weariness of systems which had so far outrun positive knowledge; and in the mind of Marius, as in that old school of Cyrene, this sense of *ennui,* combined with appetites so youthfully vigorous, brought about reaction, a sort of suicide (instances of the like have been seen since) by which a great metaphysical *acumen* was devoted to the function of proving metaphysical speculation impossible, or useless. Abstract theory was to be valued only just so far as it might serve to clear the tablet of the mind from suppositions no more than half realizable, or wholly visionary, leaving it in flawless evenness of surface to the impressions of an experience, concrete and direct.

To be absolutely virgin towards such experience, by ridding ourselves of such abstractions as are but the ghosts of bygone impressions—to be rid of the notions we have made for ourselves, and that so often only misrepresent the experience of which they profess to be the representation—*idola*, idols, false appearances, as Bacon calls them later—to neutralize the distorting influence of metaphysical system by an all-accomplished metaphysic skill: it is this bold, hard, sober recognition, under a very 'dry light', of its own proper aim, in union with a habit of feeling which on the practical side may perhaps open a wide doorway to human weakness, that gives to the Cyrenaic doctrine, to reproductions of this doctrine in the time of Marius or in our own, their gravity and importance. It was a school to which the young man might come, eager for truth, expecting much from philosophy, in no ignoble curiosity, aspiring after nothing less than an 'initiation'. He would be sent back, sooner or later, to experience, to the world of concrete impressions, to things as they may be seen, heard, felt by him; but with a wonderful machinery of observation, and free from the tyranny of mere theories.

So, in intervals of repose, after the agitation which followed the death of Flavian, the thoughts of Marius ran, while he felt himself as if returned to the fine, clear, peaceful light of that pleasant school of healthfully sensuous wisdom, in the brilliant old Greek colony, on its fresh upland by the sea. Not pleasure, but a general completeness of life, was the practical ideal to which this anti-metaphysical metaphysic really pointed. And towards such a full or complete life, a life of various yet select sensation, the most direct and effective auxiliary must be, in a word, Insight. Liberty of soul, freedom from all partial and misrepresentative doctrine which does but relieve one element in our experience at the cost of another, freedom from all embarrassment alike of regret for the past and of calculation on the future: this would be but preliminary to the real business of education—insight, insight through culture, into all that the present moment holds in trust for us, as we stand so briefly in its presence. From that maxim of *Life as the end of life*, followed, as a practical consequence, the desirableness of refining all the instruments of inward and outward intuition, of developing all their capacities, of testing and exercising one's self in them, till one's whole nature became one complex medium of reception, towards the vision—the 'beatific vision', if we really cared to make it such —of our actual experience in the world.   Not the conveyance of an abstract body of truths or principles, would be the aim of the right education of one's self, or of another, but the conveyance of an art—an art in some degree peculiar to each individual character; with the modifications, that is, due to its special constitution, and the peculiar circumstances of its growth, inasmuch as no one of us is 'like another, all in all'.

CHAPTER IX

NEW CYRENAICISM

SUCH were the practical conclusions drawn for himself by Marius, when somewhat later he had outgrown the mastery of others, from the principle that 'all is vanity'. If he could but count upon the present, if a life brief at best could not certainly be shown to conduct one anywhere beyond itself, if men's highest curiosity was indeed so persistently baffled—then, with the Cyrenaics of all ages, he would at least fill up the measure of that present with vivid sensations, and such intellectual apprehensions as, in strength and directness and their immediately realized values at the bar of an actual experience, are most like sensations. So some have spoken in every age; for, like all theories which really express a strong natural tendency of the human mind or even one of its characteristic modes of weakness, this vein of reflection is a constant tradition in philosophy. Every age of European thought has had its Cyrenaics or Epicureans, under many disguises: even under the hood of the monk. But—*Let us eat and drink, for to-morrow we die !*—is a proposal, the real import of which differs immensely, according to the natural taste, and the acquired judgment, of the guests who sit at the table. It may express nothing better than the instinct of Dante's Ciacco, the accomplished glutton, in the mud of the *Inferno*; or, since on no hypothesis does man 'live by bread alone', may come to be identical with—'My meat is to do what is just and kind'; while the soul, which can make no sincere claim to have apprehended anything beyond the veil of immediate experience, yet never loses a sense of happiness in conforming to the highest moral ideal it can clearly define for itself; and actually, though but with so faint hope, does the 'Father's business'.

In that age of Marcus Aurelius, so completely disabused of the metaphysical ambition to pass beyond 'the flaming ramparts of the world', but, on the other hand, possessed of so vast an accumulation of intellectual treasure, with so wide a view before it over all varieties of what is powerful or attractive in man and his works, the thoughts of Marius did but follow the line taken by the majority of educated persons, though to a different issue. Pitched to a really high and serious key, the precept— *Be perfect in regard to what is here and now*: the precept of 'culture', as it is called, or of a complete education—might at least save him from the vulgarity and heaviness of a generation, certainly of no general fineness of temper, though with a material well-being abundant enough. Conceded that what is secure in our existence is but the sharp apex of the present moment between two hypothetical eternities, and all that is real in our experience but a series of fleeting impressions:—so Marius continued the sceptical argument he had condensed, as the matter to hold by, from his various philosophical reading:— given, that we are never to get beyond the walls of this closely shut cell of one's own personality; that the ideas we are some-how impelled to form of an outer world, and of other minds akin to our own, are, it may be, but a day-dream, and the thought of any world beyond, a day-dream perhaps idler still: then he, at least, in whom those fleeting impressions—faces, voices, material sunshine—were very real and imperious, might well set himself to the consideration, how such actual moments as they passed might be made to yield their utmost, by the most dexterous training of capacity. Amid abstract metaphysical doubts, as to what might lie one step only beyond that experience, reinforcing the deep original materialism or earthliness of human nature itself, bound so intimately to the sensuous world, let him at least make the most of what was 'here and now'. In the actual dimness of ways from means to ends—ends in themselves desirable, yet for the most part distant, and for him, certainly, below the visible horizon—he would at all events be sure that the means, to use the well-worn terminology, should have something of finality or perfection about them, and themselves partake, in a measure, of the more excellent nature of ends— that the means should justify the end.

With this view he would demand culture, παιδεία, as the Cyrenaics said, or, in other words, a wide, a complete, education —an education partly negative, as ascertaining the true limits of man's capacities, but for the most part positive, and directed especially to the expansion and refinement of the power of reception; of those powers, above all, which are immediately relative to fleeting phenomena, the powers of emotion and sense. In such an education, an 'aesthetic' education, as it might now be termed, and certainly occupied very largely with those aspects of things which affect us pleasurably through sensation, art, of course, including all the finer sorts of literature, would have a great part to play. The study of music, in that wider Platonic sense, according to which, *music* comprehends all those matters over which the Muses of Greek mythology preside, would conduct one to an exquisite appreciation of all the finer traits of nature and of man. Nay! the products of the imagination must themselves be held to present the most perfect forms of life—spirit and matter alike under their purest and most perfect conditions—the most strictly appropriate objects of that impassioned contemplation, which, in the world of intellectual discipline, as in the highest forms of morality and religion, must be held to be the essential function of the 'perfect'. Such manner of life might come even to seem a kind of religion—an inward, visionary, mystic piety, or religion, by virtue of its effort to live days 'lovely and pleasant' in themselves, here and now, and with an all-sufficiency of well-being in the immediate sense of the object contemplated, independently of any faith, or hope that might be entertained as to their ulterior tendency. In this way, the true aesthetic culture would be realizable as a new form of the contemplative life, founding its claim on the intrinsic 'blessedness' of 'vision'—the vision of perfect men and things. One's human nature, indeed, would fain reckon on an assured and endless future, pleasing itself with the dream of a final home, to be attained at some still remote date, yet with a conscious, delightful home-coming at last, as depicted in many an old poetic Elysium. On the other hand, the world of perfected sensation, intelligence, emotion, is so close to us, and so attractive, that the most visionary of spirits must needs represent the world unseen in colours, and under a form really borrowed from it. Let me be sure then—might he not plausibly say?—that I miss no detail of this life of realized consciousness in the present! Here at least is a vision, a theory, θεωρία, which reposes on no basis of unverified hypothesis, which makes no call upon a future after all somewhat problematic; as it would be unaffected by any discovery of an Empedocles (improving on the old story of Prometheus) as to what had really been the origin, and course of development, of man's actually attained faculties and that seemingly divine particle of reason or spirit in him. Such a doctrine, at more leisurable moments, would of course have its precepts to deliver on the embellishment, generally, of what is near at hand, on the adornment of life, till, in a not impracticable rule of conduct, one's existence, from day to day, came to be like a well-executed piece of music; that 'perpetual motion' in things (so Marius figured the matter to himself, under the old Greek imageries) according itself to a kind of cadence or harmony.

It was intelligible that this 'aesthetic' philosophy might find itself (theoretically, at least, and by way of a curious question in casuistry, legitimate from its own point of view) weighing the claims of that eager, concentrated, impassioned realization of experience, against those of the received morality. Conceiving its own function in a somewhat desperate temper, and becoming, as every high-strung form of sentiment, as the religious sentiment itself, may become, somewhat antinomian, when, in its effort towards the order of experiences it prefers, it is confronted with the traditional and popular morality, at points where that morality may look very like a convention, or a mere stage-property of the world, it would be found, from time to time, breaking beyond the limits of the actual moral order; perhaps not without some pleasurable excitement in so bold a venture.

With the possibility of some such hazard as this, in thought or even in practice—that it might be, though refining, or tonic even, in the case of those strong and in health, yet, as Pascal says of the kindly and temperate wisdom of Montaigne, 'pernicious for those who have any natural tendency to impiety or vice', the line of reflection traced out above, was fairly chargeable. —Not, however, with 'hedonism' and its supposed consequences. The blood, the heart, of Marius were still pure. He knew that his carefully considered theory of practice braced him, with the effect of a moral principle duly recurring to mind every morning, towards the work of a student, for which he might seem intended. Yet there were some among his acquaintance who jumped to the conclusion that, with the 'Epicurean stye', he was making pleasure—pleasure, as they so poorly conceived it—the sole motive of life; and they precluded any exacter estimate of the situation by covering it with a high-sounding general term, through the vagueness of which they were enabled to see the severe and laborious youth in the vulgar company of Lais. Words like 'hedonism'—terms of large and vague comprehension —above all when used for a purpose avowedly controversial, have ever been the worst examples of what are called 'question-begging terms'; and in that late age in which Marius lived, amid the dust of so many centuries of philosophical debate, the air was full of them. Yet those who used that reproachful

Greek term for the philosophy of pleasure, were hardly more likely than the old Greeks themselves (on whom regarding this very subject of the theory of pleasure, their masters in the art of thinking had so emphatically to impress the necessity of 'making distinctions') to come to any very delicately correct ethical conclusions by a reasoning, which began with a general term, comprehensive enough to cover pleasures so different in quality, in their causes and effects, as the pleasures of wine and love, of art and science, of religious enthusiasm and political enterprise, and of that taste or curiosity which satisfied itself with long days of serious study. Yet, in truth, each of those pleasurable modes of activity may, in its turn, fairly become the ideal of the 'hedonistic' doctrine. Really, to the phase of reflection through which Marius was then passing, the charge of 'hedonism', whatever its true weight might be, was not properly applicable at all. Not pleasure, but fullness of life, and 'insight' as conducing to that fullness—energy, variety, and choice of experience, including noble pain and sorrow even, loves such as those in the exquisite old story of Apuleius, sincere and strenuous forms of the moral life, such as Seneca and Epictetus—whatever form of human life, in short, might be heroic, impassioned, ideal: from these the 'new Cyrenaicism' of Marius took its criterion of values. It was a theory, indeed, which might properly be regarded as in great degree coincident with the main principle of the Stoics themselves, and an older version of the precept 'Whatsoever thy hand findeth to do, do it with thy might'—a doctrine so widely acceptable among the nobler spirits of that time. And, as with that, its mistaken tendency would lie in the direction of a kind of idolatry of mere life, or natural gift, or strength—*l'idolâtrie des talents*.

To understand the various forms of ancient art and thought, the various forms of actual human feeling (the only new thing, in a world almost too opulent in what was old), to satisfy, with a kind of scrupulous equity, the claims of these concrete and actual objects on his sympathy, his intelligence, his senses—to 'pluck out the heart of their mystery', and in turn become the interpreter of them to others: this had now defined itself for Marius as a very narrowly practical design: it determined his choice of a vocation to live by. It was the era of the *rhetoricians*, or *sophists*, as they were sometimes called; of men who came in some instances to great fame and fortune, by way of a literary cultivation of 'science'. That science, it has been often said, must have been wholly an affair of words. But in a world, confessedly so opulent in what was old, the work, even of genius, must necessarily consist very much in criticism; and, in the case of the more excellent specimens of his class, the rhetorician was, after all, the eloquent and effective interpreter, for the delighted ears of others, of what understanding himself had come by, in years of travel and study, of the beautiful house of art and thought which was the inheritance of the age. The emperor Marcus Aurelius, to whose service Marius had now been called, was himself, more or less openly, a 'lecturer'. That late world, amid many curiously vivid modern traits, had this spectacle, so familiar to ourselves, of the public lecturer or essayist; in some cases adding to his other gifts that of the Christian preacher, who knows how to touch people's sensibilities on behalf of the suffering. To follow in the way of these successes was the natural instinct of youthful ambition; and it was with no vulgar egotism that Marius, at the age of nineteen, determined, like many another young man of parts, to enter as a student of rhetoric at Rome.

Though the manner of his work was changed formally from poetry to prose, he remained, and must always be, of the poetic temper: by which I mean, among other things, that quite independently of the general habit of that pensive age he lived much, and as it were by system, in reminiscence. Amid his eager grasping at the sensation, the consciousness, of the present, he had come to see that, after all, the main point of economy in the conduct of the present, was the question: How will it look to me, at what shall I value it, this day next year?—that in any given day or month one's main concern was its impression for the memory. A strange trick memory sometimes played him; for, with no natural gradation, what was of last month, or of yesterday, of to-day even, would seem as far off, as entirely detached from him, as things of ten years ago. Detached from him, yet very real, there lay certain spaces of his life, in delicate perspective, under a favourable light; and, somehow, all the less fortunate detail and circumstance had parted from them. Such hours were oftenest those in which he had been helped by work of others to the pleasurable apprehension of art, of nature, or of life. 'Not what I do, but what I am, under the power of this vision'—he would say to himself—'is what were indeed pleasing to the gods!'

And yet, with a kind of inconsistency in one who had taken for his philosophic ideal the μονόχρονος ἡδονή of Aristippus— the pleasure of the ideal present, of the mystic *now*—there would come, together with that precipitate sinking of things into the past, a desire, after all, to retain 'what was so transitive'. Could he but arrest, for others also, certain clauses of experience, as the imaginative memory presented them to himself! In those grand, hot summers, he would have imprisoned the very perfume of the flowers. To create, to live, perhaps, a little while beyond the allotted hours, if it were but in a fragment of perfect expression:—it was thus his longing defined itself for something to hold by amid the 'perpetual flux'. With men of his vocation, people were apt to say, words were things. Well! with him, words should be indeed things,—the word, the phrase, valuable in exact proportion to the transparency with which it conveyed to others the apprehension, the emotion, the mood, so vividly real within himself. *Verbaque provisam rem non invita sequentur :* Virile apprehension of the true nature of things, of the true nature of one's own impression, first of all!—words would follow that naturally, a true understanding of one's self being ever the first condition of genuine style. Language delicate and measured, the delicate Attic phrase, for instance, in which the eminent Aristeides could speak, was then a power to which people's hearts, and sometimes even their purses, readily responded. And there were many points, as Marius thought, on which the heart of that age greatly needed to be touched. He hardly knew how strong that old religious sense of responsibility, the conscience, as we call it, still was within him—a body of inward impressions, as real as those so highly valued outward ones—to offend against which, brought with it a strange feeling of disloyalty, as to a person. And the determination, adhered to with no misgiving, to add nothing, not so much as a transient sigh, to the great total of men's unhappiness, in his way through the world:—that too was something to rest on, in the drift of mere 'appearances'.

All this would involve a life of industry, of industrious study, only possible through healthy rule, keeping clear the eye alike of body and soul. For the male element, the logical conscience asserted itself now, with opening manhood—asserted itself, even in his literary style, by a certain firmness of outline, that touch of the worker in metal, amid its richness. Already he blamed instinctively alike in his work and in himself, as youth so seldom does, all that had not passed a long and liberal process of erasure. The happy phrase or sentence was really modelled upon a cleanly finished structure of scrupulous thought. The suggestive force of the one master of his development, who had battled so hard with imaginative prose; the utterance, the golden utterance, of the other, so content with its living power of persuasion that he had never written at all,—in the commixture of these two qualities he set up his literary ideal, and this rare blending of grace with an intellectual rigour or astringency, was the secret of a singular expressiveness in it.

He acquired at this time a certain bookish air, the somewhat sombre habitude of the avowed scholar, which, though it never interfered with the perfect tone, 'fresh and serenely disposed', of the Roman gentleman, yet qualified it as by an interesting oblique trait, and frightened away some of his equals in age and rank. The sober discretion of his thoughts, his sustained habit of meditation, the sense of those negative conclusions enabling him to concentrate himself, with an absorption so entire, upon what is immediately *here* and *now*, gave him a peculiar manner of intellectual confidence, as of one who had indeed been initiated into a great secret.—Though with an air so disengaged, he seemed to be living so intently in the visible world! And now, in revolt against that preoccupation with other persons, which had so often perturbed his spirit, his wistful speculations as to what the real, the greater, experience might be, determined in him, not as the longing for love—to be with Cynthia, or Aspasia—but as a thirst for existence in exquisite places. The veil that was to be lifted for him lay over the works of the old masters of art, in places where nature also had used her mastery. And it was just at this moment that a summons to Rome reached him.

CHAPTER X

Mirum est ut animus agitatione motuque corporis excitetur.
Pliny's Letters.

MANY points in that train of thought, its harder and more energetic practical details especially, at first surmised but vaguely in the intervals of his visits to the tomb of Flavian, attained the coherence of formal principle amid the stirring incidents of the journey, which took him, still in all the buoyancy of his nineteen years and greatly expectant, to Rome. That summons had come from one of the former friends of his father in the capital, who had kept himself acquainted with the lad's progress, and, assured of his parts, his courtly ways, above all of his beautiful penmanship, now offered him a place, virtually that of an *amanuensis*, near the person of the philosophic emperor. The old town-house of his family on the Caelian hill, so long neglected, might well require his personal care; and Marius, relieved a little by his preparations for travelling from a certain over-tension of spirit in which he had lived of late, was presently on his way, to await introduction to Aurelius, on his expected return home, after a first success, illusive enough as it was soon to appear, against the invaders from beyond the Danube.

The opening stage of his journey, through the firm, golden weather, for which he had lingered three days beyond the appointed time of starting—days brown with the first rains of autumn—brought him, by the byways among the lower slopes of the Apennines of Luna, to the town of Luca, a station on the Cassian Way; travelling so far mainly on foot, while the baggage followed under the care of his attendants. He wore a broad felt hat, in fashion not unlike a more modern pilgrim's, the neat head projecting from the collar of his grey *paenula*, or travelling mantle, sewed closely together over the breast, but with its two sides folded up upon the shoulders, to leave the arms free in walking, and was altogether so trim and fresh, that, as he climbed the hill from Pisa, by the long steep lane through the olive-yards, and turned to gaze where he could just discern the cypresses of the old school garden, like two black lines down the yellow walls, a little child took possession of his hand, and, looking up at him with entire confidence, paced on bravely at his side, for the mere pleasure of his company, to the spot where the road declined again into the valley beyond. From this point, leaving the servants behind, he surrendered himself, a willing subject, as he walked, to the impressions of the road, and was almost surprised, both at the suddenness with which evening came on, and the distance from his old home at which it found him.

And at the little town of Luca, he felt that indescribable sense of a welcoming in the mere outward appearance of things, which seems to mark out certain places for the special purpose of evening rest, and gives them always a peculiar amiability in retrospect. Under the deepening twilight, the rough-tiled roofs seem to huddle together side by side, like one continuous shelter over the whole township, spread low and broad above the snug sleeping-rooms within; and the place one sees for the first time, and must tarry in but for a night, breathes the very spirit of home. The cottagers lingered at their doors for a few minutes as the shadows grew larger, and went to rest early; though there was still a glow along the road through the shorn cornfields, and the birds were still awake about the crumbling grey heights of an old temple. So quiet and air-swept was the place, you could hardly tell where the country left off in it and the field-paths became its streets. Next morning he must needs change the manner of his journey. The light baggage-wagon returned, and he proceeded now more quickly, travelling a stage or two by post, along the Cassian Way, where the figures and incidents of the great high-road seemed already to tell of the capital, the one centre to which all were hastening, or had lately bidden adieu. That *Way* lay through the heart of the old, mysterious and visionary country of Etruria; and what he knew of its strange religion of the dead, reinforced by the actual sight of the funeral houses scattered so plentifully among the dwelling-places of the living, revived in him for a while, in all its strength, his old instinctive yearning towards those inhabitants of the shadowy land he had known in life. It seemed to him that he could half divine how time passed in those painted houses on the hillsides, among the gold and silver ornaments, the wrought armour and vestments, the drowsy and dead attendants; and the close consciousness of that vast population gave him no fear, but rather a sense of companionship, as he climbed the hills on foot behind the horses, through the genial afternoon.

The road, next day, passed below a town not less primitive, it might seem, than its rocky perch—white rocks, that had long been glistening before him in the distance. Down the dewy paths the people were descending from it, to keep a holiday, high and low alike in rough, white-linen smocks. A homely old play was just begun in an open-air theatre, with seats hollowed out of the turf-grown slope. Marius caught the terrified expression of a child in its mother's arms, as it turned from the yawning mouth of a great mask, for refuge in her bosom. The way mounted, and descended again, down the steep street of another place, all resounding with the noise of metal under the hammer; for every house had its brazier's workshop, the bright objects of brass and copper gleaming, like lights in a cave, out of their dark roofs and corners. Around the anvils the children were watching the work, or ran to fetch water to the hissing, red-hot metal; and Marius too watched, as he took his hasty midday refreshment, a mess of chestnut-meal and cheese, while the swelling surface of a great copper water-vessel grew flowered all over with tiny petals under the skilful strokes. Towards dusk, a frantic woman at the road-side stood and cried out the words of some philtre, or malison, in verse, with weird motion of her hands, as the travellers passed, like a wild picture drawn from Virgil.

But all along, accompanying the superficial grace of these incidents of the way, Marius noted, more and more as he drew nearer to Rome, marks of the great plague. Under Hadrian and his successors there had been many enactments to improve the condition of the slave. The *ergastula* were abolished. But no system of free labour had as yet succeeded. A whole mendicant population, artfully exaggerating every symptom and circumstance of misery, still hung around, or sheltered themselves within, the vast walls of their old, half-ruined task-houses. And for the most part they had been variously stricken by the pestilence. For once, the heroic level had been reached in rags, squints, scars—every caricature of the human type—ravaged beyond what could have been thought possible if it were to survive at all. Meantime, the farms were less carefully tended than of old: here and there they were lapsing into their natural wildness: some villas also were partly fallen into ruin. The picturesque, romantic Italy of a later time—the Italy of

Claude and Salvator Rosa—was already forming, for the delight of the modern romantic traveller.

And again Marius was aware of a real change in things, on crossing the Tiber, as if some magic effect lay in that; though here, in truth, the Tiber was but a modest enough stream of turbid water. Nature, under the richer sky, seemed readier and more affluent, and man fitter to the conditions around him: even in people hard at work there appeared to be a less burdensome sense of the mere business of life. How dreamily the women were passing up through the broad light and shadow of the steep streets with the great water-pots resting on their heads, like women of Caryae, set free from slavery in old Greek temples. With what a fresh, primeval poetry was daily existence here impressed—all the details of the threshing-floor and the vineyard; the common farm-life even; the great bakers' fires aglow upon the road in the evening. In the presence of all this Marius felt for a moment like those old, early, unconscious poets, who created the famous Greek myths of Dionysus, and the Great Mother, out of the imagery of the wine-press and the ploughshare. And still the motion of the journey was bringing his thoughts to systematic form. He seemed to have grown to the fullness of intellectual manhood, on his way hither. The formative and literary stimulus, so to call it, of peaceful exercise which he had always observed in himself, doing its utmost now, the form and the matter of thought alike detached themselves clearly and with readiness from the healthfully excited brain.—'It is wonderful,' says Pliny, 'how the mind is stirred to activity by brisk bodily exercise.' The presentable aspects of inmost thought and feeling became evident to him: the structure of all he meant, its order and outline, defined itself: his general sense of a fitness and beauty in words became effective in daintily pliant sentences, with all sorts of felicitous linking of figure to abstraction. It seemed just then as if the desire of the artist in him—that old longing to produce—might be satisfied by the exact and literal transcript of what was then passing around him, in simple prose, arresting the desirable moment as it passed, and prolonging its life a little.—To live in the concrete! To be sure, at least, of one's hold upon that! —Again, his philosophic scheme was but the reflection of the *data* of sense, and chiefly of sight, a reduction to the abstract, of the brilliant road he travelled on, through the sunshine.

But on the seventh evening there came a reaction in the cheerful flow of our traveller's thoughts, a reaction with which mere bodily fatigue, asserting itself at last over his curiosity, had much to do; and he fell into a mood, known to all passably sentimental wayfarers, as night deepens again and again over their path, in which all journeying, from the known to the unknown, comes suddenly to figure as a mere foolish truancy— like a child's running away from home—with the feeling that one had best return at once, even through the darkness. He had chosen to climb on foot, at his leisure, the long windings by which the road ascended to the place where that day's stage was to end, and found himself alone in the twilight, far behind the rest of his travelling companions. Would the last zigzag, round and round those dark masses, half natural rock, half artificial substructure, ever bring him within the circuit of the walls above? It was now that a startling incident turned those misgivings almost into actual fear. From the steep slope a heavy mass of stone was detached, after some whisperings among the trees above his head, and rushing down through the stillness fell to pieces in a cloud of dust across the road just behind him, so that he felt the touch upon his heel. That was sufficient, just then, to rouse out of its hiding-place his old vague fear of evil—of one's 'enemies'—a distress, so much a matter of constitution with him, that at times it would seem that the best pleasures of life could but be snatched, as it were hastily, in one moment's forgetfulness of its dark, besetting influence. A sudden suspicion of hatred against him, of the nearness of 'enemies', seemed all at once to alter the visible form of things, as with the child's hero, when he found the footprint on the sand of his peaceful, dreamy island. His elaborate philosophy had not put beneath his feet the terror of mere bodily evil; much less of 'inexorable fate, and the noise of greedy Acheron'.

The resting-place to which he presently came, in the keen, wholesome air of the market-place of the little hill town, was a pleasant contrast to that last effort of his journey. The room in which he sat down to supper, unlike the ordinary Roman inns at that day, was trim and sweet. The firelight danced cheerfully upon the polished, three-wicked *lucernae* burning cleanly with the best oil, upon the whitewashed walls, and the bunches of scarlet carnations set in glass goblets. The white wine of the place put before him, of the true colour and flavour of the grape, and with a ring of delicate foam as it mounted in the cup, had a reviving edge or freshness he had found in no other wine. These things had relieved a little the melancholy of the hour before; and it was just then that he heard the voice of one, newly arrived at the inn, making his way to the upper floor—a youthful voice, with a reassuring clearness of note, which completed his cure.

He seemed to hear that voice again in dreams, uttering his name: then, awake in the full morning light and gazing from the window, saw the guest of the night before, a very honourable-looking youth, in the rich habit of a military knight, standing beside his horse, and already making preparations to depart. It happened that Marius, too, was to take that day's journey on horseback. Riding presently from the inn, he overtook Cornelius—of the Twelfth Legion—advancing carefully down the steep street; and before they had issued from the gates of *Urbs-vetus*, the two young men had broken into talk together. They were passing along the street of the goldsmiths; and Cornelius must needs enter one of the workshops for the repair of some button or link of his knightly trappings. Standing in the doorway, Marius watched the work, as he had watched the brazier's business a few days before, wondering most at the simplicity of its processes, a simplicity, however, on which only genius in that craft could have lighted.—By what unguessed-at stroke of hand, for instance, had the grains of precious metal associated themselves with so daintily regular a roughness, over the surface of the little casket yonder? And the conversation which followed, hence arising, left the two travellers with sufficient interest in each other to ensure an easy companionship for the remainder of their journey. In time to come, Marius was to depend very much on the preferences, the personal judgments, of the comrade who now laid his hand so brotherly on his shoulder, as they left the workshop.

Itineris matutini gratiam capimus,—observes one of our scholarly travellers; and their road that day lay through a country, well-fitted, by the peculiarity of its landscape, to ripen a first acquaintance into intimacy; its superficial ugliness throwing the wayfarers back upon each other's entertainment in a real exchange of ideas, the tension of which, however, it would relieve, ever and anon, by the unexpected assertion of something singularly attractive. The immediate aspect of the land was, indeed, in spite of abundant olive and ilex, unpleasing enough. A river of clay seemed, 'in some old night of time', to have burst up over valley and hill, and hardened there into fantastic shelves and slides and angles of cadaverous rock, up and down among the contorted vegetation; the hoary roots and trunks seeming to confess some weird kinship with them. But

that was long ago; and these pallid hillsides needed only the
declining sun, touching the rock with purple, and throwing
deeper shadow into the immemorial foliage, to put on a peculiar,
because a very grave and austere, kind of beauty; while the
graceful outlines common to volcanic hills asserted themselves
in the broader prospect. And, for sentimental Marius, all this
was associated, by some perhaps fantastic affinity, with a
peculiar trait of severity, beyond his guesses as to the secret of
it, which mingled with the blitheness of his new companion.
Concurring, indeed, with the condition of a Roman soldier, it
was certainly something far more than the expression of military
hardness, or *ascêsis*; and what was earnest, or even austere, in
the landscape they had traversed together, seemed to have been
waiting for the passage of this figure to interpret or inform it.
Again, as in his early days with Flavian, a vivid personal
presence broke through the dreamy idealism, which had almost
come to doubt of other men's reality: reassuringly, indeed, yet
not without some sense of a constraining tyranny over him
from without.

For Cornelius, returning from the campaign, to take up his
quarters on the *Palatine*, in the imperial guard, seemed to carry
about with him, in that privileged world of comely usage to
which he belonged, the atmosphere of some still more jealously
exclusive circle. They halted on the morrow at noon, not at
an inn, but at the house of one of the young soldier's friends,
whom they found absent, indeed, in consequence of the plague
in those parts, so that after a midday rest only, they proceeded
again on their journey. The great room of the villa, to which
they were admitted, had lain long untouched; and the dust rose,
as they entered, into the slanting bars of sunlight, that fell
through the half-closed shutters. It was here, to while away
the time, that Cornelius bethought himself of displaying to his
new friend the various articles and ornaments of his knightly
array—the breastplate, the sandals and cuirass, lacing them on,
one by one, with the assistance of Marius, and finally the great
golden bracelet on the right arm, conferred on him by his general
for an act of valour. And as he gleamed there, amid that odd
interchange of light and shade, with the staff of a silken standard
firm in his hand, Marius felt as if he were face to face, for the
first time, with some new knighthood or chivalry, just then
coming into the world.

It was soon after they left this place, journeying now by
carriage, that Rome was seen at last, with much excitement on

the part of our travellers; Cornelius, and some others of whom the party then consisted, agreeing, chiefly for the sake of Marius, to hasten forward, that it might be reached by daylight, with a cheerful noise of rapid wheels as they passed over the flag-stones. But the highest light upon the mausoleum of Hadrian was quite gone out, and it was dark, before they reached the *Flaminian* Gate. The abundant sound of water was the one thing that impressed Marius, as they passed down a long street, with many open spaces on either hand: Cornelius to his military quarters, and Marius to the old dwelling-place of his fathers.

CHAPTER XI

'THE MOST RELIGIOUS CITY IN THE WORLD'

MARIUS awoke early and passed curiously from room to room, noting for more careful inspection by and by the rolls of manuscripts. Even greater than his curiosity in gazing for the first time on this ancient possession, was his eagerness to look out upon Rome itself, as he pushed back curtain and shutter, and stepped forth in the fresh morning upon one of the many balconies, with an oft-repeated dream realized at last. He was certainly fortunate in the time of his coming to Rome. That old pagan world, of which Rome was the flower, had reached its perfection in the things of poetry and art—a perfection which indicated only too surely the eve of decline. As in some vast intellectual museum, all its manifold products were intact and in their places, and with custodians also still extant, duly qualified to appreciate and explain them. And at no period of history had the material Rome itself been better worth seeing—lying there not less consummate than that world of pagan intellect which it represented in every phase of its darkness and light. The various work of many ages fell here harmoniously together, as yet untouched save by time, adding the final grace of a rich softness to its complex expression. Much which spoke of ages earlier than Nero, the great re-builder, lingered on, antique, quaint, immeasurably venerable, like the relics of the medieval city in the Paris of Louis the Fourteenth: the work of Nero's own time had come to have that sort of old-world and picturesque interest which the work of Louis has for ourselves; while without stretching a parallel too far we might perhaps liken the architectural *finesses* of the archaic Hadrian to the more excellent products of our own Gothic revival. The temple of Antoninus and Faustina was still fresh in all the majesty of its closely arrayed columns of *cipollino*; but, on the whole, little had been added under the late and present emperors, and during fifty years of public quiet, a sober brown and grey had grown apace on things. The gilding on the roof of many a temple had lost its garishness: cornice and capital of polished marble shone out with all the crisp freshness of real flowers, amid the already mouldering travertine and brickwork, though the birds had built freely among them. What Marius then saw was in many respects, after all deduction of difference, more like the modern Rome than the enumeration of particular losses might lead us to suppose; the Renaissance, in its most ambitious mood and with amplest resources, having resumed the ancient classical tradition there, with no break or obstruction, as it had happened, in any very considerable work of the Middle Age. Immediately before him, on the square, steep height, where the earliest little old Rome had huddled itself together, arose the palace of the Caesars. Half-veiling the vast substruction of rough, brown stone—line upon line of successive ages of builders—the trim, old-fashioned garden walks, under their closely-woven walls of dark glossy foliage, test of long and careful cultivation, wound gradually, among choice trees, statues and fountains, distinct and sparkling in the full morning sunlight, to the richly tinted mass of pavilions and corridors above, centring in the lofty, white-marble dwelling-place of Apollo himself.

How often had Marius looked forward to that first, free wandering through Rome, to which he now went forth, with a heat in the town sunshine (like a mist of fine gold dust spread through the air) to the height of his desire, making the dun coolness of the narrow streets welcome enough at intervals. He almost feared, descending the stair hastily, lest some unforeseen accident should snatch the little cup of enjoyment from him ere he passed the door. In such morning rambles in places new to him, life had always seemed to come at its fullest: it was then he could feel his youth, that youth the days of which he had already begun to count jealously, in entire possession. So the grave, pensive figure, a figure, be it said nevertheless, fresher far than often came across it now, moved through the old city towards the lodgings of Cornelius, certainly not by the most direct course, however eager to rejoin the friend of yesterday.

Bent as keenly on seeing as if his first day in Rome were to be also his last, the two friends descended along the *Vicus Tuscus*, with its rows of incense stalls, into the *Via Nova*, where the fashionable people were busy shopping; and Marius saw with much amusement the frizzled heads, then *à la mode*. A glimpse of the *Marmorata*, the haven at the river-side, where specimens of all the precious marbles of the world were lying amid great white blocks from the quarries of Luna, took his thoughts for a moment to his distant home. They visited the flower market, lingering where the *coronarii* pressed on them the newest species, and purchased zinnias, now in blossom (like painted flowers, thought Marius), to decorate the folds of their togas. Loitering to the other side of the Forum, past the great Galen's drug-shop, after a glance at the announcements of new poems on sale attached to the doorpost of a famous bookseller, they entered the curious library of the Temple of Peace, then a favourite resort of literary men, and read, fixed there for all to see, the *Diurnal* or Gazette of the day, which announced, together with births and deaths, prodigies and accidents, and much mere matter of business, the date and manner of the philosophic emperor's joyful return to his people; and, thereafter, with eminent names faintly disguised, what would carry that day's news, in many copies, over the provinces—a certain matter concerning the great lady, known to be dear to him, whom he had left at home. It was a story with the development of which 'society' had indeed for some time past edified or amused itself, rallying sufficiently from the panic of a year ago, not only to welcome back its ruler, but also to relish a *chronique scandaleuse*; and thus, when soon after Marius saw the world's wonder, he was already acquainted with the suspicions which have ever since hung about her name. Twelve o'clock was come before they left the Forum, waiting in a little crowd to hear the *Accensus*, according to old custom, proclaim the hour of noonday, at the moment when from the steps of the Senate-house the sun could be seen standing between the *Rostra* and the *Graecostasis*. He exerted for this function a strength of voice which confirmed in Marius a judgment the modern visitor may share with him, that Roman throats and Roman chests, namely, must, in some peculiar way, be differently constructed from those of other people. Such judgment indeed he had formed in part the evening before, noting, as a religious procession passed him, how much noise a man and a boy could make, though not without a great deal of real music, of which in truth the Romans were then as ever passionately fond.

Hence the two friends took their way through the *Via Flaminia*, almost along the line of the modern *Corso*, already bordered with handsome villas, turning presently to the left, into the *Field-of-Mars*, still the playground of Rome. But the vast public edifices were grown to be almost continuous over the grassy expanse, represented now only by occasional open spaces of verdure and wild-flowers. In one of these a crowd was standing, to watch a party of athletes stripped for exercise. Marius had been surprised at the luxurious variety of the litters borne through Rome, where no carriage horses were allowed; and just then one far more sumptuous than the rest, with dainty appointments of ivory and gold, was carried by, all the town pressing with eagerness to get a glimpse of its most beautiful woman, as she passed rapidly. Yes! there, was the wonder of the world—the empress Faustina herself: Marius could distinguish, could distinguish clearly, the well-known profile, between the floating purple curtains.

For indeed all Rome was ready to burst into gaiety again, as it awaited with much real affection, hopeful and animated, the return of its emperor, for whose *ovation* various adornments were preparing along the streets through which the imperial procession would pass. He had left Rome just twelve months before, amid immense gloom. The alarm of a barbarian insurrection along the whole line of the Danube had happened at the moment when Rome was panic-stricken by the great pestilence.

In fifty years of peace, broken only by that conflict in the East from which Lucius Verus, among other curiosities, brought back the plague, war had come to seem a merely romantic, superannuated incident of bygone history. And now it was almost upon Italian soil. Terrible were the reports of the numbers and audacity of the assailants. Aurelius, as yet untried in war, and understood by a few only in the whole scope of a really great character, was known to the majority of his subjects as but a careful administrator, though a student of philosophy, perhaps, as we say, a *dilettante*. But he was also the visible centre of government, towards whom the hearts of a whole people turned, grateful for fifty years of public happiness —its good genius, its 'Antonine'—whose fragile person might be foreseen speedily giving way under the trials of military life, with a disaster like that of the slaughter of the legions by Arminius. Prophecies of the world's impending conflagration were easily credited: 'the secular fire' would descend from heaven: superstitious fear had even demanded the sacrifice of a human victim.

Marcus Aurelius, always philosophically considerate of the humours of other people, exercising also that devout appreciation of every religious claim which was one of his characteristic habits, had invoked, in aid of the commonwealth, not only all native gods, but all foreign deities as well, however strange.—

'Help! Help! in the ocean space!' A multitude of foreign priests had been welcomed to Rome, with their various peculiar religious rites. The sacrifices made on this occasion were remembered for centuries; and the starving poor, at least, found some satisfaction in the flesh of those herds of 'white bulls' which came into the city, day after day, to yield the savour of their blood to the gods.

In spite of all this, the legions had but followed their standards despondently. But prestige, personal prestige, the name of 'Emperor', still had its magic power over the nations. The mere approach of the Roman army made an impression on the barbarians. Aurelius and his colleague had scarcely reached Aquileia when a deputation arrived to ask for peace. And now the two imperial 'brothers' were returning home at leisure; were waiting, indeed, at a villa outside the walls, till the capital had made ready to receive them. But although Rome was thus in genial reaction, with much relief, and hopefulness against the winter, facing itself industriously in damask of red and gold, those two enemies were still unmistakably extant: the barbarian army of the Danube was but overawed for a season; and the plague, as we saw when Marius was on his way to Rome, was not to depart till it had done a large part in the formation of the melancholy picturesque of modern Italy—till it had made, or prepared for the making of the Roman *Campagna*. The old, unaffected, really pagan, peace or gaiety, of Antoninus Pius—that genuine though unconscious humanist—was gone for ever. And again and again, throughout this day of varied observation, Marius had been reminded above all else, that he was not merely in 'the most religious city of the world', as one had said, but that Rome was become the romantic home of the wildest superstition. Such superstition presented itself almost as religious mania in many an incident of his long ramble,— incidents to which he gave his full attention, though contending in some measure with a reluctance on the part of his companion, the motive of which he did not understand till long afterwards. Marius certainly did not allow this reluctance to deter his own curiosity. Had he not come to Rome partly under poetic vocation, to receive all those things, the very impress of life itself, upon the visual, the imaginative, organ, as upon a mirror; to reflect them; to transmute them into golden words? He must observe that strange medley of superstition, that centuries' growth, layer upon layer, of the curiosities of religion (one faith jostling another out of place) at least for its picturesque interest, and as an indifferent outsider might, not too deeply concerned in the question which, if any of them, was to be the survivor.

Superficially, at least, the Roman religion, allying itself with much diplomatic economy to possible rivals, was in possession, as a vast and complex system of usage, intertwining itself with every detail of public and private life, attractively enough for those who had but 'the historic temper', and a taste for the past, however much a Lucian might depreciate it. Roman religion, as Marius knew, had, indeed, been always something to be done, rather than something to be thought, or believed, or loved; something to be done in minutely detailed manner, at a particular time and place, correctness in which had long been a matter of laborious learning with a whole school of ritualists—as also, now and again, a matter of heroic sacrifice with certain exceptionally devout souls, as when Caius Fabius Dorso, with his life in his hand, succeeded in passing the sentinels of the invading Gauls to perform a sacrifice on the Quirinal, and, thanks to the divine protection, had returned in safety. So jealous was the distinction between sacred and profane, that, in the matter of the 'regarding of days', it had made more than half the year a holiday. Aurelius had, indeed, ordained that there should be no more than a hundred and thirty-five festival days in the year; but in other respects he had followed in the steps of his predecessor, Antoninus Pius—commended especially for his 'religion', his conspicuous devotion to its public ceremonies—and whose coins are remarkable for their reference to the oldest and most hieratic types of Roman mythology. Aurelius had succeeded in more than healing the old feud between philosophy and religion, displaying himself, in singular combination, as at once the most zealous of philosophers and the most devout of polytheists, and lending himself, with an air of conviction, to all the pageantries of public worship. To his pious recognition of that one orderly spirit, which, according to the doctrine of the Stoics, diffuses itself through the world, and animates it—a recognition taking the form, with him, of a constant effort towards inward likeness thereto, in the harmonious order of his own soul—he had added a warm personal devotion towards the whole multitude of the old national gods, and a great many new foreign ones besides, by him, at least, not ignobly conceived. If the comparison may be reverently made, there was something here of the method by which the Catholic Church has added the *cultus* of the saints to its worship of the one Divine Being.

And to the view of the majority, though the emperor, as the personal centre of religion, entertained the hope of converting his people to philosophic faith, and had even pronounced certain public discourses for their instruction in it, that polytheistic devotion was his most striking feature. Philosophers, indeed, had, for the most part, thought with Seneca, 'that a man need not lift his hands to heaven, nor ask the sacristan's leave to put his mouth to the ear of an image, that his prayers might be heard the better'.—Marcus Aurelius, 'a master in Israel', knew all that well enough. Yet his outward devotion was much more than a concession to popular sentiment, or a mere result of that sense of fellow-citizenship with others, which had made him again and again, under most difficult circumstances, an excellent comrade. Those others, too!—amid all their ignorances, what were they but instruments in the administration of the Divine Reason, 'from end to end sweetly and strongly disposing all things'? Meantime 'Philosophy' itself had assumed much of what we conceive to be the religious character. It had even cultivated the habit, the power, of 'spiritual direction'; the troubled soul making recourse in its hour of destitution, or amid the distractions of the world, to this or that director—*philosopho suo*—who could really best understand it.

And it had been in vain that the old, grave and discreet religion of Rome had set itself, according to its proper genius, to prevent or subdue all trouble and disturbance in men's souls. In religion, as in other matters, plebeians, as such, had a taste for movement, for revolution; and it had been ever in the most populous quarters that religious changes began. To the apparatus of foreign religion, above all, recourse had been made in times of public disquietude or sudden terror; and in those great religious celebrations, before his proceeding against the barbarians, Aurelius had even restored the solemnities of Isis, prohibited in the capital since the time of Augustus, making no secret of his worship of that goddess, though her temple had been actually destroyed by authority in the reign of Tiberius. Her singular and in many ways beautiful ritual was now popular in Rome. And then—what the enthusiasm of the swarming plebeian quarters had initiated, was sure to be adopted, sooner or later, by women of fashion. A blending of all the religions of the ancient world had been accomplished. The new gods had arrived, had been welcomed, and found their places; though, certainly, with no real security, in any adequate ideal of the divine nature itself in the background of men's minds, that the presence of the new-comer should be edifying, or even refining. High and low addressed themselves to all deities alike without scruple; confusing them together when they prayed, and in the old, authorized, threefold veneration of their visible images, by flowers, incense, and ceremonial lights—those beautiful usages, which the Church, in her way through the world, ever making spoil of the world's goods for the better uses of the human spirit, took up and sanctified in her service.

And certainly 'the most religious city in the world' took no care to veil its devotion, however fantastic. The humblest house had its little chapel or shrine, its image and lamp; while almost every one seemed to exercise some religious function and responsibility. Colleges, composed for the most part of slaves and of the poor, provided for the service of the *Compitalian Lares*—the gods who presided, respectively, over the several quarters of the city. In one street, Marius witnessed an incident of the festival of the patron deity of that neighbourhood, the way being strewn with box, the houses tricked out gaily in such poor finery as they possessed, while the ancient idol was borne through it in procession, arrayed in gaudy attire the worse for wear. Numerous religious clubs had their stated anniversaries, on which the members issued with much ceremony from their guild-hall, or *schola*, and traversed the thoroughfares of Rome, preceded, like the confraternities of the present day, by their sacred banners, to offer sacrifice before some famous image. Black with the perpetual smoke of lamps and incense, oftenest old and ugly, perhaps on that account the more likely to listen to the desires of the suffering—had not those sacred effigies sometimes given sensible tokens that they were aware? The image of the Fortune of Women—*Fortuna Muliebris*, in the Latin Way, had spoken (not once only) and declared: *Bene me, Matronae ! vidistis riteque dedicastis !* The Apollo of Cumae had wept during three whole nights and days. The images in the temple of Juno Sospita had been seen to sweat. Nay! there was blood—divine blood—in the hearts of some of them: the images in the Grove of Feronia had sweated blood!

From one and all Cornelius had turned away: like the 'atheist' of whom Apuleius tells he had never once raised hand to lip in passing image or sanctuary, and had parted from Marius finally when the latter determined to enter the crowded doorway of a temple, on their return into the Forum, below the Palatine hill, where the mothers were pressing in, with a multitude of every sort of children, to touch the lightning-struck image of the wolf-nurse of Romulus—so tender to little ones!—just discernible in its dark shrine, amid a blaze of lights. Marius gazed after his companion of the day, as he mounted the steps to his lodging, singing to himself, as it seemed. Marius failed precisely to catch the words.

And, as the rich, fresh evening came on, there was heard all over Rome, far above a whisper, the whole town seeming hushed to catch it distinctly, the lively, reckless call to 'play', from the sons and daughters of foolishness, to those in whom their life was still green—*Donec virenti canities abest !—Donec virenti canities abest !* Marius could hardly doubt how Cornelius would have taken the call. And as for himself, slight as was the burden of positive moral obligation with which he had entered Rome, it was to no wasteful and vagrant affections, such as these, that his Epicureanism had committed him.

CHAPTER XII

THE DIVINITY THAT DOTH HEDGE A KING

> But ah! Maecenas is yclad in claye,
> And great Augustus long ygoe is dead,
> And all the worthies liggen wrapt in lead,
> That matter made for poets on to playe.

MARCUS AURELIUS who, though he had little relish for them himself, had ever been willing to humour the taste of his people for magnificent spectacles, was received back to Rome with the lesser honours of the *Ovation*, conceded by the Senate (so great was the public sense of deliverance) with even more than the laxity which had become its habit under imperial rule, for there had been no actual bloodshed in the late achievement. Clad in the civic dress of the chief Roman magistrate, and with a crown of myrtle upon his head, his colleague similarly attired walking beside him, he passed up to the Capitol on foot, though in solemn procession along the Sacred Way, to offer sacrifice to the national gods. The victim, a goodly sheep, whose image we may still see between the pig and the ox of the *Suovetaurilia*, filleted and stoled almost like some ancient canon of the Church, on a sculptured fragment in the Forum, was conducted by the priests, clad in rich white vestments, and bearing their sacred utensils of massive gold, immediately behind a company of flute-players, led by the great choir-master, or *conductor*, of the day, visibly tetchy or delighted, according as the instruments he ruled with his tuning-rod, rose, more or less adequately amid the difficulties of the way, to the dream of perfect music in the soul within him. The vast crowd, including the soldiers of the triumphant army, now restored to wives and children, all alike in holiday whiteness, had left their houses early in the fine, dry morning, in a real affection for 'the father of his country', to await the procession, the two princes having spent the preceding night outside the walls, at the old *Villa of the Republic*. Marius, full of curiosity, had taken his position with much care; and stood to see the world's masters pass by, at an angle from which he could command the view of a great part of the processional route, sprinkled with fine yellow sand, and punctiliously guarded from profane footsteps.

The coming of the pageant was announced by the clear sound of the flutes, heard at length above the acclamations of the people—*Salve Imperator !—Dii te servent !*—shouted in regular time, over the hills. It was on the central figure, of course, that the whole attention of Marius was fixed from the moment when the procession came in sight, preceded by the lictors with gilded *fasces*, the imperial image-bearers, and the pages carrying lighted torches; a band of knights, among whom was Cornelius in complete military array, following. Amply swathed about in the folds of a richly worked toga, after a manner now long since become obsolete with meaner persons, Marius beheld a man of about five-and-forty years of age, with prominent eyes—eyes which, although demurely downcast during this essentially religious ceremony, were by nature broadly and benignantly observant. He was still, in the main, as we see him in the busts which represent his gracious and courtly youth, when Hadrian had playfully called him, not *Verus*, after the name of his father, but *Verissimus*, for his candour of gaze, and the bland capacity of the brow, which, below the brown hair, clustering thickly as of old, shone out low, broad, and clear, and still without a trace of the trouble of his lips. You saw the brow of one who, amid the blindness or perplexity of the people about him, understood all things clearly; the dilemma, to which his experience so far had brought him, between Chance with meek resignation, and a Providence with boundless possibilities and hope, being for him at least distinctly defined.

That outward serenity, which he valued so highly as a point of manner or expression not unworthy the care of a public minister—outward symbol, it might be thought, of the inward religious serenity it had been his constant purpose to maintain —was increased to-day by his sense of the gratitude of his people; that his life had been one of such gifts and blessings as made his person seem in very deed divine to them. Yet the cloud of some reserved internal sorrow, passing from time to time into an expression of fatigue and effort, of loneliness amid the shouting multitude, might have been detected there by the more observant—as if the sagacious hint of one of his officers, 'The soldiers can't understand you, they don't know Greek', were appliable always to his relationships with other people. The nostrils and mouth seemed capable almost of peevishness; and Marius noted in them, as in the hands, and in the spare body generally, what was new to his experience—something of asceticism, as we say, of a bodily gymnastic, by which, although it told pleasantly in the clear blue humours of the eye, the flesh had scarcely been an equal gainer with the spirit. It was hardly the expression of 'the healthy mind in the healthy body', but rather of a sacrifice of the body to the soul, its needs and aspirations, that Marius seemed to divine in this assiduous student of the Greek sages—a sacrifice, in truth, far beyond the demands of their very saddest philosophy of life.

Dignify thyself with modesty and simplicity for thine ornaments!—had been ever a maxim with this dainty and high-bred Stoic, who still thought *manners* a true part of *morals*, according to the old sense of the term, and who regrets now and again that he cannot control his thoughts equally well with his countenance. That outward composure was deepened during the solemnities of this day by an air of pontifical abstraction; which, though very far from being pride—nay, a sort of humility rather—yet gave, to himself, an air of unapproachableness, and to his whole proceeding, in which every minutest act was considered, the character of a ritual. Certainly, there was no haughtiness, social, moral, or even philosophic, in Aurelius, who had realized, under more trying conditions perhaps than any one before, that no element of humanity could be alien from him. Yet, as he walked to-day, the centre of ten thousand observers, with eyes discreetly fixed on the ground, veiling his head at times and muttering very rapidly the words of the 'supplications', there was something many spectators may have noted as a thing new in their experience, for Aurelius, unlike his predecessors, took all this with absolute seriousness. The doctrine of the sanctity of kings, that, in the words of Tacitus, Princes are as gods—*Principes instar deorum esse*—seemed to have taken a novel, because a literal, sense. For Aurelius, indeed, the old legend of his descent from Numa, from Numa who had talked with the gods, meant much. Attached in very early years to the service of the altars, like many another noble youth, he was 'observed to perform all his sacerdotal functions with a constancy and exactness unusual at that age; was soon a master of the sacred music; and had all the forms and cere-monies by heart'. And now, as the emperor, who had not only a vague divinity about his person, but was actually the chief religious functionary of the state, recited from time to time the forms of invocation, he needed not the help of the prompter, or *ceremoniarius*, who then approached, to assist him by whispering the appointed words in his ear. It was that pontifical abstraction which then impressed itself on Marius as the leading outward characteristic of Aurelius; though to him alone, perhaps, in that vast crowd of observers, it was no strange thing, but a matter he had understood from of old.

Some fanciful writers have assigned the origin of these triumphal processions to the mythic pomps of Dionysus, after his conquests in the East; the very word *Triumph* being, according to this supposition, only *Thriambos*—the Dionysiac Hymn. And certainly the younger of the two imperial 'brothers', who, with the effect of a strong contrast, walked beside Aurelius, and shared the honours of the day, might well have reminded people of the delicate Greek god of flowers and wine. This new conqueror of the East was now about thirty-six years old, but with his scrupulous care for all the advantages of his person, and a soft curling beard powdered with gold, looked many years younger. One result of the more genial element in the wisdom of Aurelius had been that, amid most difficult circumstances, he had known throughout life how to act in union with persons of character very alien from his own; to be more than loyal to the colleague, the younger brother in empire, he had too lightly taken to himself, five years before, then an uncorrupt youth, 'skilled in manly exercises and fitted for war'. When Aurelius thanks the gods that a brother had fallen to his lot, whose character was a stimulus to the proper care of his own, one sees that this could only have happened in the way of an example, putting him on his guard against insidious faults. But it is with sincere amiability that the imperial writer, who was indeed little used to be ironical, adds that the lively respect and affection of the junior had often 'gladdened' him. To be able to make his use of the flower, when the fruit perhaps was useless or poisonous:— that was one of the practical successes of his philosophy; and his people noted, with a blessing, 'the concord of the two Augusti'.

The younger, certainly, possessed in full measure that charm of a constitutional freshness of aspect which may defy for a long time extravagant or erring habits of life; a physiognomy, healthy-looking, cleanly, and firm, which seemed unassociable with any form of self-torment, and made one think of the muzzle of some young hound or roe, such as human beings invariably

like to stroke—a physiognomy, in effect, with all the goodliness
of animalism of the finer sort, though still wholly animal.
The charm was that of the blond head, the unshrinking gaze,
the warm tints: neither more nor less than one may see every
English summer, in youth, manly enough, and with the stuff
which makes brave soldiers, in spite of the natural kinship it
seems to have with playthings and gay flowers. But innate
in Lucius Verus there was that more than womanly fondness
for fond things, which had made the atmosphere of the old
city of Antioch, heavy with centuries of voluptuousness, a
poison to him: he had come to love his delicacies best out of
season, and would have gilded the very flowers. But with a
wonderful power of self-obliteration, the elder brother at the
capital had directed his procedure successfully, and allowed
him, become now also the husband of his daughter Lucilla,
the credit of a 'Conquest', though Verus had certainly not
returned a conqueror over himself. He had returned, as we
know, with the plague in his company, along with many
another strange creature of his folly; and when the people saw
him publicly feeding his favourite horse *Fleet* with almonds
and sweet grapes, wearing the animal's image in gold, and
finally building it a tomb, they felt, with some unsentimental
misgiving, that he might revive the manners of Nero.—What
if, in the chances of war, he should survive the protecting
genius of that elder brother?

He was all himself to-day: and it was with much wistful
curiosity that Marius regarded him. For Lucius Verus was,
indeed, but the highly expressive type of a class—the true son
of his father, adopted by Hadrian. Lucius Verus the elder,
also, had had the like strange capacity for misusing the adornments of life, with a masterly grace; as if such misusing were,
in truth, the quite adequate occupation of an intelligence,
powerful, but distorted by cynical philosophy or some disappointment of the heart. It was almost a sort of genius, of
which there had been instances in the imperial purple: it was
to ascend the throne, a few years later, in the person of one,
now a hopeful little lad at home in the palace; and it had its
following, of course, among the wealthy youth of Rome, who
concentrated no inconsiderable force of shrewdness and tact
upon minute details of attire and manner, as upon the one
thing needful. Certainly, flowers were pleasant to the eye.
Such things had even their sober use, as making the outside
of human life superficially attractive, and thereby promoting

the first steps towards friendship and social amity. But what precise place could there be for Verus and his peculiar charm, in that *Wisdom*, that Order of divine Reason 'reaching from end to end, strongly and sweetly disposing all things', from the vision of which Aurelius came down, so tolerant of persons like him? Into such vision Marius too was certainly well-fitted to enter, yet, noting the actual perfection of Lucius Verus after his kind, his undeniable achievement of the select, in all minor things, felt, though with some suspicion of himself, that he entered into, and could understand, this other so dubious sort of character also. There was a voice in the theory he had brought to Rome with him which whispered 'nothing is either great nor small'; as there were times when he could have thought that, as the 'grammarian's' or the artist's ardour of soul may be satisfied by the perfecting of the theory of a sentence, or the adjustment of two colours, so his own life also might have been fulfilled by an enthusiastic quest after perfection;—say, in the flowering and folding of a toga.

The emperors had burned incense before the image of Jupiter, arrayed in its most gorgeous apparel, amid sudden shouts from the people of *Salve Imperator !* turned now from the living princes to the deity, as they discerned his countenance through the great open doors. The imperial brothers had deposited their crowns of myrtle on the richly embroidered lapcloth of the god; and, with their chosen guests, sat down to a public feast in the temple itself. There followed what was, after all, the great event of the day:—an appropriate discourse, a discourse almost wholly *de contemptu mundi*, delivered in the presence of the assembled Senate, by the Emperor Aurelius, who had thus, on certain rare occasions, condescended to instruct his people, with the double authority of a chief pontiff and a laborious student of philosophy. In those lesser honours of the *Ovation* there had been no attendant slave behind the emperors, to make mock of their effulgence as they went; and it was as if with the discretion proper to a philosopher, and in fear of a jealous Nemesis, he had determined himself to protest in time against the vanity of all outward success.

The Senate was assembled to hear the emperor's discourse in the vast hall of the *Curia Julia*. A crowd of high-bred youths idled around, or on the steps before the doors, with the marvellous toilets Marius had noticed in the *Via Nova*; in attendance, as usual, to learn by observation the minute points of senatorial procedure. Marius had already some acquaintance with them, and passing on found himself suddenly in the presence of what was still the most august assembly the world had seen. Under Aurelius, ever full of veneration for this ancient traditional guardian of public religion, the Senate had recovered all its old dignity and independence. Among its members many hundreds in number, visibly the most distinguished of them all, Marius noted the great sophists or rhetoricians of the day, in all their magnificence. The antique character of their attire, and the ancient mode of wearing it, still surviving with them, added to the imposing character of their persons, while they sat, with their staves of ivory in their hands, on their curule chairs—almost the exact pattern of the chair still in use in the Roman Church when a bishop *pontificates* at the divine offices—'tranquil and unmoved, with a majesty that seemed divine', as Marius thought, like the old Gaul of the Invasion. The rays of the early November sunset slanted full upon the audience, and made it necessary for the officers of the Court to draw the purple curtains over the windows, adding to the solemnity of the scene. In the depth of those warm shadows, surrounded by her ladies, the Empress Faustina was seated to listen. The beautiful Greek statue of Victory, which since the days of Augustus had presided over the assemblies of the Senate, had been brought into the hall, and placed near the chair of the emperor; who, after rising to perform a brief sacrificial service in its honour, bowing reverently to the assembled fathers left and right, took his seat and began to speak.

There was a certain melancholy grandeur in the very simplicity or triteness of the theme: as it were the very quintessence of all the old Roman epitaphs, of all that was monumental in that city of tombs, layer upon layer of dead things and people. As if in the very fervour of disillusion, he seemed to be composing —ὥσπερ ἐπιγραφὰς χρόνων καὶ ὅλων ἔθνων—the sepulchral titles of ages and whole peoples; nay! the very epitaph of the living Rome itself. The grandeur of the ruins of Rome,— heroism in ruin: it was under the influence of an imaginative anticipation of this, that he appeared to be speaking. And though the impression of the actual greatness of Rome on that day was but enhanced by the strain of contempt, falling with an accent of pathetic conviction from the emperor himself, and gaining from his pontifical pretensions the authority of a religious intimation, yet the curious interest of the discourse lay in this, that Marius, for one, as he listened, seemed to foresee a grass-grown Forum, the broken ways of the Capitol, and the

Palatine hill itself in humble occupation. That impression connected itself with what he had already noted of an actual change even then coming over Italian scenery. Throughout, he could trace something of a humour into which Stoicism at all times tends to fall, the tendency to cry, *Abase yourselves!* There was here the almost inhuman impassibility of one who had thought too closely on the paradoxical aspect of the love of posthumous fame. With the ascetic pride which lurks under all Platonism, resultant from its opposition of the seen to the unseen, as falsehood to truth—the imperial Stoic, like his true descendant, the hermit of the Middle Age, was ready, in no friendly humour, to mock, there in its narrow bed, the corpse which had made so much of itself in life. Marius could but contrast all that with his own Cyrenaic eagerness, just then, to taste and see and touch; reflecting on the opposite issues deducible from the same text. 'The world, within me and without, flows away like a river', he had said; 'therefore let me make the most of what is here and now.'—'The world and the thinker upon it, are consumed like a flame', said Aurelius, 'therefore will I turn away my eyes from vanity: renounce: withdraw myself alike from all affections.' He seemed tacitly to claim as a sort of personal dignity, that he was very familiarly versed in this view of things, and could discern a death's-head everywhere. Now and again Marius was reminded of the saying that 'with the Stoics all people are the vulgar save themselves'; and at times the orator seemed to have forgotten his audience, and to be speaking only to himself.

'Art thou in love with men's praises, get thee into the very soul of them, and see!—see what judges they be, even in those matters which concern themselves. Wouldst thou have their praise after death, bethink thee, that they who shall come hereafter, and with whom thou wouldst survive by thy great name, will be but as these, whom here thou hast found so hard to live with. For of a truth, the soul of him who is aflutter upon renown after death, presents not this aright to itself, that of all whose memory he would have each one will likewise very quickly depart, until memory herself be put out, as she journeys on by means of such as are themselves on the wing but for a while, and are extinguished in their turn.—Making so much of those thou wilt never see! It is as if thou wouldst have had those who were before thee discourse fair things concerning thee.

'To him, indeed, whose wit hath been whetted by true

doctrine, that well-worn sentence of Homer sufficeth, to guard him against regret and fear.—

> Like the race of leaves
> The race of man is:—

> The wind in autumn strows
> The earth with old leaves: then the spring the woods with new endows.

Leaves! little leaves!—thy children, thy flatterers, thine enemies! Leaves in the wind, those who would devote thee to darkness, who scorn or miscall thee here, even as they also whose great fame shall outlast them. For all these, and the like of them, are born indeed in the spring season—*ἔαρος ἐπιγίγνεται ὥρῃ*: and soon a wind hath scattered them, and thereafter the wood peopleth itself again with another generation of leaves. And what is common to all of them is but the littleness of their lives: and yet wouldst thou love and hate, as if these things should continue for ever. In a little while thine eyes also will be closed, and he on whom thou perchance hast leaned thyself be himself a burden upon another.

'Bethink thee often of the swiftness with which the things that are, or are even now coming to be, are swept past thee: that the very substance of them is but the perpetual motion of water: that there is almost nothing which continueth: of that bottomless depth of time, so close at thy side. Folly! to be lifted up, or sorrowful, or anxious, by reason of things like these! Think of infinite matter, and thy portion—how tiny a particle, of it! of infinite time, and thine own brief point there; of destiny, and the jot thou art in it; and yield thyself readily to the wheel of Clotho, to spin of thee what web she will.

'As one casting a ball from his hand, the nature of things hath had its aim with every man, not as to the ending only, but the first beginning of his course, and passage thither. And hath the ball any profit of its rising, or loss as it descendeth again, or in its fall? or the bubble, as it groweth or breaketh on the air? or the flame of the lamp, from the beginning to the end of its brief story?

'All but at this present that future is, in which nature, who disposeth all things in order, will transform whatsoever thou now seest, fashioning from its substance somewhat else, and therefrom somewhat else in its turn, lest the world grow old. We are such stuff as dreams are made of—disturbing dreams. Awake, then! and see thy dream as it is, in comparison with that erewhile it seemed to thee.

'And for me, especially, it were well to mind those many mutations of empire in time past; therein peeping also upon the future, which must needs be of like species with what hath been, continuing ever within the rhythm and number of things which really are; so that in forty years one may note of man and of his ways little less than in a thousand. Ah! from this higher place, look we down upon the shipwrecks and the calm! Consider, for example, how the world went, under the Emperor Vespasian. They are married and given in marriage, they breed children; love hath its way with them; they heap up riches for others or for themselves; they are murmuring at things as then they are; they are seeking for great place; crafty, flattering, suspicious, waiting upon the death of others:— festivals, business, war, sickness, dissolution: and now their whole life is no longer anywhere at all. Pass on to the reign of Trajan: all things continue the same: and that life also is no longer anywhere at all. Ah! but look again, and consider, one after another, as it were the sepulchral inscriptions of all peoples and times, according to one pattern.—What multitudes, after their utmost striving—a little afterwards! were dissolved again into their dust.

'Think again of life as it was far off in the ancient world; as it must be when we shall be gone; as it is now among the wild heathen. How many have never heard your names and mine, or will soon forget them! How soon may those who shout my name to-day begin to revile it, because glory, and the memory of men, and all things beside, are but vanity—a sand-heap under the senseless wind, the barking of dogs, the quarrelling of children, weeping incontinently upon their laughter.

'This hasteth to be; that other to have been: of that which now cometh to be, even now somewhat hath been extinguished. And wilt thou make thy treasure of any one of these things? It were as if one set his love upon the swallow, as it passeth out of sight through the air!

'Bethink thee often, in all contentions public and private, of those whom men have remembered by reason of their anger and vehement spirit—those famous rages, and the occasions of them—the great fortunes, and misfortunes, of men's strife of old. What are they all now, and the dust of their battles? Dust and ashes indeed; a fable, a mythus, or not so much as that. Yes! keep those before thine eyes who took this or that, the like of which happeneth to thee, so hardly; were so querulous, so agitated. And where again are they? Wouldst thou have it not otherwise with thee?

'Consider how quickly all things vanish away—their bodily structure into the general substance; the very memory of them into that great gulf and abysm of past thoughts. Ah! 'tis on a tiny space of earth thou art creeping through life—a pigmy soul carrying a dead body to its grave.

'Let death put thee upon the consideration both of thy body and thy soul: what an atom of all matter hath been distributed to thee; what a little particle of the universal mind. Turn thy body about, and consider what thing it is, and that which old age, and lust, and the languor of disease can make of it. Or come to its substantial and causal qualities, its very type: contemplate that in itself, apart from the accidents of matter, and then measure also the span of time for which the nature of things, at the longest, will maintain that special type. Nay! in the very principles and first constituents of things corruption hath its part—so much dust, humour, stench, and scraps of bone! Consider that thy marbles are but the earth's callosities, thy gold and silver its *faeces*; this silken robe but a worm's bedding, and thy purple an unclean fish. Ah! and thy life's breath is not otherwise, as it passeth out of matters like these, into the like of them again.

'For the one soul in things, taking matter like wax in the hands, moulds and remoulds—how hastily!—beast, and plant, and the babe, in turn: and that which dieth hath not slipped out of the order of nature, but, remaining therein, hath also its changes there, disparting into those elements of which nature herself, and thou too, art compacted. She changes without murmuring. The oaken chest falls to pieces with no more complaining than when the carpenter fitted it together. If one told thee certainly that on the morrow thou shouldst die, or at the furthest on the day after, it would be no great matter to thee to die on the day after to-morrow, rather than to-morrow. Strive to think it a thing no greater that thou wilt die—not to-morrow, but a year, or two years, or ten years from to-day.

'I find that all things are now as they were in the days of our buried ancestors—all things sordid in their elements, trite by long usage, and yet ephemeral. How ridiculous, then, how like a countryman in town, is he, who wonders at aught. Doth the sameness, the repetition of the public shows, weary thee? Even so doth that likeness of events in the spectacle of the world. And so must it be with thee to the end. For the wheel of the world hath ever the same motion, upward and downward, from generation to generation. When, when shall time give place to eternity?

'If there be things which trouble thee thou canst put them away, inasmuch as they have their being but in thine own notion concerning them. Consider what death is, and how, if one does but detach from it the appearances, the notions, that hang about it, resting the eye upon it as in itself it really is, it must be thought of but as an effect of nature, and that man but a child whom an effect of nature shall affright. Nay! not function and effect of nature, only; but a thing profitable also to herself.

'To cease from action—the ending of thine effort to think and do: there is no evil in that. Turn thy thought to the ages of man's life, boyhood, youth, maturity, old age: the change in every one of these also is a dying, but evil nowhere. Thou climbedst into the ship, thou hast made thy voyage and touched the shore: go forth now! Be it into some other life: the divine breath is everywhere, even there. Be it into forgetfulness for ever: at least thou wilt rest from the beating of sensible images upon thee, from the passions which pluck thee this way and that like an unfeeling toy, from those long marches of the intellect, from thy toilsome ministry to the flesh.

'Art thou yet more than dust and ashes and bare bone—a name only, or not so much as that, which, also, is but whispering and a resonance, kept alive from mouth to mouth of dying abjects who have hardly known themselves; how much less thee, dead so long ago!

'When thou lookest upon a wise man, a lawyer, a captain of war, think upon another gone. When thou seest thine own face in the glass, call up there before thee one of thine ancestors —one of those old Caesars. Lo! everywhere, thy double before thee! Thereon, let the thought occur to thee: And where are they? anywhere at all, for ever? And thou, thyself—how long? Art thou blind to that thou art—thy matter, how temporal; and thy function, the nature of thy business? Yet tarry, at least, till thou hast assimilated even these things to thine own proper essence, as a quick fire turneth into heat and light whatsoever be cast upon it.

'As words once in use are antiquated to us, so is it with the names that were once on all men's lips: Camillus, Volesus, Leonnatus: then, in a little while, Scipio and Cato, and then Augustus, and then Hadrian, and then Antoninus Pius. How many great physicians who lifted wise brows at other men's sick-beds, have sickened and died! Those wise Chaldeans, who foretold, as a great matter, another man's last hour, have themselves been taken by surprise. Aye! and all those others, in their pleasant places: those who doated on a Capreae like Tiberius, on their gardens, on the baths: Pythagoras and Socrates, who reasoned so closely upon immortality: Alexander, who used the lives of others as though his own should last for ever—he and his mule-driver alike now!—one upon another. Wellnigh the whole court of Antoninus is extinct. Panthea and Pergamus sit no longer beside the sepulchre of their lord. The watchers over Hadrian's dust have slipped from his sepulchre. —It were jesting to stay longer. Did they sit there still, would the dead feel it? or feeling it, be glad? or glad, hold those watches for ever? The time must come when they too shall be aged men and aged women, and decease, and fail from their places; and what shift were there then for imperial service? This too is but the breath of the tomb, and a skinful of dead men's blood.

'Think again of those inscriptions, which belong not to one soul only, but to whole families: Ἔσχατος τοῦ ἰδίου γένους : *He was the last of his race*. Nay! of the burial of whole cities: Helice, Pompeii: of others, whose very burial-place is unknown.

'Thou hast been a citizen in this wide city. Count not for how long, nor repine; since that which sends thee hence is no unrighteous judge, no tyrant, but Nature, who brought thee hither; as when a player leaves the stage at the bidding of the conductor who hired him. Sayest thou, "I have not played five acts"? True! but in human life, three acts only make sometimes an entire play. That is the composer's business, not thine. Withdraw thyself with a good will; for that too hath, perchance, a good will which dismisseth thee from thy part.'

The discourse ended almost in darkness, the evening having set in somewhat suddenly, with a heavy fall of snow. The torches, made ready to do him a useless honour, were of real service now, as the emperor was solemnly conducted home; one man rapidly catching light from another—a long stream of moving lights across the white Forum, up the great stairs, to the palace. And, in effect, that night winter began, the hardest that had been known for a lifetime. The wolves came from the mountains; and, led by the carrion scent, devoured the dead bodies which had been hastily buried during the plague, and, emboldened by their meal, crept, before the short day was well past, over the walls of the farmyards of the *Campagna*. The eagles were seen driving the flocks of smaller birds across the dusky sky. Only, in the city itself the winter was all the brighter for the contrast, among those who could pay for light and warmth. The habit-makers made a great sale of the spoil of all such furry creatures as had escaped wolves and eagles, for presents at the *Saturnalia*; and at no time had the winter roses from Carthage seemed more lustrously yellow and red.

CHAPTER XIII

THE 'MISTRESS AND MOTHER' OF PALACES

AFTER that sharp, brief winter, the sun was already at work, softening leaf and bud, as you might feel by a faint sweetness in the air; but he did his work behind an evenly white sky, against which the abode of the Caesars, its cypresses and bronze roofs, seemed like a picture in beautiful but melancholy colour, as Marius climbed the long flights of steps to be introduced to the Emperor Aurelius. Attired in the newest mode, his legs wound in dainty *fasciae* of white leather, with the heavy gold ring of the *ingenuus*, and in his toga of ceremony, he still retained all his country freshness of complexion. The eyes of the 'golden youth' of Rome were upon him as the chosen friend of Cornelius, and the destined servant of the emperor; but not jealously. In spite of, perhaps partly because of, his habitual reserve of manner, he had become 'the fashion', even among those who felt instinctively the irony which lay beneath that remarkable self-possession, as of one taking all things with a difference from other people, perceptible in voice, in expression, and even in his dress. It was, in truth, the air of one who, entering vividly into life, and relishing to the full the delicacies of its intercourse, yet feels all the while, from the point of view of an ideal philosophy, that he is but conceding reality to suppositions, choosing of his own will to walk in a day-dream, of the illusiveness of which he at least is aware.

In the house of the chief chamberlain Marius waited for the due moment of admission to the emperor's presence. He was admiring the peculiar decoration of the walls, coloured like rich old red leather. In the midst of one of them was depicted, under a trellis of fruit you might have gathered, the figure of a woman knocking at a door with wonderfu reality of perspective. Then the summons came; and in a few minutes, the etiquette of the imperial household being still a simple matter, he had passed the curtains which divided the central hall of the palace into three parts—three degrees of approach to the sacred person —and was speaking to Aurelius himself; not in Greek, in which the emperor oftenest conversed with the learned, but, more familiarly, in Latin, adorned however, or disfigured, by many a Greek phrase, as now and again French phrases have made the adornment of fashionable English. It was with real kindliness that Marcus Aurelius looked upon Marius, as a youth of great attainments in Greek letters and philosophy; and he liked also his serious expression, being, as we know, a believer in the doctrine of physiognomy—that, as he puts it, not love only, but every other affection of man's soul, looks out very plainly from the window of the eyes.

The apartment in which Marius found himself was of ancient aspect, and richly decorated with the favourite toys of two or three generations of imperial collectors, now finally revised by the high connoisseurship of the Stoic emperor himself, though destined not much longer to remain together there. It is the repeated boast of Aurelius that he had learned from old Antoninus Pius to maintain authority without the constant use of guards, in a robe woven by the handmaids of his own consort, with no processional lights or images, and 'that a prince may shrink himself almost into the figure of a private gentleman'. And yet, again as at his first sight of him, Marius was struck by the profound religiousness of the surroundings of the imperial presence. The effect might have been due in part to the very simplicity, the discreet and scrupulous simplicity, of the central figure in this splendid abode; but Marius could not forget that he saw before him not only the head of the Roman religion, but one who might actually have claimed something like divine worship, had he cared to do so. Though the fantastic pretensions of Caligula had brought some contempt on that claim, which had become almost a jest under the ungainly Claudius, yet, from Augustus downwards, a vague divinity had seemed to surround the Caesars even in this life; and the peculiar character of Aurelius, at once a ceremonious polytheist never forgetful of his pontifical calling, and a philosopher whose mystic speculation encircled him with a sort of saintly halo, had restored to his person, without his intending it, something of that divine prerogative, or prestige. Though he would never allow the immediate dedication of altars to himself, yet the image of his *Genius*—his spirituality or celestial counterpart—was placed among those of the deified princes of the past; and his family, including Faustina and the young Commodus, was spoken of as the 'holy' or 'divine' house. Many a Roman courtier agreed with the barbarian chief, who, after contemplating a predecessor of Aurelius, withdrew from his presence with the exclamation: 'I have seen a god to-day!' The very roof of his house, rising into a pediment or gable, like that of the sanctuary of a god, the laurels on either side its doorway, the chaplet of oak-leaves above, seemed to designate the place for religious veneration. And notwithstanding all this, the household of Aurelius was singularly modest, with none of the wasteful expense of palaces after the fashion of Louis the Fourteenth; the palatial dignity being felt only in a peculiar sense of order, the absence of all that was casual, of vulgarity and discomfort. A merely official residence of his predecessors, the *Palatine* had become the favourite dwelling-place of Aurelius; its many-coloured memories suiting, perhaps, his pensive character, and the crude splendours of Nero and Hadrian being now subdued by time. The windowless Roman abode must have had much of what to a modern would be gloom. How did the children, one wonders, endure houses with so little escape for the eye into the world outside? Aurelius, who had altered little else, choosing to *live* there, in a genuine homeliness, had shifted and made the most of the level lights, and broken out a quite medieval window here and there, and the clear daylight, fully appreciated by his youthful visitor, made pleasant shadows among the objects of the imperial collection. Some of these, indeed, by reason of their Greek simplicity and grace, themselves shone out like spaces of a purer, early light, amid the splendours of the Roman manufacture.

Though he looked, thought Marius, like a man who did not sleep enough, he was abounding and bright to-day, after one of those pitiless headaches, which since boyhood had been the 'thorn in his side', challenging the pretensions of his philosophy to fortify one in humble endurances. At the first moment, to Marius, remembering the spectacle of the emperor in ceremony, it was almost bewildering to be in private conversation with him. There was much in the philosophy of Aurelius—much consideration of mankind at large, of great bodies, aggregates and generalities, after the Stoic manner—which, on a nature less rich than his, might have acted as an inducement to care for people in inverse proportion to their nearness to him. That has sometimes been the result of the Stoic cosmopolitanism. Aurelius, however, determined to beautify by all means, great or little, a doctrine which had in it some potential sourness, had brought all the quickness of his intelligence, and long years of observation, to bear on the conditions of social intercourse.

He had early determined 'not to make business an excuse to decline the offices of humanity—not to pretend to be too much occupied with important affairs to concede what life with others may hourly demand'; and with such success, that, in an age which made much of the finer points of that intercourse, it was felt that the mere honesty of his conversation was more pleasing than other men's flattery. His agreeableness to his young visitor to-day was, in truth, a blossom of the same wisdom which had made of Lucius Verus really a brother—the wisdom of not being exigent with men, any more than with fruit-trees (it is his own favourite figure), beyond their nature. And there was another person, still nearer to him, regarding whom this wisdom became a marvel, of equity—of charity.

The centre of a group of princely children, in the same apartment with Aurelius, amid all the refined intimacies of a modern home, sat the Empress Faustina, warming her hands over a fire. With her long fingers lighted up red by the glowing coals of the brazier, Marius looked close upon the most beautiful woman in the world, who was also the great paradox of the age, among her boys and girls. As has been truly said of the numerous representations of her in art, so in life, she had the air of one curious, restless, to enter into conversation with the first comer. She had certainly the power of stimulating a very ambiguous sort of curiosity about herself. And Marius found this enigmatic point in her expression, that even after seeing her many times he could never precisely recall her features in absence. The lad of six years, looking older, who stood beside her, impatiently plucking a rose to pieces over the hearth, was, in outward appearance, his father—the young *Verissimus*—over again; but with a certain feminine length of feature, and with all his mother's alertness, or licence, of gaze.

Yet rumour knocked at every door and window of the imperial house regarding the adulterers who knocked at them, or quietly left their lovers' garlands there. Was not that likeness of the husband, in the boy beside her, really the effect of a shameful magic, in which the blood of the murdered gladiator, his true father, had been an ingredient? Were the tricks for deceiving husbands which the Roman poet describes, really hers, and her household an efficient school of all the arts of furtive love? Or, was the husband too aware, like every one beside? Were certain sudden deaths which happened there, really the work of apoplexy, or the plague?

The man whose ears, whose soul, those rumours were meant

to penetrate, was, however, faithful to his sanguine and optimist philosophy, to his determination that the world should be to him simply what the higher reason preferred to conceive it; and the life's journey Aurelius had made so far, though involving much moral and intellectual loneliness, had been ever in affectionate and helpful contact with other wayfarers, very unlike himself.   Since his days of earliest childhood in the Lateran gardens, he seemed to himself, blessing the gods for it after deliberate survey, to have been always surrounded by kinsmen, friends, servants, of exceptional virtue.   From the great Stoic idea, that we are all fellow-citizens of one city, he had derived a tenderer, a more equitable estimate than was common among Stoics, of the eternal shortcomings of men and women.   Considerations that might tend to the sweetening of his temper it was his daily care to store away, with a kind of philosophic pride in the thought that no one took more good-naturedly than he the 'oversights' of his neighbours.   For had not Plato taught (it was not paradox, but simple truth of experience) that if people sin, it is because they know no better, and are 'under the necessity of their own ignorance'?   Hard to himself, he seemed at times, doubtless, to decline too softly upon unworthy persons.   Actually, he came thereby upon many a useful instrument.   The Empress Faustina he would seem at least to have kept, by a constraining affection, from becoming altogether what most people have believed her, and won in her (we must take him at his word in the *Thoughts*, abundantly confirmed by letters, on both sides, in his correspondence with Cornelius Fronto) a consolation, the more secure, perhaps, because misknown of others.   Was the secret of her actual blamelessness, after all, with him who has at least screened her name?   At all events, the one thing quite certain about her, besides her extraordinary beauty, is her sweetness to himself.

No!   The wise, who had made due observation on the trees of the garden, would not expect to gather grapes of thorns or fig-trees: and he was the vine, putting forth his genial fruit, by natural law, again and again, after his kind, whatever use people might make of it.   Certainly, his actual presence never lost its power, and Faustina was glad in it to-day, the birthday of one of her children, a boy who stood at her knee holding in his fingers tenderly a tiny silver trumpet, one of his birthday gifts.—'For my part, unless I conceive my hurt to be such, I have no hurt at all,'—boasts the would-be apathetic emperor:— 'and how I care to conceive of the thing rests with me.'   Yet when his children fall sick or die, this pretence breaks down, and he is broken-hearted: and one of the charms of certain of his letters still extant, is his reference to those childish sicknesses.—'On my return to Lorium', he writes, 'I found my little lady—*domnulam meam*—in a fever'; and again, in a letter to one of the most serious of men: 'You will be glad to hear that our little one is better, and running about the room— *parvolam nostram melius valere et intra cubiculum discurrere*'.

The young Commodus had departed from the chamber, anxious to witness the exercises of certain gladiators, having a native taste for such company, inherited, according to popular rumour, from his true father—anxious also to escape from the too impressive company of the gravest and sweetest specimen of old age Marius had ever seen, the tutor of the imperial children, who had arrived to offer his birthday congratulations, and now, very familiarly and affectionately, made a part of the group, falling on the shoulders of the emperor, kissing the Empress Faustina on the face, the little ones on the face and hands. Marcus Cornelius Fronto, the 'Orator', favourite teacher of the emperor's youth, afterwards his most trusted counsellor, and now the undisputed occupant of the sophistic throne, whose equipage, elegantly mounted with silver, Marius had seen in the streets of Rome, had certainly turned his many personal gifts to account with a good fortune, remarkable even in that age, so indulgent to professors or rhetoricians. The gratitude of the Emperor Aurelius, always generous to his teachers, arranging their very quarrels sometimes, for they were not always fair to one another, had helped him to a really great place in the world. But his sumptuous appendages, including the villa and gardens of Maecenas, had been borne with an air perfectly becoming, by the professor of a philosophy which, even in its most accomplished and elegant phase, presupposed a gentle contempt for such things. With an intimate practical knowledge of manners, physiognomies, smiles, disguises, flatteries, and courtly tricks of every kind—a whole accomplished rhetoric of daily life—he applied them all to the promotion of humanity, and especially of men's family affection. Through a long life of now eighty years, he had been, as it were, surrounded by the gracious and soothing air of his own eloquence— the fame, the echoes, of it—like warbling birds, or murmuring bees. Setting forth in that fine medium the best ideas of matured pagan philosophy, he had become the favourite 'director' of noble youth.

Yes! it was the one instance Marius, always eagerly on the look-out for such, had yet seen of a perfectly tolerable, perfectly beautiful, old age—an old age in which there seemed, to one who perhaps habitually over-valued the expression of youth, nothing to be regretted, nothing really lost, in what years had taken away. The wise old man, whose blue eyes and fair skin were so delicate, uncontaminate, and clear, would seem to have replaced carefully and consciously each natural trait of youth, as it departed from him, by an equivalent grace of culture; and had the blitheness, the placid cheerfulness, as he had also the infirmity, the claim on stronger people, of a delightful child. And yet he seemed to be but awaiting his exit from life—that moment with which the Stoics were almost as much preoccupied as the Christians, however differently—and set Marius pondering on the contrast between a placidity like this, at eighty years, and the sort of desperateness he was aware of in his own manner of entertaining that thought. His infirmities nevertheless had been painful and long-continued, with losses of children, of pet grandchildren. What with the crowd, and the wretched streets, it was a sign of affection which had cost him something, for the old man to leave his own house at all that day; and he was glad of the emperor's support, as he moved from place to place among the children he protests so often to have loved as his own.

For a strange piece of literary good fortune, at the beginning of the present century, has set free the long-buried fragrance of this famous friendship of the old world, from below a valueless later manuscript, in a series of letters, wherein the two writers exchange, for the most part their evening thoughts, especially at family anniversaries, and with entire intimacy, on their children, on the art of speech, on all the various subtleties of the 'science of images'—rhetorical images—above all, of course, on sleep and matters of health. They are full of mutual admiration of each other's eloquence, restless in absence till they see one another again, noting, characteristically, their very dreams of each other, expecting the day which will terminate the office, the business or duty, which separates them—'as superstitious people watch for the star, at the rising of which they may break their fast'. To one of the writers, to Aurelius, the correspondence was sincerely of value. We see him once reading his letters with genuine delight on going to rest. Fronto seeks to deter his pupil from writing in Greek.—Why buy, at great cost, a foreign wine, inferior to that from one's own vineyard? Aurelius, on the other hand, with an extraordinary innate susceptibility to words—*la parole pour la parole*, as the French say—despairs, in presence of Fronto's rhetorical perfection.

Like the modern visitor to the Capitoline and some other museums, Fronto had been struck, pleasantly struck, by the family likeness among the Antonines; and it was part of his friendship to make much of it, in the case of the children of Faustina. 'Well! I have seen the little ones', he writes to Aurelius, then, apparently, absent from them: 'I have seen the little ones—the pleasantest sight of my life; for they are as like yourself as could possibly be. It has well repaid me for my journey over that slippery road, and up those steep rocks; for I beheld you, not simply face to face before me, but, more generously, whichever way I turned, to my right and my left. For the rest, I found them, Heaven be thanked! with healthy cheeks and lusty voices. One was holding a slice of white bread, like a king's son; the other a crust of brown bread, as becomes the offspring of a philosopher. I pray the gods to have both the sower and the seed in their keeping; to watch over this field wherein the ears of corn are so kindly alike. Ah! I heard too their pretty voices, so sweet that in the childish prattle of one and the other I seemed somehow to be listening—yes! in that chirping of your pretty chickens—to the limpid and harmonious notes of your own oratory. Take care! you will find me growing independent, having those I could love in your place:—love, on the surety of my eyes and ears.'

'*Magistro meo salutem!*' replies the emperor. 'I too have seen my little ones in your sight of them; as, also, I saw yourself in reading your letter. It is that charming letter forces me to write thus': with reiterations of affection, that is, which are continual in these letters, on both sides, and which may strike a modern reader perhaps as fulsome; or, again, as having something in common with the old Judaic unction of friendship. They were certainly sincere.

To one of those children Fronto had now brought the birthday gift of the silver trumpet, upon which he ventured to blow softly now and again, turning away with eyes delighted at the sound, when he thought the old man was not listening. It was the well-worn, valetudinarian subject of sleep on which Fronto and Aurelius were talking together; Aurelius always feeling it a burden, Fronto a thing of magic capacities, so that he had written an *encomium* in its praise, and often by ingenious arguments recommends his imperial pupil not to be sparing of it. To-day, with his younger listeners in mind, he had a story to tell about it:

'They say that our father Jupiter, when he ordered the world at the beginning, divided time into two parts exactly equal: the one part he clothed with light, the other with darkness: he called them Day and Night; and he assigned rest to the night and to day the work of life. At that time Sleep was not yet born and men passed the whole of their lives awake: only, the quiet of the night was ordained for them, instead of sleep. But it came to pass, little by little, being that the minds of men are restless, that they carried on their business alike by night as by day, and gave no part at all to repose. And Jupiter, when he perceived that even in the night-time they ceased not from trouble and disputation, and that even the courts of law remained open' (it was the pride of Aurelius, as Fronto knew, to be assiduous in those courts till far into the night), 'resolved to appoint one of his brothers to be the overseer of the night and have authority over man's rest. But Neptune pleaded in excuse the gravity of his constant charge of the seas, and Father Dis the difficulty of keeping in subjection the spirits below; and Jupiter, having taken counsel with the other gods, perceived that the practice of nightly vigils was somewhat in favour. It was then, for the most part, that Juno gave birth to her children: Minerva, the mistress of all art and craft, loved the midnight lamp: Mars delighted in the darkness for his plots and sallies; and the favour of Venus and Bacchus was with those who roused by night. Then it was that Jupiter formed the design of creating Sleep; and he added him to the number of the gods, and gave him the charge over night and rest, putting into his hands the keys of human eyes. With his own hands he mingled the juices wherewith Sleep should soothe the hearts of mortals—herb of Enjoyment and herb of Safety, gathered from a grove in Heaven; and, from the meadows of Acheron, the herb of Death; expressing from it one single drop only, no bigger than a tear one might hide. "With this juice", he said: "pour slumber upon the eyelids of mortals. So soon as it hath touched them they will lay themselves down motionless, under thy power. But be not afraid: they shall revive, and in a while stand up again upon their feet." Thereafter, Jupiter gave wings to Sleep, attached, not, like Mercury's, to his heels, but to his shoulders, like the wings of Love. For he said: "It becomes thee not to approach men's eyes as with the noise

of chariots, and the rushing of a swift courser, but in placid
and merciful flight, as upon the wings of a swallow—nay!
with not so much as the flutter of the dove". Besides all this,
that he might be yet pleasanter to men, he committed to him
also a multitude of blissful dreams, according to every man's
desire. One watched his favourite actor; another listened to
the flute, or guided a charioteer in the race: in his dream, the
soldier was victorious, the general was borne in triumph, the
wanderer returned home. Yes!—and sometimes those dreams
come true!'

Just then Aurelius was summoned to make the birthday
offerings to his household gods. A heavy curtain of tapestry
was drawn back; and beyond it Marius gazed for a few moments
into the *Lararium*, or imperial chapel. A patrician youth, in
white habit, was in waiting, with a little chest in his hand
containing incense for the use of the altar. On richly carved
consoles, or sideboards, around this narrow chamber, were
arranged the rich apparatus of worship and the golden or
gilded images, adorned to-day with fresh flowers, among them
that image of Fortune from the apartment of Antoninus Pius,
and such of the emperor's own teachers as were gone to their
rest. A dim fresco on the wall commemorated the ancient
piety of Lucius Albinius, who in flight from Rome on the
morrow of a great disaster, overtaking certain priests on foot
with their sacred utensils, descended from the wagon in which
he rode and yielded it to the ministers of the gods. As he
ascended into the chapel the emperor paused, and with a grave
but friendly look at his young visitor, delivered a parting
sentence, audible to him alone: *Imitation is the most acceptable
part of worship : the gods had much rather mankind should
resemble than flatter them :—Make sure that those to whom you
come nearest be the happier by your presence !*

It was the very spirit of the scene and the hour—the hour
Marius had spent in the imperial house. How temperate, how
tranquillizing! what humanity! Yet, as he left the eminent
company concerning whose ways of life at home he had been
so youthfully curious, and sought, after his manner, to determine
the main trait in all this, he had to confess that it was a sentiment
of mediocrity, though of a mediocrity for once really golden.

CHAPTER XIV

MANLY AMUSEMENT

DURING the Eastern war there came a moment when schism in the empire had seemed possible through the defection of Lucius Verus; when to Aurelius it had also seemed possible to confirm his allegiance by no less a gift than his beautiful daughter Lucilla, the eldest of his children—the *domnula*, probably, of those letters. The *little lady*, grown now to strong and stately maidenhood, had been ever something of the good genius, the better soul, to Lucius Verus, by the law of contraries, her somewhat cold and apathetic modesty acting as counterfoil to the young man's tigerish fervour. Conducted to Ephesus, she had become his wife by form of civil marriage, the more solemn wedding rites being deferred till their return to Rome.

The ceremony of the *Confarreation*, or religious marriage, in which bride and bridegroom partook together of a certain mystic bread, was celebrated accordingly, with due pomp, early in the spring; Aurelius himself assisting, with much domestic feeling. A crowd of fashionable people filled the space before the entrance to the apartments of Lucius on the Palatine hill, richly decorated for the occasion, commenting, not always quite delicately, on the various details of the rite, which only a favoured few succeeded in actually witnessing. 'She comes!' Marius could hear them say, 'escorted by her young brothers: it is the young Commodus who carries the torch of whitethorn-wood, the little basket of work-things, the toys for the children':—and then, after a watchful pause, 'she is winding the woollen thread round the doorposts. Ah! I see the marriage-cake: the bridegroom presents the fire and water.' Then, in a longer pause, was heard the chorus, *Thalassie! Thalassie!* and for just a few moments, in the strange light of many wax tapers at noonday, Marius could see them both, side by side, while the bride was lifted over the doorstep: Lucius Verus heated and handsome—the pale, impassive Lucilla looking very long and slender, in her closely folded yellow veil, and high nuptial crown.

As Marius turned away, glad to escape from the pressure of the crowd, he found himself face to face with Cornelius, an infrequent spectator on occasions such as this. It was a relief to depart with him—so fresh and quiet he looked, though in all his splendid equestrian array in honour of the ceremony—from the garish heat of the marriage scene. The reserve which had puzzled Marius so much on his first day in Rome, was but an instance of many, to him wholly unaccountable, avoidances alike of things and persons, which must certainly mean that an intimate companionship would cost him something in the way of seemingly indifferent amusements. Some inward standard Marius seemed to detect there (though wholly unable to estimate its nature), of distinction, selection, refusal, amid the various elements of the fervid and corrupt life across which they were moving together:—some secret, constraining motive, ever on the alert at eye and ear, which carried him through Rome as under a charm, so that Marius could not but think of that figure of the white bird in the market-place as undoubtedly made true of him. And Marius was still full of admiration for this companion, who had known how to make himself very pleasant to him. Here was the clear, cold corrective, which the fever of his present life demanded. Without it, he would have felt alternately suffocated and exhausted by an existence, at once so gaudy and overdone, and yet so intolerably empty; in which people, even at their best, seemed only to be brooding, like the wise emperor himself, over a world's disillusion. For with all the severity of Cornelius, there was such a breeze of hopefulness—freshness and hopefulness, as of new morning, about him. For the most part, as I said, those refusals, that reserve of his, seemed unaccountable. But there were cases where the unknown monitor acted in a direction with which the judgment, or instinct, of Marius himself wholly concurred; the effective decision of Cornelius strengthening him further therein, as by a kind of outwardly embodied conscience. And the entire drift of his education determined him, on one point at least, to be wholly of the same mind with this peculiar friend (they two, it might be, together, against the world!) when, alone of a whole company of brilliant youth, he had withdrawn from his appointed place in the amphitheatre, at a grand public show, which, after an interval of many months, was presented there, in honour of the nuptials of Lucius Verus and Lucilla.

And it was still to the eye, through visible movement and

aspect, that the character, or genius of Cornelius made itself felt by Marius; even as on that afternoon when he had girt on his armour, among the expressive lights and shades of the dim old villa at the roadside, and every object of his knightly array had seemed to be but sign or symbol of some other thing far beyond it. For, consistently with his really poetic temper, all influence reached Marius, even more exclusively than he was aware, through the medium of sense. From Flavian, in that brief early summer of his existence, he had derived a powerful impression of the 'perpetual flux': he had caught there, as in cipher or symbol, or low whispers more effective than any definite language, his own Cyrenaic philosophy, presented thus, for the first time, in an image or person, with much attractiveness, touched also, consequently, with a pathetic sense of personal sorrow:—a concrete image, the abstract equivalent of which he could recognize afterwards, when the agitating personal influence had settled down for him, clearly enough, into a theory of practice. But of what possible intellectual formula could this mystic Cornelius be the sensible exponent; seeming, as he did, to live ever in close relationship with, and recognition of, a mental view, a source of discernment, a light upon his way, which had certainly not yet sprung up for Marius? Meantime, the discretion of Cornelius, his energetic clearness and purity, were a charm rather physical than moral: his exquisite correctness of spirit, at all events, accorded so perfectly with the regular beauty of his person, as to seem to depend upon it. And wholly different as was this later friendship, with its exigency, its warnings, its restraints, from the feverish attachment to Flavian, which had made him at times like an uneasy slave, still, like that, it was a reconciliation to the world of sense, the visible world. From the hopefulness of this gracious presence, all visible things around him, even the commonest objects of everyday life—if they but stood together to warm their hands at the same fire—took for him a new poetry, a delicate fresh bloom, and interest. It was as if his bodily eyes had been indeed mystically washed, renewed, strengthened.

And how eagerly, with what a light heart, would Flavian have taken his place in the amphitheatre, among the youth of his own age! with what an appetite for every detail of the entertainment, and its various accessories:—the sunshine, filtered into soft gold by the *vela*, with their serpentine patterning, spread over the more select part of the company; the Vestal virgins, taking their privilege of seats near the Empress Faustina, who sat there in a maze of double-coloured gems, changing, as she moved, like the waves of the sea; the cool circle of shadow, in which the wonderful toilets of the fashionable told so effectively around the blazing arena, covered again and again during the many hours' show with clean sand for the absorption of certain great red patches there, by troops of white-shirted boys, for whom the good-natured audience provided a scramble of nuts and small coin, flung to them over a trellis-work of silver-gilt and amber, precious gift of Nero, while a rain of flowers and perfume fell over themselves, as they paused between the parts of their long feast upon the spectacle of animal suffering.

During his sojourn at Ephesus, Lucius Verus had readily become a patron, patron or *protégé*, of the great goddess of Ephesus, the goddess of hunters; and the show, celebrated by way of a compliment to him to-day, was to present some incidents of her story, where she figures almost as the genius of madness, in animals, or in the humanity which comes in contact with them. The entertainment would have an element of old Greek revival in it, welcome to the taste of a learned and Hellenizing society; and, as Lucius Verus was in some sense a lover of animals, was to be a display of animals mainly. There would be real wild and domestic creatures, all of rare species; and a real slaughter. On so happy an occasion, it was hoped, the elder emperor might even concede a point, and a living criminal fall into the jaws of the wild beasts. And the spectacle was, certainly, to end in the destruction, by one mighty shower of arrows, of a hundred lions, 'nobly' provided by Aurelius himself for the amusement of his people.—*Tam magnanimus fuit !*

The arena, decked and in order for the first scene, looked delightfully fresh, reinforcing on the spirits of the audience the actual freshness of the morning, which at this season still brought the dew. Along the subterranean ways that led up to it, the sound of an advancing chorus was heard at last, chanting the words of a sacred song, or hymn to Diana; for the spectacle of the amphitheatre was, after all, a religious occasion. To its grim acts of bloodshedding a kind of sacrificial character still belonged in the view of certain religious casuists, tending conveniently to soothe the humane sensibilities of so pious an emperor as Aurelius, who, in his fraternal complacency, had consented to preside over the shows.

Artemis or Diana, as she may be understood in the actual development of her worship, was, indeed, the symbolical

expression of two allied yet contrasted elements of human
temper and experience—man's amity, and also his enmity,
towards the wild creatures, when they were still, in a certain
sense, his brothers. She is the complete, and therefore highly
complex, representative of a state, in which man was still much
occupied with animals, not as his flock, or as his servants after
the pastoral relationship of our later, orderly world, but rather
as his equals, on friendly terms or the reverse—a state full of
primeval sympathies and antipathies, of rivalries and common
wants—while he watched, and could enter into, the humours
of those 'younger brothers', with an intimacy, the 'survivals'
of which in a later age seem often to have had a kind of madness
about them. Diana represents alike the bright and the dark
side of such relationship. But the humanities of that relationship were all forgotten to-day in the excitement of a show, in
which mere cruelty to animals, their useless suffering and death,
formed the main point of interest. People watched their
destruction, batch after batch, in a not particularly inventive
fashion; though it was expected that the animals themselves,
as living creatures are apt to do when hard put to it, would
become inventive, and make up, by the fantastic accidents of
their agony, for the deficiencies of an age fallen behind in this
matter of manly amusement. It was as a Deity of Slaughter—
the Taurian goddess who demands the sacrifice of the ship-
wrecked sailors thrown on her coasts—the cruel, moonstruck
huntress, who brings not only sudden death, but *rabies*, among
the wild creatures that Diana was to be presented, in the
person of a famous courtesan. The aim at an actual theatrical
illusion, after the first introductory scene, was frankly surrendered to the display of the animals, artificially stimulated
and maddened to attack each other. And as Diana was also
a special protectress of new-born creatures, there would be a
certain curious interest in the dexterously contrived escape of
the young from their mothers' torn bosoms; as many pregnant
animals as possible being carefully selected for the purpose.

The time had been, and was to come again, when the pleasures
of the amphitheatre centred in a similar practical joking upon
human beings. What more ingenious diversion had stage
manager ever contrived than that incident, itself a practical
epigram never to be forgotten, when a criminal, who, like slaves
and animals, had no rights, was compelled to present the part
of Icarus; and, the wings failing him in due course, had fallen
into a pack of hungry bears? For the long shows of the

amphitheatre were, so to speak, the novel-reading of that age—a current help provided for sluggish imaginations, in regard, for instance, to grisly accidents, such as might happen to one's self; but with every facility for comfortable inspection. Scaevola might watch his own hand, consuming, crackling, in the fire, in the person of a culprit, willing to redeem his life by an act so delightful to the eyes, the very ears, of a curious public. If the part of Marsyas was called for, there was a criminal condemned to lose his skin. It might be almost edifying to study minutely the expression of his face, while the assistants corded and pegged him to the bench, cunningly; the servant of the law waiting by, who, after one short cut with his knife, would slip the man's leg from his skin, as neatly as if it were a stocking —a *finesse* in providing the due amount of suffering for wrong-doers only brought to its height in Nero's living bonfires. But then, by making his suffering ridiculous, you enlist against the sufferer some real, and all would-be manliness, and do much to stifle any false sentiment of compassion. The philosophic emperor, having no great taste for sport, and asserting here a personal scruple, had greatly changed all that; had provided that nets should be spread under the dancers on the tight-rope, and buttons for the swords of the gladiators. But the gladiators were still there. Their bloody contests had, under the form of a popular amusement, the efficacy of a human sacrifice; as, indeed, the whole system of the public shows was understood to possess a religious import. Just at this point, certainly, the judgment of Lucretius on pagan religion is without reproach:

Tantum religio potuit suadere malorum.

And Marius, weary and indignant, feeling isolated in the great slaughter-house, could not but observe that, in his habitual complaisance to Lucius Verus, who, with loud shouts of applause from time to time, lounged beside him, Aurelius had sat impassibly through all the hours Marius himself had remained there. For the most part, indeed, the emperor had actually averted his eyes from the show, reading, or writing on matters of public business, but had seemed, after all, indifferent. He was revolving, perhaps, that old Stoic paradox of the *Imperceptibility of pain*; which might serve as an excuse, should those savage popular humours ever again turn against men and women. Marius remembered well his very attitude and expression on this day, when, a few years later, certain things came to pass in Gaul, under his full authority; and that attitude and expression defined already, even thus early in their so friendly intercourse, and though he was still full of gratitude for his interest, a permanent point of difference between the emperor and himself—between himself, with all the convictions of his life taking centre to-day in his merciful, angry heart, and Aurelius, as representing all the light, all the apprehensive power there might be in pagan intellect. There was something in a tolerance such as this, in the bare fact that he could sit patiently through a scene like this, which seemed to Marius to mark Aurelius as his inferior now and for ever on the question of righteousness; to set them on opposite sides, in some great conflict, of which that difference was but a single presentment. Due, in whatever proportions, to the abstract principles he had formulated for himself, or in spite of them, there was the loyal conscience within him, deciding, judging himself and every one else, with a wonderful sort of authority:—You ought, methinks, to be something quite different from what you are; here! and here! Surely Aurelius must be lacking in that decisive conscience at first sight, of the intimations of which Marius could entertain no doubt—which he looked for in others. He at least, the humble follower of the bodily eye, was aware of a crisis in life, in this brief, obscure existence, a fierce opposition of real good and real evil around him, the issues of which he must by no means compromise or confuse; of the antagonisms of which the 'wise' Marcus Aurelius was unaware.

That long chapter of the cruelty of the Roman public shows may, perhaps, leave with the children of the modern world a feeling of self-complacency. Yet it might seem well to ask ourselves—it is always well to do so, when we read of the slave-trade, for instance, or of great religious persecutions on this side or on that, or of anything else which raises in us the question, 'Is thy servant a dog, that he should do this thing?'— not merely, what germs of feeling we may entertain which, under fitting circumstances, would induce us to the like; but, even more practically, what thoughts, what sort of considerations, may be actually present to our minds such as might have furnished us, living in another age, and in the midst of those legal crimes, with plausible excuses for them: each age in turn, perhaps, having its own peculiar point of blindness, with its consequent peculiar sin — the touchstone of an unfailing conscience in the select few.

Those cruel amusements were, certainly, the sin of blindness, of deadness and stupidity, in the age of Marius; and his light had not failed him regarding it. Yes! what was needed was the heart that would make it impossible to witness all this; and the future would be with the forces that could beget a heart like that. His chosen philosophy had said: Trust the eye: Strive to be right always in regard to the concrete experience: Beware of falsifying your impressions. And its sanction had at least been effective here, in protesting: 'This, and this, is what you may not look upon!'—Surely evil was a real thing, and the wise man wanting in the sense of it, where, not to have been, by instinctive election, on the right side, was to have failed in life.

PART THE THIRD

CHAPTER XV

STOICISM AT COURT

THE very finest flower of the same company—Aurelius, with the gilded *fasces* borne before him, a crowd of exquisites, the Empress Faustina herself, and all the elegant blue-stockings of the day, who maintained, people said, their private 'sophists' to whisper philosophy into their ears winsomely as they performed the duties of the toilet—was assembled again a few months later, in a different place and for a very different purpose. The temple of Peace, a 'modernizing' foundation of Hadrian, enlarged by a library and lecture-rooms, had grown into an institution like something between a college and a literary club; and here Cornelius Fronto was to pronounce a discourse on the *Nature of Morals*. There were some, indeed, who had desired the Emperor Aurelius himself to declare his whole mind on this matter. Rhetoric was become almost a function of the state: philosophy was upon the throne; and had from time to time, by request, delivered an official utterance with wellnigh divine authority. And it was as the delegate of this authority, under the full sanction of the philosophic emperor—emperor and pontiff, that the aged Fronto purposed to-day to expound some parts of the Stoic doctrine, with the view of recommending morals to that refined but perhaps prejudiced company, as being, in effect, one mode of comeliness in things—as it were music, or a kind of artistic order, in life. And he did this earnestly, with an outlay of all his science of mind, and that eloquence of which he was known to be a master. For Stoicism was no longer a rude and unkempt thing. Received at court, it had largely decorated itself: it was grown persuasive and insinuating, and sought not only to convince men's intelligence but to allure their souls. Associated with the beautiful old age of the great rhetorician, and his winning voice, it was almost Epicurean. And the old man was at his best on the occasion; the last on which he ever appeared in this way. To-day was his own birthday. Early in the morning the imperial letter of congratulation had reached him; and all the pleasant animation

143

it had caused was in his face, when assisted by his daughter Gratia he took his place on the ivory chair, as president of the *Athenaeum* of Rome, wearing with a wonderful grace the philosophic pall—in reality neither more nor less than the loose woollen cloak of the common soldier, but fastened on his right shoulder with a magnificent clasp, the emperor's birthday gift.

It was an age, as abundant evidence shows, whose delight in rhetoric was but one result of a general susceptibility—an age not merely taking pleasure in words, but experiencing a great moral power in them. Fronto's quaintly fashionable audience would have wept, and also assisted with their purses, had his present purpose been, as sometimes happened, the recommendation of an object of charity. As it was, arranging themselves at their ease among the images and flowers, these amateurs of exquisite language, with their tablets open for careful record of felicitous word or phrase, were ready to give themselves wholly to the intellectual treat prepared for them, applauding, blowing loud kisses through the air sometimes, at the speaker's triumphant exit from one of his long, skilfully modulated sentences; while the younger of them meant to imitate everything about him, down to the inflexions of his voice and the very folds of his mantle. Certainly there was rhetoric enough:—a wealth of imagery; illustrations from painting, music, mythology, the experiences of love; a management, by which subtle, unexpected meaning was brought out of familiar terms, like flies from morsels of amber, to use Fronto's own figure. But with all its richness, the higher claim of his style was rightly understood to lie in gravity and self-command, and an especial care for the purities of a vocabulary which rejected every expression unsanctioned by the authority of approved ancient models.

And it happened with Marius, as it will sometimes happen, that this general discourse to a general audience had the effect of an utterance adroitly designed for him. His conscience still vibrating painfully under the shock of that scene in the amphitheatre, and full of the ethical charm of Cornelius, he was questioning himself with much impatience as to the possibility of an adjustment between his own elaborately thought-out intellectual scheme and the 'old morality'. In that intellectual scheme indeed the old morality had so far been allowed no place, as seeming to demand from him the admission of certain first principles such as might misdirect or retard him in his efforts towards a complete, many-sided existence; or distort the revelations of the experience of life; or curtail his natural liberty of heart and mind. But now (his imagination being occupied for the moment with the noble and resolute air, the gallantry, so to call it, which composed the outward mien and presentment of his strange friend's inflexible ethics) he felt already some nascent suspicion of his philosophic programme, in regard, precisely, to the question of good taste. There was the taint of a graceless 'antinomianism' perceptible in it, a dissidence, a revolt against accustomed modes, the actual impression of which on other men might rebound upon himself in some loss of that personal pride to which it was part of his theory of life to allow so much. And it was exactly a moral situation such as this that Fronto appeared to be contemplating. He seemed to have before his mind the case of one—Cyrenaic or Epicurean, as the courtier tends to be, by habit and instinct, if not on principle—who yet experiences, actually, a strong tendency to moral assents, and a desire, with as little logical inconsistency as may be, to find a place for duty and righteousness in his house of thought.

And the Stoic professor found the key to this problem in the purely aesthetic beauty of the old morality, as an element in things, fascinating to the imagination, to good taste in its most highly developed form, through association—a system or order, as a matter of fact, in possession, not only of the larger world, but of the rare minority of *élite* intelligences; from which, therefore, least of all would the sort of Epicurean he had in view endure to become, so to speak, an outlaw. He supposed his hearer to be, with all sincerity, in search after some principle of conduct (and it was here that he seemed to Marius to be speaking straight to him) which might give unity of motive to an actual rectitude, a cleanness and probity of life, determined partly by natural affection, partly by enlightened self-interest or the feeling of honour, due in part even to the mere fear of penalties; no element of which, however, was distinctively moral in the agent himself as such, and providing him, therefore, no common ground with a really moral being like Cornelius, or even like the philosophic emperor. Performing the same offices; actually satisfying, even as they, the external claims of others; rendering to all their dues—one thus circumstanced would be wanting, nevertheless, in the secret of inward adjustment to the moral agents around him. How tenderly—more tenderly than many stricter souls—he might yield himself to

kindly instinct! what fineness of charity in passing judgment
on others! what an exquisite conscience of other men's susceptibilities! He knows for how much the manner, because
the heart itself, counts, in doing a kindness. He goes beyond
most people in his care for all weakly creatures; judging,
instinctively, that to be but sentient is to possess rights. He
conceives a hundred duties, though he may not call them by
that name, of the existence of which purely duteous souls may
have no suspicion. He has a kind of pride in doing more than
they, in a way of his own. Sometimes, he may think that
those men of line and rule do not really understand their own
business. How narrow, inflexible, unintelligent! what poor
guardians (he may reason) of the inward spirit of righteousness,
are some supposed careful walkers according to its letter and
form. And yet all the while he admits, as such, no moral world
at all: no theoretic equivalent to so large a proportion of the
facts of life.

But, over and above such practical rectitude, thus determined
by natural affection or self-love or fear, he may notice that
there is a remnant of right conduct, what he does, still more
what he abstains from doing, not so much through his own free
election, as from a deference, an 'assent', entire, habitual,
unconscious, to custom—to the actual habit or fashion of
others, from whom he could not endure to break away, any
more than he would care to be out of agreement with them
on questions of mere manner, or, say, even, of dress. Yes!
there were the evils, the vices, which he avoided as, essentially,
a failure in good taste. An assent, such as this, to the
preferences of others, might seem to be the weakest of motives,
and the rectitude it could determine the least considerable
element in a moral life. Yet here, according to Cornelius
Fronto, was in truth the revealing example, albeit operating
upon comparative trifles, of the general principle required.
There was one great idea associated with which that determination to conform to precedent was elevated into the clearest,
the fullest, the weightiest principle of moral action; a principle
under which one might subsume men's most strenuous efforts
after righteousness. And he proceeded to expound the idea of
Humanity—of a universal commonwealth of mind, which
becomes explicit, and as if incarnate, in a select communion
of just men made perfect.

Ὁ κόσμος ὡσανεὶ πόλις ἔστιν—the world is as it were a
commonwealth, a city: and there are observances, customs,

usages, actually current in it, things our friends and companions will expect of us, as the condition of our living there with them at all, as really their peers or fellow-citizens. Those observances were, indeed, the creation of a visible or invisible aristocracy in it, whose actual manners, whose preferences from of old, become now a weighty tradition as to the way in which things should or should not be done, are like a music, to which the intercourse of life proceeds—such a music as no one who had once caught its harmonies would willingly jar. In this way, the *becoming*, as in Greek—τὸ πρέπον: or τὰ ἤθη, *mores*, *manners*, as both Greeks and Romans said, would indeed be a comprehensive term for duty. Righteousness would be, in the words of 'Caesar' himself, of the philosophic Aurelius, but a 'following of the reasonable will of the oldest, the most venerable, of cities, of polities—of the royal, the law-giving element, therein—forasmuch as we are citizens also in that supreme city on high, of which all other cities beside are but as single habitations'. But as the old man spoke with animation of this supreme city, this invisible society, whose conscience was become explicit in its inner circle of inspired souls, of whose common spirit, the trusted leaders of human conscience had been but the mouthpiece, of whose successive personal preferences in the conduct of life, the 'old morality' was the sum,— Marius felt that his own thoughts were passing beyond the actual intention of the speaker; not in the direction of any clearer theoretic or abstract definition of that ideal commonwealth, but rather as if in search of its visible locality and abiding-place, the walls and towers of which, so to speak, he might really trace and tell, according to his own old, natural habit of mind. It would be the fabric, the outward fabric, of a system reaching, certainly, far beyond the great city around him, even if conceived in all the machinery of its visible and invisible influences at their grandest—as Augustus or Trajan might have conceived of them—however well the visible Rome might pass for a figure of that new, unseen, Rome on high. At moments, Marius even asked himself with surprise, whether it might be some vast secret society the speaker had in view:— that august community, to be an outlaw from which, to be foreign to the manners of which, was a loss so much greater than to be excluded, into the ends of the earth, from the sovereign Roman commonwealth. Humanity, a universal order, the great polity, its aristocracy of elect spirits, the mastery of their example over their successors—these were the ideas, stimulating enough in their way, by association with which the Stoic professor had attempted to elevate, to unite under a single principle, men's moral efforts, himself lifted up with so genuine an enthusiasm. But where might Marius search for all this, as more than an intellectual abstraction? Where were those elect souls in whom the claim of Humanity became so amiable, winning, persuasive—whose footsteps through the world were so beautiful in the actual order he saw—whose faces averted from him, would be more than he could bear? Where was that comely order, to which as a great fact of experience he must give its due; to which, as to all other beautiful 'phenomena' in life, he must, for his own peace, adjust himself?

Rome did well to be serious. The discourse ended somewhat abruptly, as the noise of a great crowd in motion was heard below the walls; whereupon, the audience, following the humour of the younger element in it, poured into the colonnade, from the steps of which the famous procession, or *transvectio*, of the military knights was to be seen passing over the Forum, from their trysting-place at the temple of Mars, to the temple of the Dioscuri. The ceremony took place this year, not on the day accustomed—anniversary of the victory of Lake Regillus, with its pair of celestial assistants—and amid the heat and roses of a Roman July, but, by anticipation, some months earlier, the almond-trees along the way being still in leafless flower. Through that light trellis-work Marius watched the riders, arrayed in all their gleaming ornaments, and wearing wreaths of olive around their helmets, the faces below which, what with battle and the plague, were almost all youthful. It was a flowery scene enough, but had to-day its fullness of warlike meaning; the return of the army to the north, where the enemy was again upon the move, being now imminent. Cornelius had ridden along in his place, and, on the dismissal of the company, passed below the steps where Marius stood, with that new song he had heard once before floating from his lips.

CHAPTER XVI

SECOND THOUGHTS

AND Marius, for his part, was grave enough. The discourse of
Cornelius Fronto, with its wide prospect over the human, the
spiritual, horizon, had set him on a review—on a review of the
isolating narrowness, in particular, of his own theoretic scheme.
Long after the very latest roses were faded, when 'the town'
had departed to country villas, or the baths, or the war, he
remained behind in Rome; anxious to try the lastingness of his
own Epicurean rose garden; setting to work over again, and
deliberately passing from point to point of his old argument
with himself, down to its practical conclusions. That age and
our own have much in common—many difficulties and hopes.
Let the reader pardon me if here and there I seem to be passing
from Marius to his modern representatives—from Rome, to
Paris or London.

What really were its claims as a theory of practice, of the
sympathies that determine practice? It had been a theory,
avowedly, of loss and gain (so to call it), of an economy. If,
therefore, it missed something in the commerce of life which
some other theory of practice was able to include, if it made a
needless sacrifice, then it must be, in a manner, inconsistent
with itself, and lack theoretic completeness. Did it make such
a sacrifice? What did it lose, or cause one to lose?

And we may note, as Marius could hardly have done, that
Cyrenaicism is ever the characteristic philosophy of youth,
ardent, but narrow in its survey—sincere, but apt to become
one-sided, or even fanatical. It is one of those subjective and
partial ideals, based on vivid, because limited, apprehension of
the truth of one aspect of experience (in this case, of the beauty
of the world and the brevity of man's life there) which it may
be said to be the special vocation of the young to express.
In the school of Cyrene, in that comparatively fresh Greek
world, we see this philosophy where it is least *blasé*, as we say;
in its most pleasant, its blithest and yet perhaps its wisest form,
youthfully bright in the youth of European thought. But it

grows young again for a while in almost every youthful soul. It is spoken of sometimes as the appropriate utterance of jaded men; but in them it can hardly be sincere, or, by the nature of the case, an enthusiasm. 'Walk in the ways of thine heart, and in the sight of thine eyes,' is, indeed, most often, according to the supposition of the book from which I quote it, the counsel of the young, who feel that the sunshine is pleasant along their veins, and wintry weather, though in a general sense foreseen, a long way off. The youthful enthusiasm or fanaticism, the self-abandonment to one favourite mode of thought or taste, which occurs, quite naturally, at the outset of every really vigorous intellectual career, finds its special opportunity in a theory such as that so carefully put together by Marius, just because it seems to call on one to make the sacrifice, accompanied by a vivid sensation of power and will, of what others value— sacrifice of some conviction, or doctrine, or supposed first principle—for the sake of that clear-eyed intellectual consistency, which is like spotless bodily cleanliness, or scrupulous personal honour, and has itself for the mind of the youthful student, when he first comes to appreciate it, the fascination of an ideal.

The Cyrenaic doctrine, then, realized as a motive of strenuousness or enthusiasm, is not so properly the utterance of the 'jaded Epicurean', as of the strong young man in all the freshness of thought and feeling, fascinated by the notion of raising his life to the level of a daring theory, while, in the first genial heat of existence, the beauty of the physical world strikes potently upon his wide-open, unwearied senses. He discovers a great new poem every spring, with a hundred delightful things he too has felt, but which have never been expressed, or at least never so truly, before. The workshops of the artists, who can select and set before us what is really most distinguished in visible life, are open to him. He thinks that the old Platonic, or the new Baconian philosophy, has been better explained than by the authors themselves, or with some striking original development, this very month. In the quiet heat of early summer, on the dusty gold morning, the music comes, louder at intervals, above the hum of voices from some neighbouring church, among the flowering trees, valued now, perhaps, only for the poetically rapt faces among priests or worshippers, or the mere skill and eloquence, it may be, of its preachers of faith and righteousness. In his scrupulous idealism, indeed, he too feels himself to be something of a priest, and that devotion of his days to the contemplation of what is beautiful, a sort of perpetual religious service. Afar off, how many fair cities and delicate sea-coasts await him! At that age, with minds of a certain constitution, no very choice or exceptional circumstances are needed to provoke an enthusiasm something like this. Life in modern London even, in the heavy glow of summer, is stuff sufficient for the fresh imagination of a youth to build its 'palace of art' of; and the very sense and enjoyment of an experience in which all is new, are but enhanced, like that glow of summer itself, by the thought of its brevity, giving him something of a gambler's zest, in the apprehension, by dexterous act or diligently appreciative thought, of the highly coloured moments which are to pass away so quickly. At bottom, perhaps, in his elaborately developed self-consciousness, his sensibilities, his almost fierce grasp upon the things he values at all, he has, beyond all others, an inward need of something permanent in its character, to hold by: of which circumstance, also, he may be partly aware, and that, as with the brilliant Claudio in *Measure for Measure*, it is, in truth, but darkness he is 'encountering, like a bride'. But the inevitable falling of the curtain is probably distant; and in the daylight, at least, it is not often that he really shudders at the thought of the grave—the weight above, the narrow world and its company, within. When the thought of it does occur to him, he may say to himself: Well! and the rude monk, for instance, who has renounced all this, on the security of some dim world beyond it, really acquiesces in that 'fifth act', amid all the consoling ministries around him, as little as I should at this moment; though I may hope that, as at the real ending of a play, however well acted, I may already have had quite enough of it, and find a true well-being in eternal sleep.

And precisely in this circumstance, that, consistently with the function of youth in general, Cyrenaicism will always be more or less the special philosophy, or 'prophecy', of the young, when the ideal of a rich experience comes to them in the ripeness of the receptive, if not of the reflective, powers—precisely in this circumstance, if we rightly consider it, lies the duly prescribed corrective of that philosophy. For it is by its exclusiveness, and by negation rather than positively, that such theories fail to satisfy us permanently; and what they really need for their correction, is the complementary influence of some greater system, in which they may find their due place. That *Sturm und Drang* of the spirit, as it has been called, that ardent and special apprehension of half-truths, in the enthusiastic, and as

*F 903

it were 'prophetic' advocacy of which, devotion to truth, in the case of the young—apprehending but one point at a time in the great circumference—most usually embodies itself, is levelled down, safely enough, afterwards, as in history so in the individual, by the weakness and mere weariness, as well as by the maturer wisdom, of our nature. And though truth, indeed, resides, as has been said, 'in the whole'—in harmonizings and adjustments like this—yet those special apprehensions may still owe their full value, in this sense of 'the whole', to that earlier, one-sided but ardent preoccupation with them.

Cynicism and Cyrenaicism:—they are the earlier Greek forms of Roman Stoicism and Epicureanism, and in that world of old Greek thought, we may notice with some surprise that, in a little while, the nobler form of Cyrenaicism—Cyrenaicism cured of its faults—met the nobler form of Cynicism half-way. Starting from opposed points, they merged, each in its most refined form, in a single ideal of temperance or moderation. Something of the same kind may be noticed regarding some later phases of Cyrenaic theory. If it starts with considerations opposed to the religious temper, which the religious temper holds it a duty to repress, it is like it, nevertheless, and very unlike any lower development of temper, in its stress and earnestness, its serious application to the pursuit of a very unworldly type of perfection. The saint, and the Cyrenaic lover of beauty, it may be thought, would at least understand each other better than either would understand the mere man of the world. Carry their respective positions a point further, shift the terms a little, and they might actually touch.

Perhaps all theories of practice tend, as they rise to their best, as understood by their worthiest representatives, to identification with each other. For the variety of men's possible reflections on their experience, as of that experience itself, is not really so great as it seems; and as the highest and most disinterested ethical *formulae*, filtering down into men's everyday existence, reach the same poor level of vulgar egotism, so we may fairly suppose that all the highest spirits, from whatever contrasted points they have started, would yet be found to entertain, in the moral consciousness realized by themselves, much the same kind of mental company; to hold, far more than might be thought probable, at first sight, the same personal types of character, and even the same artistic and literary types, in esteem or aversion; to convey, all of them alike, the same savour of unworldliness. And Cyrenaicism or

Epicureanism too, new or old, may be noticed, in proportion to the completeness of its development, to approach, as to the nobler form of Cynicism, so also to the more nobly developed phases of the old, or traditional morality. In the gravity of its conception of life, in its pursuit after nothing less than a perfection, in its apprehension of the value of time—the passion and the seriousness which are like a consecration—*la passion et le sérieux qui consacrent*—it may be conceived, as regards its main drift, to be not so much opposed to the old morality, as an exaggeration of one special motive in it.

Some cramping, narrowing, costly preference of one part of his own nature, and of the nature of things, to another, Marius seemed to have detected in himself, meantime—in himself, as also in those old masters of the Cyrenaic philosophy. If they did realize the μονόχρονος ἡδονή, as it was called—the pleasure of the 'Ideal Now'—if certain moments of their lives were high-pitched, passionately coloured, intent with sensation, and a kind of knowledge which, in its vivid clearness, was like sensation —if, now and then, they apprehended the world in its fullness, and had a vision, almost 'beatific', of ideal personalities in life and art, yet these moments were a very costly matter: they paid a great price for them, in the sacrifice of a thousand possible sympathies, of things only to be enjoyed through sympathy, from which they detached themselves, in intellectual pride, in loyalty to a mere theory that would take nothing for granted, and assent to no approximate or hypothetical truths. In their unfriendly, repellent attitude towards the Greek religion, and the old Greek morality, surely, they had been but faulty economists. The Greek religion was then alive: then, still more than in its later day of dissolution, the higher view of it was possible, even for the philosopher. Its story made little or no demand for a reasoned or formal acceptance. A religion, which had grown through and through man's life, with so much natural strength; had meant so much for so many generations; which expressed so much of their hopes, in forms so familiar and so winning; linked by associations so manifold to man as he had been and was—a religion like this, one would think, might have had its uses, even for a philosophic sceptic. Yet those beautiful gods, with the whole round of their poetic worship, the school of Cyrene definitely renounced.

The old Greek morality, again, with all its imperfections, was certainly a comely thing.—Yes! a harmony, a music, in men's ways, one might well hesitate to jar. The merely aesthetic sense might have had a legitimate satisfaction in the spectacle of that fair order of choice manners, in those attractive conventions, enveloping, so gracefully, the whole of life, ensuring some sweetness, some security at least against offence, in the intercourse of the world. Beyond an obvious utility, it could claim, indeed, but custom—use-and-wont, as we say—for its sanction. But then, one of the advantages of that liberty of spirit among the Cyrenaics (in which, through theory, they had become dead to theory, so that all theory, as such, was really indifferent to them, and indeed nothing valuable but in its tangible ministration to life) was precisely this, that it gave them free play in using as their ministers or servants, things which, to the uninitiated, must be masters or nothing. Yet, how little the followers of Aristippus made of that whole comely system of manners or morals, then actually in possession of life, is shown by the bold practical consequence which one of them maintained (with a hard, self-opinionated adherence to his peculiar theory of values) in the not very amiable paradox that friendship and patriotism were things one could do without; while another—*Deaths-advocate*, as he was called—helped so many to self-destruction, by his pessimistic eloquence on the evils of life, that his lecture-room was closed. That this was in the range of their consequences—that this was a possible, if remote, deduction from the premises of the discreet Aristippus— was surely an inconsistency in a thinker who professed above all things an economy of the moments of life. And yet those old Cyrenaics felt their way, as if in the dark, we may be sure, like other men in the ordinary transactions of life, beyond the narrow limits they drew of clear and absolutely legitimate knowledge, admitting what was not of immediate sensation, and drawing upon that 'fantastic' future which might never come. A little more of such 'walking by faith', a little more of such not unreasonable 'assent', and they might have profited by a hundred services to their culture, from Greek religion and Greek morality, as they actually were. The spectacle of their fierce, exclusive, tenacious hold on their own narrow apprehension, makes one think of a picture with no relief, no soft shadows nor breadth of space, or of a drama without proportionate repose.

Yet it was of perfection that Marius (to return to him again from his masters, his intellectual heirs) had been really thinking all the time: a narrow perfection it might be objected, the perfection of but one part of his nature—his capacities of feeling,

of exquisite physical impressions, of an imaginative sympathy—
but still, a true perfection of those capacities, wrought out to
their utmost degree, admirable enough in its way. He too is
an economist: he hopes, by that 'insight' of which the old
Cyrenaics made so much, by skilful apprehension of the conditions of spiritual success as they really are, the special circumstances of the occasion with which he has to deal, the special
felicities of his own nature, to make the most, in no mean or
vulgar sense, of the few years of life; few, indeed, for the attainment of anything like general perfection! With the brevity of
that sum of years his mind is exceptionally impressed; and this
purpose makes him no frivolous *dilettante*, but graver than other
men: his scheme is not that of a trifler, but rather of one who
gives a meaning of his own, yet a very real one, to those old
words—*Let us work while it is day!* He has a strong apprehension, also, of the beauty of the visible things around him; their
fading, momentary, graces and attractions. His natural susceptibility in this direction, enlarged by experience, seems to
demand of him an almost exclusive preoccupation with the
aspects of things; with their aesthetic character, as it is called—
their revelations to the eye and the imagination: not so much
because those aspects of them yield him the largest amount of
enjoyment, as because to be occupied, in this way, with the
aesthetic or imaginative side of things, is to be in real contact
with those elements of his own nature, and of theirs, which,
for him at least, are matter of the most real kind of apprehension.
As other men are concentrated upon truths of number, for
instance, or on business, or it may be on the pleasures of appetite,
so he is wholly bent on living in that full stream of refined
sensation. And in the prosecution of this love of beauty, he
claims an entire personal liberty, liberty of heart and mind,
liberty, above all, from what may seem conventional answers
to first questions.

But, without him there is a venerable system of sentiment
and idea, widely extended in time and place, in a kind of
impregnable possession of human life—a system which, like
some other great products of the conjoint efforts of human
mind through many generations, is rich in the world's experience;
so that, in attaching one's self to it, one lets in a great tide of
that experience, and makes, as it were with a single step, a
great experience of one's own, and with great consequent
increase to one's sense of colour, variety, and relief, in the
spectacle of men and things. The mere sense that one belongs

to a system—an imperial system or organization—has, in itself, the expanding power of a great experience; as some have felt who have been admitted from narrower sects into the communion of the Catholic Church; or as the old Roman citizen felt. It is, we might fancy, what the coming into possession of a very widely spoken language might be, with a great literature, which is also the speech of the people we have to live among.

A wonderful order, actually in possession of human life!—grown inextricably through and through it; penetrating into its laws, its very language, its mere habits of decorum, in a thousand half-conscious ways; yet still felt to be, in part, an unfulfilled ideal; and, as such, awakening hope, and an aim, identical with the one only consistent aspiration of mankind! In the apprehension of that, just then, Marius seemed to have joined company once more with his own old self; to have overtaken on the road the pilgrim who had come to Rome, with absolute sincerity, on the search for perfection. It defined not so much a change of practice, as of sympathy—a new departure, an expansion, of sympathy. It involved, certainly, some curtailment of his liberty, in concession to the actual manner, the distinctions, the enactments of that great crowd of admirable spirits, who have elected so, and not otherwise, in their conduct of life, and are not here to give one, so to term it, an 'indulgence'. But then, under the supposition of their disapproval, no roses would ever seem worth plucking again. The authority they exercised was like that of classic taste—an influence so subtle, yet so real, as defining the loyalty of the scholar; or of some beautiful and venerable ritual, in which every observance is become spontaneous and almost mechanical, yet is found, the more carefully one considers it, to have a reasonable significance and a natural history.

And Marius saw that he would be but an inconsistent Cyrenaic, mistaken in his estimate of values, of loss and gain, and untrue to the well-considered economy of life which he had brought with him to Rome—that some drops of the great cup would fall to the ground—if he did not make that concession, if he did but remain just there.

CHAPTER XVII

BEATA URBS

Many prophets and kings have desired to see the things which ye see.

THE enemy on the Danube was, indeed, but the vanguard of the mighty invading hosts of the fifth century. Illusively repressed just now, those confused movements along the northern boundary of the empire were destined to unite triumphantly at last, in the barbarism which, powerless to destroy the Christian Church, was yet to suppress for a time the achieved culture of the pagan world. The kingdom of Christ was to grow up in a somewhat false alienation from the light and beauty of the kingdom of nature, of the natural man, with a partly mistaken tradition concerning it, and an incapacity, as it might almost seem at times, for eventual reconciliation thereto. Meantime Italy had armed itself once more, in haste, and the imperial brothers set forth for the Alps.

Whatever misgiving the Roman people may have felt as to the leadership of the younger was unexpectedly set at rest; though with some temporary regret for the loss of what had been, after all, a popular figure on the world's stage. Travelling fraternally in the same litter with Aurelius, Lucius Verus was struck with sudden and mysterious disease, and died as he hastened back to Rome. His death awoke a swarm of sinister rumours, to settle on Lucilla, jealous, it was said, of Fabia her sister, perhaps of Faustina — on Faustina herself, who had accompanied the imperial progress, and was anxious now to hide a crime of her own—even on the elder brother, who, beforehand with the treasonable designs of his colleague, should have helped him at supper to a favourite morsel, cut with a knife poisoned ingeniously on one side only. Aurelius, certainly, with sincere distress, his long irritations, so dutifully concealed or repressed, turning now into a single feeling of regret for the human creature, carried the remains back to Rome, and demanded of the Senate a public funeral, with a decree for the *apotheôsis*, or canonization, of the dead.

For three days the body lay in state in the Forum, enclosed

in an open coffin of cedar-wood, on a bed of ivory and gold, in the centre of a sort of temporary chapel, representing the temple of his patroness *Venus Genetrix*. Armed soldiers kept watch around it, while choirs of select voices relieved one another in the chanting of hymns or monologues from the great tragedians. At the head of the couch were displayed the various personal decorations which had belonged to Verus in life. Like all the rest of Rome, Marius went to gaze on the face he had seen last scarcely disguised under the hood of a travelling-dress, as the wearer hurried, at nightfall, along one of the streets below the palace, to some amorous appointment. Unfamiliar as he still was with dead faces, he was taken by surprise, and touched far beyond what he had reckoned on, by the piteous change there; even the skill of Galen having been not wholly successful in the process of embalming. It was as if a brother of his own were lying low before him, with that meek and helpless expression, it would have been a sacrilege to treat rudely.

Meantime, in the centre of the *Campus Martius*, within the grove of poplars which enclosed the space where the body of Augustus had been burnt, the great funeral pyre, stuffed with shavings of various aromatic woods, was built up in many stages, separated from each other by a light entablature of woodwork, and adorned abundantly with carved and tapestried images. Upon this pyramidal or flame-shaped structure lay the corpse, hidden now under a mountain of flowers and incense brought by the women, who from the first had had their fondness for the wanton graces of the deceased. The dead body was surmounted by a waxen effigy of great size, arrayed in the triumphal ornaments. At last the Centurions to whom that office belonged, drew near, torch in hand, to ignite the pile at its four corners, while the soldiers, in wild excitement, flung themselves around it, casting into the flames the decorations they had received for acts of valour under the dead emperor's command.

It had been a really heroic order, spoiled a little, at the last moment, through the somewhat tawdry artifice, by which an eagle—not a very noble or youthful specimen of its kind—was caused to take flight amid the real or affected awe of the spectators, above the perishing remains; a court chamberlain, according to ancient etiquette, subsequently making official declaration before the Senate, that the imperial 'genius' had been seen in this way, escaping from the fire. And Marius was present when the Fathers, duly certified of the fact, by 'acclamation', muttering their judgment all together, in a kind of low, rhythmical chant, decreed *Caelum*—the privilege of divine rank to the departed.

The actual gathering of the ashes in a white cerecloth by the widowed Lucilla, when the last flicker had been extinguished by drops of wine; and the conveyance of them to the little cell, already populous, in the central mass of the sepulchre of Hadrian, still in all the splendour of its statued colonnades, were a matter of private or domestic duty; after the due accomplishment of which Aurelius was at liberty to retire for a time into the privacy of his beloved apartments of the Palatine. And hither, not long afterwards, Marius was summoned a second time, to receive from the imperial hands the great pile of manuscripts it would be his business to revise and arrange.

One year had passed since his first visit to the palace; and as he climbed the stairs to-day, the great cypresses rocked against the sunless sky, like living creatures in pain. He had to traverse a long subterranean gallery, once a secret entrance to the imperial apartments, and in our own day, amid the ruin of all around it, as smooth and fresh as if the carpets were but just removed from its floor after the return of the emperor from the shows. It was here, on such an occasion, that the Emperor Caligula, at the age of twenty-nine, had come by his end, the assassins gliding along it as he lingered a few moments longer to watch the movements of a party of noble youths at their exercise in the courtyard below. As Marius waited, a second time, in that little red room in the house of the chief chamberlain, curious to look once more upon its painted walls—the very place whither the assassins were said to have turned for refuge after the murder—he could all but see the figure, which in its surrounding light and darkness seemed to him the most melancholy in the entire history of Rome. He called to mind the greatness of that popularity and early promise—the stupefying height of irresponsible power, from which, after all, only men's viler side had been clearly visible—the overthrow of reason—the seemingly irredeemable memory; and still, above all, the beautiful head in which the noble lines of the race of Augustus were united to, he knew not what expression of sensibility and fineness, not theirs, and for the like of which one must pass onward to the Antonines. Popular hatred had been careful to destroy its semblance wherever it was to be found; but one bust, in dark bronze-like basalt of a wonderful perfection of finish, preserved in the museum of the Capitol, may have seemed to some visitors there perhaps the finest extant relic of Roman art. Had the very seal of empire upon those sombre brows, reflected from his mirror, suggested his insane attempt upon the liberties, the dignity of men?—'O humanity!' he seems to ask, 'what hast thou done to me that I should so despise thee?'—And might not this be indeed the true meaning of kingship, if the world would have one man to reign over it? The like of this: or, some incredible, surely never to be realized, height of disinterestedness, in a king who should be the servant of all, quite at the other extreme of the practical dilemma involved in such a position. Not till some while after his death had the body been decently interred by the piety of the sisters he had driven into exile. Fraternity of feeling had been no invariable feature in the incidents of Roman story. One long *Vicus Sceleratus*, from its first dim foundation in fraternal quarrel on the morrow of a common deliverance so touching—had not almost every step in it some gloomy memory of unnatural violence? Romans did well to fancy the traitress Tarpeia still 'green in earth', crowned, enthroned, at the roots of the Capitoline rock. If in truth the religion of Rome was everywhere in it, like that perfume of the funeral incense still upon the air, so also was the memory of crime prompted by a hypocritical cruelty, down to the erring, or not erring, Vesta calmly buried alive there, only eighty years ago, under Domitian.

It was with a sense of relief that Marius found himself in the presence of Aurelius, whose gesture of friendly intelligence, as he entered, raised a smile at the gloomy train of his own thoughts just then, although since his first visit to the palace a great change had passed over it. The clear daylight found its way now into empty rooms. To raise funds for the war, Aurelius, his luxurious brother being no more, had determined to sell by auction the accumulated treasures of the imperial household. The works of art, the dainty furniture, had been removed, and were now 'on view' in the Forum, to be the delight or dismay, for many weeks to come, of the large public of those who were curious in these things. In such wise had Aurelius come to the condition of philosophic detachment he had affected as a boy, hardly persuaded to wear warm clothing, or to sleep in more luxurious manner than on the bare floor. But, in his empty house, the man of mind, who had always made so much of the pleasures of philosophic contemplation, felt freer in thought than ever. He had been reading, with less self-reproach than usual, in the *Republic* of Plato, those passages which describe the life of the philosopher-kings—like that of hired servants in their own house—who, possessed of the 'gold undefiled' of intellectual vision, forgo so cheerfully all other riches. It was one of his happy days: one of those rare days, when, almost with none of the effort, otherwise so constant with him, his thoughts came rich and full, and converged in a mental view, as exhilarating to him as the prospect of some wide expanse of landscape to another man's bodily eye. He seemed to lie readier than was his wont to the imaginative influence of the philosophic reason—to its suggestions of a possible open country, commencing just where all actual experience leaves off, but which experience, one's own and not another's, may one day occupy. In fact, he was seeking strength for himself, in his own way, before he started for that ambiguous earthly warfare which was to occupy the remainder of his life. 'Ever remember this,' he writes, 'that a happy life depends, not on *many* things—ἐν ὀλιγίστοις κεῖται.' And to-day, committing himself with a steady effort of volition to the mere silence of the great empty apartments, he might be said to have escaped, according to Plato's promise to those who live closely with philosophy, from the evils of the world.

In his 'conversations with himself' Marcus Aurelius speaks often of that *City on high*, of which all other cities are but single habitations. From him in fact Cornelius Fronto, in his late discourse, had borrowed the expression; and he certainly meant by it more than the whole commonwealth of Rome, in any idealization of it, however sublime. Incorporate somehow with the actual city whose goodly stones were lying beneath his gaze, it was also implicate in that reasonable constitution of nature, by devout contemplation of which it is possible for man to associate himself to the consciousness of God. In that *New Rome* he had taken up his rest for a while on this day, deliberately feeding his thoughts on the better air of it, as another might have gone for mental renewal to a favourite villa.

'Men seek retirement in country-houses,' he writes, 'on the sea-coast, on the mountains; and you have yourself as much fondness for such places as another. But there is little proof of culture therein; since the privilege is yours of retiring into yourself whensoever you please—into that little farm of one's own mind, where a silence so profound may be enjoyed.' That it could make these retreats, was a plain consequence of the kingly prerogative of the mind, its dominion over circumstance, its inherent liberty.—'It is in thy power to think as thou wilt:

The essence of things is in thy thoughts about them: All is opinion, conception: No man can be hindered by another: What is outside thy circle of thought is nothing at all to it; hold to this, and you are safe: One thing is needful—to live close to the divine genius within thee, and minister thereto worthily.' And the first point in this true ministry, this culture, was to maintain one's soul in a condition of indifference and calm. How continually had public claims, the claims of other persons, with their rough angularities of character, broken in upon him, the shepherd of the flock. But after all he had at least this privilege he could not part with, of thinking as he would; and it was well, now and then, by a conscious effort of will, to indulge it for a while, under systematic direction. The duty of thus making discreet, systematic use of the power of imaginative vision for purposes of spiritual culture, 'since the soul takes colour from its fantasies', is a point he has frequently insisted on.

The influence of these seasonable meditations—a symbol, or sacrament, because an intensified condition, of the soul's own ordinary and natural life—would remain upon it, perhaps for many days. There were experiences he could not forget, intuitions beyond price, he had come by in this way, which were almost like the breaking of a physical light upon his mind; as the great Augustus was said to have seen a mysterious physical splendour, yonder, upon the summit of the Capitol, where the altar of the Sibyl now stood. With a prayer, therefore, for inward quiet, for conformity to the divine reason, he read some select passages of Plato, which bear upon the harmony of the reason, in all its forms, with itself.—'Could there be *Cosmos*, that wonderful, reasonable order, in him, and nothing but disorder in the world without?' It was from this question he had passed on to the vision of a reasonable, a divine, order, not in nature, but in the condition of human affairs—that unseen Celestial City, Uranopolis, Callipolis, *Urbs Beata*—in which, a consciousness of the divine will being everywhere realized, there would be, among other felicitous differences from this lower visible world, no more quite hopeless death, of men, or children, or of their affections. He had tried to-day, as never before, to make the most of this vision of a New Rome, to realize it as distinctly as he could, and, as it were, find his way along its streets, ere he went down into a world so irksomely different, to make his practical effort towards it, with a soul full of compassion for men as they were. However distinct the mental image might have been to him, with the descent of but one flight of steps into the market-place below, it must have retreated again, as if at touch of some malign magic wand, beyond the utmost verge of the horizon. But it had been actually, in his clearest vision of it, a confused place, with but a recognizable entry, a tower or fountain, here or there, and haunted by strange faces, whose novel expression he, the great physiognomist, could by no means read. Plato, indeed, had been able to articulate, to see, at least in thought, his ideal city. But just because Aurelius had passed beyond Plato, in the scope of the gracious charities he presupposed there, he had been unable really to track his way about it. Ah! after all, according to Plato himself, all vision was but reminiscence, and this, his heart's desire, no place his soul could ever have visited in any region of the old world's achievements. He had but divined, by a kind of generosity of spirit, the void place, which another experience than his must fill.

Yet Marius noted the wonderful expression of peace, of quiet pleasure, on the countenance of Aurelius, as he received from him the rolls of fine clear manuscript, fancying the thoughts of the emperor occupied at the moment with the famous prospect towards the Alban hills, from those lofty windows.

CHAPTER XVIII

'THE CEREMONY OF THE DART'

THE ideas of Stoicism, so precious to Marcus Aurelius, ideas of large generalization, have sometimes induced, in those over whose intellects they have had real power, a coldness of heart. It was the distinction of Aurelius that he was able to harmonize them with the kindness, one might almost say the amenities, of a humorist, as also with the popular religion and its many gods. Those vasty conceptions of the later Greek philosophy had in them, in truth, the germ of a sort of austerely opinionative 'natural theology', and how often has that led to religious dryness—a hard contempt of everything in religion, which touches the senses, or charms the fancy, or really concerns the affections. Aurelius had made his own the secret of passing, naturally, and with no violence to his thought, to and fro, between the richly coloured and romantic religion of those old gods who had still been human beings, and a very abstract speculation upon the impassive, universal soul—that circle whose centre is everywhere, the circumference nowhere—of which a series of purely logical necessities had evolved the *formula*. As in many another instance, those traditional pieties of the place and the hour had been derived by him from his mother:—παρὰ τῆς μητρὸς τὸ θεοσεβές. Purified, as all such religion of concrete time and place needs to be, by frequent confronting with the ideal of godhead as revealed to that innate religious sense in the possession of which Aurelius differed from the people around him, it was the ground of many a sociability with their simpler souls, and for himself, certainly, a consolation, whenever the wings of his own soul flagged in the trying atmosphere of purely intellectual vision. A host of companions, guides, helpers, about him from of old time, 'the very court and company of heaven', objects for him of personal reverence and affection—the supposed presence of the ancient popular gods determined the character of much of his daily life, and might prove the last stay of human nature at its weakest. 'In every time and place', he had said, 'it rests with thyself to use the event of the hour religiously: at all seasons worship the gods.' And when he said 'Worship the gods!' he did it, as strenuously as everything else.

Yet here again, how often must he have experienced disillusion, or even some revolt of feeling, at that contact with coarser natures to which his religious conclusions exposed him. At the beginning of the year one hundred and seventy-three public anxiety was as great as ever; and as before, it brought people's superstition into unreserved play. For seven days the images of the old gods, and some of the graver new ones, lay solemnly exposed in the open air, arrayed in all their ornaments, each in his separate resting-place, amid lights and burning incense, while the crowd, following the imperial example, daily visited them, with offerings of flowers to this or that particular divinity, according to the devotion of each.

But supplementing these older official observances, the very wildest gods had their share of worship—strange creatures with strange secrets startled abroad into open daylight. The delirious sort of religion of which Marius was a spectator in the streets of Rome, during the seven days of the *Lectisternium*, reminded him now and again of an observation of Apuleius: it was 'as if the presence of the gods did not do men good, but disordered or weakened them'. Some jaded women of fashion, especially, found in certain oriental devotions, at once relief for their religiously tearful souls and an opportunity for personal display; preferring this or that 'mystery', chiefly because the attire required in it was suitable to their peculiar manner of beauty. And one morning Marius encountered an extraordinary crimson object, borne in a litter through an excited crowd—the famous courtesan Benedicta, still fresh from the bath of blood, to which she had submitted herself, sitting below the scaffold where the victims provided for that purpose were slaughtered by the priests. Even on the last day of the solemnity, when the emperor himself performed one of the oldest ceremonies of the Roman religion, this fantastic piety had asserted itself. There were victims enough certainly, brought from the choice pastures of the Sabine mountains, and conducted around the city they were to die for, in almost continuous procession, covered with flowers and wellnigh worried to death before the time by the crowds of people superstitiously pressing to touch them. But certain old-fashioned Romans, in these exceptional circumstances, demanded something more than this, in the way of a human sacrifice after the ancient pattern; as when, not so long since, some Greeks or

Gauls had been buried alive in the Forum. At least, human blood should be shed; and it was through a wild multitude of fanatics, cutting their flesh with knives and whips and licking up ardently the crimson stream, that the emperor repaired to the temple of Bellona, and in solemn symbolic act cast the bloodstained spear, or 'dart', carefully preserved there, towards the enemy's country—towards that unknown world of German homes, still warm, as some believed under the faint northern twilight, with those innocent affections of which Romans had lost the sense. And this at least was clear, amid all doubts of abstract right or wrong on either side, that the ruin of those homes was involved in what Aurelius was then preparing for, with—Yes! the gods be thanked for that achievement of an invigorating philosophy!—almost with a light heart.

For, in truth, that departure, really so difficult to him, for which Marcus Aurelius had needed to brace himself so strenuously, came to test the power of a long-studied theory of practice; and it was the development of this theory—a *theôria*, literally— a view, an intuition, of the most important facts, and still more important possibilities, concerning man in the world, that Marius now discovered, almost as if by accident, below the dry surface of the manuscripts entrusted to him. The great purple rolls contained, first of all, statistics, a general historical account of the writer's own time, and an exact diary; all alike, though in three different degrees of nearness to the writer's own personal experience, laborious, formal, self-suppressing. This was for the instruction of the public; and part of it has, perhaps, found its way into the *Augustan Histories*. But it was for the especial guidance of his son Commodus that he had permitted himself to break out, here and there, into reflections upon what was passing, into conversations with the reader. And then, as though he were put off his guard in this way, there had escaped into the heavy matter-of-fact, of which the main portion was composed, morsels of his conversation with himself. It was the romance of a soul (to be traced only in hints, wayside notes, quotations from older masters), as it were in lifelong and often baffled search after some vanished or elusive golden fleece, or Hesperidean fruit-trees, or some mysterious light of doctrine, ever retreating before him. A man, he had seemed to Marius from the first, of two lives, as we say. Of what nature, he had sometimes wondered, on the day, for instance, when he had interrupted the emperor's musings in the empty palace, might be that placid inward guest or inhabitant, who

from amid the preoccupations of the man of practical affairs
looked out, as if surprised, at the things and faces around.
Here, then, under the tame surface of what was meant for a
life of business, Marius discovered, welcoming a brother, the
spontaneous self-revelation of a soul as delicate as his own—a
soul for which conversation with itself was a necessity of
existence. Marius, indeed, had always suspected that the
sense of such necessity was a peculiarity of his. But here,
certainly, was another, in this respect like himself; and again
he seemed to detect the advent of some new or changed spirit
into the world, mystic, inward, hardly to be satisfied with that
wholly external and objective habit of life which had been
sufficient for the old classic soul. His purely literary curiosity
was greatly stimulated by this example of a book of self-
portraiture. It was in fact the position of the modern essayist—
creature of efforts rather than of achievements, in the matter of
apprehending truth, but at least conscious of lights by the way,
which he must needs record, acknowledge. What seemed to
underlie that position was the desire to make the most of every
experience that might come, outwardly or from within: to
perpetuate, to display, what was so fleeting, in a kind of
instinctive, pathetic protest against the imperial writer's own
theory—that theory of the 'perpetual flux' of all things—to
Marius himself, so plausible from of old.

There was, besides, a special moral or doctrinal significance
in the making of such conversation with one's self at all.
The *Logos*, the reasonable spark, in man, is common to him with
the gods—κοινὸς αὐτῷ πρὸς τοὺς θεούς—*cum diis communis.*
That might seem but the truism of a certain school of philosophy;
but in Aurelius was clearly an original and lively apprehension.
There could be no inward conversation with one's self such as
this, unless there were indeed someone else, aware of our actual
thoughts and feelings, pleased or displeased at one's disposition
of one's self. Cornelius Fronto too could enounce that theory
of the reasonable community between men and God, in many
different ways. But then, he was a cheerful man, and Aurelius
a singularly sad one; and what to Fronto was but a doctrine,
or a motive of mere rhetoric, was to the other a consolation.
He walks and talks, for a spiritual refreshment lacking which
he would faint by the way, with what to the learned professor
is but matter of philosophic eloquence.

In performing his public religious functions Marcus Aurelius
had ever seemed like one who took part in some great process,

a great thing really done, with more than the actually visible
assistants about him.   Here, in these manuscripts, in a hundred
marginal flowers of thought or language, in happy new phrases
of his own like the impromptus of an actual conversation, in
quotations from other older masters of the inward life, taking
new significance from the chances of such intercourse, was the
record of his communion with that eternal reason, which was
also his own proper self, with the divine companion, whose
tabernacle was in the intelligence of men—the journal of his
daily commerce with that.

Chance: or Providence!   Chance: or Wisdom, one with
nature and man, reaching from end to end, through all time
and all existence, orderly disposing all things, according to
fixed periods, as he describes it, in terms very like certain well-
known words of the book of *Wisdom*:—those are the 'fenced
opposites' of the speculative dilemma, the tragic *embarras*, of
which Aurelius cannot too often remind himself as the summary
of man's situation in the world.   If there be, however, a
provident soul like this 'behind the veil', truly, even to him,
even in the most intimate of those conversations, it has never
yet spoken with any quite irresistible assertion of its presence.
Yet one's choice in that speculative dilemma, as he has found
it, is on the whole a matter of will.—''Tis in thy power', here
too, again, 'to think as thou wilt.'   For his part he has asserted
his will, and has the courage of his opinion.   'To the better of
two things, if thou findest that, turn with thy whole heart:
eat and drink ever of the best before thee.'   'Wisdom', says
that other disciple of the *Sapiential* philosophy, 'hath mingled
Her wine, she hath also prepared Herself a table.'   Τοῦ ἀρίστου
ἀπόλαυε : 'Partake ever of Her best!'   And what Marius,
peeping now very closely upon the intimacies of that singular
mind, found a thing actually pathetic and affecting, was the
manner of the writer's bearing as in the presence of this supposed
guest; so elusive, so jealous of any palpable manifestation of
himself, so taxing to one's faith, never allowing one to lean
frankly upon him and feel wholly at rest.   Only, he would do
his part, at least, in maintaining the constant fitness, the
sweetness and quiet, of the guest-chamber.   Seeming to vary
with the intellectual fortune of the hour, from the plainest
account of experience, to a sheer fantasy, only 'believed because
it was impossible', that one hope was, at all events, sufficient
to make men's common pleasures and their common ambition,
above all their commonest vices, seem very petty indeed, too

petty to know of. It bred in him a kind of *magnificence* of character, in the old Greek sense of the term; a temper incompatible with any merely plausible advocacy of his convictions, or merely superficial thoughts about anything whatever, or talk about other people, or speculation as to what was passing in their so visibly little souls, or much talking of any kind, however clever or graceful. A soul thus disposed had 'already entered into the better life':—was indeed in some sort 'a priest, a minister of the gods'. Hence his constant 'recollection'; a close watching of his soul, of a kind almost unique in the ancient world.—*Before all things examine into thyself : strive to be at home with thyself !*—Marius, a sympathetic witness of all this, might almost seem to have had a foresight of monasticism itself in the prophetic future. With this mystic companion he had gone a step onward out of the merely objective pagan existence. Here was already a master in that craft of self-direction, which was about to play so large a part in the forming of human mind, under the sanction of the Christian Church.

Yet it was in truth a somewhat melancholy service, a service on which one must needs move about, solemn, serious, depressed, with the hushed footsteps of those who move about the house where a dead body is lying. Such was the impression which occurred to Marius again and again as he read, with a growing sense of some profound dissidence from his author. By certain quite traceable links of association he was reminded, in spite of the moral beauty of the philosophic emperor's ideas, how he had sat, essentially unconcerned, at the public shows. For, actually, his contemplations had made him of a sad heart, inducing in him that melancholy—*Tristitia*—which even the monastic moralists have held to be of the nature of deadly sin, akin to the sin of *Desidia* or Inactivity. Resignation, a sombre resignation, a sad heart, patient bearing of the burden of a sad heart:—Yes! this belonged doubtless to the situation of an honest thinker upon the world. Only, in this case there seemed to be too much of a complacent acquiescence in the world as it is. And there could be no true *Théodicée* in that; no real accommodation of the world as it is, to the divine pattern of the *Logos*, the eternal reason, over against it. It amounted to a tolerance of evil.

The soul of good, though it moveth upon a way thou canst but little understand, yet prospereth on the journey:

If thou sufferest nothing contrary to nature, there can be naught of evil with thee therein:

If thou hast done aught in harmony with that reason in which men
are communicant with the gods, there also can be nothing of evil
with thee—nothing to be afraid of:
Whatever is, is right; as from the hand of one dispensing to every
man according to his desert:
If reason fulfil its part in things, what more dost thou require?
Dost thou take it ill that thy stature is but of four cubits?
That which happeneth to each of us is for the profit of the whole:
The profit of the whole—that was sufficient!

—Links, in a train of thought really generous! of which, nevertheless, the forced and yet facile optimism, refusing to see evil
anywhere, might lack, after all, the secret of genuine cheerfulness.
It left in truth a weight upon the spirits; and with that weight
unlifted, there could be no real justification of the ways of
Heaven to man. 'Let thine air be cheerful', he had said;
and, with an effort, did himself at times attain to that serenity
of aspect, which surely ought to accompany, as their outward
flower and favour, hopeful assumptions like those. Still, what
in Aurelius was but a passing expression, was with Cornelius
(Marius could but note the contrast) nature, and a veritable
physiognomy. With Cornelius, in fact, it was nothing less
than the joy which Dante apprehended in the blessed spirits
of the perfect, the outward semblance of which, like a reflex
of physical light upon human faces from 'the land which is very
far off', we may trace from Giotto onward to its consummation
in the work of Raphael—the serenity, the durable cheerfulness,
of those who have been indeed delivered from death, and of
which the utmost degree of that famed 'blitheness' of the
Greeks had been but a transitory gleam, as in careless and
wholly superficial youth. And yet, in Cornelius, it was certainly
united with the bold recognition of evil as a fact in the world;
real as an aching in the head or heart, which one instinctively
desires to have cured; an enemy with whom no terms could be
made, visible, hatefully visible, in a thousand forms—the
apparent waste of men's gifts in an early, or even in a late grave;
the death, as such, of men, and even of animals; the disease
and pain of the body.

And there was another point of dissidence between Aurelius
and his reader.—The philosophic emperor was a despiser of
the body. Since it is 'the peculiar privilege of reason to move
within herself, and to be proof against corporeal impressions,
suffering neither sensation nor passion to break in upon her',
it follows that the true interest of the spirit must ever be to
treat the body—Well! as a corpse attached thereto, rather than

as a living companion—nay, actually to promote its dissolution. In counterpoise to the inhumanity of this, presenting itself to the young reader as nothing less than a sin against nature, the very person of Cornelius was nothing less than a sanction of that reverent delight Marius had always had in the visible body of man. Such delight indeed had been but a natural consequence of the sensuous or materialistic character of the philosophy of his choice. Now to Cornelius the body of man was unmistakably, as a later seer terms it, the one true temple in the world; or rather itself the proper object of worship, of a sacred service, in which the very finest gold might have its seemliness and due symbolic use:—Ah! and of what awe-stricken pity also, in its dejection, in the perishing grey bones of a poor man's grave!

Some flaw of vision, thought Marius, must be involved in the philosopher's contempt for it—some diseased point of thought, or moral dullness, leading logically to what seemed to him the strangest of all the emperor's inhumanities, the temper of the suicide; for which there was just then, indeed, a sort of *mania* in the world. ''Tis part of the business of life', he read, 'to lose it handsomely.' On due occasion, 'one might give life the slip'. The moral or mental powers might fail one; and then it were a fair question, precisely, whether the time for taking leave was not come:—'Thou canst leave this prison when thou wilt. Go forth boldly!' Just there, in the bare capacity to entertain such question at all, there was what Marius, with a soul which must always leap up in loyal gratitude for mere physical sunshine, touching him as it touched the flies in the air, could not away with. There, surely, was a sign of some crookedness in the natural power of apprehension. It was the attitude, the melancholy intellectual attitude, of one who might be greatly mistaken in things—who might make the greatest of mistakes.

A heart that could forget itself in the misfortune, or even in the weakness of others:—of this Marius had certainly found the trace, as a confidant of the emperor's conversations with himself, in spite of those jarring inhumanities, of that pretension to a stoical indifference, and the many difficulties of his manner of writing. He found it again not long afterwards, in still stronger evidence, in this way. As he read one morning early, there slipped from the rolls of manuscript a sealed letter with the emperor's superscription, which might well be of importance, and he felt bound to deliver it at once in person; Aurelius being then absent from Rome in one of his favourite retreats, at

Praeneste, taking a few days of quiet with his young children, before his departure for the war. A whole day passed as Marius crossed the *Campagna* on horseback, pleased by the random autumn lights bringing out in the distance the sheep at pasture, the shepherds in their picturesque dress, the golden elms, tower and villa; and it was after dark that he mounted the steep street of the little hill town to the imperial residence. He was struck by an odd mixture of stillness and excitement about the place. Lights burned at the windows. It seemed that numerous visitors were within, for the courtyard was crowded with litters and horses in waiting. For the moment, indeed, all larger cares, even the cares of war, of late so heavy a pressure, had been forgotten in what was passing with the little Annius Verus; who for his part had forgotten his toys, lying all day across the knees of his mother, as a mere child's earache grew rapidly to alarming sickness with great and manifest agony, only suspended a little, from time to time, when from very weariness he passed into a few moments of unconsciousness. The country surgeon called in had removed the imposthume with the knife. There had been a great effort to bear this operation, for the terrified child, hardly persuaded to submit himself, when his pain was at its worst, and even more for the parents. At length, amid a company of pupils pressing in with him, as the custom was, to watch the proceedings in the sick-room, the eminent Galen had arrived, only to pronounce the thing done visibly useless, the patient falling now into longer intervals of delirium. And thus, thrust on one side by the crowd of departing visitors, Marius was forced into the privacy of a grief, the desolate face of which went deep into his memory, as he saw the emperor carry the child away—quite conscious at last, but with a touching expression upon it of weakness and defeat—pressed close to his bosom, as if he yearned just then for one thing only, to be united, to be absolutely one with it, in its obscure distress.

CHAPTER XIX

THE WILL AS VISION

Paratum cor meum deus! paratum cor meum!

THE emperor demanded a senatorial decree for the erection of images in memory of the dead prince; that a golden one should be carried, together with the other images, in the great procession of the *Circus*, and the addition of the child's name to the Hymn of the Salian Priests: and so, stifling private grief, without further delay set forth for the war.

True kingship, as Plato, the old master of Aurelius, had understood it, was essentially of the nature of a service. If so be, you can discover a mode of life more desirable than the being a king, for those who shall be kings; then, the true Ideal of the State will become a possibility; but not otherwise. And if the life of Beatific Vision be indeed possible, if philosophy really 'concludes in an ecstasy', affording full fruition to the entire nature of man; then, for certain elect souls at least, a mode of life will have been discovered more desirable than to be a king. By love or fear you might induce such persons to forgo their privilege; to take upon them the distasteful task of governing other men, or even of leading them to victory in battle. But, by the very conditions of its tenure, their dominion would be wholly a ministry to others: they would have taken upon them 'the form of a servant': they would be reigning for the well-being of others rather than their own. The true king, the righteous king, would be Saint Louis, exiling himself from the better land and its perfected company—so real a thing to him, definite and real as the pictured scenes of his psalter—to take part in or to arbitrate men's quarrels, about the transitory appearances of things. In a lower degree (lower, in proportion as the highest Platonic dream is lower than any Christian vision) the true king would be Marcus Aurelius, drawn from the meditation of books, to be the ruler of the Roman people in peace, and still more, in war.

To Aurelius, certainly, the philosophic mood, the visions, however dim, which this mood brought with it, were sufficiently pleasant to him, together with the endearments of his home, to make public rule nothing less than a sacrifice of himself according to Plato's requirement, now consummated in his setting forth for the campaign on the Danube. That it was such a sacrifice was to Marius visible fact, as he saw him ceremoniously lifted into the saddle amid all the pageantry of an imperial departure, yet with the air less of a sanguine and self-reliant leader than of one in some way or other already defeated. Through the fortune of the subsequent years, passing and repassing so inexplicably from side to side, the rumour of which reached him amid his own quiet studies, Marius seemed always to see that central figure, with its habitually dejected hue grown now to an expression of positive suffering, all the stranger from its contrast with the magnificent armour worn by the emperor on this occasion, as it had been worn by his predecessor Hadrian.

—Totus et argento contextus et auro:

clothed in its gold and silver, dainty as that old divinely constructed armour of which Homer tells, but without its miraculous lightsomeness—he looked out baffled, labouring, moribund; a mere comfortless shadow taking part in some shadowy reproduction of the labours of Hercules, through those northern, mist-laden confines of the civilized world. It was as if the familiar soul which had been so friendly disposed towards him were actually departed to Hades; and when he read the *Conversations* afterwards, though his judgment of them underwent no material change, it was nevertheless with the allowance we make for the dead. The memory of that suffering image, while it certainly strengthened his adhesion to what he could accept at all in the philosophy of Aurelius, added a strange pathos to what must seem the writer's mistakes. What, after all, had been the meaning of that incident, observed as so fortunate an omen long since, when the prince, then a little child much younger than was usual, had stood in ceremony among the priests of Mars and flung his crown of flowers with the rest at the sacred image reclining on the *Pulvinar* ? The other crowns lodged themselves here or there; when, Lo! the crown thrown by Aurelius, the youngest of them all, alighted upon the very brows of the god, as if placed there by a careful hand! He was still young, also, when on the day of his adoption by Antoninus Pius he saw himself in a dream, with as it were shoulders of ivory, like the images of the gods, and found them more capable than shoulders of flesh. Yet he was now wellnigh fifty years of age, setting out with two-thirds of life behind him, upon a labour which would fill the remainder of it with anxious cares—a labour for which he had perhaps no capacity, and certainly no taste.

That ancient suit of armour was almost the only object Aurelius now possessed from all those much cherished articles of *vertu* collected by the Caesars, making the imperial residence like a magnificent museum. Not men alone were needed for the war, so that it became necessary, to the great disgust alike of timid persons and of the lovers of sport, to arm the gladiators, but money also was lacking. Accordingly, at the sole motion of Aurelius himself, unwilling that the public burden should be further increased, especially on the part of the poor, the whole of the imperial ornaments and furniture, a sumptuous collection of gems formed by Hadrian, with many works of the most famous painters and sculptors, even the precious ornaments of the emperor's chapel or *Lararium*, and the wardrobe of the Empress Faustina, who seems to have borne the loss without a murmur, were exposed for public auction. 'These treasures,' said Aurelius, 'like all else that I possess, belong by right to the Senate and People.' Was it not a characteristic of the true kings in Plato that they had in their houses nothing they could call their own? Connoisseurs had a keen delight in the mere reading of the *Praetor's* list of the property for sale. For two months the learned in these matters were daily occupied in the appraising of the embroidered hangings, the choice articles of personal use selected for preservation by each succeeding age, the great outlandish pearls from Hadrian's favourite cabinet, the marvellous plate lying safe behind the pretty iron wicker-work of the shops in the goldsmiths' quarter. Meantime ordinary persons might have an interest in the inspection of objects which had been as daily companions to people so far above and remote from them—things so fine also in workmanship and material as to seem, with their antique and delicate air, a worthy survival of the grand bygone eras, like select thoughts or utterances embodying the very spirit of the vanished past. The town became more pensive than ever over old fashions.

The welcome amusement of this last act of preparation for the great war being now over, all Rome seemed to settle down into a singular quiet, likely to last long, as though bent only on watching from afar the languid, somewhat uneventful course of the contest itself. Marius took advantage of it as an opportunity for still closer study than of old, only now and then going out to one of his favourite spots on the Sabine or Alban hills for a quiet even greater than that of Rome in the country air. On one of these occasions, as if by favour of an invisible power withdrawing some unknown cause of dejection from around him, he enjoyed a quite unusual sense of self-possession—the possession of his own best and happiest self. After some gloomy thoughts overnight, he awoke under the full tide of the rising sun, himself full, in his entire refreshment, of that almost religious appreciation of sleep, the graciousness of its influence on men's spirits, which had made the old Greeks conceive of it as a god. It was like one of those old joyful wakings of childhood, now becoming rarer and rarer with him, and looked back upon with much regret as a measure of advancing age. In fact, the last bequest of this serene sleep had been a dream, in which, as once before, he overheard those he loved best pronouncing his name very pleasantly, as they passed through the rich light and shadow of a summer morning, along the pavement of a city—Ah! fairer far than Rome! In a moment, as he arose, a certain oppression of late setting very heavily upon him was lifted away, as though by some physical motion in the air.

That flawless serenity, better than the most pleasurable excitement, yet so easily ruffled by chance collision even with the things and persons he had come to value as the greatest treasure in life, was to be wholly his to-day, he thought, as he rode towards Tibur, under the early sunshine; the marble of its villas glistening all the way before him on the hillside. And why could he not hold such serenity of spirit ever at command? he asked, expert as he was at last become in the art of setting the house of his thoughts in order. ''Tis in thy power to think as thou wilt': he repeated to himself: it was the most serviceable of all the lessons enforced on him by those imperial *Conversations*. —''Tis in thy power to think as thou wilt.' And were the cheerful, sociable, restorative beliefs, of which he had there read so much, that bold adhesion, for instance, to the hypothesis of an eternal friend to man, just hidden behind the veil of a mechanical and material order, but only just behind it, ready perhaps even now to break through:—were they, after all, really a matter of choice, dependent on some deliberate act of volition on his part? Were they doctrines one might take for granted, generously take for granted, and led on by them, at first as but well-defined objects of hope, come at last into the region of a corresponding certitude of the intellect? 'It is the truth I seek,' he had read, 'the truth, by which no one', grey and depressing though it might seem, 'was ever really injured.' And yet, on the other hand, the imperial wayfarer, he had been able to go along with so far on his intellectual pilgrimage, let fall many things concerning the practicability of a methodical and self-forced assent to certain principles or pre-suppositions 'one could not do without'. Were there, as the expression '*one could not do without*' seemed to hint, beliefs without which life itself must be almost impossible, principles which had their sufficient ground of evidence in that very fact? Experience certainly taught that, as regarding the sensible world he could attend or not, almost at will, to this or that colour, this or that train of sounds, in the whole tumultuous concourse of colour and sound, so it was also, for the well-trained intelligence, in regard to that hum of voices which besiege the inward no less than the outward ear. Might it be not otherwise with those various and competing hypotheses, the permissible hypotheses, which, in that open field for hypothesis—one's own actual ignorance of the origin and tendency of our being—present themselves so importunately, some of them with so emphatic a reiteration, through all the mental changes of successive ages? Might the will itself be an organ of knowledge, of vision?

On this day truly no mysterious light, no irresistibly leading hand from afar reached him; only the peculiarly tranquil influence of its first hour increased steadily upon him, in a manner with which, as he conceived, the aspects of the place he was then visiting had something to do. The air there, air supposed to possess the singular property of restoring the whiteness of ivory, was pure and thin. An even veil of lawn-like white cloud had now drawn over the sky; and under its broad, shadowless light every hue and tone of time came out upon the yellow old temples, the elegant pillared circle of the shrine of the patronal Sibyl, the houses seemingly of a piece with the ancient fundamental rock. Some half-conscious motive of poetic grace would appear to have determined their grouping; in part resisting, partly going along with the natural wildness and harshness of the place, its floods and precipices. An air of immense age possessed, above all, the vegetation around—a world of evergreen trees—the olives especially, older than how many generations of men's lives! fretted and twisted by the combining forces of life and death into every conceivable caprice of form. In the windless weather all seemed to be listening to the roar of the immemorial waterfall, plunging down so unassociably among these human habitations, and with a motion so unchanging from age to age as to count, even in this time-worn place, as an image of unalterable rest. Yet the clear sky all but broke to let through the ray which was silently quickening everything in the late February afternoon, and the unseen violet refined itself through the air. It was as if the spirit of life in nature were but withholding any too precipitate revelation of itself, in its slow, wise, maturing work.

Through some accident to the trappings of his horse at the inn where he rested, Marius had an unexpected delay. He sat down in an olive garden, and, all around him and within still turning to reverie, the course of his own life hitherto seemed to withdraw itself into some other world, disparted from this spectacular point where he was now placed to survey it, like that distant road below, along which he had travelled this morning across the *Campagna*. Through a dreamy land he could see himself moving, as if in another life, and like another person, through all his fortunes and misfortunes, passing from point to point, weeping, delighted, escaping from various dangers. That prospect brought him, first of all, an impulse of lively gratitude: it was as if he must look round for someone else to share his joy with: for someone to whom he might tell the thing, for his own relief. Companionship, indeed, familiarity with others, gifted in this way or that, or at least pleasant to him, had been, through one or another long span of it, the chief delight of the journey. And was it only the resultant general sense of such familiarity, diffused through his memory, that in a while suggested the question whether there had not been—besides Flavian, besides Cornelius even, and amid the solitude which in spite of ardent friendship he had perhaps loved best of all things—some other companion, an unfailing companion, ever at his side throughout; doubling his pleasure in the roses by the way, patient of his peevishness or depression, sympathetic above all with his grateful recognition, onward from his earliest days, of the fact that he was there at all? Must not the whole world around have faded away for him altogether, had he been left for one moment really alone in it? In his deepest apparent solitude there had been rich entertainment. It was as if there were not one only, but two wayfarers, side by side, visible there across the plain, as he indulged his fancy. A bird came and sang among the wattled hedge-roses: an animal feeding crept nearer: the child who kept it was gazing quietly: and the scene and the hours still conspiring, he passed from that mere fantasy of a self not himself, beside him in his coming and going, to those divinations of a living and companionable spirit at work in all things, of which he had become aware from time to time in his old philosophic readings—in Plato and others, last but not least, in Aurelius. Through one reflection upon another, he passed from such instinctive divinations, to the thoughts which give them logical consistency, formulating at last, as the necessary exponent of our own and the world's life, that reasonable Ideal to which the Old Testament gives the name of *Creator*, which for the philosophers of Greece is the *Eternal Reason*, and in the New Testament the *Father of Men*—even as one builds up from act and word and expression of the friend actually visible at one's side, an ideal of the spirit within him.

In this peculiar and privileged hour, his bodily frame, as he could recognize, although just then, in the whole sum of its capacities, so entirely possessed by him—Nay! actually his very self—was yet determined by a far-reaching system of material forces external to it, a thousand combining currents from earth and sky. Its seemingly active powers of apprehension were, in fact, but susceptibilities to influence. The perfection of its capacity might be said to depend on its passive surrender, as of a leaf on the wind, to the motions of the great stream of physical energy without it. And might not the intellectual frame also, still more intimately himself as in truth it was, after the analogy of the bodily life, be a moment only, an impulse or series of impulses, a single process, in an intellectual or spiritual system external to it, diffused through all time and place—that great stream of spiritual energy, of which his own imperfect thoughts, yesterday or to-day, would be but the remote, and therefore imperfect, pulsations? It was the hypothesis (boldest, though in reality the most conceivable of all hypotheses) which had dawned on the contemplations of the two opposed great masters of the old Greek thought, alike:—the 'World of Ideas', existent only because, and in so far as, they are known, as Plato conceived; the 'creative, incorruptible, informing mind', supposed by Aristotle, so sober-minded, yet as regards this matter left something of a mystic after all. Might not this entire material world, the very scene around him, the immemorial rocks, the firm marble, the olive gardens, the falling water, be themselves but reflections in, or a creation of, that one indefectible mind, wherein he too became conscious, for an hour, a day, for so many years? Upon what other hypothesis could he so well understand the persistency of all these things for his own intermittent consciousness of them, for the intermittent consciousness of so many generations, fleeting away one after another? It was easier to conceive of the material fabric of things as but an element in a world of thought—as a thought in a mind, than of mind as an element, or accident, or passing condition in a world of matter, because mind was really nearer to himself: it was an explanation of what was less known by what was known better. The purely material world, that close, impassable prison-wall, seemed just then the unreal thing, to be actually dissolving away all around him: and he felt a quiet hope, a quiet joy dawning faintly, in the dawning of this doctrine upon him as a really credible opinion. It was like the break of day over some vast prospect with the 'new city', as it were some celestial New Rome, in the midst of it. That divine companion figured no longer as but an occasional wayfarer beside him; but rather as the unfailing 'assistant', without whose inspiration and concurrence he could not breathe or see, instrumenting his bodily senses, rounding, supporting his imperfect thoughts. How often had the thought of their brevity spoiled for him the most natural pleasures of life, confusing even his present sense of them by the suggestion of disease, of death, of a coming end, in everything! How had he longed, sometimes, that there were indeed one to whose boundless power of memory he could commit his own most fortunate moments, his admiration, his love, Aye! the very sorrows of which he could not bear quite to lose the sense:—one strong to retain them even though he forgot, in whose more vigorous consciousness they might subsist for ever, beyond that mere quickening of capacity which was all that remained of them in himself! 'Oh! that they might live before Thee'—To-day at least, in the peculiar clearness of one privileged hour, he seemed to have apprehended that in which the experiences he valued most might find, one by one, an abiding-place. And again, the resultant sense of companionship, of a person beside him, evoked the faculty of conscience—of conscience, as of old and when he had been at his best, in the form, not of fear, nor of self-reproach even, but of a certain lively gratitude.

Himself—his sensations and ideas—never fell again precisely into focus as on that day, yet he was the richer by its experience. But for once only to have come under the power of that peculiar mood, to have felt the train of reflections which belong to it really forcible and conclusive, to have been led by them to a conclusion, to have apprehended the *Great Ideal*, so palpably that it defined personal gratitude and the sense of a friendly hand laid upon him amid the shadows of the world, left this one particular hour a marked point in life never to be forgotten. It gave him a definitely ascertained measure of his moral or intellectual need, of the demand his soul must make upon the powers, whatsoever they might be, which had brought him, as he was, into the world at all. And again, would he be faithful to himself, to his own habits of mind, his leading suppositions, if he did but remain just there? Must not all that remained of life be but a search for the equivalent of that Ideal, among so-called actual things—a gathering together of every trace or token of it, which his actual experience might present?

PART THE FOURTH

CHAPTER XX

TWO CURIOUS HOUSES

I. GUESTS

Your old men shall dream dreams.

A NATURE like that of Marius, composed, in about equal parts, of instincts almost physical, and of slowly accumulated intellectual judgments, was perhaps even less susceptible than other men's characters of essential change. And yet the experience of that fortunate hour, seeming to gather into one central act of vision all the deeper impressions his mind had ever received, did not leave him quite as he had been. For his mental view, at least, it changed measurably the world about him, of which he was still indeed a curious spectator, but which looked farther off, was weaker in its hold, and, in a sense, less real to him than ever. It was as if he viewed it through a diminishing glass. And the permanency of this change he could note, some years later, when it happened that he was a guest at a feast, in which the various exciting elements of Roman life, its physical and intellectual accomplishments, its frivolity and far-fetched elegances, its strange, mystic essays after the unseen, were elaborately combined. The great Apuleius, the literary ideal of his boyhood, had arrived in Rome—was now visiting Tusculum, at the house of their common friend, a certain aristocratic poet who loved every sort of superiorities; and Marius was favoured with an invitation to a supper given in his honour.

It was with a feeling of half-humorous concession to his own early boyish hero-worship, yet with some sense of superiority in himself, seeing his old curiosity grown now almost to indifference when on the point of satisfaction at last, and upon a juster estimate of its object, that he mounted to the little town on the hillside, the footways of which were so many flights of easy-going steps gathered round a single great house under shadow of the 'haunted' ruins of Cicero's villa on the wooded heights. He found a touch of weirdness in the circumstance that in so romantic a place he had been bidden to meet the

writer who was come to seem almost like one of the personages
in his own fiction. As he turned now and then to gaze at the
evening scene through the tall narrow openings of the street,
up which the cattle were going home slowly from the pastures
below, the Alban mountains, stretched between the great walls
of the ancient houses, seemed close at hand—a screen of
vaporous dun purple against the setting sun—with those waves
of surpassing softness in the boundary lines which indicate
volcanic formation. The coolness of the little brown market-
place, for profit of which even the working people, in long file
through the olive-gardens, were leaving the plain for the night,
was grateful, after the heats of Rome. Those wild country
figures, clad in every kind of fantastic patchwork, stained by
wind and weather fortunately enough for the eye, under that
significant light inclined him to poetry. And it was a very
delicate poetry of its kind that seemed to enfold him, as passing
into the poet's house he paused for a moment to glance back
towards the heights above; whereupon, the numerous cascades
of the precipitous garden of the villa, framed in the doorway
of the hall, fell into a harmless picture, in its place among the
pictures within, and scarcely more real than they—a landscape-
piece, in which the power of water (plunging into what unseen
depths!), done to the life, was pleasant, and without its natural
terrors.

At the farther end of this bland apartment, fragrant with
the rare woods of the old inlaid panelling, the falling of aromatic
oil from the ready-lighted lamps, the iris-root clinging to the
dresses of the guests, as with odours from the altars of the gods,
the supper-table was spread, in all the daintiness characteristic
of the agreeable *petit-maître*, who entertained. He was already
most carefully dressed, but, like Martial's Stella, perhaps
consciously, meant to change his attire once and again during
the banquet; in the last instance, for an ancient vesture (object
of much rivalry among the young men of fashion, at that great
sale of the imperial wardrobes), a toga, of altogether lost hue
and texture. He wore it with a grace which became the leader
of a thrilling movement then on foot for the restoration of that
disused garment, in which, laying aside the customary evening
dress, all the visitors were requested to appear, setting off the
delicate sinuosities and well-disposed 'golden ways' of its folds,
with harmoniously tinted flowers. The opulent sunset, blending
pleasantly with artificial light, fell across the quiet ancestral
effigies of old consular dignitaries, along the wide floor strewn

with sawdust of sandal-wood, and lost itself in the heap of cool coronals, lying ready for the foreheads of the guests on a sideboard of old citron. The crystal vessels darkened with old wine, the hues of the early autumn fruit—mulberries, pomegranates, and grapes that had long been hanging under careful protection upon the vines, were almost as much a feast for the eye as the dusky fires of the rare twelve-petalled roses. A favourite animal, white as snow, brought by one of the visitors, purred its way gracefully among the wine-cups, coaxed onward from place to place by those at table, as they reclined easily on their cushions of German eider-down, spread over the long-legged, carved couches.

A highly refined modification of the *acroama*—a musical performance during supper for the diversion of the guests—was presently heard hovering round the place, soothingly, and so unobtrusively that the company could not guess, and did not like to ask, whether or not it had been designed by their entertainer. They inclined on the whole to think it some wonderful peasant-music peculiar to that wild neighbourhood, turning, as it did now and then, to a solitary reed-note, like a bird's, while it wandered into the distance. It wandered quite away at last, as darkness with a bolder lamplight came on, and made way for another sort of entertainment. An odd, rapid, phantasmal glitter, advancing from the garden by torchlight, defined itself, as it came nearer, into a dance of young men in armour. Arrived at length in a portico, open to the supper chamber, they contrived that their mechanical march-movement should fall out into a kind of highly expressive dramatic action; and with the utmost possible emphasis of dumb motion, their long swords weaving a silvery network in the air, they danced the *Death of Paris*. The young Commodus, already an adept in these matters, who had condescended to welcome the eminent Apuleius at the banquet, had mysteriously dropped from his place to take his share in the performance; and at its conclusion reappeared, still wearing the dainty accoutrements of Paris, including a breastplate, composed entirely of overlapping tigers' claws, skilfully gilt. The youthful prince had lately assumed the dress of manhood, on the return of the emperor for a brief visit from the north; putting up his hair, in imitation of Nero, in a golden box dedicated to Capitoline Jupiter. His likeness to Aurelius, his father, was become, in consequence, more striking than ever; and he had one source of genuine interest in the great literary guest of the occasion, in that the latter was the fortunate possessor of a monopoly for the exhibition of wild beasts and gladiatorial shows in the province of Carthage, where he resided.

Still, after all complaisance to the perhaps somewhat crude tastes of the emperor's son, it was felt that with a guest like Apuleius, whom they had come prepared to entertain as veritable *connoisseurs*, the conversation should be learned and superior, and the host at last deftly led his company round to literature, by the way of bindings. Elegant rolls of manuscript from his fine library of ancient Greek books passed from hand to hand about the table. It was a sign for the visitors themselves to draw their own choicest literary curiosities from their bags, as their contribution to the banquet; and one of them, a famous reader, choosing his lucky moment, delivered in *tenor* voice the piece which follows, with a preliminary query as to whether it could indeed be the composition of Lucian of Samosata, understood to be the great mocker of that day:

'What sound was that, Socrates?' asked Chaerephon. 'It came from the beach under the cliff yonder, and seemed a long way off.—And how melodious it was! Was it a bird, I wonder. I thought all sea-birds were songless.'

'Aye! a sea-bird,' answered Socrates, 'a bird called the Halcyon, and has a note full of plaining and tears. There is an old story people tell of it. It was a mortal woman once, daughter of Aeolus, god of the winds. Ceyx, the son of the morning-star, wedded her in her early maidenhood. The son was not less fair than the father; and when it came to pass that he died, the crying of the girl as she lamented his sweet usage, was—Just that! And some while after, as Heaven willed, she was changed into a bird. Floating now on bird's wings over the sea she seeks her lost Ceyx there; since she was not able to find him after long wandering over the land.'

'That then is the Halcyon—the kingfisher', said Chaerephon. 'I never heard a bird like it before. It has truly a plaintive note. What kind of a bird is it, Socrates?'

'Not a large bird, though she has received large honour from the gods on account of her singular conjugal affection. For whensoever she makes her nest, a law of nature brings round what is called Halcyon's weather—days distinguishable among all others for their serenity, though they come sometimes amid the storms of winter—days like to-day! See how transparent is the sky above us, and how motionless the sea!—like a smooth mirror.'

'True! A Halcyon day, indeed! and yesterday was the same. But tell me, Socrates, what is one to think of those stories which have been told from the beginning, of birds changed into mortals and mortals into birds? To me nothing seems more incredible.'

'Dear Chaerephon,' said Socrates, 'methinks we are but half-blind judges of the impossible and the possible. We try the question by the standard of our human faculty, which avails neither for true knowledge, nor for faith, nor vision. Therefore many things seem to us impossible which are really easy, many things unattainable which are within our reach; partly through inexperience, partly through the childishness of our minds. For in truth, every man, even the oldest of us, is like a little child, so brief and babyish are the years of our life in comparison of eternity. Then, how can we, who comprehend not the faculties of gods and of the heavenly host, tell whether aught of that kind be possible or no?—What a tempest you saw three days ago! One trembles but to think of the lightning, the thunderclaps, the violence of the wind! You might have thought the whole world was going to ruin. And then, after a little, came this wonderful serenity of weather, which has continued till to-day. Which do you think the greater and more difficult thing to do:—to exchange the disorder of that irresistible whirlwind to a clarity like this, and becalm the whole world again, or to refashion the form of a woman into that of a bird? We can teach even little children to do something of that sort—to take wax or clay, and mould out of the same material many kinds of form, one after another, without difficulty. And it may be that to the Deity, whose power is too vast for comparison with ours, all processes of that kind are manageable and easy. How much wider is the whole circle of heaven than thyself?—Wider than thou canst express.

'Among ourselves also, how vast the difference we may observe in men's degrees of power! To you and me, and many another like us, many things are impossible which are quite easy to others. For those who are unmusical, to play on the flute; to read or write, for those who have not yet learned; is no easier than to make birds of women, or women of birds. From the dumb and lifeless egg Nature moulds her swarms of winged creatures, aided, as some will have it, by a divine and secret art in the wide air around us. She takes from the honeycomb a little memberless live thing; she brings it wings and feet, brightens and beautifies it with quaint variety of colour:—and

Lo! the bee in her wisdom, making honey worthy of the gods.

'It follows, that we mortals, being altogether of little account, able wholly to discern no great matter, sometimes not even a little one, for the most part at a loss regarding what happens even with ourselves, may hardly speak with security as to what may be the powers of the immortal gods concerning Kingfisher, or Nightingale. Yet the glory of thy mythus, as my fathers bequeathed it to me, O tearful songstress! that will I too hand on to my children, and tell it often to my wives, Xanthippe and Myrto:—the story of thy pious love to Ceyx, and of thy melodious hymns; and, above all, of the honour thou hast with the gods!'

The reader's well-turned periods seemed to stimulate, almost uncontrollably, the eloquent stirrings of the eminent man of letters then present. The impulse to speak masterfully was visible, before the recital was well over, in the moving lines about his mouth, by no means designed, as detractors were wont to say, simply to display the beauty of his teeth. One of the company, expert in his humours, made ready to transcribe what he would say, the sort of things of which a collection was then forming, the 'Florida' or Flowers, so to call them, he was apt to let fall by the way—no *impromptu* ventures at random; but rather elaborate, carved ivories of speech, drawn, at length, out of the rich treasure-house of a memory stored with such, and as with a fine savour of old musk about them. Certainly in this case, as Marius thought, it was worth while to hear a charming writer speak. Discussing, quite in our modern way, the peculiarities of those suburban views, especially the sea-views, of which he was a professed lover, he was also every inch a priest of Aesculapius, patronal god of Carthage. There was a piquancy in his *rococo*, very African, and as it were perfumed personality, though he was now wellnigh sixty years old, a mixture there of that sort of Platonic spiritualism which can speak of the soul of man as but a sojourner in the prison of the body—a blending of that with such a relish for merely bodily graces as availed to set the fashion in matters of dress, deportment, accent, and the like, nay! with something also which reminded Marius of the vein of coarseness he had found in the 'Golden Book'. All this made the total impression he conveyed a very uncommon one. Marius did not wonder, as he watched him speaking, that people freely attributed to him many of the marvellous adventures he had recounted in that famous romance, over and above the wildest version of his own actual story—his extraordinary marriage, his religious initiations, his acts of mad generosity, his trial as a sorcerer.

But a sign came from the imperial prince that it was time for the company to separate. He was entertaining his immediate neighbours at the table with a trick from the streets; tossing his olives in rapid succession into the air, and catching them, as they fell, between his lips. His dexterity in this performance made the mirth around him noisy, disturbing the sleep of the furry visitor: the learned party broke up; and Marius withdrew, glad to escape into the open air. The courtesans in their large wigs of false blond hair were lurking for the guests, with groups of curious idlers. A great conflagration was visible in the distance. Was it in Rome; or in one of the villages of the country? Pausing for a few minutes on the terrace to watch it, Marius was for the first time able to converse intimately with Apuleius; and in this moment of confidence the 'illuminist', himself with locks so carefully arranged, and seemingly so full of affectations, almost like one of those light women there, dropped a veil as it were, and appeared, though still permitting the play of a certain element of theatrical interest in his *bizarre* tenets, to be ready to explain and defend his position reasonably. For a moment his fantastic foppishness and his pretensions to ideal vision seemed to fall into some intelligible congruity with each other. In truth, it was the Platonic Idealism, as he conceived it, which for him literally animated, and gave him so lively an interest in, this world of the purely outward aspects of men and things.—Did material things, such things as they had had around them all that evening, really need apology for being there, to interest one, at all? Were not all visible objects—the whole material world indeed, according to the consistent testimony of philosophy in many forms—'full of souls'? embarrassed perhaps, partly imprisoned, but still eloquent souls? Certainly, the contemplative philosophy of Plato, with its figurative imagery and apologue, its manifold aesthetic colouring, its measured eloquence, its music for the outward ear, had been, like Plato's old master himself, a two-sided or two-coloured thing. Apuleius was a Platonist: only, for him, the *Ideas* of Plato were no creatures of logical abstraction, but in very truth informing souls, in every type and variety of sensible things. Those noises in the house all supper-time, sounding through the tables and along the walls:—were they only startings in the old rafters, at the impact of the music and laughter; or rather importunities of the secondary selves, the true unseen selves, of the persons, nay! of the very things around, essaying to break through their frivolous, merely transitory surfaces, to remind one of abiding essentials beyond them, which might have their say, their judgment to give, by and by, when the shifting of the meats and drinks at life's table would be over? And was not this the true significance of the Platonic doctrine? — a hierarchy of divine beings, associating themselves with particular things and places, for the purpose of mediating between God and man—man, who does but need due attention on his part to become aware of his celestial company, filling the air about him, thick as motes in the sunbeam, for the glance of sympathetic intelligence he casts through it.

'Two kinds there are, of animated beings', he exclaimed: 'Gods, entirely differing from men in the infinite distance of their abode, since one part of them only is seen by our blunted vision—those mysterious stars!—in the eternity of their existence, in the perfection of their nature, infected by no contact with ourselves; and men, dwelling on the earth,.with frivolous and anxious minds, with infirm and mortal members, with variable fortunes; labouring in vain; taken altogether and in their whole species perhaps, eternal; but, severally, quitting the scene in irresistible succession.

'What then? Has nature connected itself together by no bond, allowed itself to be thus crippled, and split into the divine and human elements? And you will say to me: If so it be, that man is thus entirely exiled from the immortal gods, that all communication is denied him, that not one of them occasionally visits us, as a shepherd his sheep—to whom shall I address my prayers? Whom shall I invoke as the helper of the unfortunate, the protector of the good?

'Well! there are certain divine powers of a middle nature, through whom our aspirations are conveyed to the gods, and theirs to us. Passing between the inhabitants of earth and heaven, they carry from one to the other prayers and bounties, supplication and assistance, being a kind of interpreters. This interval of the air is full of them! Through them, all revelations, miracles, magic processes, are effected. For, specially appointed members of this order have their special provinces, with a ministry according to the disposition of each. They go to and fro without fixed habitation: or dwell in men's houses——'

Just then a companion's hand laid in the darkness on the

shoulder of the speaker carried him away, and the discourse broke off suddenly. Its singular intimations, however, were sufficient to throw back on this strange evening, in all its detail—the dance, the readings, the distant fire—a kind of allegoric expression: gave it the character of one of those famous Platonic figures or apologues which had then been in fact under discussion. When Marius recalled its circumstances he seemed to hear once more that voice of genuine conviction, pleading, from amidst a scene at best of elegant frivolity, for so boldly mystical a view of man and his position in the world. For a moment, but only for a moment, as he listened, the trees had seemed, as of old, to be growing 'close against the sky'. Yes! the reception of theory, of hypothesis, of beliefs, did depend a great deal on temperament. They were, so to speak, mere equivalents of temperament. A celestial ladder, a ladder from heaven to earth: that was the assumption which the experience of Apuleius had suggested to him: it was what, in different forms, certain persons in every age had instinctively supposed: they would be glad to find their supposition accredited by the authority of a grave philosophy. Marius, however, yearning not less than they, in that hard world of Rome, and below its unpeopled sky, for the trace of some celestial wing across it, must still object that they assumed the thing with too much facility, too much of self-complacency. And his second thought was, that to indulge but for an hour fantasies, fantastic visions of that sort, only left the actual world more lonely than ever. For him certainly, and for his solace, the little godship for whom the rude countryman, an unconscious Platonist, trimmed his twinkling lamp, would never slip from the bark of these immemorial olive-trees.—No! not even in the wildest moonlight. For himself, it was clear, he must still hold by what his eyes really saw. Only, he had to concede also, that the very boldness of such theory bore witness, at least, to a variety of human disposition and a consequent variety of mental view, which might—who could tell?—be correspondent to, be defined by and define, varieties of facts, of truths, just 'behind the veil', regarding the world all alike had actually before them as their original premise or starting-point; a world wider, perhaps, in its possibilities, than all possible fancies concerning it.

CHAPTER XXI

II. THE CHURCH IN CECILIA'S HOUSE

Your old men shall dream dreams, and your young men shall see visions.

CORNELIUS had certain friends in or near Rome, whose household, to Marius, as he pondered now and again what might be the determining influences of that peculiar character, presented itself as possibly its main secret—the hidden source from which the beauty and strength of a nature, so persistently fresh in the midst of a somewhat jaded world, might be derived. But Marius had never yet seen these friends; and it was almost by accident that the veil of reserve was at last lifted, and, with strange contrast to his visit to the poet's villa at Tusculum, he entered another curious house.

'The house in which she lives', says that mystical German writer quoted once before, 'is for the orderly soul, which does not live on blindly before her, but is ever, out of her passing experiences, building and adorning the parts of a many-roomed abode for herself, only an expansion of the body; as the body, according to the philosophy of Swedenborg, is but a process, an expansion, of the soul. For such an orderly soul, as life proceeds, all sorts of delicate affinities establish themselves, between herself and the doors and passage-ways, the lights and shadows, of her outward dwelling-place, until she may seem incorporate with it—until at last, in the entire expressiveness of what is outward, there is for her, to speak properly, between outward and inward, no longer any distinction at all; and the light which creeps at a particular hour on a particular picture or space upon the wall, the scent of flowers in the air at a particular window, become to her, not so much apprehended objects, as themselves powers of apprehension and doorways to things beyond—the germ or rudiment of certain new faculties, by which she, dimly yet surely, apprehends a matter lying beyond her actually attained capacities of spirit and sense.'

So it must needs be in a world which is itself, we may think, together with that bodily 'tent' or 'tabernacle', only one of many vestures for the clothing of the pilgrim soul, to be left by her, surely, as if on the wayside, worn out one by one, as it was from her, indeed, they borrowed what momentary value or significance they had.

The two friends were returning to Rome from a visit to a country-house, where again a mixed company of guests had been assembled; Marius, for his part, a little weary of gossip, and those sparks of ill-tempered rivalry which would seem sometimes to be the only sort of fire the intercourse of people in general society can strike out of them. A mere reaction upon this, as they started in the clear morning, made their companionship, at least for one of them, hardly less tranquillizing than the solitude he so much valued. Something in the south-west wind, combining with their own intention, favoured increasingly, as the hours wore on, a serenity like that Marius had felt once before in journeying over the great plain towards Tibur—a serenity that was to-day brotherly amity also, and seemed to draw into its own charmed circle whatever was then present to eye or ear, while they talked or were silent together, and all petty irritations, and the like, shrank out of existence, or kept certainly beyond its limits. The natural fatigue of the long journey overcame them quite suddenly at last, when they were still about two miles distant from Rome. The seemingly endless line of tombs and cypresses had been just where a cross-road from the *Latin Way* fell into the *Appian*, that Cornelius halted at a doorway in a long, low wall—the outer wall of some villa courtyard, it might be supposed—as if at liberty to enter, and rest there awhile. He held the door open for his companion to enter also, if he would; with an expression, as he lifted the latch, which seemed to ask Marius, apparently shrinking from a possible intrusion: 'Would you like to see it?' Was he willing to look upon that, the seeing of which might define—yes! define the critical turning-point in his days?

The little doorway in this long, low wall admitted them, in fact, into the court or garden of a villa, disposed in one of those abrupt natural hollows which give its character to the country in this place; the house itself, with all its dependent buildings, the spaciousness of which surprised Marius as he entered, being thus wholly concealed from passengers along the road. All around, in those well-ordered precincts, were the quiet signs of wealth, and of a noble taste—a taste, indeed, chiefly evidenced

in the selection and juxtaposition of the material it had to deal
with, consisting almost exclusively of the remains of older art,
here arranged and harmonized, with effects, both as regards
colour and form, so delicate as to seem really derivative from
some finer intelligence in these matters than lay within the
resources of the ancient world. It was the old way of true
Renaissance—being indeed the way of Nature with her roses,
the divine way with the body of man, perhaps with his soul—
conceiving the new organism by no sudden and abrupt creation,
but rather by the action of a new principle upon elements, all
of which had in truth already lived and died many times.
The fragments of older architecture, the mosaics, the spiral
columns, the precious corner-stones of immemorial building,
had put on, by such juxtaposition, a new and singular expressiveness, an air of grave thought, of an intellectual purpose, in
itself, aesthetically, very seductive. Lastly, herb and tree had
taken possession, spreading their seed-bells and light branches,
just astir in the trembling air, above the ancient garden wall,
against the wide realms of sunset. And from the first they
could hear singing, the singing of children mainly, it would
seem, and of a new kind; so novel indeed in its effect, as to
bring suddenly to the recollection of Marius, Flavian's early
essays towards a new world of poetic sound. It was the
expression not altogether of mirth, yet of some wonderful sort
of happiness—the blithe self-expansion of a joyful soul in
people upon whom some all-subduing experience had wrought
heroically, and who still remembered, on this bland afternoon,
the hour of a great deliverance.

His old native susceptibility to the spirit, the special sympathies, of places—above all, to any hieratic or religious significance they might have—was at its liveliest, as Marius, still
encompassed by that peculiar singing, and still amid the
evidences of a grave discretion all around him, passed into the
house. That intelligent seriousness about life, the absence of
which had ever seemed to remove those who lacked it into
some strange species wholly alien from himself, accumulating
all the lessons of his experience since those first days at White-
nights, was as it were translated here, as if in designed congruity
with his favourite precepts of the power of physical vision,
into an actual picture. If the true value of souls is in proportion to what they can admire, Marius was just then an
acceptable soul. As he passed through the various chambers,
great and small, one dominant thought increased upon him, the

thought of chaste women and their children—of all the various affections of family life under its most natural conditions, yet developed, as if in devout imitation of some sublime new type of it, into large controlling passions.   There reigned throughout, an order and purity, an orderly disposition, as if by way of making ready for some gracious spousals.   The place itself was like a bride adorned for her husband; and its singular cheerfulness, the abundant light everywhere, the sense of peaceful industry, of which he received a deep impression though without precisely reckoning wherein it resided, as he moved on rapidly, were in forcible contrast just at first to the place to which he was next conducted by Cornelius still with a sort of eager, hurried, half-troubled reluctance,. and as if he forbore the explanation which might well be looked for by his companion.

An old flower garden in the rear of the house, set here and there with a venerable olive-tree—a picture in pensive shade and fiery blossom, as transparent, under that afternoon light, as the old miniature-painters' work on the walls of the chambers within—was bounded towards the west by a low, grass-grown hill.   A narrow opening cut in its steep side, like a solid blackness there, admitted Marius and his gleaming leader into a hollow cavern or crypt, neither more nor less in fact than the family burial-place of the Cecilii, to whom this residence belonged, brought thus, after an arrangement then becoming not unusual, into immediate connexion with the abode of the living, in bold assertion of that instinct of family life, which the sanction of the *Holy Family* was, hereafter, more and more to reinforce. Here, in truth, was the centre of the peculiar religious expressiveness, of the sanctity, of the entire scene.   That 'any person may, at his own election, constitute the place which belongs to him a *religious* place, by the carrying of his dead into it':—had been a maxim of old Roman law, which it was reserved for the early Christian societies, like that established here by the piety of a wealthy Roman matron, to realize in all its consequences. Yet this was certainly unlike any cemetery Marius had ever before seen; most obviously in this, that these people had returned to the older fashion of disposing of their dead by burial instead of burning.   Originally a family sepulchre, it was growing to a vast *necropolis*, a whole township of the deceased, by means of some free expansion of the family interest beyond its amplest natural limits.   That air of venerable beauty which characterized the house and its precincts above, was maintained also here.   It was certainly with a great outlay of labour that these long, apparently endless, yet elaborately designed galleries, were increasing so rapidly, with their layers of beds or berths, one above another, cut, on either side the pathway, in the porous *tufa*, through which all the moisture filters downwards, leaving the parts above dry and wholesome. All alike were carefully closed, and with all the delicate costliness at command; some with simple tiles of baked clay, many with slabs of marble, enriched by fair inscriptions: marble taken, in some cases, from older pagan tombs—the inscription sometimes a *palimpsest*, the new epitaph being woven into the faded letters of an earlier one.

As in an ordinary Roman cemetery, an abundance of utensils for the worship or commemoration of the departed was disposed around—incense, lights, flowers, their flame or their freshness being relieved to the utmost by contrast with the coal-like blackness of the soil itself, a volcanic sandstone, cinder of burnt-out fires. Would they ever kindle again?—possess, transform, the place?—Turning to an ashen pallor where, at regular intervals, an air-hole or *luminare* let in a hard beam of clear but sunless light, with the heavy sleepers, row upon row within, leaving a passage so narrow that only one visitor at a time could move along, cheek to cheek with them, the high walls seemed to shut one in into the great company of the dead. Only the long straight pathway lay before him; opening, however, here and there, into a small chamber, around a broad, table-like coffin or 'altar-tomb', adorned even more profusely than the rest as if for some anniversary observance. Clearly, these people, concurring in this with the special sympathies of Marius himself, had adopted the practice of burial from some peculiar feeling of hope they entertained concerning the body; a feeling which, in no irreverent curiosity, he would fain have penetrated. The complete and irreparable disappearance of the dead in the funeral fire, so crushing to the spirits, as he for one had found it, had long since induced in him a preference for that other mode of settlement to the last sleep, as having something about it more homelike and hopeful, at least in outward seeming. But whence the strange confidence that these 'handfuls of white dust' would hereafter recompose themselves once more into exulting human creatures? By what heavenly alchemy, what reviving dew from above, such as was certainly never again to reach the dead violets?—*Januarius, Agapetus, Felicitas ; Martyrs ! refresh, I pray you, the soul of Cecil, of Cornelius !* said an inscription, one of many, scratched, like a passing sigh, when it was still fresh in the mortar that had closed up the prison door. All critical estimate of this bold hope, as sincere apparently as it was audacious in its claim, being set aside, here at least, carried further than ever before, was that pious, systematic commemoration of the dead, which, in its chivalrous refusal to forget or finally desert the helpless, had ever counted with Marius as the central exponent or symbol of all natural duty.

The stern soul of the excellent Jonathan Edwards, applying the faulty theology of John Calvin, afforded him, we know, the vision of infants not a span long, on the floor of hell. Every visitor to the Catacombs must have observed, in a very different theological connexion, the numerous children's graves there— beds of infants, but a span long indeed, lowly 'prisoners of hope', on these sacred floors. It was with great curiosity, certainly, that Marius considered them, decked in some instances with the favourite toys of their tiny occupants—toy soldiers, little chariot wheels, the entire paraphernalia of a baby-house; and when he saw afterwards the living children, who sang and were busy above—sang their psalm *Laudate Pueri Dominum !*— their very faces caught for him a sort of quaint unreality from the memory of those others, the children of the Catacombs, but a little way below them.

Here and there, mingling with the record of merely natural decease, and sometimes even at these children's graves, were the signs of violent death or 'martyrdom'—proofs that some 'had loved not their lives unto the death'—in the little red phial of blood, the palm-branch, the red flowers for their heavenly 'birthday'. About one sepulchre in particular, dis- tinguished in this way, and devoutly arrayed for what, by a bold paradox, was thus treated as, *natalitia*—a birthday, the peculiar arrangements of the whole place visibly centred. And it was with a singular novelty of feeling, like the dawning of a fresh order of experiences upon him, that, standing beside those mournful relics, snatched in haste from the common place of execution not many years before, Marius became, as by some gleam of foresight, aware of the whole force of evidence for a certain strange, new hope, defining in its turn some new and weighty motive of action, which lay in deaths so tragic for the 'Christian superstition'. Something of them he had heard indeed already. They had seemed to him but one savagery the more, savagery self-provoked, in a cruel and stupid world.

And yet these poignant memorials seemed also to draw him onwards to-day, as if towards an image of some still more pathetic suffering, in the remote background. Yes! the interest, the expression, of the entire neighbourhood was instinct with it, as with the savour of some priceless incense. Penetrating the whole atmosphere, touching everything around with its peculiar sentiment, it seemed to make all this visible mortality, death's very self—Ah! lovelier than any fable of old mythology had ever thought to render it, in the utmost limits of fantasy; and this, in simple candour of feeling about a supposed fact. *Peace ! Pax ! Pax tecum !*—the word, the thought—was put forth everywhere, with images of hope, snatched sometimes from that jaded pagan world which had really afforded men so little of it from first to last; the various consoling images it had thrown off, of succour, of regeneration, of escape from the grave—Hercules wrestling with Death for possession of Alcestis, Orpheus taming the wild beasts, the Shepherd with his sheep, the Shepherd carrying the sick lamb upon his shoulders. Yet these imageries after all, it must be confessed, formed but a slight contribution to the dominant effect of tranquil hope there—a kind of heroic cheerfulness and grateful expansion of heart, as with the sense, again, of some real deliverance, which seemed to deepen the longer one lingered through these strange and awful passages. A figure, partly pagan in character, yet most frequently repeated of all these visible parables—the figure of one just escaped from the sea, still clinging as for life to the shore in surprised joy, together with the inscription beneath it, seemed best to express the prevailing sentiment of the place. And it was just as he had puzzled out this inscription—

> *I went down to the bottom of the mountains :*
> *The earth with her bars was about me for ever :*
> *Yet hast Thou brought up my life from corruption !*

—that with no feeling of suddenness or change Marius found himself emerging again, like a later mystic traveller through similar dark places 'quieted by hope', into the daylight.

They were still within the precincts of the house, still in possession of that wonderful singing, although almost in the open country, with a great view of the *Campagna* before them, and the hills beyond. The orchard or meadow, through which their path lay, was already grey with twilight, though the western sky, where the greater stars were visible, was still afloat in crimson splendour. The colour of all earthly things seemed repressed by the contrast, yet with a sense of great richness lingering in their shadows. At that moment the voice of the singers, a 'voice of joy and health', concentrated itself with solemn antistrophic movement into an evening, or 'candle' hymn.

> Hail! Heavenly Light, from His pure glory poured,
> Who is the Almighty Father, heavenly, blest:—
> Worthiest art Thou, at all times to be sung
> With undefilèd tongue.—

It was like the evening itself made audible, its hopes and fears, with the stars shining in the midst of it. Half above, half below the level white mist, dividing the light from the darkness, came now the mistress of this place, the wealthy Roman matron, left early a widow a few years before, by Cecilius, 'Confessor and Saint'. With a certain antique severity in the gathering of the long mantle, and with coif or veil folded decorously below the chin, 'grey within grey', to the mind of Marius her temperate beauty brought reminiscences of the serious and virile character of the best female statuary of Greece. Quite foreign, however, to any Greek statuary was the expression of pathetic care with which she carried a little child at rest in her arms. Another, a year or two older, walked beside, the fingers of one hand within her girdle. She paused for a moment with a greeting for Cornelius.

That visionary scene was the close, the fitting close, of the afternoon's strange experiences. A few minutes later, passing forward on his way along the public road, he could have fancied it a dream. The house of Cecilia grouped itself beside that other curious house he had lately visited at Tusculum. And what a contrast was presented by the former, in its suggestions of hopeful industry, of immaculate cleanness, of responsive affection!—all alike determined by that transporting discovery of some fact, or series of facts, in which the old puzzle of life had found its solution. In truth, one of his most characteristic and constant traits had ever been a certain longing for escape— for some sudden, relieving interchange, across the very spaces of life, it might be, along which he had lingered most pleasantly— for a lifting, from time to time, of the actual horizon. It was like the necessity under which the painter finds himself, to set a window or open doorway in the background of his picture; or like a sick man's longing for northern coolness, and the whispering willow-trees, amid the breathless evergreen forests

of the south. To some such effect had this visit occurred to
him, and through so slight an accident. Rome and Roman
life, just then, were come to seem like some stifling forest of
bronze-work, transformed, as if by malign enchantment, out of
the generations of living trees, yet with roots in a deep, down-
trodden soil of poignant human susceptibilities. In the midst
of its suffocation, that old longing for escape had been satisfied
by this vision of the church in Cecilia's house, as never before.
It was still, indeed, according to the unchangeable law of his
temperament, to the eye, to the visual faculty of mind, that
those experiences appealed—the peaceful light and shade, the
boys whose very faces seemed to sing, the virginal beauty of
the mother and her children. But, in his case, what was thus
visible constituted a moral or spiritual influence, of a somewhat
exigent and controlling character, added anew to life, a new
element therein, with which, consistently with his own chosen
maxim, he must make terms.

The thirst for every kind of experience, encouraged by a
philosophy which taught that nothing was intrinsically great
or small, good or evil, had ever been at strife in him with a
hieratic refinement, in which the boy-priest survived, prompting
always the selection of what was perfect of its kind, with
subsequent loyal adherence of his soul thereto. This had carried
him along in a continuous communion with ideals, certainly
realized in part, either in the conditions of his own being, or in
the actual company about him, above all, in Cornelius. Surely,
in this strange new society he had touched upon for the first
time to-day—in this strange family, like 'a garden enclosed'—
was the fulfilment of all the preferences, the judgments, of that
half-understood friend, which of late years had been his protection so often amid the perplexities of life. Here, it might be,
was, if not the cure, yet the solace or anodyne of his great
sorrows—of that constitutional sorrowfulness, not peculiar to
himself perhaps, but which had made his life certainly like one
long 'disease of the spirit'. Merciful intention made itself
known remedially here, in the mere contact of the air, like a
soft touch upon aching flesh. On the other hand, he was aware
that new responsibilities also might be awakened—new and
untried responsibilities—a demand for something from him in
return. Might this new vision, like the malignant beauty of
pagan Medusa, be exclusive of any admiring gaze upon anything
but itself? At least he suspected that, after the beholding of
it, he could never again be altogether as he had been before.

CHAPTER XXII

FAITHFUL to the spirit of his early Epicurean philosophy and the impulse to surrender himself, in perfectly liberal inquiry about it, to anything that, as a matter of fact, attracted or impressed him strongly, Marius informed himself with much pains concerning the church in Cecilia's house; inclining at first to explain the peculiarities of that place by the establishment there of the *schola* or common hall of one of those burial-guilds, which then covered so much of the unofficial, and, as it might be called, subterranean enterprise of Roman society.

And what he found, thus looking, literally, for the dead among the living, was the vision of a natural, a scrupulously natural, love, transforming, by some new gift of insight into the truth of human relationships, and under the urgency of some new motive by him so far unfathomable, all the conditions of life. He saw, in all its primitive freshness and amid the lively facts of its actual coming into the world, as a reality of experience, that regenerate type of humanity, which, centuries later, Giotto and his successors, down to the best and purest days of the young Raphael, working under conditions very friendly to the imagination, were to conceive as an artistic ideal. He felt there, felt amid the stirring of some wonderful new hope within himself, the genius, the unique power of Christianity; in exercise then, as it has been exercised ever since, in spite of many hindrances, and under the most inopportune circumstances. Chastity—as he seemed to understand—the chastity of men and women, amid all the conditions, and with the results, proper to such chastity, is the most beautiful thing in the world and the truest conservation of that creative energy by which men and women were first brought into it. The nature of the family, for which the better genius of old Rome itself had sincerely cared, of the family and its appropriate affections—all that love of one's kindred by which obviously one does triumph in some degree over death—had never been so felt before. Here, surely! in its genial warmth, its jealous exclusion of all that was opposed to it, to its own immaculate naturalness, in the hedge set around the sacred thing on every side, this development of the family did but carry forward, and give effect to, the purposes, the kindness, of nature itself, friendly to man.   As if by way of a due recognition of some immeasurable divine condescension manifest in a certain historic fact, its influence was felt more especially at those points which demanded some sacrifice of one's self, for the weak, for the aged, for little children, and even for the dead.   And then, for its constant outward token, its significant manner or index, it issued in a certain debonair grace, and a certain mystic attractiveness, a courtesy, which made Marius doubt whether that famed Greek 'blitheness', or gaiety, or grace, in the handling of life, had been, after all, an unrivalled success.   Contrasting with the incurable insipidity even of what was most exquisite in the higher Roman life, of what was still truest to the primitive soul of goodness amid its evil, the new creation he now looked on—as it were a picture beyond the craft of any master of old pagan beauty—had indeed all the appropriate freshness of a 'bride adorned for her husband'. Things new and old seemed to be coming as if out of some goodly treasure-house, the brain full of science, the heart rich with various sentiment, possessing withal this surprising healthfulness, this reality of heart.

'You would hardly believe', writes Pliny—to his own wife!— 'what a longing for you possesses me.   Habit—that we have not been used to be apart—adds herein to the primary force of affection.   It is this keeps me awake at night fancying I see you beside me.   That is why my feet take me unconsciously to your sitting-room at those hours when I was wont to visit you there.   That is why I turn from the door of the empty chamber, sad and ill at ease, like an excluded lover.'—

There, is a real idyll from that family life, the protection of which had been the motive of so large a part of the religion of the Romans, still surviving among them; as it survived also in Aurelius, his disposition and aims, and, spite of slanderous tongues, in the attained sweetness of his interior life.   What Marius had been permitted to see was a realization of such life higher still: and with—Yes! with a more effective sanction and motive than it had ever possessed before, in that fact, or series of facts, to be ascertained by those who would.

The central glory of the reign of the Antonines was that society had attained in it, though very imperfectly, and for the most part by cumbrous effort of law, many of those ends to which Christianity went straight, with the sufficiency, the success, of a direct and appropriate instinct. Pagan Rome, too, had its touching charity sermons on occasions of great public distress; its charity children in long file, in memory of the elder Empress Faustina; its prototype under patronage of Aesculapius, of the modern hospital for the sick on the island of Saint Bartholomew. But what pagan charity was doing tardily, and as if with the painful calculation of old age, the Church was doing, almost without thinking about it, with all the liberal enterprise of youth, because it was her very being thus to do. 'You fail to realize your own good intentions', she seems to say, to pagan virtue, pagan kindness. She identified herself with those intentions and advanced them with an unparalleled freedom and largeness. The gentle Seneca would have reverent burial provided even for the dead body of a criminal. Yet when a certain woman collected for interment the insulted remains of Nero, the pagan world surmised that she must be a Christian: only a Christian would have been likely to conceive so chivalrous a devotion towards mere wretchedness. 'We refuse to be witnesses even of a homicide commanded by the law,' boasts the dainty conscience of a Christian apologist, 'we take no part in your cruel sports nor in the spectacles of the amphitheatre, and we hold that to witness a murder is the same thing as to commit one.' And there was another duty almost forgotten, the sense of which Rousseau brought back to the degenerate society of a later age. In an impassioned discourse the sophist Favorinus counsels mothers to suckle their own infants; and there are Roman epitaphs erected to mothers, which gratefully record this proof of natural affection as a thing then unusual. In this matter too, what a sanction, what a provocative to natural duty, lay in that image discovered to Augustus by the Tiburtine Sibyl, amid the aurora of a new age, the image of the Divine Mother and the Child, just then rising upon the world like the dawn!

Christian belief, again, had presented itself as a great inspirer of chastity. Chastity, in turn, realized in the whole scope of its conditions, fortified that rehabilitation of peaceful labour, after the mind, the pattern, of the workman of Galilee, which was another of the natural instincts of the Catholic Church, as being indeed the long-desired initiator of a religion of cheerfulness, as a true lover of the industry—so to term it—the labour, the creation, of God.

And this severe yet genial assertion of the ideal of woman, of the family, of industry, of man's work in life, so close to the truth of nature, was also, in that charmed hour of the minor 'Peace of the Church', realized as an influence tending to beauty, to the adornment of life and the world. The sword in the world, the right eye plucked out, the right hand cut off, the spirit of reproach which those images express, and of which monasticism is the fulfilment, reflect one side only of the nature of the divine missionary of the New Testament. Opposed to, yet blent with, this ascetic or militant character, is the function of the Good Shepherd, serene, blithe, and debonair, beyond the gentlest shepherd of Greek mythology; of a king under whom the beatific vision is realized of a reign of peace—peace of heart —among men. Such aspect of the divine character of Christ, rightly understood, is indeed the final consummation of that bold and brilliant hopefulness in man's nature, which had sustained him so far through his immense labours, his immense sorrows, and of which pagan gaiety in the handling of life is but a minor achievement. Sometimes one, sometimes the other, of those two contrasted aspects of its Founder, have, in different ages and under the urgency of different human needs, been at work also in the Christian Church. Certainly, in that brief 'Peace of the Church' under the Antonines, the spirit of a pastoral security and happiness seems to have been largely expanded. There, in the Early Church of Rome, was to be seen, and on sufficiently reasonable grounds, that satisfaction and serenity on a dispassionate survey of the facts of life, which all hearts had desired, though for the most part in vain, con-trasting itself for Marius, in particular, very forcibly, with the imperial philosopher's so heavy burden of unrelieved melancholy. It was Christianity in its humanity, or even its humanism, in its generous hopes for man, its common sense and alacrity of cheerful service, its sympathy with all creatures, its appreciation of beauty and daylight.

'The angel of righteousness', says the *Shepherd of Hermas*, the most characteristic religious book of that age, its *Pilgrim's Progress*—'the angel of righteousness is modest and delicate and meek and quiet. Take from thyself grief, for (as Hamlet will one day discover) 'tis the sister of doubt and ill-temper. Grief is more evil than any other spirit of evil, and is most dreadful to the servants of God, and beyond all spirits destroyeth man. For, as when good news is come to one in grief, straight-way he forgetteth his former grief, and no longer attendeth to anything except the good news which he hath heard, so do ye, also! having received a renewal of your soul through the beholding of these good things. Put on therefore gladness that hath always favour before God, and is acceptable unto Him, and delight thyself in it; for every man that is glad doeth the things that are good, and thinketh good thoughts, despising grief.'—Such were the commonplaces of this new people, among whom so much of what Marius had valued most in the old world seemed to be under renewal and further promotion. Some transforming spirit was at work to harmonize contrasts, to deepen expression—a spirit which, in its dealing with the elements of ancient life, was guided by a wonderful tact of selection, exclusion, juxtaposition, begetting thereby a unique effect of freshness, a grave yet wholesome beauty, because the world of sense, the whole outward world was understood to set forth the veritable unction and royalty of a certain priesthood and kingship of the soul within, among the prerogatives of which was a delightful sense of freedom.

The reader may think, perhaps, that Marius, who, Epicurean as he was, had his visionary aptitudes, by an inversion of one of Plato's peculiarities with which he was of course familiar, must have descended, by *foresight*, upon a later age than his own, and anticipated Christian poetry and art as they came to be under the influence of Saint Francis of Assisi. But if he dreamed on one of those nights of the beautiful house of Cecilia, its lights and flowers, of Cecilia herself moving among the lilies, with an enhanced grace as happens sometimes in healthy dreams, it was indeed hardly an anticipation. He had lighted, by one of the peculiar intellectual good-fortunes of his life, upon a period when, even more than in the days of austere *ascêsis* which had preceded and were to follow it, the Church was true for a moment, truer perhaps than she would ever be again, to that element of profound serenity in the soul of her Founder, which reflected the eternal goodwill of God to man, 'in whom', according to the oldest version of the angelic message, 'He is well pleased'.

For what Christianity did many centuries afterwards in the way of informing an art, a poetry, of graver and higher beauty, we may think, than that of Greek art and poetry at their best, was in truth conformable to the original tendency of its genius. The genuine capacity of the Catholic Church in this direction, discoverable from the first in the New Testament, was also really at work, in that earlier 'Peace', under the Antonines—

the minor 'Peace of the Church', as we might call it, in distinction
from the final 'Peace of the Church', commonly so called, under
Constantine. Saint Francis, with his following in the sphere of
poetry and of the arts—the voice of Dante, the hand of Giotto—
giving visible feature and colour, and a palpable place among
men, to the regenerate race, did but re-establish a continuity,
only suspended in part by those troublous intervening centuries
—the 'Dark Ages', properly thus named—with the gracious
spirit of the primitive church, as manifested in that first early
springtide of her success. The greater 'Peace' of Constantine,
on the other hand, in many ways, does but establish the exclusiveness, the puritanism, the ascetic gloom which, in the period
between Aurelius and the first Christian emperor, characterized
a church under misunderstanding or oppression, driven back,
in a world of tasteless controversy, inwards upon herself.

Already, in the reign of Antoninus Pius, the time was gone
by when men became Christians under some sudden and overpowering impression, and with all the disturbing results of
such a crisis. At this period the larger number, perhaps, had
been born Christians, had been ever with peaceful hearts in
their 'Father's house'. That earlier belief in the speedy coming
of judgment and of the end of the world, with the consequences
it so naturally involved in the temper of men's minds, was
dying out. Every day the contrast between the Church and
the world was becoming less pronounced. And now also, as
the Church rested awhile from opposition, that rapid self-
development outward from within, proper to times of peace,
was in progress. Antoninus Pius, it might seem, more truly
even than Marcus Aurelius himself, was of that group of pagan
saints for whom Dante, like Augustine, has provided in his
scheme of the house with many mansions. A sincere old Roman
piety had urged his fortunately constituted nature to no mistakes,
no offences against humanity. And of his entire freedom from
guile one reward had been this singular happiness, that under
his rule there was no shedding of Christian blood. To him
belonged that half-humorous placidity of soul, of a kind
illustrated later very effectively by Montaigne, which, starting
with an instinct of mere fairness towards human nature and the
world, seems at last actually to qualify its possessor to be
almost the friend of the people of Christ. Amiable, in its own
nature, and full of a reasonable gaiety, Christianity has often
had its advantage of characters such as that. The geniality of
Antoninus Pius, like the geniality of the earth itself, had per-

mitted the Church, as being in truth no alien from that old mother earth, to expand and thrive for a season as by natural process. And that charmed period under the Antonines, extending to the later years of the reign of Aurelius (beautiful, brief chapter of ecclesiastical history!), contains, as one of its motives of interest, the earliest development of Christian ritual under the presidence of the Church of Rome.

Again as in one of those mystical, quaint visions of the *Shepherd of Hermas*, 'the aged woman was become by degrees more and more youthful. And in the third vision she was quite young, and radiant with beauty: only her hair was that of an aged woman. And at the last she was joyous, and seated upon a throne—seated upon a throne, because her position is a strong one'. The subterranean worship of the Church belonged properly to those years of her early history in which it was illegal for her to worship at all. But, hiding herself for a while as conflict grew violent, she resumed, when there was felt to be no more than ordinary risk, her natural freedom. And the kind of outward prosperity she was enjoying in those moments of her first 'Peace', her modes of worship now blossoming freely above-ground, was reinforced by the decision at this point of a crisis in her internal history.

In the history of the Church, as throughout the moral history of mankind, there are two distinct ideals, either of which it is possible to maintain—two conceptions, under one or the other of which we may represent to ourselves men's efforts towards a better life—corresponding to those two contrasted aspects, noted above, as discernible in the picture afforded by the New Testament itself of the character of Christ. The ideal of asceticism represents moral effort as essentially a sacrifice, the sacrifice of one part of human nature to another, that it may live the more completely in what survives of it; while the ideal of culture represents it as a harmonious development of all the parts of human nature, in just proportion to each other. It was to the latter order of ideas that the Church, and especially the Church of Rome in the age of the Antonines, freely lent herself. In that earlier 'Peace' she had set up for herself the ideal of spiritual development, under the guidance of an instinct by which, in those serene moments, she was absolutely true to the peaceful soul of her Founder. 'Goodwill to men,' she said, 'in whom God Himself is well pleased!' For a little while, at least, there was no forced opposition between the soul and the body, the world and the spirit, and the grace of graciousness itself was pre-eminently with the people of Christ. Tact, good sense, ever the note of a true orthodoxy, the merciful compromises of the church, indicative of her imperial vocation in regard to all the varieties of human kind, with a universality of which the old Roman pastorship she was superseding is but a prototype, was already become conspicuous, in spite of a discredited, irritating, vindictive society, all around her.

Against that divine urbanity and moderation the old error of Montanus we read of dimly, was a fanatical revolt—sour, falsely anti-mundane, ever with an air of ascetic affectation, and a bigoted distaste in particular for all the peculiar graces of womanhood. By it the desire to please was understood to come of the author of evil. In this interval of quietness, it was perhaps inevitable, by the law of reaction, that some such extravagances of the religious temper should arise. But again the Church of Rome, now becoming every day more and more completely the capital of the Christian world, checked the nascent Montanism, or puritanism of the moment, vindicating for all Christian people a cheerful liberty of heart, against many a narrow group of sectaries, all alike, in their different ways, accusers of the genial creation of God. With her full, fresh faith in the *Evangele*—in a veritable regeneration of the earth and the body, in the dignity of man's entire personal being—for a season, at least, at that critical period in the development of Christianity, she was for reason, for common sense, for fairness to human nature, and, generally, for what may be called the naturalness of Christianity.—As also for its comely order: she would be 'brought to her king in raiment of needlework'. It was by the bishops of Rome, diligently transforming themselves, in the true catholic sense, into universal pastors, that the path of what we must call humanism was thus defined.

And then, in this hour of expansion, as if now at last the Catholic Church might venture to show her outward lineaments as they really were, worship—'the beauty of holiness', nay! the elegance of sanctity—was developed, with a bold and confident gladness, the like of which has hardly been the ideal of worship in any later age. The tables in fact were turned: the prize of a cheerful temper on a candid survey of life was no longer with the pagan world. The aesthetic charm of the Catholic Church, her evocative power over all that is eloquent and expressive in the better mind of man, her outward comeliness, her dignifying convictions about human nature:—all this, as abundantly realized centuries later by Dante and Giotto, by the great medieval church builders, by the great ritualists like Saint Gregory, and the masters of sacred music in the Middle Age—we may see already, in dim anticipation, in those charmed moments towards the end of the second century. Dissipated or turned aside, partly through the fatal mistake of Marcus Aurelius himself, for a brief space of time we may discern that influence clearly predominant there. What might seem harsh as dogma was already justifying itself as worship; according to the sound rule: *Lex orandi, lex credendi*—Our creeds are but the brief abstract of our prayer and song.

The wonderful liturgical spirit of the Church, her wholly unparalleled genius for worship, being thus awake, she was rapidly reorganizing both pagan and Jewish elements of ritual, for the expanding therein of her own new heart of devotion. Like the institutions of monasticism, like the Gothic style of architecture, the ritual system of the Church, as we see it in historic retrospect, ranks as one of the great, conjoint, and (so to term them) *necessary*, products of human mind. Destined for ages to come to direct with so deep a fascination men's religious instincts, it was then already recognizable as a new and precious fact in the sum of things. What has been on the whole the method of the Church, as 'a power of sweetness and patience', in dealing with matters like pagan art, pagan literature, was even then manifest; and has the character of the moderation, the divine moderation of Christ himself. It was only among the ignorant, indeed, only in the 'villages', that Christianity, even in conscious triumph over paganism, was really betrayed into iconoclasm. In the final 'Peace' of the Church under Constantine, while there was plenty of destructive fanaticism in the country, the revolution was accomplished in the larger towns, in a manner more orderly and discreet—in the Roman manner. The faithful were bent less on the destruction of the old pagan temples than on their conversion to a new and higher use; and, with much beautiful furniture ready to hand, they became Christian sanctuaries.

Already, in accordance with such maturer wisdom, the Church of the 'Minor Peace' had adopted many of the graces of pagan feeling and pagan custom; as being indeed a living creature, taking up, transforming, accommodating still more closely to the human heart what of right belonged to it. In this way an obscure synagogue was expanded into the Catholic Church. Gathering, from a richer and more varied field of sound than had remained for him, those old Roman harmonies,

some notes of which Gregory the Great, centuries later, and
after generations of interrupted development, formed into the
Gregorian music, she was already, as we have heard, the house of
song—of a wonderful new music and poesy.   As if in anticipation
of the sixteenth century, the Church was becoming 'humanistic',
in an earlier and unimpeachable *Renaissance*.   Singing there
had been in abundance from the first; though often it dared
only be 'of the heart'.   And it burst forth, when it might,
into the beginnings of a true ecclesiastical music; the Jewish
psalter, inherited from the synagogue, turning now, gradually,
from Greek into Latin—broken Latin, into Italian, as the ritual
use of the rich, fresh, expressive vernacular superseded the
earlier authorized language of the Church.   Through certain
surviving remnants of Greek in the later Latin liturgies, we may
still discern a highly interesting intermediate phase of ritual
development, when the Greek and the Latin were in combination; the poor, surely!—the poor and the children of that liberal
Roman Church—responding already in their own 'vulgar tongue',
to an office said in the original, liturgical Greek.   That hymn
sung in the early morning, of which Pliny had heard, was
kindling into the service of the Mass.

The Mass, indeed, would appear to have been said continuously
from the Apostolic age.   Its details, as one by one they become
visible in later history, have already the character of what is
ancient and venerable.   'We are very old, and ye are young!'
they seem to protest, to those who fail to understand them.
Ritual, in fact, like all other elements of religion, must grow
and cannot be made—grow by the same law of development
which prevails everywhere else, in the moral as in the physical
world.   As regards this special phase of the religious life,
however, such development seems to have been unusually
rapid in the subterranean age which preceded Constantine;
and in the very first days of the final triumph of the Church
the Mass emerges to general view already substantially complete.
'Wisdom' was dealing, as with the dust of creeds and philosophies, so also with the dust of outworn religious usage, like the
very spirit of life itself, organizing soul and body out of the lime
and clay of the earth.   In a generous eclecticism, within the
bounds of her liberty, and as by some providential power within
her, she gathers and serviceably adopts, as in other matters so
in ritual, one thing here, another there, from various sources—
Gnostic, Jewish, Pagan—to adorn and beautify the greatest
act of worship the world has seen.   It was thus the liturgy of

the Church came to be—full of consolations for the human soul, and destined, surely! one day, under the sanction of so many ages of human experience, to take exclusive possession of the religious consciousness.

> TANTUM ERGO SACRAMENTUM
> VENEREMUR CERNUI:
> ET ANTIQUUM DOCUMENTUM
> NOVO CEDAT RITUI.

CHAPTER XXIII

DIVINE SERVICE

Wisdom hath builded herself a house: she hath mingled her wine: she hath also prepared for herself a table.

THE more highly favoured ages of imaginative art present instances of the summing up of an entire world of complex associations under some single form, like the *Zeus* of Olympia, or the series of frescoes which commemorate *The Acts of Saint Francis*, at Assisi, or like the play of *Hamlet* or *Faust*. It was not in an image, or series of images, yet still in a sort of dramatic action, and with the unity of a single appeal to eye and ear, that Marius about this time found all his new impressions set forth, regarding what he had already recognized, intellectually, as for him at least the most beautiful thing in the world.

To understand the influence upon him of what follows, the reader must remember that it was an experience which came amid a deep sense of vacuity in life. The fairest products of the earth seemed to be dropping to pieces, as if in men's very hands, around him. How real was their sorrow, and his! 'His observation of life' had come to be like the constant telling of a sorrowful rosary, day after day; till, as if taking infection from the cloudy sorrow of the mind, the eye also, the very senses, were grown faint and sick. And now it happened as with the actual morning on which he found himself a spectator of this new thing. The long winter had been a season of unvarying sullenness. At last, on this day he awoke with a sharp flash of lightning in the earliest twilight: in a little while the heavy rain had filtered the air: the clear light was abroad; and, as though the spring had set in with a sudden leap in the heart of things, the whole scene around him lay like some untarnished picture beneath a sky of delicate blue. Under the spell of his late depression, Marius had suddenly determined to leave Rome for a while. But desiring first to advertise Cornelius of his movements, and failing to find him in his lodgings, he had ventured, still early in the day, to seek him in the Cecilian villa. Passing through its silent and empty courtyard he loitered for a moment, to admire. Under the clear but immature light of winter morning after a storm, all the details of form and colour in the old marbles were distinctly visible, and with a kind of severity or sadness—so it struck him—amid their beauty: in them, and in all other details of the scene—the cypresses, the bunches of pale daffodils in the grass, the curves of the purple hills of Tusculum, with the drifts of virgin snow still lying in their hollows.

The little open door, through which he passed from the courtyard, admitted him into what was plainly the vast *Lararium*, or domestic sanctuary, of the Cecilian family, transformed in many particulars, but still richly decorated, and retaining much of its ancient furniture in metal-work and costly stone. The peculiar half-light of dawn seemed to be lingering beyond its hour upon the solemn marble walls; and here, though at that moment in absolute silence, a great company of people was assembled. In that brief period of peace, during which the Church emerged for a while from her jealously guarded subterranean life, the rigour of an earlier rule of exclusion had been relaxed. And so it came to pass that on this morning Marius saw for the first time the wonderful spectacle—wonderful, especially, in its evidential power over himself, over his own thoughts—of those who believe.

There were noticeable, among those present, great varieties of rank, of age, of personal type. The Roman *ingenuus*, with the white toga and gold ring, stood side by side with his slave; and the air of the whole company was, above all, a grave one, an air of recollection. Coming thus unexpectedly upon this large assembly, so entirely united, in a silence so profound, for purposes unknown to him, Marius felt for a moment as if he had stumbled by chance upon some great conspiracy. Yet that could scarcely be, for the people here collected might have figured as the earliest handsel, or pattern, of a new world, from the very face of which discontent had passed away. Corresponding to the variety of human type there present, was the various expression of every form of human sorrow assuaged. What desire, what fulfilment of desire, had wrought so pathetically on the features of these ranks of aged men and women of humble condition? Those young men, bent down so discreetly on the details of their sacred service, had faced life and were glad, by some science, or light of knowledge they had, to which there had certainly been no parallel in the older world. Was some credible message from beyond 'the flaming ramparts

of the world'—a message of hope, regarding the place of men's
souls and their interest in the sum of things—already moulding
anew their very bodies, and looks, and voices, now and here?
At least, there was a cleansing and kindling flame at work in
them, which seemed to make everything else Marius had ever
known look comparatively vulgar and mean.   There were the
children, above all—troops of children—reminding him of those
pathetic children's graves, like cradles or garden-beds, he had
noticed in his first visit to these places; and they more than
satisfied the odd curiosity he had then conceived about them,
wondering in what quaintly expressive forms they might come
forth into the daylight, if awakened from sleep.   Children of
the Catacombs, some but 'a span long', with features not so
much beautiful as heroic (that world of new, refining sentiment
having set its seal even on childhood), they retained certainly
no stain or trace of anything subterranean this morning, in
the alacrity of their worship—as ready as if they had been at
play—stretching forth their hands, crying, chanting in a resonant
voice, and with boldly upturned faces, *Christe Eleison !*

For the silence—silence, amid those lights of early morning
to which Marius had always been constitutionally impressible,
as having in them a certain reproachful austerity—was broken
suddenly by resounding cries of *Kyrie Eleison ! Christe Eleison !*
repeated alternately, again and again, until the bishop, rising
from his chair, made sign that this prayer should cease.   But
the voices burst out once more presently, in richer and more
varied melody, though still of an antiphonal character; the
men, the women and children, the deacons, the people, answering
one another, somewhat after the manner of a Greek chorus.
But again with what a novelty of poetic accent; what a genuine
expansion of heart; what profound intimations for the intellect,
as the meaning of the words grew upon him!   *Cum grandi
affectu et compunctione dicatur*—says an ancient eucharistic
order; and certainly, the mystic tone of this praying and singing
was one with the expression of deliverance, of grateful assurance
and sincerity, upon the faces of those assembled.   As if some
searching correction, a regeneration of the body by the spirit,
had begun, and was already gone a great way, the countenances
of men, women, and children alike had a brightness on them
which he could fancy reflected upon himself—an amenity, a
mystic amiability and unction, which found its way most readily
of all to the hearts of children themselves.   The religious poetry
of those Hebrew psalms—*Benedixisti Domine terram tuam:*

Dixit Dominus Domino meo, sede a dextris meis—was certainly in marvellous accord with the lyrical instinct of his own character. Those august hymns, he thought, must thereafter ever remain by him as among the well-tested powers in things to soothe and fortify the soul. One could never grow tired of them!

In the old pagan worship there had been little to call the understanding into play. Here, on the other hand, the utterance, the eloquence, the music of worship conveyed, as Marius readily understood, a fact, or series of facts, for intellectual reception. That became evident, more especially, in those lessons, or sacred readings, which, like the singing, in broken vernacular Latin, occurred at certain intervals, amid the silence of the assembly. There were readings, again with bursts of chanted invocation between for fuller light on a difficult path, in which many a vagrant voice of human philosophy, haunting men's minds from of old, recurred with clearer accent than had ever belonged to it before, as if lifted, above its first intention, into the harmonies of some supreme system of knowledge or doctrine, at length complete. And last of all came a narrative which, with a thousand tender memories, every one appeared to know by heart, displaying, in all the vividness of a picture for the eye, the mournful figure of him towards whom this whole act of worship still consistently turned—a figure which seemed to have absorbed, like some rich tincture in his garment, all that was deep-felt and impassioned in the experiences of the past.

It was the anniversary of his birth as a little child they celebrated to-day. *Astiterunt reges terrae:* so the Gradual, the 'Song of Degrees', proceeded, the young men on the steps of the altar responding in deep, clear antiphon or chorus:

> Astiterunt reges terrae—
> Adversus sanctum puerum tuum, Jesum:
> Nunc, Domine, da servis tuis loqui verbum tuum—
> Et signa fieri, per nomen sancti pueri Jesu.

And the proper action of the rite itself, like a half-opened book to be read by the duly initiated mind, took up those suggestions, and carried them forward into the present, as having reference to a power still efficacious, still after some mystic sense even now in action among the people there assembled. The entire office, indeed, with its interchange of lessons, hymns, prayer, silence, was itself like a single piece of highly composite, dramatic music; a 'song of degrees', rising steadily to a climax. Notwithstanding the absence of any central image visible to the eye, the entire ceremonial process, like the place in which it was enacted, was weighty with symbolic significance, seemed to express a single leading motive. The mystery, if such in fact it was, centred indeed in the actions of one visible person, distinguished among the assistants, who stood ranged in semicircle around him, by the extreme fineness of his white vestments, and the pointed cap with the golden ornaments upon his head.

Nor had Marius ever seen the pontifical character, as he conceived it—*sicut unguentum in capite, descendens in oram vestimenti*—so fully realized, as in the expression, the manner and voice, of this novel pontiff, as he took his seat on the white chair placed for him by the young men, and received his long staff into his hand, or moved his hands—hands which seemed endowed in very deed with some mysterious power—at the *Lavabo*, or at the various benedictions, or to bless certain objects on the table before him, chanting in cadence of a grave sweetness the leading parts of the rite. What profound unction and mysticity! The solemn character of the singing was at its height when he opened his lips. Like some new sort of *rhapsôdos*, it was for the moment as if he alone possessed the words of the office, and they flowed anew from some permanent source of inspiration within him. The table or altar at which he presided, below a canopy on delicate spiral columns, was in fact the tomb of a youthful 'witness', of the family of the Cecilii, who had shed his blood not many years before, and whose relics were still in this place. It was for his sake the bishop put his lips so often to the surface before him; the regretful memory of that death entwining itself, though not without certain notes of triumph, as a matter of special inward significance, throughout a service which was, before all else, from first to last, a commemoration of the dead.

A sacrifice also—a sacrifice, it might seem, like the most primitive, the most natural and enduringly significant of old pagan sacrifices, of the simplest fruits of the earth. And in connexion with this circumstance again, as in the actual stones of the building so in the rite itself, what Marius observed was not so much new matter as a new spirit, moulding, informing, with a new intention, many observances not witnessed for the first time to-day. Men and women came to the altar successively, in perfect order, and deposited below the lattice-work of pierced white marble, their baskets of wheat and grapes, incense, oil for the sanctuary lamps; bread and wine especially—

pure wheaten bread, the pure white wine of the Tusculan vineyards. There was here a veritable consecration, hopeful and animating, of the earth's gifts, of old dead and dark matter itself, now in some way redeemed at last, of all that we can touch or see, in the midst of a jaded world that had lost the true sense of such things, and in strong contrast to the wise emperor's renunciant and impassive attitude towards them. Certain portions of that bread and wine were taken into the bishop's hands; and thereafter, with an increasing mysticity and effusion the rite proceeded. Still in a strain of inspired supplication, the antiphonal singing developed, from this point, into a kind of dialogue between the chief minister and the whole assisting company:

> SURSUM CORDA!
> HABEMUS AD DOMINUM.
> GRATIAS AGAMUS DOMINO DEO NOSTRO!—

It might have been thought the business, the duty or service of young men more particularly, as they stood there in long ranks, and in severe and simple vesture of the purest white— a service in which they would seem to be flying for refuge, as with their precious, their treacherous and critical youth in their hands, to one—Yes! one like themselves, who yet claimed their worship, a worship, above all, in the way of Aurelius, in the way of imitation. *Adoramus te Christe, quia per crucem tuam redemisti mundum!*—they cry together. So deep is the emotion that at moments it seems to Marius as if some there present apprehend that prayer prevails, that the very object of this pathetic crying himself draws near. From the first there had been the sense, an increasing assurance, of one coming:— actually with them now, according to the oft-repeated affirmation or petition, *Dominus vobiscum!* Some at least were quite sure of it; and the confidence of this remnant fired the hearts, and gave meaning to the bold, ecstatic worship, of all the rest about them.

Prompted especially by the suggestions of that mysterious old Jewish psalmody, so new to him—lesson and hymn—and catching therewith a portion of the enthusiasm of those beside him, Marius could discern dimly, behind the solemn recitation which now followed, at once a narrative and a prayer, the most touching image truly that had ever come within the scope of his mental or physical gaze. It was the image of a young man giving up voluntarily, one by one, for the greatest of ends, the

greatest gifts; actually parting with himself, above all, with
the serenity, the divine serenity, of his own soul; yet from the
midst of his desolation crying out upon the greatness of his
success, as if foreseeing this very worship.[1]   As centre of the
supposed facts which for these people were become so constraining a motive of hopefulness, of activity, that image seemed
to display itself with an overwhelming claim on human gratitude.
What Saint Louis of France discerned, and found so irresistibly
touching, across the dimness of many centuries, as a painful
thing done for love of him by one he had never seen, was to
them almost as a thing of yesterday; and their hearts were
whole with it.   It had the force, among their interests, of an
almost recent event in the career of one whom their fathers'
fathers might have known.   From memories so sublime, yet
so close at hand, had the narrative descended in which these
acts of worship centred; though again the names of some more
recently dead were mingled in it.   And it seemed as if the very
dead were aware; to be stirring beneath the slabs of the
sepulchres which lay so near, that they might associate themselves to this enthusiasm—to this exalted worship of Jesus.

One by one, at last, the faithful approach to receive from the
chief minister morsels of the great, white, wheaten cake he had
taken into his hands—*Perducat vos ad vitam aeternam !* he prays,
half-silently, as they depart again, after discreet embraces.
The Eucharist of those early days was, even more entirely than
at any later or happier time, an act of thanksgiving; and while
the remnants of the feast are borne away for the reception of
the sick, the sustained gladness of the rite reaches its highest
point in the singing of a hymn: a hymn like the spontaneous
product of two opposed militant companies, contending accord-
antly together, heightening, accumulating their witness, pro-
voking one another's worship, in a kind of sacred rivalry.

Ite ! Missa est !—cried the young deacons: and Marius
departed from that strange scene along with the rest.   What
was it?—Was it this made the way of Cornelius so pleasant
through the world?   As for Marius himself—the natural soul
of worship in him had at last been satisfied as never before.
He felt, as he left that place, that he must hereafter experience
often a longing memory, a kind of thirst, for all this, over again.
And it seemed moreover to define what he must require of the
powers, whatsoever they might be, that had brought him into
the world at all, to make him not unhappy in it.

[1] Psalm xxii 22-31.

CHAPTER XXIV

A CONVERSATION NOT IMAGINARY

IN cheerfulness is the success of our studies, says Pliny—
studia hilaritate proveniunt. It was still the habit of Marius,
encouraged by his experience that sleep is not only a sedative
but the best of stimulants, to seize the morning hours for
creation, making profit when he might of the wholesome serenity
which followed a dreamless night. 'The morning for creation',
he would say; 'the afternoon for the perfecting labour of the
file; the evening for reception—the reception of matter from
without one, of other men's words and thoughts—matter for
our own dreams, or the merely mechanic exercise of the brain,
brooding thereon silently, in its dark chambers.' To leave
home early in the day was therefore a rare thing for him. He
was induced so to do on the occasion of a visit to Rome of the
famous writer Lucian, whom he had been bidden to meet.
The breakfast over, he walked away with the learned guest,
having offered to be his guide to the lecture-room of a well-
known Greek rhetorician and expositor of the Stoic philosophy,
a teacher then much in fashion among the studious youth of
Rome. On reaching the place, however, they found the doors
closed, with a slip of writing attached, which proclaimed 'a
holiday'; and the morning being a fine one, they walked farther,
along the Appian Way. Mortality, with which the *Queen of
Ways*—in reality the favourite cemetery of Rome—was so
closely crowded, in every imaginable form of sepulchre, from
the tiniest baby-house, to the massive monument out of which
the Middle Age would adapt a fortress-tower, might seem, on a
morning like this, to be 'smiling through tears'. The flower-
stalls just beyond the city gates presented to view an array of
posies and garlands, fresh enough for a wedding. At one and
another of them groups of persons, gravely clad, were making
their bargains before starting for some perhaps distant spot on
the highway, to keep a *dies rosationis*, this being the time of
roses, at the grave of a deceased relation. Here and there, a
funeral procession was slowly on its way, in weird contrast to
the gaiety of the hour.

The two companions, of course, read the epitaphs as they strolled along. In one, reminding them of the poet's—*Si lacrimae prosunt, visis te ostende videri !*—a woman prayed that her lost husband might visit her dreams. Their characteristic note, indeed, was an imploring cry, still to be sought after by the living. 'While I live,' such was the promise of a lover to his dead mistress, 'you will receive this homage: after my death —who can tell?'—*post mortem nescio.* 'If ghosts, my sons, do feel anything after death, my sorrow will be lessened by your frequent coming to me here!'—'This is a *privileged* tomb; to my family and descendants has been conceded the right of visiting this place as often as they please.'—'This is an eternal habitation; here lie I; here I shall lie for ever.'—'Reader! if you doubt that the soul survives, make your oblation and a prayer for me; and you shall understand!'

The elder of the two readers, certainly, was little affected by those pathetic suggestions. It was long ago that after visiting the banks of the Padus, where he had sought in vain for the poplars (sisters of Phaethon erewhile) whose tears became amber, he had once for all arranged for himself a view of the world exclusive of all reference to what might lie beyond its 'flaming barriers'. And at the age of sixty he had no misgivings. His elegant and self-complacent but far from unamiable scepticism, long since brought to perfection, never failed him. It surrounded him, as some are surrounded by a magic ring of fine aristocratic manners, with 'a rampart', through which he himself never broke, nor permitted any thing or person to break upon him. Gay, animated, content with his old age as it was, the aged student still took a lively interest in studious youth.—Could Marius inform him of any such, now known to him in Rome? What did the young men learn, just then? and how?

In answer, Marius became fluent concerning the promise of one young student, the son, as it presently appeared, of parents of whom Lucian himself knew something: and soon afterwards the lad was seen coming along briskly—a lad with gait and figure well enough expressive of the sane mind in the healthy body, though a little slim and worn of feature, and with a pair of eyes expressly designed, it might seem, for fine glancings at the stars. At the sight of Marius he paused suddenly, and with a modest blush on recognizing his companion, who straightway took with the youth, so prettily enthusiastic, the freedom of an old friend.

In a few moments the three were seated together, immediately above the fragrant borders of a rose farm, on the marble bench of one of the *exhedrae* for the use of foot-passengers at the roadside, from which they could overlook the grand, earnest prospect of the *Campagna*, and enjoy the air. Fancying that the lad's plainly written enthusiasm had induced in the elder speaker somewhat more fervour than was usual with him, Marius listened to the conversation which follows.—

'Ah! Hermotimus! Hurrying to lecture!—if I may judge by your pace, and that volume in your hand. You were thinking hard as you came along, moving your lips and waving your arms. Some fine speech you were pondering, some knotty question, some viewy doctrine—not to be idle for a moment, to be making progress in philosophy, even on your way to the schools. To-day, however, you need go no farther. .We read a notice at the schools that there would be no lecture Stay, therefore, and talk awhile with us.

—With pleasure, Lucian.—Yes! I was ruminating yesterday's conference. One must not lose a moment. *Life is short and art is long!* And it was of the art of medicine that was first said—a thing so much easier than divine philosophy, to which one can hardly attain in a lifetime, unless one be ever wakeful, ever on the watch. And here the hazard is no little one:— By the attainment of a true philosophy to attain happiness; or, having missed both, to perish, as one of the vulgar herd.

—The prize is a great one, Hermotimus! and you must needs be near it, after these months of toil, and with that scholarly pallor of yours. Unless, indeed, you have already laid hold upon it, and kept us in the dark.

—How could that be, Lucian? Happiness, as Hesiod says, abides very far hence; and the way to it is long and steep and rough. I see myself still at the beginning of my journey; still but at the mountain's foot. I am trying with all my might to get forward. What I need is a hand, stretched out to help me.

—And is not the master sufficient for that? Could he not, like Zeus in Homer, let down to you, from that high place, a golden cord, to draw you up thither, to himself and to that Happiness, to which he ascended so long ago?

—The very point, Lucian! Had it depended on him I should long ago have been caught up. 'Tis I, am wanting.

—Well! keep your eye fixed on the journey's end, and that happiness there above, with confidence in his goodwill.

—Ah! there are many who start cheerfully on the journey and proceed a certain distance, but lose heart when they light on the obstacles of the way. Only, those who endure to the end do come to the mountain's top, and thereafter live in Happiness:—live a wonderful manner of life, seeing all other people from that great height no bigger than tiny ants.

—What little fellows you make of us—less than the pygmies—down in the dust here. Well! we, "the vulgar herd", as we creep along, will not forget you in our prayers, when you are seated up there above the clouds, whither you have been so long hastening. But tell me, Hermotimus!—when do you expect to arrive there?

—Ah! that I know not. In twenty years, perhaps, I shall be really on the summit.—A great while! you think. But then, again, the prize I contend for is a great one.

—Perhaps! But as to those twenty years—that you will live so long. Has the master assured you of that? Is he a prophet as well as a philosopher? For I suppose you would not endure all this upon a mere chance—toiling day and night, though it might happen that just ere the last step, Destiny seized you by the foot and plucked you thence, with your hope still unfulfilled.

—Hence, with these ill-omened words, Lucian! Were I to survive but for a day, I should be happy, having once attained wisdom.

—How?—Satisfied with a single day, after all those labours?

—Yes! one blessed moment were enough!

—But again, as you have never been, how know you that happiness is to be had up there, at all—the happiness that is to make all this worth while?

—I believe what the master tells me. Of a certainty he knows, being now far above all others.

—And what was it he told you about it? Is it riches, or glory, or some indescribable pleasure?

—Hush! my friend! All those are nothing in comparison of the life there.

—What, then, shall those who come to the end of this discipline — what excellent thing shall they receive, if not these?

—Wisdom, the absolute goodness and the absolute beauty, with the sure and certain knowledge of all things—how they are. Riches and glory and pleasure—whatsoever belongs to the body—they have cast from them: stripped bare of all that, they mount up, even as Hercules, consumed in the fire, became a god. He too cast aside all that he had of his earthly mother, and bearing with him the divine element, pure and undefiled, winged his way to heaven from the discerning flame. Even so do they, detached from all that others prize, by the burning fire of a true philosophy, ascend to the highest degree of happiness.

—Strange! And do they never come down again from the heights to help those whom they left below? Must they, when they be once come thither, there remain for ever, laughing, as you say, at what other men prize?

—More than that! They whose initiation is entire are subject no longer to anger, fear, desire, regret. Nay! They scarcely feel at all.

—Well! as you have leisure to-day, why not tell an old friend in what way you first started on your philosophic journey? For, if I might, I should like to join company with you from this very day.

—If you be really willing, Lucian! you will learn in no long time your advantage over all other people. They will seem but as children, so far above them will be your thoughts.

—Well! Be you my guide! It is but fair. But tell me—Do you allow learners to contradict, if anything is said which they don't think right?

—No, indeed! Still, if you wish, oppose your questions. In that way you will learn more easily.

—Let me know, then—Is there one only way which leads to a true philosophy—your own way—the way of the Stoics: or is it true, as I have heard, that there are many ways of approaching it?

—Yes! Many ways! There are the Stoics, and the Peripatetics, and those who call themselves after Plato: there are the enthusiasts for Diogenes, and Antisthenes, and the followers of Pythagoras, besides others.

—It was true, then. But again, is what they say the same or different?

—Very different.

—Yet the truth, I conceive, would be one and the same, from all of them. Answer me, then—In what, or in whom, did you confide when you first betook yourself to philosophy, and seeing so many doors open to you, passed them all by and went in to the Stoics, as if there alone lay the way of truth? What token had you? Forget, please, all you are to-day—half-way, or more, on the philosophic journey: answer me as you would have done then, a mere outsider as I am now.

—Willingly! It was there the great majority went! 'Twas by that I judged it to be the better way.

—A majority how much greater than the Epicureans, the Platonists, the Peripatetics? You, doubtless, counted them respectively, as with the votes in a scrutiny.

—No! But this was not my only motive. I heard it said by every one that the Epicureans were soft and voluptuous, the Peripatetics avaricious and quarrelsome, and Plato's followers puffed up with pride. But of the Stoics, not a few pronounced that they were true men, that they knew everything, that theirs was the royal road, the one road, to wealth, to wisdom, to all that can be desired.

—Of course those who said this were not themselves Stoics: you would not have believed them—still less their opponents. They were the vulgar, therefore.

—True! But you must know that I did not trust to others exclusively. I trusted also to myself—to what I saw. I saw the Stoics going through the world after a seemly manner, neatly clad, never in excess, always collected, ever faithful to the mean which all pronounce "golden".

—You are trying an experiment on me. You would fain see how far you can mislead me as to your real ground. The kind of probation you describe is applicable, indeed, to works of art, which are rightly judged by their appearance to the eye. There is something in the comely form, the graceful drapery, which tells surely of the hand of Pheidias or Alcamenes. But if philosophy is to be judged by outward appearances, what would become of the blind man, for instance, unable to observe the attire and gait of your friends the Stoics?

—It was not of the blind I was thinking.

—Yet there must needs be some common criterion in a matter so important to all. Put the blind, if you will, beyond the privileges of philosophy; though they perhaps need that inward vision more than all others. But can those who are not blind, be they as keen-sighted as you will, collect a single fact of mind from a man's attire, from anything outward?—Understand me! You attached yourself to these men—did you not?—because of a certain love you had for the mind in them, the thoughts they possessed desiring the mind in you to be improved thereby?

—Assuredly!

—How, then, did you find it possible, by the sort of signs you just now spoke of, to distinguish the true philosopher from the false? Matters of that kind are not wont so to reveal themselves. They are but hidden mysteries, hardly to be guessed at through the words and acts which may in some sort be conformable to them. You, however, it would seem, can look straight into the heart in men's bosoms, and acquaint yourself with what really passes there.

—You are making sport of me, Lucian! In truth, it was with God's help I made my choice, and I don't repent it.

—And still you refuse to tell me, to save me from perishing in that "vulgar herd".

—Because nothing I can tell you would satisfy you.

—You are mistaken, my friend! But since you deliberately conceal the thing, grudging me, as I suppose, that true philosophy which would make me equal to you, I will try, if it may be, to find out for myself the exact criterion in these matters—how to make a perfectly safe choice. And, do you listen.

—I will; there may be something worth knowing in what you will say.

—Well!—only don't laugh if I seem a little fumbling in my efforts. The fault is yours, in refusing to share your lights with me. Let philosophy, then, be like a city—a city whose citizens within it are a happy people, as your master would tell you, having lately come thence, as we suppose. All the virtues are theirs, and they are little less than gods. Those acts of violence which happen among us are not to be seen in their streets. They live together in one mind, very seemly; the things which beyond everything else cause men to contend against each other, having no place among them. Gold and silver, pleasure, vainglory, they have long since banished, as being unprofitable to the commonwealth; and their life is an unbroken calm, in liberty, equality, an equal happiness.

—And is it not reasonable that all men should desire to be of a city such as that, and take no account of the length and difficulty of the way thither, so only they may one day become its freemen?

—It might well be the business of life:—leaving all else, forgetting one's native country here, unmoved by the tears, the restraining hands, of parents or children, if one had them—only bidding them follow the same road; and if they would not or could not, shaking them off, leaving one's very garment in their hands if they took hold on us, to start off straightway for that happy place! For there is no fear, I suppose, of being shut out if one came thither naked. I remember, indeed, long ago an aged man related to me how things passed there, offering himself to be my leader, and enrol me on my arrival in the number of the citizens. I was but fifteen—certainly very foolish: and it may be that I was then actually within the suburbs, or at the very gates, of the city. Well, this aged man told me, among other things, that all the citizens were way-farers from afar. Among them were barbarians and slaves, poor men—aye! and cripples—all indeed who truly desired that citizenship. For the only legal conditions of enrolment were—not wealth, nor bodily beauty, nor noble ancestry—things not named among them—but intelligence, and the desire for moral beauty, and earnest labour. The last comer, thus qualified, was made equal to the rest: master and slave, patrician, plebeian, were words they had not—in that blissful place. And believe me, if that blissful, that beautiful place, were set on a hill visible to all the world, I should long ago have journeyed thither. But, as you say, it is far off: and one must needs find out for one's self the road to it, and the best possible guide. And I find a multi-tude of guides, who press on me their services, and protest, all alike, that they have themselves come thence. Only, the roads they propose are many, and towards adverse quarters. And one of them is steep and stony, and through the beating sun; and the other is through green meadows, and under grateful shade, and by many a fountain of water. But howsoever the road may be, at each one of them stands a credible guide; he puts out his hand and would have you come his way. All other ways are wrong, all other guides false. Hence my difficulty!—The number and variety of the ways! For you know, *There is but one road that leads to Corinth.*

—Well! If you go the whole round, you will find no better guides than those. If you wish to get to Corinth, you will follow the traces of Zeno and Chrysippus. It is impossible otherwise.

—Yes! The old, familiar language! Were one of Plato's fellow-pilgrims here, or a follower of Epicurus—or fifty others—each would tell me that I should never get to Corinth except in his company. One must therefore credit all alike, which would be absurd; or, what is far safer, distrust all alike, until one has discovered the truth. Suppose now, that, being as I am, ignorant which of all philosophers is really in possession of truth, I choose your sect, relying on yourself—my friend, indeed, yet still acquainted only with the way of the Stoics; and that then some divine power brought Plato, and Aristotle, and Pythagoras, and the others, back to life again. Well!

They would come round about me, and put me on my trial for my presumption, and say: "In whom was it you confided when you preferred Zeno and Chrysippus to me?—and me?—masters of far more venerable age than those, who are but of yesterday; and though you have never held any discussion with us, nor made trial of our doctrine? It is not thus that the law would have judges do—listen to one party and refuse to let the other speak for himself. If judges act thus, there may be an appeal to another tribunal." What should I answer? Would it be enough to say: "I trusted my friend Hermotimus"?—"We know not Hermotimus, nor he us", they would tell me; adding, with a smile, "your friend thinks he may believe all our adversaries say of us whether in ignorance or in malice. Yet if he were umpire in the games, and if he happened to see one of our wrestlers, by way of a preliminary exercise, knock to pieces an antagonist of mere empty air, he would not thereupon pronounce him a victor. Well! don't let your friend Hermotimus suppose, in like manner, that his teachers have really prevailed over us in those battles of theirs, fought with our mere shadows. That, again, were to be like children, lightly overthrowing their own card-castles; or like boy-archers, who cry out when they hit the target of straw. The Persian and Scythian bowmen as they speed along, can pierce a bird on the wing."

—Let us leave Plato and the others at rest. It is not for me to contend against them. Let us rather search out together if the truth of philosophy be as I say. Why summon the athletes, and archers from Persia?

—Yes! let them go, if you think them in the way. And now do you speak! You really look as if you had something wonderful to deliver.

—Well then, Lucian! to me it seems quite possible for one who has learned the doctrines of the Stoics only, to attain from those a knowledge of the truth, without proceeding to inquire into all the various tenets of the others. Look at the question in this way. If one told you that twice two make four, would it be necessary for you to go the whole round of the arithmeticians, to see whether any one of them will say that twice two make five, or seven? Would you not see at once that the man tells the truth?

—At once.

—Why then do you find it impossible that one who has fallen in with the Stoics only, in their enunciation of what is true, should adhere to them, and seek after no others; assured that four could never be five, even if fifty Platos, fifty Aristotles said so?

—You are beside the point, Hermotimus! You are likening open questions to principles universally received. Have you ever met any one who said that twice two make five, or seven?

—No! only a madman would say that.

—And have you ever met, on the other hand, a Stoic and an Epicurean who were agreed upon the beginning and the end, the principle and the final cause, of things? Never! Then your parallel is false. We are inquiring to which of the sects philosophic truth belongs, and you seize on it by anticipation, and assign it to the Stoics, alleging, what is by no means clear, that it is they for whom twice two make four. But the Epicureans, or the Platonists, might say that it is they, in truth, who make two and two equal four, while you make them five or seven. Is it not so, when you think *virtue* the only good, and the Epicureans *pleasure*; when you hold all things to be *material*, while the Platonists admit something *immaterial*? As I said, you resolve offhand, in favour of the Stoics, the very point which needs a critical decision. If it is clear beforehand that the Stoics alone make two and two equal four, then the others must hold their peace. But so long as that is the very point of debate, we must listen to all sects alike, or be well assured that we shall seem but partial in our judgment.

—I think, Lucian! that you do not altogether understand my meaning. To make it clear, then, let us suppose that two men had entered a temple, of Aesculapius—say! or Bacchus: and that afterwards one of the sacred vessels is found to be missing. And the two men must be searched to see which of them has hidden it under his garment. For it is certainly in the possession of one or the other of them. Well! if it be found on the first there will be no need to search the second; if it is not found on the first, then the other must have it; and again, there will be no need to search him.

—Yes! So let it be.

—And we too, Lucian! if we have found the holy vessel in possession of the Stoics, shall no longer have need to search other philosophers, having attained that we were seeking. Why trouble ourselves further?

—No need, if something had indeed been found, and you knew it to be that lost thing: if, at the least, you could recognize the sacred object when you saw it. But truly, as the matter now stands, not two persons only have entered the temple, one or the other of whom must needs have taken the golden cup, but a whole crowd of persons. And then, it is not clear what the lost object really is—cup, or flagon, or diadem; for one of the priests avers this, another that; they are not even in agreement as to its material: some will have it to be of brass, others of silver, or gold. It thus becomes necessary to search the garments of all persons who have entered the temple, if the lost vessel is to be recovered. And if you find a golden cup on the first of them, it will still be necessary to proceed in searching the garments of the others; for it is not certain that this cup really belonged to the temple. Might there not be many such golden vessels?—No! we must go on to every one of them, placing all that we find in the midst together, and then make our guess which of all those things may fairly be supposed to be the property of the god. For, again, this circumstance adds greatly to our difficulty, that without exception every one searched is found to have something upon him—cup, or flagon, or diadem, of brass, of silver, of gold: and still, all the while, it is not ascertained which of all these is the sacred thing. And you must still hesitate to pronounce any one of them guilty of the sacrilege—those objects may be their own lawful property: one cause of all this obscurity being, as I think, that there was no inscription on the lost cup, if cup it was. Had the name of the god, or even that of the donor, been upon it, at least we should have had less trouble, and having detected the inscription, should have ceased to trouble any one else by our search.

—I have nothing to reply to that.

—Hardly anything plausible. So that if we wish to find who it is has the sacred vessel, or who will be our best guide to Corinth, we must needs proceed to every one and examine him with the utmost care, stripping off his garment and considering him closely. Scarcely, even so, shall we come at the truth. And if we are to have a credible adviser regarding this question of philosophy—which of all philosophies one ought to follow— he alone who is acquainted with the *dicta* of every one of them can be such a guide: all others must be inadequate. I would give no credence to them if they lacked information as to one only. If somebody introduced a fair person and told us he was the fairest of all men, we should not believe that, unless we knew that he had seen all the people in the world. Fair he might be; but, fairest of all—none could know, unless he had seen all. And we too desire, not a fair one, but the fairest of all. Unless we find him, we shall think we have failed. It is no casual beauty that will content us; what we are seeking after is that supreme beauty which must of necessity be unique.

—What then is one to do, if the matter be really thus? Perhaps you know better than I. All I see is that very few of us would have time to examine all the various sects of philosophy in turn, even if we began in early life. I know not how it is; but though you seem to me to speak reasonably, yet (I must confess it) you have distressed me not a little by this exact exposition of yours. I was unlucky in coming out to-day, and in my falling in with you, who have thrown me into utter perplexity by your proof that the discovery of truth is impossible, just as I seemed to be on the point of attaining my hope.

—Blame your parents, my child, not me! Or rather, blame mother Nature herself, for giving us but seventy or eighty years instead of making us as long-lived as Tithonus. For my part, I have but led you from premise to conclusion.

—Nay! you are a mocker! I know not wherefore, but you have a grudge against philosophy; and it is your entertainment to make a jest of her lovers.

—Ah! Hermotimus! what the Truth may be, you philosophers may be able to tell better than I. But so much at least I know of her, that she is one by no means pleasant to those who hear her speak: in the matter of pleasantness, she is far surpassed by Falsehood: and Falsehood has the pleasanter countenance. She, nevertheless, being conscious of no alloy within, discourses with boldness to all men, who therefore have little love for her. See how angry you are now because I have stated the truth about certain things of which we are both alike enamoured—that they are hard to come by. It is as if you had fallen in love with a statue and hoped to win its favour, thinking it a human creature; and I, understanding it to be but an image of brass or stone, had shown you, as a friend, that your love was impossible, and thereupon you had conceived that I bore you some ill-will.

—But still, does it not follow from what you said, that we must renounce philosophy and pass our days in idleness?

—When did you hear me say that? I did but assert that if we are to seek after philosophy, whereas there are many ways professing to lead thereto, we must with much exactness distinguish them.

—Well, Lucian! that we must go to all the schools in turn, and test what they say, if we are to choose the right one, is perhaps reasonable; but surely ridiculous, unless we are to live as many years as the Phoenix, to be so lengthy in the trial of each; as if it were not possible to learn the whole by the part! They say that Pheidias, when he was shown one of the talons of a lion, computed the stature and age of the animal it belonged to, modelling a complete lion upon the standard of a single part of it. You too would recognize a human hand were the rest of the body concealed. Even so with the schools of philosophy:— the leading doctrines of each might be learned in an afternoon That over-exactness of yours, which required so long a time, is by no means necessary for making the better choice.

—You are forcible, Hermotimus! with this theory of *The Whole by the Part*. Yet, methinks, I heard you but now propound the contrary. But tell me; would Pheidias when he saw the lion's talon have known that it was a lion's, if he had never seen the animal? Surely, the cause of his recognizing the part was his knowledge of the whole. There is a way of choosing one's philosophy even less troublesome than yours. Put the names of all the philosophers into an urn. Then call a little child, and let him draw the name of the philosopher you shall follow all the rest of your days.

—Nay! be serious with me. Tell me; did you ever buy wine?

—Surely.

—And did you first go the whole round of the wine merchants, tasting and comparing their wines?

—By no means.

—No! You were contented to order the first good wine you found at your price. By tasting a little you were ascertained of the quality of the whole cask. How if you had gone to each of the merchants in turn, and said: "I wish to buy a *cotylé* of wine. Let me drink out the whole cask. Then I shall be able to tell which is best, and where I ought to buy". Yet this is what you would do with the philosophies. Why drain the cask when you might taste, and see?

—How slippery you are; how you escape from one's fingers! Still, you have given me an advantage, and are in your own trap.

—How so?

—Thus! You take a common object known to every one, and make *wine* the figure of a thing which presents the greatest variety in itself, and about which all men are at variance, because it is an unseen and difficult thing. I hardly know wherein philosophy and wine are alike unless it be in this, that the philosophers exchange their ware for money, like the wine merchants; some of them with a mixture of water or worse, or giving short measure. However, let us consider your parallel. The wine in the cask, you say, is of one kind throughout. But have the philosophers—has your own master even—but one and the same thing only to tell you, every day and all days, on a subject so manifold? Otherwise, how can you know the whole by the tasting of one part? The whole is not the same—Ah! and it may be that God has hidden the good wine of philosophy at the bottom of the cask. You must drain it to the end if you are to find those drops of divine sweetness you seem so much to thirst for! Yourself, after drinking so deeply, are still but at the beginning, as you said. But is not philosophy rather like this? Keep the figure of the merchant and the cask: but let it be filled, not with wine, but with every sort of grain. You come to buy. The merchant hands you a little of the wheat which lies at the top. Could you tell by looking at that, whether the chick-peas were clean, the lentils tender, the beans full? And then, whereas in selecting our wine we risk only our money; in selecting our philosophy we risk ourselves, as you told me—might ourselves sink into the dregs of "the vulgar herd". Moreover, while you may not drain the whole cask of wine by way of tasting, Wisdom grows no less by the depth of your drinking. Nay! if you take of her, she is increased thereby.

And then I have another similitude to propose, as regards this tasting of philosophy. Don't think I blaspheme her if I say that it may be with her as with some deadly poison, hemlock or aconite. These too, though they cause death, yet kill not if one tastes but a minute portion. You would suppose that the tiniest particle must be sufficient.

—Be it as you will, Lucian! One must live a hundred years: one must sustain all this labour; otherwise philosophy is unattainable.

—Not so! Though there were nothing strange in that, if it be true, as you said at first, that *Life is short and art is long*. But now you take it hard that we are not to see you this very day, before the sun goes down, a Chrysippus, a Pythagoras, a Plato.

—You overtake me, Lucian! and drive me into a corner; in jealousy of heart, I believe, because I have made some progress in doctrine whereas you have neglected yourself.

—Well! Don't attend to me! Treat me as a Corybant, a fanatic: and do you go forward on this road of yours. Finish the journey in accordance with the view you had of these matters at the beginning of it. Only, be assured that my judgment on it will remain unchanged. Reason still says, that without criticism, without a clear, exact, unbiased intelligence to try them, all those theories—all things—will have been seen but in vain. "To that end", she tells us, "much time is necessary, many delays of judgment, a cautious gait; repeated inspection." And we are not to regard the outward appearance, or the reputation of wisdom, in any of the speakers; but like the judges of Areopagus, who try their causes in the darkness of the night, look only to what they *say*.

—Philosophy, then, is impossible, or possible only in another life!

—Hermotimus! I grieve to tell you that all this, even, may be in truth insufficient. After all, we may deceive ourselves in the belief that we have found something:—like the fishermen! Again and again they let down the net. At last they feel something heavy, and with vast labour draw up, not a load of fish, but only a pot full of sand, or a great stone.

—I don't understand what you mean by the net. It is plain that you have caught me in it.

—Try to get out! You can swim as well as another. We may go to all philosophers in turn and make trial of them. Still, I for my part, hold it by no means certain that any one of them really possesses what we seek. The truth may be a thing that not one of them has yet found. You have twenty beans in your hand, and you bid ten persons guess how many: one says five, another fifteen; it is possible that one of them may tell the true number; but it is not impossible that all may be wrong. So it is with the philosophers. All alike are in search of Happiness—what kind of thing it is. One says one thing, one another: it is pleasure; it is virtue;—what not? And Happiness may indeed be one of those things. But it is possible also that it may be still something else, different and distinct from them all.

—What is this?—There is something, I know not how, very sad and disheartening in what you say. We seem to have come round in a circle to the spot whence we started, and to our first incertitude. Ah! Lucian, what have you done to me? You have proved my priceless pearl to be but ashes, and all my past labour to have been in vain.

—Reflect, my friend, that you are not the first person who has thus failed of the good thing he hoped for. All philosophers, so to speak, are but fighting about the "ass's shadow". To me you seem like one who should weep, and reproach fortune because he is not able to climb up into heaven, or go down into the sea by Sicily and come up at Cyprus, or sail on wings in one day from Greece to India. And the true cause of his trouble is that he has based his hope on what he has seen in a dream, or his own fancy has put together; without previous thought whether what he desires is in itself attainable and within the compass of human nature. Even so, methinks, has it happened with you. As you dreamed, so largely, of those wonderful things, came Reason, and woke you up from sleep, a little roughly: and then you are angry with Reason, your eyes being still but half open, and find it hard to shake off sleep for the pleasure of what you saw therein. Only, don't be angry with me, because, as a friend, I would not suffer you to pass your life in a dream, pleasant perhaps, but still only a dream— because I wake you up and demand that you should busy yourself with the proper business of life, and send you to it possessed of common sense. What your soul was full of just now is not very different from those Gorgons and Chimeras and the like, which the poets and the painters construct for us, fancy-free:—things which never were, and never will be, though many believe in them, and all like to see and hear of them, just because they are so strange and odd.

And you too, methinks, having heard from some such maker of marvels of a certain woman of a fairness beyond nature— beyond the Graces, beyond Venus Urania herself—asked not if he spoke truth, and whether this woman be really alive in the world, but straightway fell in love with her; as they say that Medea was enamoured of Jason in a dream. And what more than anything else seduced you, and others like you, into that passion, for a vain idol of the fancy, is, that he who told you about that fair woman, from the very moment when you first believed that what he said was true, brought forward all the rest in consequent order. Upon her alone your eyes were fixed; by her he led you along, when once you had given him a hold upon you—led you along the straight road, as he said, to the beloved one. All was easy after that. None of you asked again whether it was the true way; following one after another, like sheep led by the green bough in the hand of the shepherd. He moved you hither and thither with his finger, as easily as water spilt on a table!

My friend! Be not so lengthy in preparing the banquet,

lest you die of hunger! I saw one who poured water into a mortar, and ground it with all his might with a pestle of iron, fancying he did a thing useful and necessary: but it remained water only, none the less.'

Just there the conversation broke off suddenly, and the disputants parted. The horses were come for Lucian. The boy went on his way, and Marius onward, to visit a friend whose abode lay farther. As he returned to Rome towards evening, the melancholy aspect, natural to a city of the dead, had triumphed over the superficial gaudiness of the early day. He could almost have fancied Canidia there, picking her way among the rickety lamps, to rifle some neglected or ruined tomb; for these tombs were not all equally well cared for (*Post mortem nescio!*), and it had been one of the pieties of Aurelius to frame a severe law to prevent the defacing of such monuments. To Marius there seemed to be some new meaning in that terror of isolation, of being left alone in these places, of which the sepulchral inscriptions were so full. A blood-red sunset was dying angrily, and its wild glare upon the shadowy objects around helped to combine the associations of this famous way, its deeply graven marks of immemorial travel, together with the earnest questions of the morning as to the true way of that other sort of travelling, around an image, almost ghastly in the traces of its great sorrows—bearing along for ever, on bleeding feet, the instrument of its punishment—which was all Marius could recall distinctly of a certain Christian legend he had heard. The legend told of an encounter at this very spot, of two wayfarers on the Appian Way, as also upon some very dimly discerned mental journey, altogether different from himself and his late companions—an encounter between Love, literally fainting by the road, and Love 'travelling in the greatness of his strength', Love itself, suddenly appearing to sustain that other. A strange contrast to anything actually presented in that morning's conversation, it seemed nevertheless to echo its very words—'Do they never come down again', he heard once more the well-modulated voice: 'Do they never come down again from the heights, to help those whom they left here below?'—'And we too desire, not a fair one, but the fairest of all. Unless we find him, we shall think we have failed.'

CHAPTER XXV

SUNT LACRIMAE RERUM

It was become a habit with Marius—one of his modernisms—developed by his assistance at the emperor's 'conversations with himself', to keep a register of the movements of his own private thoughts and humours; not continuously indeed, yet sometimes for lengthy intervals, during which it was no idle self-indulgence, but a necessity of his intellectual life, to 'confess himself', with an intimacy, seemingly rare among the ancients; ancient writers, at all events, having been jealous, for the most part, of affording us so much as a glimpse of that interior self, which in many cases would have actually doubled the interest of their objective informations.

'If a particular tutelary or *genius*,' writes Marius, 'according to old belief, walks through life beside each one of us, mine is very certainly a capricious creature. He fills one with wayward, unaccountable, yet quite irresistible humours, and seems always to be in collusion with some outward circumstance, often trivial enough in itself—the condition of the weather, forsooth!—the people one meets by chance—the things one happens to overhear them say, veritable ἐνόδιοι σύμβολοι, or omens by the wayside, as the old Greeks fancied—to push on the unreasonable prepossessions of the moment into weighty motives. It was doubtless a quite explicable, physical fatigue that presented me to myself, on awaking this morning, so lack-lustre and trite. But I must needs take my petulance, contrasting it with my accustomed morning hopefulness, as a sign of the ageing of appetite, of a decay in the very capacity of enjoyment. We need some imaginative stimulus, some not impossible ideal such as may shape vague hope, and transform it into effective desire, to carry us year after year, without disgust, through the routine work which is so large a part of life.

'Then, how if appetite, be it for real or ideal, should itself fail one after awhile? Ah, yes! it is of cold always that men die; and on some of us it creeps very gradually. In truth, I can remember just such a lack-lustre condition of feeling once or twice before. But I note that it was accompanied then by an odd indifference, as the thought of them occurred to me, in regard to the sufferings of others—a kind of callousness, so unusual with me, as at once to mark the humour it accompanied as a palpably morbid one that could not last. Were those sufferings, great or little, I asked myself then, of more real consequence to them than mine to me, as I remind myself that "nothing that will end is really long"—long enough to be thought of importance? But to-day, my own sense of fatigue, the pity I conceive for myself, disposed me strongly to a tenderness for others. For a moment the whole world seemed to present itself as a hospital of sick persons; many of them sick in mind; all of whom it would be a brutality not to humour, not to indulge.

'Why, when I went out to walk off my wayward fancies, did I confront the very sort of incident (my unfortunate *genius* had surely beckoned it from afar to vex me) likely to irritate them further? A party of men were coming down the street. They were leading a fine race-horse; a handsome beast, but badly hurt somewhere, in the circus, and useless. They were taking him to slaughter; and I think the animal knew it: he cast such looks, as if of mad appeal, to those who passed him, as he went among the strangers to whom his former owner had committed him, to die, in his beauty and pride, for just that one mischance or fault; although the morning air was still so animating, and pleasant to snuff. I could have fancied a human soul in the creature, swelling against its luck. And I had come across the incident just when it would figure to me as the very symbol of our poor humanity, in its capacities for pain, its wretched accidents, and those imperfect sympathies, which can never quite identify us with one another; the very power of utterance and appeal to others seeming to fail us, in proportion as our sorrows come home to ourselves, are really our own. We are constructed for suffering! What proofs of it does but one day afford, if we care to note them, as we go—a whole long chaplet of sorrowful mysteries! *Sunt lacrimae rerum et mentem mortalia tangunt.*

'Men's fortunes touch us! The little children of one of those institutions for the support of orphans, now become fashionable among us by way of memorial of eminent persons deceased, are going, in long file, along the street, on their way to a holiday in the country. They halt, and count themselves with an air of triumph, to show that they are all there. Their gay chatter has disturbed a little group of peasants; a young woman and her husband, who have brought the old mother, now past work and witless, to place her in a house provided for such afflicted people. They are fairly affectionate, but anxious how the thing they have to do may go—hope only she may permit them to leave her there behind quietly. And the poor old soul is excited by the noise made by the children, and partly aware of what is going to happen with her. She too begins to count—one, two, three, five—on her trembling fingers, misshapen by a life of toil. "Yes! yes! and twice five make ten"—they say, to pacify her. It is her last appeal to be taken home again; her proof that all is not yet up with her; that she is, at all events, still as capable as those joyous children.

'At the baths, a party of labourers are at work upon one of the great brick furnaces, in a cloud of black dust. A frail young child has brought food for one of them, and sits apart, waiting till his father comes—watching the labour, but with a sorrowful distaste for the din and dirt. He is regarding wistfully his own place in the world, there before him. His mind, as he watches, is grown up for a moment; and he foresees, as it were, in that moment, all the long tale of days, of early awakings, of his own coming life of drudgery at work like this.

'A man comes along carrying a boy whose rough work has already begun—the only child—whose presence beside him sweetened the father's toil a little. The boy has been badly injured by a fall of brickwork, yet, with an effort, rides boldly on his father's shoulders. It will be the way of natural affection to keep him alive as long as possible, though with that miserably shattered body—"Ah! with us still, and feeling our care beside him!"—and yet surely not without a heartbreaking sigh of relief, alike from him and them, when the end comes.

'On the alert for incidents like these, yet of necessity passing them by on the other side, I find it hard to get rid of a sense that I, for one, have failed in love. I could yield to the humour till I seemed to have had my share in those great public cruelties, the shocking legal crimes which are on record, like that cold-blooded slaughter, according to law, of the four hundred slaves in the reign of Nero, because one of their number was thought to have murdered his master. The reproach of that, together with the kind of facile apologies those who had no share in the deed may have made for it, as they went about quietly on their own affairs that day, seems to come very close to me, as I think upon it. And to how many of those now actually around me, whose life is a sore one, must I be indifferent, if I ever become aware of their soreness at all? To some, perhaps, the necessary conditions of my own life may cause me to be opposed, in a kind of natural conflict, regarding those interests which actually determine the happiness of theirs. I would that a stronger love might arise in my heart!

'Yet there is plenty of charity in the world. My patron, the Stoic emperor, has made it even fashionable. To celebrate one of his brief returns to Rome lately from the war, over and above a largess of gold pieces to all who would, the public debts were forgiven. He made a nice show of it: for once, the Romans entertained themselves with a good-natured spectacle, and the whole town came to see the great bonfire in the Forum, into which all bonds and evidence of debt were thrown on delivery, by the emperor himself; many private creditors following his example. That was done well enough! But still the feeling returns to me, that no charity of ours can get at a certain natural unkindness which I find in things themselves.

'When I first came to Rome, eager to observe its religion, especially its antiquities of religious usage, I assisted at the most curious, perhaps, of them all, the most distinctly marked with that immobility which is a sort of ideal in the Roman religion. The ceremony took place at a singular spot some miles distant from the city, among the low hills on the bank of the Tiber, beyond the Aurelian Gate. There, in a little wood of venerable trees, piously allowed their own way, age after age— ilex and cypress remaining where they fell at last, one over the other, and all caught, in that early May-time, under a riotous tangle of wild clematis—was to be found a magnificent sanctuary, in which the members of the Arval College assembled themselves on certain days. The axe never touched those trees—Nay! it was forbidden to introduce any iron thing whatsoever within the precincts; not only because the deities of these quiet places hate to be disturbed by the harsh noise of metal, but also in memory of that better age—the lost *Golden Age*—the homely age of the potters, of which the central act of the festival was a commemoration.

'The preliminary ceremonies were long and complicated, but of a character familiar enough. Peculiar to the time and place was the solemn exposition, after lavation of hands, processions backwards and forwards, and certain changes of vestments, of the identical earthen vessels—veritable relics of the old religion of Numa!—the vessels from which the holy Numa himself had eaten and drunk, set forth above a kind of altar, amid a cloud of flowers and incense, and many lights, for the veneration of the credulous or the faithful.

'They were, in fact, cups or vases of burnt clay, rude in form: and the religious veneration thus offered to them expressed men's desire to give honour to a simpler age, before iron had found place in human life: the persuasion that that age was worth remembering: a hope that it might come again.

'That a Numa, and his age of gold, would return, has been the hope or the dream of some, in every period. Yet if he did come back, or any equivalent of his presence, he could but weaken, and by no means smite through, that root of evil, certainly of sorrow, of outraged human sense, in things, which one must carefully distinguish from all preventible accidents. Death, and the little perpetual daily dyings, which have something of its sting, he must necessarily leave untouched. And, methinks, that were all the rest of man's life framed entirely to his liking, he would straightway begin to sadden himself, over the fate—say, of the flowers! For there is, there has come to be since Numa lived perhaps, a capacity for sorrow in his heart, which grows with all the growth, alike of the individual and of the race, in intellectual delicacy and power, and which *will* find its aliment.

'Of that sort of golden age, indeed, one discerns even now a trace, here and there. Often have I maintained that, in this generous southern country at least, Epicureanism is the special philosophy of the poor. How little I myself really need, when people leave me alone, with the intellectual powers at work serenely. The drops of falling water, a few wild flowers with their priceless fragrance, a few tufts even of half-dead leaves, changing colour in the quiet of a room that has but light and shadow in it; these, for a susceptible mind, might well do duty for all the glory of Augustus. I notice sometimes what I conceive to be the precise character of the fondness of the roughest working-people for their young children, a fine appreciation, not only of their serviceable affection, but of their visible graces: and indeed, in this country, the children are almost always worth looking at. I see daily, in fine weather, a child like a delicate nosegay, running to meet the rudest of brickmakers as he comes from work. She is not at all afraid to hang upon his rough hand: and through her, he reaches out to, he makes his own, something from that strange region, so distant from him yet so real, of the world's refinement. What is of finer soul, or of finer stuff in things, and demands delicate touching—to him the delicacy of the little child represents that: it initiates him into that. There, surely, is a touch of the *secular* gold, of a perpetual age of gold. But then again, think for a moment, with what a hard humour at the nature of things, his struggle for bare life will go on, if the child should happen to die. I observed to-day, under one of the archways of the baths, two children at play, a little seriously—a fair girl and her crippled younger brother. Two toy chairs and a little table, and sprigs of fir set upright in the sand for a garden! They played at housekeeping. Well! the girl thinks her life a perfectly good thing in the service of this crippled brother. But she will have a jealous lover in time: and the boy, though his face is not altogether unpleasant, is after all a hopeless cripple.

'For there is a certain grief in things as they are, in man as he has come to be, as he certainly is, over and above those griefs of circumstance which are in a measure removable— some inexplicable shortcoming, or misadventure, on the part of nature itself—death, and old age as it must needs be, and that watching for their approach, which makes every stage of life like a dying over and over again. Almost all death is painful, and in every thing that comes to an end a touch of death, and therefore of wretched coldness struck home to one, of remorse, of loss and parting, of outraged attachments. Given faultless men and women, given a perfect state of society which should have no need to practise on men's susceptibilities for its own selfish ends, adding one turn more to the wheel of the great rack for its own interest or amusement, there would still be this evil in the world, of a certain necessary sorrow and desolation, felt, just in proportion to the moral or nervous perfection men have attained to. And what we need in the world, over against that, is a certain permanent and general power of compassion—humanity's standing force of self-pity— as an elementary ingredient of our social atmosphere, if we are to live in it at all. I wonder, sometimes, in what way man has cajoled himself into the bearing of his burden thus far, seeing how every step in the capacity of apprehension his labour has won for him, from age to age, must needs increase his dejection. It is as if the increase of knowledge were but an increasing revelation of the radical hopelessness of his position: and I would that there were one even as I, behind this vain show of things!

'At all events, the actual conditions of our life being as they

are, and the capacity for suffering so large a principle in things—
since the only principle, perhaps, to which we may always
safely trust is a ready sympathy with the pain one actually
sees—it follows that the practical and effective difference
between men will lie in their power of insight into those
conditions, their power of sympathy. The future will be with
those who have most of it; while for the present, as I persuade
myself, those who have much of it, have something to hold by,
even in the dissolution of a world, or in that dissolution of self,
which is, for every one, no less than the dissolution of the world
it represents for him. Nearly all of us, I suppose, have had our
moments, in which any effective sympathy for us on the part
of others has seemed impossible; in which our pain has seemed
a stupid outrage upon us, like some overwhelming physical
violence, from which we could take refuge, at best, only in
some mere general sense of goodwill—somewhere in the world
perhaps. And then, to one's surprise, the discovery of that
goodwill, if it were only in a not unfriendly animal, may seem
to have explained, to have actually justified to us, the fact of
our pain. There have been occasions, certainly, when I have
felt that if others cared for me as I cared for them, it would be,
not so much a consolation, as an equivalent, for what one has
lost or suffered: a realized profit on the summing up of one's
accounts: a touching of that absolute ground amid all the
changes of phenomena, such as our philosophers have of late
confessed themselves quite unable to discover. In the mere
clinging of human creatures to each other, nay! in one's own
solitary self-pity, amid the effects even of what might appear
irredeemable loss, I seem to touch the eternal. Something in
that pitiful contact, something new and true, fact or apprehension of fact, is educed, which, on a review of all the perplexities
of life, satisfies our moral sense, and removes that appearance
of unkindness in the soul of things themselves, and assures us
that not everything has been in vain.

'And I know not how, but in the thought thus suggested, I
seem to take up, and re-knit myself to, a well-remembered
hour, when by some gracious accident—it was on a journey—
all things about me fell into a more perfect harmony than is
their wont. Everything seemed to be, for a moment, after all,
almost for the best. Through the train of my thoughts, one
against another, it was as if I became aware of the dominant
power of another person in controversy, wrestling with me.
I seem to be come round to the point at which I left off then.

The antagonist has closed with me again. A protest comes, out of the very depths of man's radically hopeless condition in the world, with the energy of one of those suffering yet prevailing deities of which old poetry tells. Dared one hope that there is a heart, even as ours, in that divine "Assistant" of one's thoughts—a heart even as mine, behind this vain show of things!'

CHAPTER XXVI

THE MARTYRS

Ah! voilà les âmes qu'il falloit à la mienne!
ROUSSEAU.

THE charm of its poetry, a poetry of the affections, wonderfully fresh in the midst of a threadbare world, would have led Marius, if nothing else had done so, again and again, to Cecilia's house. He found a range of intellectual pleasures, altogether new to him, in the sympathy of that pure and elevated soul. Elevation of soul, generosity, humanity—little by little it came to seem to him as if these existed nowhere else. The sentiment of maternity, above all, as it might be understood there—its claims, with the claims of all natural feeling everywhere, down to the sheep bleating on the hills, nay! even to the mother-wolf, in her hungry cave—seemed to have been vindicated, to have been enforced anew, by the sanction of some divine pattern thereof. He saw its legitimate place in the world given at last to the bare capacity for suffering in any creature, however feeble or apparently useless. In this chivalry, seeming to leave the world's heroism a mere property of the stage, in this so scrupulous fidelity to what could not help itself, could scarcely claim not to be forgotten, what a contrast to the hard contempt of one's own or other's pain, of death, of glory even, in those discourses of Aurelius!

But if Marius thought at times that some long-cherished desires were now about to blossom for him, in the sort of home he had sometimes pictured to himself, the very charm of which would lie in its contrast to any random affections: that in this woman, to whom children instinctively clung, he might find such a sister, at least, as he had always longed for; there were also circumstances which reminded him that a certain rule forbidding second marriages was among these people still in force; ominous incidents, moreover, warning a susceptible conscience not to mix together the spirit and the flesh, nor make the matter of a heavenly banquet serve for earthly meat and drink.

246

One day he found Cecilia occupied with the burial of one of the children of her household. It was from the tiny brow of such a child, as he now heard, that the new light had first shone forth upon them—through the light of mere physical life, glowing there again, when the child was dead, or supposed to be dead. The aged servant of Christ had arrived in the midst of their noisy grief; and mounting to the little chamber where it lay, had returned, not long afterwards, with the child stirring in his arms as he descended the stair rapidly; bursting open the closely wound folds of the shroud and scattering the funeral flowers from them, as the soul kindled once more through its limbs.

Old Roman common sense had taught people to occupy their thoughts as little as might be with children who died young. Here, to-day, however, in this curious house, all thoughts were tenderly bent on the little waxen figure, yet with a kind of exultation and joy, notwithstanding the loud weeping of the mother. The other children, its late companions, broke with it, suddenly, into the place where the deep black bed lay open to receive it. Pushing away the grim *fossores*, the gravediggers, they ranged themselves around it in order, and chanted that old psalm of theirs—*Laudate pueri dominum!* Dead children, children's graves—Marius had been always half aware of an old superstitious fancy in his mind concerning them; as if in coming near them he came near the failure of some lately born hope or purpose of his own. And now, perusing intently the expression with which Cecilia assisted, directed, returned afterwards to her house, he felt that he too had had to-day his funeral of a little child. But it had always been his policy, through all his pursuit of 'experience', to take flight in time from any too disturbing passion, from any sort of affection likely to quicken his pulses beyond the point at which the quiet work of life was practicable. Had he, after all, been taken unawares, so that it was no longer possible for him to fly? At least, during the journey he took, by way of testing the existence of any chain about him, he found a certain disappointment at his heart, greater than he could have anticipated; and as he passed over the crisp leaves, nipped off in multitudes by the first sudden cold of winter, he felt that the mental atmosphere within himself was perceptibly colder.

Yet it was, finally, a quite successful resignation which he achieved, on a review, after his manner, during that absence, of loss or gain. The image of Cecilia, it would seem, was already become for him like some matter of poetry, or of another man's story, or a picture on the wall. And on his return to Rome there had been a rumour in that singular company, of things which spoke certainly not of any merely tranquil loving: hinted rather that he had come across a world, the lightest contact with which might make appropriate to himself also the precept that 'They which have wives be as they that have none'.

This was brought home to him when, in early spring, he ventured once more to listen to the sweet singing of the Eucharist. It breathed more than ever the spirit of a wonderful hope—of hopes more daring than poor, labouring humanity had ever seriously entertained before, though it was plain that a great calamity was befallen. Amid stifled sobbing, even as the pathetic words of the psalter relieved the tension of their hearts, the people around him still wore upon their faces their habitual gleam of joy, of placid satisfaction. They were still under the influence of an immense gratitude in thinking, even amid their present distress, of the hour of a great deliverance. As he followed again that mystical dialogue, he felt also again, like a mighty spirit about him, the potency, the half-realized presence, of a great multitude, as if thronging along those awful passages, to hear the sentence of its release from prison; a company which represented nothing less than—*orbis terrarum*— the whole company of mankind. And the special note of the day expressed that relief—a sound new to him, drawn deep from some old Hebrew source, as he conjectured, *Alleluia !* repeated over and over again, *Alleluia ! Alleluia !* at every pause and movement of the long Easter ceremonies.

And then, in its place, by way of sacred lection, although in shocking contrast with the peaceful dignity of all around, came the *Epistle of the Churches of Lyons and Vienne*, to 'their sister', the Church of Rome. For the 'Peace' of the Church had been broken—broken, as Marius could not but acknowledge, on the responsibility of the Emperor Aurelius himself, following tamely, and as a matter of course, the traces of his predecessors, gratuitously enlisting, against the good as well as the evil of that great pagan world, the strange new heroism of which this singular message was full. The greatness of it certainly lifted away all merely private regret, inclining one, at last, actually to draw sword for the oppressed, as if in some new order of knighthood:

'The pains which our brethren have endured we have no power fully to tell, for the enemy came upon us with his whole strength. But the grace of God fought for us, set free the weak, and made ready those who, like pillars, were able to bear the weight. These, coming now into close strife with the foe, bore every kind of pang and shame. At the time of the fair which is held here with a great crowd, the governor led forth the Martyrs as a show. Holding what was thought great but little, and that the pains of to-day are not deserving to be measured against the glory that shall be made known, these worthy wrestlers went joyfully on their way; their delight and the sweet favour of God mingling in their faces, so that their bonds seemed but a goodly array, or like the golden bracelets of a bride. Filled with the fragrance of Christ, to some they seemed to have been touched with earthly perfumes.

'Vettius Epagathus, though he was very young, because he would not endure to see unjust judgment given against us, vented his anger, and sought to be heard for the brethren, for he was a youth of high place. Whereupon the governor asked him whether he also were a Christian. He confessed in a clear voice, and was added to the number of the Martyrs. But he had the Paraclete within him; as, in truth, he showed by the fullness of his love; glorying in the defence of his brethren, and to give his life for theirs.

'Then was fulfilled the saying of the Lord that the day should come, *When he that slayeth you will think that he doeth God service.* Most madly did the mob, the governor and the soldiers, rage against the handmaiden Blandina, in whom Christ showed that what seems mean among men is of price with Him. For whilst we all, and her earthly mistress, who was herself one of the contending Martyrs, were fearful lest through the weakness of the flesh she should be unable to profess the faith, Blandina was filled with such power that her tormentors following upon each other from morning until night, owned that they were overcome, and had no more that they could do to her; admiring that she still breathed after her whole body was torn asunder.

'But this blessed one, in the very midst of her "witness", renewed her strength; and to repeat, *I am Christ's !* was to her rest, refreshment, and relief from pain. As for Alexander, he neither uttered a groan nor any sound at all, but in his heart talked with God. Sanctus, the deacon, also, having borne beyond all measure pains devised by them, hoping that they would get something from him, did not so much as tell his name; but to all questions answered only, *I am Christ's !* For this he confessed instead of his name, his race, and everything beside.

Whence also a strife in torturing him arose between the
governor and those tormentors, so that when they had nothing
else they could do they set red-hot plates of brass to the most
tender parts of his body. But he stood firm in his profession,
cooled and fortified by that stream of living water which flows
from Christ. His corpse, a single wound, having wholly lost
the form of man, was the measure of his pain. But Christ,
paining in him, set forth an ensample to the rest—that there is
nothing fearful, nothing painful, where the love of the Father
overcomes. And as all those cruelties were made null through
the patience of the Martyrs, they bethought them of other
things; among which was their imprisonment in a dark and
most sorrowful place, where many were privily strangled. But,
destitute of man's aid, they were filled with power from the
Lord, both in body and mind, and strengthened their brethren.
Also, much joy was in our virgin mother, the Church; for, by
means of these, such as were fallen away retraced their steps—
were again conceived, were filled again with lively heat, and
hastened to make the profession of their faith.

'The holy bishop Pothinus, who was now past ninety years
old and weak in body, yet in his heat of soul and longing for
martyrdom, roused what strength he had, and was also cruelly
dragged to judgment, and gave witness. Thereupon he suffered
many stripes, all thinking it would be a wickedness if they fell
short in cruelty towards him, for that thus their own gods would
be avenged. Hardly drawing breath, he was thrown into
prison, and after two days there died.

'After these things their martyrdom was parted into divers
manners. Plaiting as it were one crown of many colours and
every sort of flowers, they offered it to God. Maturus, therefore,
Sanctus and Blandina, were led to the wild beasts. And
Maturus and Sanctus passed through all the pains of the
amphitheatre, as if they had suffered nothing before: or rather,
as having in many trials overcome, and now contending for the
prize itself, were at last dismissed.

'But Blandina was bound and hung upon a stake, and set
forth as food for the assault of the wild beasts. And as she
thus seemed to be hung upon the Cross, by her fiery prayers
she imparted much alacrity to those contending Witnesses.
For as they looked upon her with the eye of flesh, through her,
they saw Him that was crucified. But as none of the beasts
would then touch her, she was taken down from the Cross, and
sent back to prison for another day: that, though weak and mean,

yet clothed with the mighty wrestler, Christ Jesus, she might by many conquests give heart to her brethren.

'On the last day, therefore, of the shows, she was brought forth again, together with Ponticus, a lad of about fifteen years old. They were brought in day by day to behold the pains of the rest. And when they wavered not, the mob was full of rage; pitying neither the youth of the lad, nor the sex of the maiden. Hence, they drave them through the whole round of pain. And Ponticus, taking heart from Blandina, having borne well the whole of those torments, gave up his life. Last of all, the blessed Blandina herself, as a mother that had given life to her children, and sent them like conquerors to the great King, hastened to them, with joy at the end, as to a marriage-feast; the enemy himself confessing that no woman had ever borne pain so manifold and great as hers.

'Nor even so was their anger appeased; some among them seeking for us pains, if it might be, yet greater; that the saying might be fulfilled, *He that is unjust, let him be unjust still.* And their rage against the Martyrs took a new form, insomuch that we were in great sorrow for lack of freedom to entrust their bodies to the earth. Neither did the night-time, nor the offer of money, avail us for this matter; but they set watch with much carefulness, as though it were a great gain to hinder their burial. Therefore, after the bodies had been displayed to view for many days, they were at last burned to ashes, and cast into the river Rhone, which flows by this place, that not a vestige of them might be left upon the earth. For they said, *Now shall we see whether they will rise again, and whether their God can save them out of our hands.*'

CHAPTER XXVII

THE TRIUMPH OF MARCUS AURELIUS

Not many months after the date of that epistle, Marius, then expecting to leave Rome for a long time, and in fact about to leave it for ever, stood to witness the triumphal entry of Marcus Aurelius, almost at the exact spot from which he had watched the emperor's solemn return to the capital on his own first coming thither. His triumph was now a 'full' one—*Justus Triumphus*—justified, by far more than the due amount of bloodshed in those northern wars, at length, it might seem, happily at an end. Among the captives, amid the laughter of the crowds at his blowsy upper garment, his trousered legs and conical wolf-skin cap, walked our own ancestor, representative of subject Germany, under a figure very familiar in later Roman sculpture; and, though certainly with none of the grace of the *Dying Gaul*, yet with plenty of uncouth pathos in his misshapen features, and the pale, servile, yet angry eyes. His children, white-skinned and golden-haired 'as angels', trudged beside him. His brothers, of the animal world, the ibex, the wild-cat, and the reindeer stalking and trumpeting grandly, found their due place in the procession; and among the spoil, set forth on a portable frame that it might be distinctly seen (no mere model, but the very house he had lived in), a wattled cottage, in all the simplicity of its snug contrivances against the cold, and well calculated to give a moment's delight to his new sophisticated masters.

Andrea Mantegna, working at the end of the fifteenth century, for a society full of antiquarian fervour at the sight of the earthy relics of the old Roman people, day by day returning to light out of the clay—childish still, moreover, and with no more suspicion of pasteboard than the old Romans themselves, in its unabashed love of open-air pageantries, has invested this, the greatest, and alas! the most characteristic, of the splendours of imperial Rome, with a reality livelier than any description. The homely sentiments for which he has found place in his learned paintings are hardly more lifelike than the great public incidents of the show, there depicted. And then, with all that vivid realism, how refined, how dignified, how select in type, is this reflection of the old Roman world!—now especially, in its time-mellowed red and gold, for the modern visitor to the old English palace.

It was under no such selected types that the great procession presented itself to Marius; though, in effect, he found something there prophetic, so to speak, and evocative of ghosts, as susceptible minds will do, upon a repetition after long interval of some notable incident, which may yet perhaps have no direct concern for themselves. In truth, he had been so closely bent of late on certain very personal interests that the broad current of the world's doings seemed to have withdrawn into the distance, but now, as he witnessed this procession, to return once more into evidence for him. The world, certainly, had been holding on its old way, and was all its old self, as it thus passed by dramatically, accentuating, in this favourite spectacle, its mode of viewing things. And even apart from the contrast of a very different scene, he would have found it, just now, a somewhat vulgar spectacle. The temples, wide open, with their ropes of roses flapping in the wind against the rich, reflecting marble, their startling draperies and heavy cloud of incense, were but the centres of a great banquet spread through all the gaudily coloured streets of Rome, for which the carnivorous appetite of those who thronged them in the glare of the midday sun was frankly enough asserted. At best, they were but calling their gods to share with them the cooked, sacrificial, and other meats, reeking to the sky. The child, who was concerned for the sorrows of one of those northern captives as he passed by, and explained to his comrade: 'There's feeling in that hand, you know!' benumbed and lifeless as it looked in the chain, seemed, in a moment, to transform the entire show into its own proper tinsel. Yes! these Romans were a coarse, a vulgar people; and their vulgarities of soul in full evidence here. And Aurelius himself seemed to have undergone the world's coinage, and fallen to the level of his reward, in a mediocrity no longer golden.

Yet if, as he passed by, almost filling the quaint old circular chariot with his magnificent golden-flowered attire, he presented himself to Marius, chiefly as one who had made the great mistake; to the multitude he came as a more than magnanimous conqueror. That he had 'forgiven' the innocent wife and children of the dashing and almost successful rebel Avidius Cassius, now no more, was a recent circumstance still in memory.

As the children went past—not among those who, ere the emperor ascended the steps of the Capitol, would be detached from the great progress for execution, happy rather, and radiant, as adopted members of the imperial family—the crowd actually enjoyed an exhibition of the *moral* order, such as might become rpehaps the fashion. And it was in consideration of some possible touch of a heroism herein that might really have cost him something, that Marius resolved to seek the emperor once more, with an appeal for common sense, for reason and justice.

He had set out at last to revisit his old home; and knowing that Aurelius was then in retreat at a favourite villa, which lay almost on his way thither, determined there to present himself. Although the great plain was dying steadily, a new race of wild birds establishing itself there, as he knew enough of their habits to understand, and the idle *contadino*, with his never-ending ditty of decay and death, replacing the lusty Roman labourer, never had that poetic region between Rome and the sea more deeply impressed him than on this sunless day of early autumn, under which all that fell within the immense horizon was presented in one uniform tone of a clear, penitential blue. Stimulating to the fancy as was that range of low hills to the northwards, already troubled with the upbreaking of the Apennines, yet a want of quiet in their outline, the record of wild fracture there, of sudden upheaval and depression, marked them as but the ruins of nature; while at every little descent and ascent of the road might be noted traces of the abandoned work of man. From time to time, the way was still redolent of the floral relics of summer, daphne and myrtle blossom, sheltered in the little hollows and ravines. At last, amid rocks here and there piercing the soil, as those descents became steeper, and the main line of the Apennines, now visible, gave a higher accent to the scene, he espied over the *plateau*, almost like one of those broken hills, cutting the horizon towards the sea, the old brown villa itself, rich in memories of one after another of the family of the Antonines. As he approached it, such reminiscences crowded upon him, above all of the life there of the aged Antoninus Pius, in its wonderful mansuetude and calm. Death had overtaken him here at the precise moment when the tribune of the watch had received from his lips the word *Aequanimitas!* as the watchword of the night. To see their emperor living there like one of his simplest subjects, his hands red at vintage-time with the juice of the grapes, hunting, teaching his children, starting betimes, with all who cared to join him, for long days of antiquarian research in the country around:—this, and the like of this, had seemed to mean the peace of mankind.

Upon that had come—like a stain! it seemed to Marius just then—the more intimate life of Faustina, the life of Faustina at home. Surely, that marvellous but malign beauty must still haunt those rooms, like an unquiet, dead goddess, who might have perhaps, after all, something reassuring to tell surviving mortals about her ambiguous self. When, two years since, the news had reached Rome that those eyes, always so persistently turned to vanity, had suddenly closed for ever, a strong desire to pray had come over Marius, as he followed in fancy on its wild way the soul of one he had spoken with now and again, and whose presence in it for a time the world of art could so ill have spared. Certainly, the honours freely accorded to embalm her memory were poetic enough—the rich temple left among those wild villagers at the spot, now it was hoped sacred for ever, where she had breathed her last; the golden image, in her old place at the amphitheatre; the altar at which the newly married might make their sacrifice; above all, the great foundation for orphan girls, to be called after her name.

The latter, precisely, was the cause why Marius failed in fact to see Aurelius again, and make the chivalrous effort at enlightenment he had proposed to himself. Entering the villa, he learned from an usher, at the door of the long gallery, famous still for its grand prospect in the memory of many a visitor, and then leading to the imperial apartments, that the emperor was already in audience: Marius must await his turn—he knew not how long it might be. An odd audience it seemed; for at that moment, through the closed door, came shouts of laughter, the laughter of a great crowd of children—the 'Faustinian Children' themselves, as he afterwards learned—happy and at their ease, in the imperial presence. Uncertain, then, of the time for which so pleasant a reception might last, so pleasant that he would hardly have wished to shorten it, Marius finally determined to proceed, as it was necessary that he should accomplish the first stage of his journey on this day. The thing was not to be—*Vale! anima infelicissima!*—He might at least carry away that sound of the laughing orphan children, as a not unamiable last impression of kings and their houses.

The place he was now about to visit, especially as the resting-place of his dead, had never been forgotten. Only, the first eager period of his life in Rome had slipped on rapidly; and, almost on a sudden, that old time had come to seem very long ago. An almost burdensome solemnity had grown about his memory of the place, so that to revisit it seemed a thing that needed preparation: it was what he could not have done hastily. He half feared to lessen, or disturb, its value for himself. And then, as he travelled leisurely towards it, and so far with quite tranquil mind, interested also in many another place by the way, he discovered a shorter road to the end of his journey, and found himself indeed approaching the spot that was to him like no other. Dreaming now only of the dead before him, he journeyed on rapidly through the night; the thought of them increasing on him, in the darkness. It was as if they had been waiting for him there through all those years, and felt his footsteps approaching now, and understood his devotion, quite gratefully, in that lowliness of theirs, in spite of its tardy fulfilment. As morning came, his late tranquillity of mind had given way to a grief which surprised him by its freshness. He was moved more than he could have thought possible by so distant a sorrow. 'To-day!'—they seemed to be saying as the hard dawn broke—'To-day, he will come!' At last, amid all his distractions, they were become the main purpose of what he was then doing. The world around it, when he actually reached the place later in the day, was in a mood very different from his:—so workaday, it seemed, on that fine afternoon, and the villages he passed through so silent; the inhabitants being, for the most part, at their labour in the country. Then, at length, above the tiled outbuildings, were the walls of the old villa itself, with the tower for the pigeons; and, not among cypresses, but half-hidden by aged poplar-trees, their leaves like golden fruit, the birds floating around it, the conical roof of the tomb itself. In the presence of an old servant who remembered him, the great seals were broken, the rusty key turned at last in the lock, the door was forced out among the weeds grown thickly about it, and Marius was actually in the place which had been so often in his thoughts.

He was struck, not however without a touch of remorse thereupon, chiefly by an odd air of neglect, the neglect of a place allowed to remain as when it was last used, and left in a hurry, till long years had covered it all alike with thick dust—the faded flowers, the burnt-out lamps, the tools and hardened mortar of the workmen who had had something to do there. A heavy fragment of woodwork had fallen and chipped open one of the oldest of the mortuary urns, many hundreds in number ranged around the walls. It was not properly an urn, but a minute coffin of stone, and the fracture had revealed a piteous spectacle of the mouldering, unburned remains within; the bones of a child, as he understood, which might have died, in ripe age, three times over, since it slipped away from among his great-grandfathers, so far up in the line. Yet the protruding baby hand seemed to stir up in him feelings vivid enough, bringing him intimately within the scope of dead people's grievances. He noticed, side by side with the urn of his mother, that of a boy of about his own age—one of the serving-boys of the household—who had descended hither, from the lightsome world of childhood, almost at the same time with her. It seemed as if this boy of his own age had taken filial place beside her there, in his stead. That hard feeling, again, which had always lingered in his mind with the thought of the father he had scarcely known, melted wholly away, as he read the precise number of his years, and reflected suddenly: He was of my own present age; nor had old man, but with interests, as he looked round him on the world for the last time, even as mine to-day! And with that came a blinding rush of kindness, as if two alienated friends had come to understand each other at last. There was weakness in all this; as there is in all care for dead persons, to which nevertheless people will always yield in proportion as they really care for one another. With a vain yearning, as he stood there, still to be able to do something for them, he reflected that such doing must be, after all, in the nature of things, mainly for himself. His own epitaph might be that old one—*Ἔσχατος τοῦ ἰδίου γένους*—*He was the last of his race!* Of those who might come hither after himself, probably no one would ever again come quite as he had done to-day; and it was under the influence of this thought that he determined to bury all that, deep below the surface, to be remembered only by him, and in a way which would claim no sentiment from the indifferent. That took many days—was like a renewal of lengthy old burial rites—as he himself watched the work, early and late; coming on the last day very early, and anticipating, by stealth, the last touches, while the workmen were absent; one young lad only, finally smoothing down the earthy bed, greatly surprised at the seriousness with which Marius flung in his flowers, one by one, to mingle with the dark mould.

CHAPTER XXVIII

THOSE eight days at his old home, so mournfully occupied, had been for Marius in some sort a forcible disruption from the world and the roots of his life in it. He had been carried out of himself as never before; and when the time was over, it was as if the claim over him of the earth below had been vindicated, over against the interests of that living world around. Dead, yet sentient and caressing hands seemed to reach out of the ground and to be clinging about him. Looking back sometimes now, from about the midway of life—the age, as he conceived, at which one begins to redescend one's life—though antedating it a little, in his sad humour, he would note, almost with surprise, the unbroken placidity of the contemplation in which it had been passed. His own temper, his early theoretic scheme of things, would have pushed him on to movement and adventure. Actually, as circumstances had determined, all its movement had been inward; movement of observation only, or even of pure meditation; in part, perhaps, because throughout it had been something of a *meditatio mortis*, ever facing towards the act of final detachment. Death, however, as he reflected, must be for every one nothing less than the fifth or last act of a drama, and, as such, was likely to have something of the stirring character of a *dénouement*. And, in fact, it was in form tragic enough that his end not long afterwards came to him.

In the midst of the extreme weariness and depression which had followed those last days, Cornelius, then, as it happened, on a journey and travelling near the place, finding traces of him, had become his guest at White-nights. It was just then that Marius felt, as he had never done before, the value to himself, the overpowering charm, of his friendship. 'More than brother!'—he felt—'like a son also!' contrasting the fatigue of soul which made himself in effect an older man, with the irrepressible youth of his companion. For it was still the marvellous hopefulness of Cornelius, his seeming prerogative over the future, that determined, and kept alive, all other sentiment concerning him. A new hope had sprung up in the world of which he, Cornelius, was a depositary, which he was to bear onward in it. Identifying himself with Cornelius in so dear a friendship, through him, Marius seemed to touch, to ally himself to, actually to become a possessor of the coming world; even as happy parents reach out, and take possession of it, in and through the survival of their children. For in these days their intimacy had grown very close, as they moved hither and thither, leisurely, among the country-places thereabout, Cornelius being on his way back to Rome, till they came one evening to a little town (Marius remembered that he had been there on his first journey to Rome) which had even then its church and legend—the legend and holy relics of the martyr Hyacinthus, a young Roman soldier, whose blood had stained the soil of this place in the reign of the Emperor Trajan.

The thought of that so recent death haunted Marius through the night, as if with audible crying and sighs above the restless wind, which came and went around their lodging. But towards dawn he slept heavily; and awaking in broad daylight, and finding Cornelius absent, set forth to seek him. The plague was still in the place—had indeed just broken out afresh; with an outbreak also of cruel superstition among its wild and miserable inhabitants. Surely, the old gods were wroth at the presence of this new enemy among them! And it was no ordinary morning into which Marius stepped forth. There was a menace in the dark masses of hill, and motionless wood, against the grey, although apparently unclouded sky. Under this sunless heaven the earth itself seemed to fret and fume with a heat of its own, in spite of the strong night wind. And now the wind had fallen. Marius felt that he breathed some strange heavy fluid, denser than any common air. He could have fancied that the world had sunken in the night, far below its proper level, into some close, thick abysm of its own atmosphere. The Christian people of the town, hardly less terrified and overwrought by the haunting sickness about them than their pagan neighbours, were at prayer before the tomb of the martyr; and even as Marius pressed among them to a place beside Cornelius, on a sudden the hills seemed to roll like a sea in motion, around the whole compass of the horizon. For a moment Marius supposed himself attacked with some sudden sickness of brain, till the fall of a great mass of building convinced him that not himself but the earth under his feet was giddy. A few moments later the little market-place was alive with the rush of the distracted inhabitants from their tottering houses; and as they waited anxiously for the second shock of earthquake, a long-smouldering suspicion leapt precipitately into well-defined purpose, and the whole body of people was carried forward towards the band of worshippers below. An hour later, in the wild tumult which followed, the earth had been stained afresh with the blood of the martyrs Felix and Faustinus — *Flores apparuerunt in terra nostra!* — and their brethren, together with Cornelius and Marius, thus, as it had happened, taken among them, were prisoners, reserved for the action of the law. Marius and his friend, with certain others, exercising the privilege of their rank, made claim to be tried in Rome, or at least in the chief town of the district; where, indeed, in the troublous days that had now begun, a legal process had been already instituted. Under the care of a military guard the captives were removed on the same day, one stage of their journey; sleeping, for security, during the night, side by side with their keepers, in the rooms of a shepherd's deserted house by the wayside.

It was surmised that one of the prisoners was not a Christian: the guards were forward to make the utmost pecuniary profit of this circumstance, and in the night, Marius, taking advantage of the loose charge kept over them, and by means partly of a large bribe, had contrived that Cornelius, as the really innocent person, should be dismissed in safety on his way, to procure, as Marius explained, the proper means of defence for himself, when the time of trial came.

And in the morning Cornelius in fact set forth alone, from their miserable place of detention. Marius believed that Cornelius was to be the husband of Cecilia; and that, perhaps strangely, had but added to the desire to get him away safely.— We wait for the great crisis which is to try what is in us: we can hardly bear the pressure of our hearts, as we think of it: the lonely wrestler, or victim, which imagination foreshadows to us, can hardly be one's self; it seems an outrage of our destiny that we should be led along so gently and imperceptibly, to so terrible a leaping-place in the dark, for more perhaps than life or death. At last, the great act, the critical moment itself comes, easily, almost unconsciously. Another motion of the clock, and our fatal line—the 'great climacteric point'—has been passed, which changes ourselves or our lives. In one quarter of an hour, under a sudden, uncontrollable impulse, hardly weighing what he did, almost as a matter of course and as lightly as one hires a bed for one's night's rest on a journey, Marius had taken upon himself all the heavy risk of the position in which Cornelius had then been—the long and wearisome delays of judgment which were possible; the danger and wretchedness of a long journey in this manner; possibly the danger of death. He had delivered his brother, after the manner he had sometimes vaguely anticipated as a kind of distinction in his destiny; though indeed always with wistful calculation as to what it might cost him: and in the first moment after the thing was actually done, he felt only satisfaction at his courage, at the discovery of his possession of 'nerve'.

Yet he was, as we know, no hero, no heroic martyr—had indeed no right to be; and when he had seen Cornelius depart, on his blithe and hopeful way, as he believed, to become the husband of Cecilia; actually, as it had happened, without a word of farewell, supposing Marius was almost immediately afterwards to follow (Marius indeed having avoided the moment of leave-taking with its possible call for an explanation of the circumstances), the reaction came. He could only guess, of course, at what might really happen. So far, he had but taken upon himself, in the stead of Cornelius, a certain amount of personal risk; though he hardly supposed himself to be facing the danger of death. Still, especially for one such as he, with all the sensibilities of which his whole manner of life had been but a promotion, the situation of a person under trial on a criminal charge was actually full of distress. To him, in truth, a death such as the recent death of those saintly brothers, seemed no glorious end. In his case, at least, the Martyrdom, as it was called—the overpowering act of testimony that Heaven had come down among men—would be but a common execution; from the drops of his blood there would spring no miraculous, poetic flowers; no eternal aroma would indicate the place of his burial; no plenary grace, overflowing for ever upon those who might stand around it. Had there been one to listen just then, there would have come, from the very depth of his desolation, an eloquent utterance at last, on the irony of men's fates, on the singular accidents of life and death.

The guards, now safely in possession of whatever money and other valuables the prisoners had had on them, pressed them forward, over the rough mountain paths, altogether careless of their sufferings. The great autumn rains were falling. At night the soldiers lighted a fire; but it was impossible to keep warm. From time to time they stopped to roast portions of the meat they carried with them, making their captives sit round the fire, and pressing it upon them. But weariness and depression of spirits had deprived Marius of appetite, even if the food had been more attractive, and for some days he partook of nothing but bad bread and water. All through the dark mornings they dragged over boggy plains, up and down hills, wet through sometimes with the heavy rain. Even in those deplorable circumstances, he could but notice the wild, dark beauty of those regions—the stormy sunrise, and placid spaces of evening. One of the keepers, a very young soldier, won him at times, by his simple kindness, to talk a little, with wonder at the lad's half-conscious, poetic delight in the adventures of the journey. At times, the whole company would lie down for rest at the roadside, hardly sheltered from the storm; and in the deep fatigue of his spirit, his old longing for inopportune sleep overpowered him.—Sleep anywhere, and under any conditions, seemed just then a thing one might well exchange the remnants of one's life for.

It must have been about the fifth night, as he afterwards conjectured, that the soldiers, believing him likely to die, had finally left him, unable to proceed farther, under the care of some country people, who to the extent of their power certainly treated him kindly in his sickness. He awoke to consciousness after a severe attack of fever, lying alone on a rough bed, in a kind of hut. It seemed a remote, mysterious place, as he looked around in the silence; but so fresh—lying, in fact, in a high pasture-land among the mountains—that he felt he should recover, if he might but just lie there in quiet long enough. Even during those nights of delirium he had felt the scent of the new-mown hay pleasantly, with a dim sense for a moment that he was lying safe in his old home. The sunlight lay clear beyond the open door; and the sounds of the cattle reached him softly from the green places around. Recalling confusedly the torturing hurry of his late journeys, he dreaded, as his consciousness of the whole situation returned, the coming of the guards. But the place remained in absolute stillness. He was, in fact, at liberty, but for his own disabled condition. And it was certainly a genuine clinging to life that he felt just then, at the very bottom of his mind. So it had been, obscurely, even through all the wild fancies of his delirium, from the moment which followed his decision against himself, in favour of Cornelius.

The occupants of the place were to be heard presently, coming and going about him on their business: and it was as if the approach of death brought out in all their force the merely human sentiments. There is that in death which certainly makes indifferent persons anxious to forget the dead: to put them—those aliens—away out of their thoughts altogether, as soon as may be. Conversely, in the deep isolation of spirit which was now creeping upon Marius, the faces of these people, casually visible, took a strange hold on his affections; the link of general brotherhood, the feeling of human kinship, asserting itself most strongly when it was about to be severed for ever. At nights he would find this face or that impressed deeply on his fancy; and, in a troubled sort of manner, his mind would follow them onwards, on the ways of their simple, humdrum, everyday life, with a peculiar yearning to share it with them, envying the calm, earthy cheerfulness of all their days to be, still under the sun, though so indifferent, of course, to him!— as if these rude people had been suddenly lifted into some height of earthly good fortune, which must needs isolate them from himself.

Tristem neminem fecit—he repeated to himself; his old prayer shaping itself now almost as his epitaph. Yes! so much the very hardest judge must concede to him. And the sense of satisfaction which that thought left with him disposed him to a conscious effort of recollection, while he lay there, unable now even to raise his head, as he discovered on attempting to reach a pitcher of water which stood near. Revelation, vision, the discovery of a vision, the *seeing* of a perfect humanity, in a perfect world—through all his alternations of mind, by some dominant instinct, determined by the original necessities of his own nature and character, he had always set that above the *having*, or even the *doing*, of anything. For, such vision, if received with due attitude on his part, was, in reality, the *being* something, and as such was surely a pleasant offering or sacrifice to whatever gods there might be, observant of him. And how goodly had the vision been!—one long unfolding of beauty and energy in things, upon the closing of which he might gratefully utter his '*Vixi!*' Even then, just ere his eyes were to be shut for ever, the things they had seen seemed a veritable possession in hand; the persons, the places, above all, the touching image of Jesus, apprehended dimly through the expressive faces, the crying of the children, in that mysterious drama, with a sudden sense of peace and satisfaction now, which he could not explain to himself. Surely, he had prospered in life! And again, as of old, the sense of gratitude seemed to bring with it the sense also of a living person at his side.

For still, in a shadowy world, his deeper wisdom had ever been, with a sense of economy, with a jealous estimate of gain and loss, to use life, not as the means to some problematic end, but, as far as might be, from dying hour to dying hour, an end in itself—a kind of music, all-sufficing to the duly trained ear, even as it died out on the air. Yet now, aware still in that suffering body of such vivid powers of mind and sense, as he anticipated from time to time how his sickness, practically without aid as he must be in this rude place, was likely to end, and that the moment of taking final account was drawing very near, a consciousness of waste would come, with half-angry tears of self-pity, in his great weakness—a blind, outraged, angry feeling of wasted power, such as he might have experienced himself standing by the death-bed of another in condition like his own.

And yet it was the fact, again, that the vision of men and things, actually revealed to him on his way through the world, had developed, with a wonderful largeness, the faculties to which it addressed itself, his general capacity of vision; and in that too was a success, in the view of certain, very definite, well-considered, undeniable possibilities. Throughout that elaborate and lifelong education of his receptive powers, he had ever kept in view the purpose of preparing himself towards possible further revelation some day—towards some ampler vision, which should take up into itself and explain this world's delightful shows, as the scattered fragments of a poetry, till then but half-understood, might be taken up into the text of a lost epic, recovered at last. At this moment, his unclouded receptivity of soul, grown so steadily through all those years, from experience to experience, was at its height; the house ready for the possible guest; the tablet of the mind white and smooth, for whatsoever divine fingers might choose to write there. And was not this precisely the condition, the attitude of mind, to which something higher than he, yet akin to him, would be likely to reveal itself; to which that influence he had felt now and again like a friendly hand upon his shoulder, amid the actual obscurities of the world, would be likely to make a further explanation? Surely, the aim of a true philosophy must lie, not in futile efforts towards the complete accommodation of man to the circumstances in which he chances to find himself, but in the maintenance of a kind of candid discontent, in the face of the very highest achievement; the unclouded and receptive soul quitting the world finally, with the same fresh wonder with which it had entered the world still unimpaired, and going on its blind way at last with the consciousness of some profound enigma in things, as but a pledge of something further to come. Marius seemed to understand how one might look back upon life here, and its excellent visions, as but the portion of a racecourse left behind him by a runner still swift of foot: for a moment, he experienced a singular curiosity, almost an ardent desire to enter upon a future, the possibilities of which seemed so large.

And just then, again amid the memory of certain touching actual words and images, came the thought of the great hope, that hope against hope, which, as he conceived, had arisen—*Lux sedentibus in tenebris*—upon the aged world; the hope Cornelius had seemed to bear away upon him in his strength, with a buoyancy which had caused Marius to feel, not so much that by a caprice of destiny he had been left to die in his place, as that Cornelius was gone on a mission to deliver him also from death. There had been a permanent protest established in the world, a plea, a perpetual afterthought, which humanity henceforth would ever possess in reserve, against any wholly mechanical and disheartening theory of itself and its conditions. That was a thought which relieved for him the iron outline of the horizon about him, touching it as if with soft light from beyond; filling the shadowy, hollow places to which he was on his way with the warmth of definite affections; confirming also certain considerations by which he seemed to link himself to the generations to come in the world he was leaving. Yes! through the survival of their children, happy parents are able to think calmly, and with a very practical affection, of a world in which they are to have no direct share; planting with a cheerful good-humour, the acorns they carry about with them, that their grandchildren may be shaded from the sun by the broad oak-trees of the future. That is nature's way of easing death to us. It was thus too, surprised, delighted, that Marius, under the power of that new hope among men, could think of the generations to come after him. Without it, dim in truth as it was, he could hardly have dared to ponder the world which limited all he really knew, as it would be when he should have departed from it. A strange lonesomeness, like physical darkness, seemed to settle upon the thought of it; as if its business hereafter must be, as far as he was concerned, carried on in some inhabited, but distant and alien, star. Contrariwise, with the sense of that hope warm about him, he seemed to anticipate some kindly care for himself, never to fail even on earth, a care for his very body—that dear sister and companion of his soul, outworn, suffering, and in the very article of death, as it was now.

For the weariness came back tenfold; and he had finally to abstain from thoughts like these, as from what caused physical pain. And then, as before in the wretched, sleepless nights of those forced marches, he would try to fix his mind, as it were impassively, and like a child thinking over the toys it loves, one after another, that it may fall asleep thus, and forget all about them the sooner, on all the persons he had loved in life— on his love for them, dead or living, grateful for his love or not, rather than on theirs for him—letting their images pass away again, or rest with him, as they would. In the bare sense of having loved he seemed to find, even amid this foundering of the ship, that on which his soul might 'assuredly rest and depend'. One after another, he suffered those faces and voices to come and go, as in some mechanical exercise, as he might have repeated all the verses he knew by heart, or like the telling of beads one by one, with many a sleepy nod between-whiles.

For there remained also, for the old earthy creature still within him, that great blessedness of physical slumber. To sleep, to lose one's self in sleep—that, as he had always recognized, was a good thing. And it was after a space of deep sleep that he awoke amid the murmuring voices of the people who had kept and tended him so carefully through his sickness, now kneeling around his bed: and what he heard confirmed, in the then perfect clearness of his soul, the inevitable suggestion of his own bodily feelings. He had often dreamt he was condemned to die, that the hour, with wild thoughts of escape, was arrived; and waking, with the sun all around him, in complete liberty of life, had been full of gratitude for his place there, alive still, in the land of the living. He read surely, now, in the manner, the doings, of these people, some of whom were passing out through the doorway, where the heavy sunlight in very deed lay, that his last morning was come, and turned to think once more of the beloved. Often had he fancied of old that not to die on a dark or rainy day might itself have a little alleviating grace or favour about it. The people around his bed were praying fervently—*Abi ! Abi ! Anima Christiana !* In the moments of his extreme helplessness their mystic bread had been placed, had descended like a snowflake from the sky, between his lips. Gentle fingers had applied to hands and feet, to all those old passage-ways of the senses, through which the world had come and gone for him, now so dim and obstructed, a medicinable oil. It was the same people who, in the grey, austere evening of that day, took up his remains, and buried them secretly, with their accustomed prayers; but with joy also, holding his death, according to their generous view in this matter, to have been of the nature of a martyrdom; and martyrdom, as the Church had always said, a kind of sacrament with plenary grace.

1881-1884.